1/01

Blood of My Blood

Blood of My Blood

BARRY LYGA

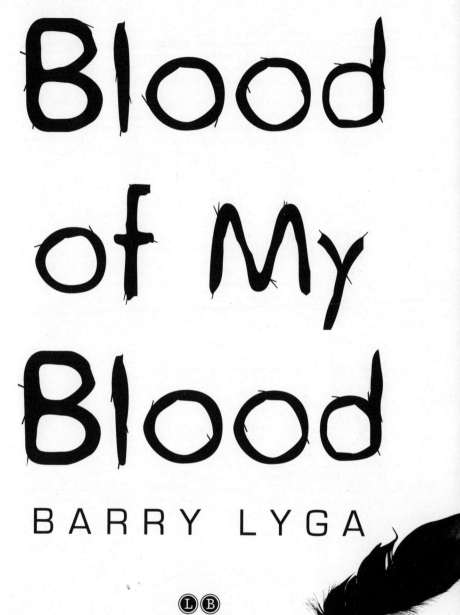

Little, Brown and Company

New York   Boston

Little, Brown and Company

Hachette Book Group
1290 Avenue of the Americas, New York, NY 10104
Visit our website at lb-teens.com

Little, Brown and Company is a division of Hachette Book Group, Inc.
The Little, Brown name and logo are trademarks of Hachette Book Group, Inc.

The publisher is not responsible for websites (or their content) that are not owned by the publisher.

First Edition: September 2014

Library of Congress Cataloging-in-Publication Data

Lyga, Barry.
 Blood of my blood / Barry Lyga.
  pages cm. — (I hunt killers ; 3)
 Summary: Jazz Dent, who has been shot and left to die in New York City, his girlfriend, Connie, who is in the clutches of Jazz's serial killer father, Billy, and his best friend, Howie, who is bleeding to death on the floor of Jazz's own home in tiny Lobo's Nod, must all rise above the horrors their lives have become and find a way to come together in pursuit of Billy.
 ISBN 978-0-316-19870-7 (hardback) — ISBN 978-0-316-33349-8 (ebook)
 [1. Serial murderers—Fiction.   2. Fathers and sons—Fiction.   3. Mystery and detective stories.   4. New York (N.Y.)—Fiction.]   I. Title.
 PZ7.L97967Blo 2014
 [Fic]—dc23

                                                            2014003643

10 9 8 7 6 5 4 3 2 1

RRD-C

Printed in the United States of America

For my parents. Ironically.

Part One

Up the Cliff

CHAPTER 1

Jazz opened his eyes.

Connie opened her eyes.

Howie opened his eyes.

CHAPTER 2

Jazz realized he had been floating. Floating in dreams. But the dreams weren't really dreams—not entirely. They were memories, filtered through a dream haze.

He'd seen himself in the Hideout again, with Connie. Telling her how happy it would make him to know that his mom had escaped Billy, rather than been killed.

He'd seen himself at his mother's grave, weeping for her at Connie's side.

And she wasn't dead, Jazz knew, both in and out of the dream. She wasn't dead; she was alive, and he'd said that would make him happy, but now he was hurt and he was angry and he was also—damn it!—happy at the same time because she was alive and that was great, but why didn't she, why, why, why didn't she take *him*—

Which is when he'd jerked awake, still in the dark, still locked in unit 83F. Cramped and stagnant, the place still reeked of formaldehyde and bleach, with a growing note of blood and meat. Nothing had changed.

Nothing except...

He opened Dog's ancient cell phone again, burning precious battery life. The storage unit lit up with the image of his mother.

That part wasn't a dream. She's alive. She's really still alive.

For now.

He shivered. It was cold in the storage unit, but that wasn't the cause of his sudden chill.

Who did you come to New York to find? he had asked Billy, and Billy had answered with the photo.

She could be dead by now. Or tortured. Or anything, really.

"LET ME OUT OF HERE!"

The scream nearly ripped his throat to shreds; in the close echo chamber of unit 83F, it battered his eardrums. His heart skipped at the sound of his own voice, so raw and desperate. He hadn't even known he was going to scream until the words were out of his mouth.

Don't lose it, Jazz. Don't lose it. Stay in control.

But he couldn't stop himself. His leg had settled into a dull, forceful throb of pain, and he found he could maneuver well enough to get to the door of the storage unit, where he proceeded to howl and scream and pound at the door until the corrugated metal made his fists slick with his own blood.

He slumped down in the darkness. His hands were numb, but that—he knew—wouldn't last. The pain would find him.

The pain always found him.

Pain means you're alive. Pain is good. Pain is life.

It wouldn't matter soon. Soon enough, he would be dead. His makeshift bandage wouldn't keep the blood stanched forever. And if he didn't bleed out, he would die of infection. Or thirst.

According to the clock on the screen of Dog's phone, it had been less than fifteen minutes since he'd first seen the photo. Fifteen minutes to pass into a fugue state, to wake up again. Time was losing all meaning.

His mother stared back at him, caught unawares by Billy's prying, prospecting camera.

"Mom," he said, but it sounded wrong. After a moment, he realized why. She'd gone away when he was so young. And yes, he'd sometimes called her *Mom*, but most often he'd called her...

"Mommy," he said, the word wrenched from him as though stuck fast.

"Mommy," he said again, and wept.

CHAPTER 3

It wasn't a dream. It really was Billy Dent standing in front of her.

Connie shook her head to clear it, but the action only made a smallish pulse at the base of her skull become a throbbing headache that she couldn't ignore. She gasped with the pain of it, and Billy smiled.

"Just breathe in and out," he advised. "Only gave you a small dose. You should be clearin' up in no time."

Connie listened, but the headache didn't—it kept pounding at her, a tiny man wearing gigantic concrete boots stomping away inside her brain.

Oh, God, Connie, stop worrying about your headache.

She was tied to a chair, she realized, as she tried to put one hand to her head to steady the pulsating beat there. She flexed the muscles of her arms, back, legs. The chair was depressingly sturdy; the ropes confidently tied. Billy was no amateur.

The room was exactly as she'd expected from this run-down building's exterior—walls stained with mold and dirty water, floors dinged and marred with substances she didn't want to know. There was Billy, of course, lurking dead ahead, but off to her left, she could just barely make out the edge of a table, on which lay two cell phones: her own iPhone and some kind of cheap flip phone.

Billy looked different from the photos she'd seen of him over the years. He wore absurd muttonchops and a goatee trimmed to elongate his face. His hair was grayish brown, not dirty blond. It was the face she'd seen when the apartment door had opened, and she'd recognized him not by his face, but by his *expression*, his evil glee, and that voice.

Her stomach lifted and lowered, then lifted again.

"I'm gonna throw up," she whispered.

Billy shrugged. "Ain't gonna stop you."

She wondered if she could aim her puke at Billy's shoes. She wondered what the punishment would be for vomiting on the world's most notorious serial killer.

She managed to keep her guts in check.

"It's called Darkene," Billy said suddenly. He had pulled another chair over and now sat on it, no more than two feet from her.

"What's called Darkene?" she asked. She could suddenly remember—with crystal clarity—Jazz's attempt to lecture her on surviving serial killers. She had screwed up most of the basics, but "keep them talking" was still on the list. Maybe if she kept Billy talking, someone would...

"Stuff I shot you up with," Billy said.

Would...

Connie couldn't remember being "shot up" with any-thing. The last thing she remembered was the door to the apartment opening. Seeing Billy there. Recognizing him—instantly—despite his facial hair and hair color. That drawl...

"Well now, ain't you just the sweetest piece of chocolate I ever seen."

"Some kinda European version of Rohypnol," Billy went on. "They gone and put it in an alcohol solution to make it injectable, see? Found out about it on the Internet. And ain't that thing a marvel? You can find out anything about any-body. Amazing. Sure makes my job easier. Hell, when I started out, back in the day, you couldn't just push a few buttons and get what you needed. Had to do the *legwork* back then. More chances to get sloppy. Wouldn't go back to that for all the tea in China, darlin'."

At the mention of Rohypnol, Connie's gut surged again, and she only barely kept herself from throwing up. Roofies. The date rape drug. She—

"Oh, now, darlin'," Billy said soothingly, "you ain't thinkin' unkindly thoughts toward ol' Billy, are you?" He laughed. "It's all over your face. You thinkin' 'date rape drug' and you know I got certain, well, let's call 'em *predilections*, shall we? I ain't gonna lie to you—I have been known to engage in what the prison shrink calls 'nonconsensual liaisons' with certain ladies. And I'll tell you, Connie—if a single one of them women had been a real person or mattered in the slightest, there's a chance I might even regret it. But they weren't, so I don't."

He cleared his throat and leaned in close. "But you think real hard now, and you realize that your drawers are still on and I ain't taken a stitch of clothin' off you. Ain't done nothing untoward. Not to my boy's girl."

Except drug me, she wanted to say. *And tie me to a chair.*

Wanted to say. But couldn't. Wouldn't. She was six inches from the mouth of a man who had bitten the throat out of a woman. Six inches from a man who had cut the nipples off a victim and switched them with those of another. Six inches from the monster who stalked the earth in a suit of human flesh and blood, raping, torturing, and murdering.

She walked into Melissa Hoover's house with Jazz ahead of her and Howie behind her. Billy had been here. G. William told them that much on the phone. And then, suddenly, Jazz looked through a doorway and spun around and shoved at her and at Howie, shoved with more force than was necessary, as though he didn't care that Connie was his girlfriend, didn't care about Howie's hemophilia.

"You can't see this," he said. "You'll have nightmares for the rest of your lives."

He had never told Connie exactly *what* Billy Dent had done to poor Melissa Hoover. But Connie and Howie had waited outside as Jazz stalked the crime scene with G. William and the cops. She'd seen a cop come outside and lean against the house, then hang—openmouthed—over a rosemary bush, as if begging his guts to let him puke. Nothing had come.

She'd watched the medical examiner go in, grim, and come out, gray-skinned and shaking his head.

Billy Dent didn't just kill people. He didn't just rape them. He *ruined* them. He *destroyed* them.

She was, she realized in a moment of stark, hot clarity, terrified.

Now was not the time for sass. Now was not the time to show how tough she was or to be a "strong woman." Now was the time to do or say whatever she had to do or say in order to survive this.

"I'm sorry I doubted you," she whispered.

Billy roared with laughter, slapping one knee. "Black girls!" he howled. "God love 'em! Where's the sass, girl? Where's the head toss and the attitude? You're disappointing me. I see on the TV how badass y'all are supposed to be, but here? Now? You ain't impressin' me. Not a credit to the African American species, if you don't mind my saying. More like a nothing-special colored girl. Beaten down like a slave, you know?"

He stood up with a hand behind his back, and when the hand came into view, it held a large, wicked knife.

"You think you're good enough for my boy, Conscience Hall? You think you got what it takes to be with him? Oh, that's right—I know all about you and him. I know. I first heard about it, I thought, 'Well, damn, Jasper's got himself some strange.' And I laughed—well, no. Didn't quite laugh. *Sniggered*."

Connie tensed. She couldn't keep her eyes from following the knife as Billy gestured with it. But her ears couldn't help hearing—

"Oh, no!" Billy said in mock chagrin. "Did he say *that word*? No, no, of course not. I said *sniggered*, Connie. Stop being so sensitive. It's a real problem with your particular breed. I ain't sayin' that out of a sense of racial entitlement, you understand. I'm just speaking honest with you. I'm trying to help you."

He paused, and Connie realized — to her horror — that he expected a response.

"Thank you," she managed to say. "Thank you, Mr. Dent."

"'Mr. Dent?'" Billy clucked his tongue. "Damn, girl, we're practically family, what with you spreadin' your legs for my son." He sighed heavily. "It's gonna kill my poor momma, if you 'n' Jasper get hitched, Connie. Don't mind telling you that. She ain't as progressive-minded as I am. Know what I mean?"

"Yes, Mr. . . . Yes."

"Call me Billy, darlin'." He tilted his head like a confused puppy, grinning, the knife dancing slowly back and forth in her field of vision, throwing off flares from the overhead light.

"Yes, Billy. I understand."

Billy nodded in satisfaction. "Good. Good." He started pacing now, still gesturing with the knife. And Connie's fear had abated enough that she began looking for a way out . . . only to realize there was none. She could scream, sure, but this was Billy Dent — he'd have her throat cut before the first syllable passed her lips.

"'Sniggering.' Perfectly fine word. Nothin' wrong with it. Won't hear ol' Billy usin' *that* word," Billy said, grinning. "Little old *niggling* thing like that? Drives people bonkers, it does. Why, it would be *politically incorrect* to say that! Insensitive! I say something like that, people might *really* hate me. Not just black folk, either. Got a lot of white folk get upset by it, too. But you want to know something? I'll tell you a secret, Connie. I'll tell you a secret, if you tell me one. Do we have a deal?"

What choice did she have? Connie nodded.

Billy considered. "You gonna live up to your end of the bargain?"

Another nod.

"You sure?"

Nod.

"Good. I don't want to be dealing with no *reneger*." He howled with laughter again, wiping tears from his eyes. He was out of control, helpless in the throes of his own idiotic, racist humor.

"I won't hold back," he told her. "Gonna tell you a good secret. All the details. I won't be...*niggardly* about it." No laughter now as he sat across from her again, a wicked gleam in his eye.

Connie bit her bottom lip, hard. She'd made the worst mistake she could possibly make with him. *His idiotic, racist humor*, she'd thought. Nothing Billy Dent did was idiotic. Nothing was uncalculated or left to chance.

He's trying to get inside your head, someone said to her, and she was surprised—a little, at least—to find that it was Jazz's voice. That was new.

Once he gets inside your head, it's game over, Jazz went on. *Once he gets inside your head, you're dead.*

Billy did the head tilt again. "Thinkin', ain't you? Thinkin' way back in that head of yours. You're thinkin' that if you can keep me talking, maybe someone will come to rescue you." He did something extraordinary just then — he tapped his knife against his chin, the sharp, lethal point just under his mouth. Absentmindedly. As though he did this all the time to keep himself focused. Connie hissed in a breath in some sort of strange sympathy — the idea of that blade so close to her, *touching* her . . .

He held the knife so casually, as if it were just an extension of his hand. *Does he have special ones?* she wondered. *Or will any old knife do?*

He winked at her, and in that moment, she knew she was doomed. Billy was in her head. He was playing two games at once, talking to her while also sussing her out. Figuring out what would make her scream the most, maybe. Or possibly what would make her scream the best. He probably had a grading scale for screams, after all. And he knew how to take a victim from a one to a ten, no problem.

"So, here's my secret," he said. "Ain't much difference between me and one of you 'people' running around out there in the world. Ain't much difference at all, Connie. Truly. Know how I know?"

She shook her head.

"Well, I'll tell you. I performed . . . Well, I performed what you might call an *experiment*, Connie. See, I got a whole lotta deaths to my name. Most of 'em are women. I guess you know that." He stroked his chin with his free hand. "Got a lot of people sayin' I got, well, issues with women. Whole buncha experts thinkin' they can understand ol' Billy. But, damn, Connie. Damn! They don't know me! You think they know me?"

She shook her head again. Agreeing with Billy Dent had become absurdly easy.

"I love women, Connie. Truly, I do. Love my momma, for example. That's just one right there. But the problem here is that there just ain't a lot of real women in the world. Oh, I know you like to think there are. You like to walk around all day and see. You see these things, Connie. These creatures, these dolls. Pretty things, sometimes. They got long hair and they got a bosom and they got fine legs with a nice spot between 'em, but they ain't *real*, you hear me?"

He suddenly screamed: "YOU HEAR ME?"

"Yes!" she cried. "Yes, I hear you!"

"I DON'T BELIEVE YOU!" He brandished the knife before her eyes, the deadly point staring at her, unmoving, held so unbelievably still that it couldn't have moved less if Billy had been a statue.

"I believe you!" she yelped. "I really do! I swear, Billy! I swear!"

He chuckled and went from outrage to easygoing in less time than it took her to blink. The knife pulled back.

"You get it. I'm startin' to think maybe you're real, Connie. Maybe that's why my boy ain't cut you open yet. Might could be."

If I'm real, does he kill me? Does he let me go? Or does it even matter 'cause I'm black?

"Anyway, I tried this out. My little experiment. Scientific

method, Connie. See, the newspeople, they sure loved talkin' about what I did and who I did it to and why. And I ain't gonna lie to you—my pride surely goeth before my fall because I was pretty dang fascinated with what they had to say. Read every story I could get my hands on." He dropped a sly, conspiratorial wink. "Even had one of them— whatchacallit—Google Alerts for a little while. Make sure I catch everything.

"So here's where the experiment comes in. Here's the secret, Connie: I purposely killed me some homely girls. Not many. I'm a man, after all, and I got my tastes and I ain't one to deny myself. But I picked out some girls who weren't nothin' to write home about, and I did 'em just as done as the others, and you know what?"

She shrugged. It felt offhand and deliberate and provocative, so she quickly added, "No. What?"

"I'll tell you what: The media reported on them *less* than on the others. Fewer pictures. Fewer words written. Less detail. Know why?"

He didn't wait for an answer. He leaned in even closer than before: Five inches, then four, then three, now his lips at her ear—right at her ear—and he could bite it off or even just suck her brain out because he was Billy Dent and maybe he could.

"Because," he whispered, his breath incongruously warm and soft in her ear, "*they* want to do the pretty ones, just like I do. They live through me, Connie. They want what I have. What I get. What I take. They don't have the guts, though. For the blood and the bodies and the rape and the rest. So they just report on it. They tell you the details. And all the time, they wish it had been them. Holding them down. Cutting the clothes from their bodies. Doing all the rest.

"They all want it, Connie," he said, and leaned away from her, still grinning. "Nice secret, right?"

She remembered then the conversation she'd had. On the phone. The Auto-Tuned voice, goading her, telling her that when Connie died, there'd be no 24/7 memorial on TV. No follow-up reports.

What if it's just true that your life is ___ *than a white girl's?* the v___

"Like v___ ___, she said, the words ___ ___ she could stop them. "Some people are worth less than others." *To you,* she added mentally but didn't have the guts to speak aloud.

Billy pursed his lips. "Don't quite know what was said to you on the phone," he admitted. "Wasn't me you were talkin' to."

You're gonna die anyway, Connie. Might as well satisfy your curiosity. "So you have a partner?"

"A partner? In a manner of speakin', I suppose."

"Like the Impressionist. And the Hat-Dog Killer."

"Those peckerheads?" Billy said, heated. "You mockin' me, girl? The three of them ain't got two full gonads between 'em. Useful jackasses is all. Tools, like a wrench or a"—he held up the knife, surprised and delighted, as though he'd forgotten it was there—"or a knife!"

Three of them? she thought.

"But now it's your turn," Billy said. "Your turn to tell me a secret."

17

Connie's lips parted, but no sound came out. She could not move her tongue, which lay dry and heavy in her mouth, useless. She couldn't imagine a single secret, all of a sudden. Nothing at all. Certainly nothing that would interest Billy Dent.

It doesn't matter, anyway. He's going to kill you no matter what you say.

"Cat got your tongue?" Billy asked.

"I don't have any secrets," she managed at last. "I'm sorry."

"Everyone's got secrets, darlin'. Everyone. And you and me, hell, we just met. This is our first time talkin'. You got a lot of secrets from me."

"You know who I am," she told him. "You know all about me."

"Secondhand," Billy said, sniffing at the very idea. He waved it out of the air like stink. "Other folks, tellin' me what they seen. I want to know *you*, Connie. *From* you." This time, he tapped his teeth with the knife, and for a single, glorious instant, Connie imagined throwing her weight forward, knocking into him, the knife skidding up those teeth, carving open his upper lip, sliding up into his nose, through the sinus cavity, into his brain —

But in the small glitch of time it took for the thought to occur to her, the moment was over.

"Tell me about my boy," Billy said. "About your first time."

"First time?" she asked dully. She felt like an idiot. First time *what*?

Billy smiled, and for a split second, Connie relaxed before

she realized that Billy's smiles were artifacts of his derelict humanity, tools used to put prey at ease.

"Don't fiddle with me, girl. I been treating you humanely, but that can change real quick. Your first time. With Jasper. Tell me what it was like."

"We didn't!" Connie blurted out. "We haven't!"

Billy's expression and posture changed not one iota. But Connie knew—instantly—that she'd said the wrong thing.

"I—" she began, but Billy hushed her with a glance.

He moved the knife, lifting it to his eyes, then turned it slowly until every angle of it had fallen beneath his gaze.

"Is this a dagger which I see before me?" he said in a surprisingly accurate British accent. Connie blinked, unsure what to do or say in response, and then Billy darted forward and the blade was at the corner of her eye. She jerked away out of reflex, but Billy slapped his free palm against the side of her head, forcing her to stare directly into the blade.

"Is this the goddamn dagger?" Billy demanded in his familiar drawl. "Am I losing my mind, girl, or is this a knife I got in my hand?"

Connie whimpered.

"Answer me!" Billy yelled, his spittle flecking her cheek.

"It's a knife!" she yelped. "You have the knife!"

"And do you believe I will cut you and gut you if you lie to me? Do you?"

"I know you will!" she cried. "But I'm telling the truth!"

"I want to know!" Billy roared. "Tell me about your first time with my boy! Tell me, or I'll rip you open and cut you into little bitty pieces and let you watch yourself die!"

"We haven't!" Connie pleaded. "We haven't had sex yet! I swear to God!"

Billy exploded with a wrathful, rageful bellow. His free hand slid to the back of her head, and he grabbed a handful of her braids, yanking her head back. He came around to the front of her, straddling her, and moved the knife to her bare, vulnerable throat, pressing the edge of the blade against her flesh. There was pressure, but no pain.

Not yet.

"To *God*? You swear to God? You think God was watching or caring when I nailed that silly, crazy girl to the ceiling of that church in Pennsylvania? You think God was payin' attention when I slipped my knife inside her, when I found all her dark and bloody secrets? You think God gave a good damn when I popped out her eyeballs, easy as you please, and fed 'em to the strays in the alley? Do you? Do you?" He licked his lips. "So if you're gonna swear to somethin', little girl, if you're gonna try to *persuade* Dear Old Dad, you best swear to something that *matters*."

Connie swallowed. What had been dry now went slick. She couldn't help it. She—she swallowed again. This time, there was pain along with the wetness of her own blood.

"I swear to you!" she whispered, trying to move her throat as little as possible. She was now raw and open there, keenly aware of how thin the skin was between the blade and her windpipe, the blade and her jugular. "I swear, Billy!" Tears dripped down her cheeks, slid over the curve of her jaw, and melded with the slippery blood.

Tears. She was used to a lifetime of tears doing *something*.

Tears slowed down the conversation. Tears made people apologize. Sometimes tears just pissed off the other person, and he or she stomped out of the room.

She wasn't used to nothing.

For all Billy's demeanor changed, she might as well have been dry-eyed and not bleeding.

"You think I'm gonna believe that?" he asked. "Fine-lookin' girl like you? Sweet talker like my Jasper? You think I believe you could hold out? That boy could talk your legs open in no time, make you think it was your idea all along."

It's not me; it's him, she wanted to say. But would he believe that? Could Billy Dent believe the truth?

Billy began sawing the blade back and forth, almost gently. Connie felt her skin part.

"Please," she said. She didn't want to say it. She struggled with herself, ordered herself to shut up, to no avail.

Connie didn't want to beg for her life. She didn't want to do that. But she would. She knew it. She could feel it crawling up her throat like something that hadn't quite been dead when she'd eaten it. She would whimper. And cry. Her nose would run streamers of snot. And it would be useless because that was the sort of thing you did to play on someone's pity, but Billy Dent had no pity. He was born without it, the way some people were born without detached earlobes or the ability to curl their tongues. Her tears and her pleas would do nothing to him, and she knew it, but she wouldn't be able to stop herself. She would beg and wheedle and swear and importune, and in the end, he would do horrible, horrible things to her, anyway.

Suddenly, he stopped with the knife and looked over her, over her head, his eyes marveling.

She realized that he was still holding her by the braids with his knifeless hand. Now he pulled them up and was gazing at them, almost in awe.

"I ain't never touched a colored girl's hair before," he said with a gentleness that both surprised and frightened her.

Touch my hair as much as you want. I don't care. Just let me live.

With a smooth motion, he removed the blade from her throat and sliced through one of her braids, almost at her scalp, cutting through the knotted hair with a swiftness that offered further proof—along with her bleeding throat—of the sharpness of the knife.

He took a step back and held the knife by its handle in his teeth as he—with quick efficiency and no fumbling—tied the severed braid around his right wrist.

Oh, God. A trophy. His trophy. Oh, Jesus. Oh, Jesus. I don't know what I did wrong; I was stupid to come here, but stupid's not a sin. I don't know what I did to get here, but I promise I'll never do it again. Please get me out of here, and I will never, ever do anything bad again as long as I live. I will be a good girl for the rest of my life.

Billy took the knife out of his mouth and studied the crimsoned length of the blade for a moment. Connie swallowed again, this time causing a stitch of flame to race along her neck where she was open to the air.

Her mind went blank. She had nothing in her. Nothing to say. Nothing to think. Nothing to pray.

And then she was literally saved by the bell.

The phone rang.

It was, Connie thought, bizarre to see Billy Dent answer the phone.

He'd been built up in her mind as the Boogeyman, the Creature, the Devil Himself. But when the flip phone on the table next to him buzzed, his eyebrows quirked for an instant like anyone else's, and he picked up the phone and said into it—politely—"Hello?"

Just like a human being.

Bizarre.

"No, you can't talk to Ugly J." Beat. "Well, I don't rightly care. Tell me."

Saved by the bell, she thought. *Saved by the freakin' bell.*

Connie flashed away from the oddly prosaic tableau of Billy Dent on the phone, back to the box she'd unearthed in his old backyard.

A bell. The bell. A bit of Poe surfaced from sophomore English: *the tintinnabulation that so musically wells / From the bells, bells, bells, bells, / Bells, bells, bells—*

Oh my God, I'm losing it.

Billy listened for a moment. His expression did not change from its studied, frozen neutrality as he said, "And you left him there?" and yet Connie felt as though the temperature in the room had dropped fifteen degrees. She fantasized that she could see her breath.

She tried not to get too excited about her temporary reprieve. Blood still ran down her neck and pooled in the hollow of her clavicle. She didn't have Jazz's intimate understanding of the fragility of the human body. How bad was the cut? How much blood had she lost? How much would she lose?

Chill out, Connie. You're not Howie. If he'd cut your jugular or your carotid, you'd probably be dead or unconscious already.

Then again, maybe that was the Darkene talking. She knew Rohypnol could linger in the body.

"You left him there?" Billy repeated, again without heat, but then he spun the knife—still rubied and glimmering with a wet veneer of her blood—and jabbed it at the table, where it *thunked* into place, point down and vibrating slightly. Connie knew that would be the sound it would make if it hit her bones.

"You go nowhere," Billy said now. "Stay where you are, and don't even think of killing anyone else until I tell you it's okay." He paused. "If you want to be a Crow, you'll rethink arguin' with me." Another pause. "That's what I thought."

Billy snapped the phone shut and stared at it, small, black, and dead in his palm.

"Stupid son of a bitch," he said calmly, then dropped the phone to the table, snatched up the knife, and began methodically stabbing the phone, his face expressionless, his eyes fixated on the spot where the point of the knife cracked the plastic of the phone, then broke through, then finally crunched its way to the table again—*thunk*.

Connie's blood sloughed off the knife and onto the carcass of the phone; it looked like Billy had stabbed the phone to death.

I'm going to die. This is how I'm going to die, and this is where I'm going to die. Because I did all the stupid things you yell at stupid people for doing in stupid movies.

"Right," Billy said. "You."

He was staring at her, as though he'd just remembered she was here. With two steps, he was at her side, and then his fingers pressed against her neck, right where he'd cut her open. Connie hissed in pain and pulled away. Billy thumped the top of her head with the side of his fist.

"Sit still."

He ran a finger along the gash. Connie sniveled.

"Quit it," he said coldly. "This is nothing. You ain't dyin'." He studied his bloodied fingertips for a moment, then licked one clean. Connie gagged.

"Thought it would taste different," he remarked, as though to himself.

He wiped his other fingers clean on Connie's shirt, quick and efficient, not pausing to linger at her breasts, as if she was nothing more than a towel to him.

"Ain't done with you yet," he told her. "You still owe me that secret. That memory of my boy. And I aim to collect. But right now, I got something important to do. So you'll have to sit still for me."

With no further preamble, Billy produced a handkerchief and shoved it in Connie's mouth before she could move or protest. Then he grabbed the back of her chair and rocked her onto the back legs. She went dizzy with the sudden movement and the lingering aftereffects of the Darkene. One-handed, Billy hauled her, backward, across the floor, the chair rattling, the legs scraping the hardwood as she went. He opened a door and dragged her in, righting the chair a few feet inside. Connie had only a moment as Billy stepped around her and over the threshold—she desperately fired her vision everywhere she could, even twisting her raw and abused neck to look around. Small room. Some kind of rubberized egg carton–looking stuff was stapled to the walls. The only furniture was a bed, covered with an unruly hump of blankets.

Standing in the doorway—the only source of light—Billy fixed her with a hard stare.

"Now, I got a couple chores on my list. While I'm gone, I want you to think about two things, and two things only: One, I want you to think about what I want to know, about your first time makin' my kid happy. Second, you think about how persuasive I can be when I need to be. Got it?"

Connie nodded wildly.

Billy held up the wrist on which he wore Connie's severed braid. "I'm keeping you real close, girl. I'll be back for you soon."

And then he closed the door. The room went starkly, immediately black. There was the depressing and unmistakable click of a lock.

From outside, she heard Billy's footfalls on the floor. Then the apartment door. Then nothing.

Connie waited for her eyes to adjust to the darkness. Billy

had turned out the light in the outer room when he left, so there was only a bit of gray murk around the doorframe, light only in comparison to the pitch black around it. She looked down and could barely make out her own sleeves. So that was it, then.

Think, Connie. You have some time. Maybe five minutes, maybe five hours. Who knows. Use it. Now.

She wondered: Could she somehow hop the chair over to the bed she'd seen? Maybe there was a rough edge or an exposed screw or nail that she could use to saw through her ropes. As best she could tell, Billy had tied her by her ankles and wrists to the legs and arms of the chair, using what felt like coarse, thick rope. It chafed her skin at the wrists. She was bound tightly. She could move her feet a little and waggle her fingers, but that was it. At least she still had some circulation going.

Okay, Connie, enough with the medical exam. He could be right back. Get moving.

She took a deep breath through her nose (thank God the handkerchief was clean—it tasted only of fresh cotton) and pushed against the floor with all her might, hoping to lift the chair an inch or two. At the same time, she flung her weight back, toward the bed.

She teetered for a moment, then fell over backward, her entire body rattling with impact. Her head smacked against the floor, and she whooshed out all her air and a scream into the handkerchief, both muted, then tried to suck in another breath, couldn't, panicked, and began sucking on the handkerchief for a starry, terrified moment before her reflexes took over and she greedily snorted great wallops of air in through her nose, exhaling noisily, gustily.

Oh, crap. Crap. Now I'm screwed. Damn it.

Her head throbbed and pounded. Something wet ran along her cheek; her still-bleeding neck had squirted a little puddle on the floor, and in her contorted, breathless moments, she'd rolled into it.

Get up, Connie! Get up*! Do it! Before he gets back! Figure this out! Now!*

Her hammering heart threatened to burst. She forced herself to walk away from her own panic, imagining it as a boulder fallen in her path. Thank God for all that guided imagery and meditation she did. *Yoga saves lives*, she thought.

Stepped away from her own fear, she began to calm her breathing and bring her heart rate back to normal. She was, she knew, flooded with all kinds of endorphins and fear hormones right now. There was nothing she could do about that. She would have to take the best action she could imagine and hope that it was the right one.

First order of business had to be getting to the bed. It was the only thing in the room. It was the only tool she had.

She struggled for a moment, willing her restricted body to find a way to sit upright again, but it was fruitless. Then again…why sit up? Could she somehow inch along the floor as she was? Thrash around just the right way and make it to the bed?

She took another deep breath. This wouldn't be easy. She couldn't rely on her legs or arms. She would have to use her core. She had a great core. The solitary yoga instructor in Lobo's Nod wasn't very good, but in the few classes Connie had taken, the woman was big on boat pose. Which was suddenly a very good thing for Connie.

Just then, something in the room shifted.

Connie froze. Her breath was suddenly enormously loud. Impossibly loud.

Another sound. Arms and legs shifted under cloth.

That mound on the bed.

Not just blankets.

Oh, God. She wasn't alone.

CHAPTER 4

Howie came to with a lot on his mind and wanted to say it all. All he managed, though, was "Guh!"

"He's awake!" a man called.

"Stay still, kid," another voice said. It was a woman. Under normal circumstances, Howie would be inclined to listen, but his head was on fire and he ached all over, so he tried to lift his arms, but something strong held him down. Pinned him.

Even through the fire in his head, he was keenly aware of the bruises that had just been inflicted on him. He groaned with pain and closed his eyes against it.

"What the hell?" the man said. Definitely a man. Or a woman with a frog in her throat. One or the other.

"Jesus!" the woman barked. "You hardly touched him—"

"Kid, are you a hemophiliac?" the man asked.

Well, duh! Howie thought, and then realized he'd actually said it out loud.

The woman swore like someone who'd just dropped a

chainsaw on her own foot. Howie couldn't help it. He laughed.

And then passed out again.

"You have *got* to start wearing your medical bracelet," a familiar voice said.

Howie blinked sleep gunk out of his eyes, but his ears told him the tale long before his eyes came on line—he was in the hospital. Again. The steady *beep-beep* of his heart monitor and the sound of squeaky IV-pole wheels on linoleum in the distance were unmistakable.

For a moment, he considered how sad it was that he'd been in the hospital enough times to recognize it with his eyes closed. Then he decided that this was probably a decent superpower. He was Ear-Man.

"I'm totally Ear-Man," he said, his voice clogged and unfamiliar. He cleared his throat with a disgusting hawking sound.

"Of course you're human," said Dr. Mogelof, standing at his bedside and obviously mishearing him.

"Hey, it's my favorite ER doctor!" Howie clapped a little, then got too tired.

"We have to stop meeting like this, Howie. People will talk." Dr. Mogelof tapped a few spots on her iPad and nodded as though satisfied. "Get some rest. Your parents are on their way."

Oh, joy.

The last thing he remembered was Jazz's aunt Samantha knocking him to the floor and ripping the shotgun out of his hands. The bandages on his right hand told the tale—he'd been stitched up well there. And it was the hand he jerked off with, too. Damn.

Had he passed out from the pain? The blood loss? He didn't know.

Wait. *Not* the last thing he remembered.

He called out to Dr. Mogelof as she was leaving, "Hey, before you go—how's Gramma?"

"What?"

"The old lady. At the house with me. How is she?"

"Kid, you need to worry about yourself right now."

"C'mon. I need to know."

"I can't tell you about another patient. Besides, someone else got her. I was lucky—they gave me you again."

"Flattery will get you everywhere with me, doc, but seriously." Howie pushed himself up in bed, gritting his teeth against the pain. He was bruised all over from his fall to the floor, and now that he was fully awake, he could feel the zone of null-sensation on his forehead where Dr. Mogelof had injected him with lidocaine before stitching him back together. Yeah, he'd passed out, all right. The last thing he remembered was Sam standing over him with the shotgun. He'd probably smacked his head a good one when he blacked out. He wondered if he would have yet another scar. Probably.

"Anyway, the other person they brought in. That's Jazz's grandmother. I think she had a heart attack. And Sammy J was with us and where the heck is *she* and did anyone call me 'cause Connie's on a plane to New York and oh man what time is it and did G. William show up and—"

"Whoa! Whoa!" Dr. Mogelof darted a nervous glance at Howie's heart monitor. "Don't make me knock you out for your own good."

"Doc, honest, there's a lot of shizz going down, and I gotta get back in the game." If Howie hadn't noticed the thudding in his own chest, the heart monitor would have given it away. As it was, the two of them in syncopation was kind of like the world's worst hip-hop backbeat. "I gotta call people and check on people and—"

"Slow down. Start from the beginning."

Howie considered. What *was* the beginning? You could go all the way back to age ten, really, to that day when Jazz had kicked the hell out of the bullies poking bruises into Howie's arms, but that seemed like a lot of effort, and he was getting tired.

"I think I'm in love with my best friend's aunt," he blurted out.

"Well, that's...nice."

"I also think she might be a serial killer."

Dr. Mogelof stared at him. "You know how to pick 'em, don't you?"

"I'm sort of unlucky in love," Howie admitted. He finally managed to sit up, wincing. "How soon can I get out of here, doc?"

"Probably in the morning. This is nothing like when you were stabbed."

"Not stabbed," Howie admonished her. "Slashed. There's a difference."

"Believe me, I know. I'm the one who sewed you back together. Anything else? I need to get back."

"Gramma. The old woman. I need to know about her. And there might have been a younger woman with her. That's Sammy J." *Sister to Billy Dent, but I'm not telling you that 'cause who knows if you'll call the media. Patient confidentiality doesn't extend to the relatives, right?* "I need to know, really."

"Look, there's nothing I can tell you. We picked you up on a nine-one-one call from the Dent house." There was a slight pause in her voice between *the* and *Dent*. Like from pretty much everyone else in Lobo's Nod. "You'll be okay. Try not to walk into any more knives or floors, hmm?"

"Can I at least have my cell phone?"

Dr. Mogelof rolled her eyes and pointed. Howie craned his neck to follow her finger; his cell was next to him, on the bed's tray.

"Right. Thanks."

As soon as she left, he snatched up the phone. There was a text from Connie that made no sense. It was an address in New York, followed by *bell, guns, Eliot Ness? Mean anything?*

Uh, no.

First he texted Connie back: *wht up, girl? you ok?*

Then he took a deep breath and tapped on JAZZ in his contacts list. *in hospital. again. ok, though.* He started to gnaw at his lower lip and stopped when he realized he would now have a bruised lip to add to his troubles. *call me*, he finished. He couldn't bring himself to text *your gramma might be dead* to his best friend.

He sighed. This was supposed to be easy. Keep an eye on Gramma. Keep the other eye on Aunt Samantha. He wasn't supposed to end up in a hospital bed.

He figured he'd better get as much done as possible before his parents arrived. He called the Lobo's Nod Sheriff's Office, depressingly noting that he was probably one of the few people in town to have the number stored in his phone.

"Hey," he said when Lana, the sheriff's dispatcher, answered, "can I speak to G. William?"

"Sure," said a nearby voice, and Howie looked up to see G. William Tanner, sheriff of Lobo's Nod, standing in his doorway.

Oh, goody, Howie thought. *Here we go.*

CHAPTER 5

Connie froze on the floor, stupidly hoping against hope that as long as she didn't move, the other person in the room wouldn't be able to find her. But it was a small room. And there was nowhere to hide. Even in the dark, she'd be found. Easily.

"Who's there?" a voice asked.

In her panic, Connie felt her blood rush into her ears. She heard the voice as though it came from a seashell. Connie went silent, but the sucking sound of her own breath through her nose seemed as loud as hurricane winds.

"Who's there?" the voice demanded again, and this time Connie thought she detected a tremble in it. Was it possible...

Was it possible she wasn't Billy's only prisoner?

She heard more movement on the bed, and then—yes!—she heard the sweetest sound ever.

Metal on metal.

Handcuffs. She was sure of it. At the very least, it was definitely the *clink* of a chain of some sort.

Connie grunted and struggled against her ropes, fruit-lessly. Her fall had loosened them a tiny bit, but not nearly enough. Not that she had expected to be able to wriggle out of them.

She shifted gears, straining her jaw to its widest, then poking at the handkerchief with her tongue. It was, without a doubt, the most ridiculous thing she'd ever done in her life, but in that moment, it was also the most serious. She had to get the handkerchief out. She had to be able to talk.

"I'm not totally helpless," the voice said, and Connie's panic subsided enough to return her hearing to normal; she realized it was a woman's voice. Her slight quaver could have meant a lie or an adrenaline-fueled truth. With the right length of chain, someone on the bed could still stomp Connie's head in as long as she was on the floor.

Connie made muted grunting and moaning noises, trying to sound as docile as possible as she worked at the handkerchief.

Billy had stuffed it in there tight, but not tight enough. With a gagging, near-vomiting lurch, she finally managed to spit it out and hauled in a huge breath through her mouth.

"Don't come near me!" the woman on the bed shrieked.

"I'm not going to hurt you!" Connie let her head droop until it touched the floor. She was still feeling some buzz from the Darkene. "I'm not going to hurt you, I swear."

"Are you on the floor?" the woman asked.

"Yes. I'm a prisoner here." She waited a moment. "Like you."

The woman said nothing for what seemed a long, long time. Connie heard her breathing—slow, even. Then she heard the *clink* of the chain again.

"How do I know that?" the woman asked softly. Scared.

"Because I'm tied to a chair and pretty much helpless on the floor," Connie admitted. "Look, my name's Connie." *Humanize yourself to them.* Good advice for dealing with serial killers, but also with their captives, she imagined.

Her fellow prisoner once again fell silent for a while. Then, at last, she said, "There's a light switch, Connie. Maybe if we work together, we can get to it somehow?"

Even though she was bound and helpless, sweet relief flooded every cell of Connie's body, anyway.

CHAPTER 6

Jazz hadn't even realized he'd passed out again until the sensation of something crawling on his leg woke him with a panicked, heart-choking jolt. Without thinking, he slapped at whatever it was, bringing the heel of his palm down—hard—on the makeshift bandage he'd wrapped around the bullet wound. For a moment, the pain was so huge and broad and blinding that he froze, mouth agape, utterly silent, unable to move even his lips for the shock of it.

But in the next instant, he screamed—once, short. He had nothing else in him. No fuel for a further bellow of pain. He whimpered instead, desperate to cradle his leg in both hands, terrified to do so. The space around the entry wound felt swollen and ripe, the bandage tighter than it had been. Tears spilled down his cheeks.

It wasn't some rodent or insect on his leg as he'd feared. And he dearly wished it was as simple and as easy to deal with as a stray roach or rat.

No, it was blood. His own blood, of course. The wound

was bleeding again. Or still. Maybe it had never stopped in the first place. He didn't know.

He flipped open Dog's cell and shined it on his bare leg. A trickle of blood wended its way down to his knee. That's what he'd felt in his sleep.

Damn it. Damn it. Damn. It.

He didn't know what else to do. The thought of trying to dig in there for the bullet again made him swoon. Could he rewrap the wound? Even tighter? Apply a tourniquet?

You put a tourniquet on there and you'll end up losing the leg.

Ah, but if you don't, you'll end up losing, period.

He picked at the edge of the duct tape with which he'd circled his thigh. As he peeled it away, it pulled on the hair on his legs, but that pain was nothing compared with when he had to tear the makeshift bandage—his shirt sleeve—away from the open wound itself. He bit down on the same shoe tongue he'd bit down on when getting his pants off.

Felt like years ago, he'd done that. Years. It had been hours, maybe. He no longer bothered to check the time on either of the cell phones. Pointless.

Sure enough, fresh blood was oozing out of the wound. He'd somehow pulled the wound open further.

"Somehow?" With all the thrashing around I've been doing, I'm surprised the whole damn leg didn't fall off.

He flashed on a brief tableau of himself without that leg, crutching along a sidewalk somewhere. Or limping the hallways of Lobo's Nod High on a blade, more of a freak than ever. At least the outside would match the inside.

He had to stop the bleeding. But he had no idea how to do it, other than a tourniquet up high on his leg. Right up around the groin, really. He'd lose everything from an inch or two below the hip all the way down to his toes.

Was this really a debate to be having? Didn't staying alive matter more than anything else?

He felt around for his pants in the dark. His fingers glided along something thin and sharp. The butcher knife. The one Dog had had in his laptop bag. Jazz had forgotten that he'd snagged it and kept it nearby. Just in case Hat came back. He laughed at himself. The very idea...What would he do if that door slid up and Duncan Hershey wandered in? Gesture threateningly from the floor before Hat put a bullet between his eyes?

And you told the cops Hershey wasn't the guy. Soooo confident, weren't you? He's not the guy, you said. It's not him, you said. Moron. How's that working out for you now?

Skipping the knife, he slapped his hand in the dark until he found his pants. Dragging them over to him, he lay on his back, the pants piled on his chest as he threaded his belt out from the loops. It would suffice as a tourniquet.

Wait. Wait. Do I need to do this? Dummy...

With his elbows and his one good leg, he managed to drag himself across the storage unit until he bumped against the body of Oliver Belsamo, the deceased half of the Hat-Dog Killer. Good. He'd left Belsamo's body near one of the workbenches.

Gritting his teeth against the strain and the pain, Jazz used his hands to lift his shot leg as high as he could, then—gently—lowered it until he felt the solid wood of the workbench at his heel. He ended up with his leg high in the air, stuck at a nearly right angle from his body. For comfort's sake, he had no choice but to lean back, resting his head against Dog's corpse.

He'd done this before, propping the leg on Belsamo himself. Maybe if he could keep the leg elevated higher this time... That might stop the blood loss enough to keep from needing a tourniquet. He would try it, at least. Give it a little while. See what happened.

He took a deep breath and let it out. It felt like the first real, clean breath he'd had since being shot.

He settled back against Dog. Until rigor set in, Belsamo would make a decent enough pillow.

And that's how Billy found him.

*　*

Jazz refused to allow himself to drift into unconsciousness or sleep (he wasn't sure which) again, so he was alert and did not miss the unmistakable sound of a key turning in the padlock that held the door to unit 83F shut.

Hat. Hat was back. To finish the job.

Jazz rolled partly onto his right side, trying to keep his leg elevated. The awkward movement twisted his left leg a bit, and a new pulse of pain lanced up and down that side of his body, but it wasn't as bad as it would have been if he'd dragged it across the floor. The elevation was already numbing the leg.

He heard a slight grunt, and then the door to the unit clanked and rolled up to the ceiling. Jazz's eyes recoiled at the sudden bright light that spilled in, and he shaded them with a cupped hand, peering into the light, his mind racing. Unless Hat shot him immediately, Jazz figured he had a chance to talk the killer closer to him....He cast about blindly for the butcher knife. If he could get Hat close enough, he could jam the butcher knife right into that bastard's heart.

Ain't I taught you nothin', Jasper? Billy's voice whispered. *Heart's protected by ribs and the sternum. Especially in your weakened condition, better to go for the carotid or the jugular. Or, if you can't reach that, go for the femoral artery.*

Right. Of course. More fatherly wisdom from Dear Old Dad.

"Numb, stupid, self-absorbed prick don't even bother to drag the body in!" the figure silhouetted against the hallway light said, and Jazz blinked rapidly, his quest for the knife forgotten. He was astonished that he wasn't just hearing Billy's voice in his head anymore—he was now imagining that Hat sounded like his father, too.

He shook his head, and his eyes adjusted to the light, and *Oh my God. I'm not hearing things after all.*

Billy tsked and kicked lazily at Morales's body. A whispering sound came from her, and anyone other than Billy or Jazz might have thought—miracle of miracles!—she was still alive, but both Dents knew that sometimes gases built up in corpses are released when the body is moved or further damaged. Morales's dead sigh was nothing more than that. Her last breath, perhaps, drawn in and never exhaled until now.

43

With a swift and sure stride, Billy crossed from the entrance to where Jazz had propped his leg up. Billy had disguised himself—new hair color and length, facial hair, things like that—but no mask could hide Jazz's father from him. Even if he hadn't heard the voice, he would have recognized the walk; the way the lips moved; those cold, dead blue eyes.

His father inhaled deeply and chuckled. "Ah, smell it! Preservative and rigor mortis! My two favorite smells."

Billy held a leather satchel in one hand and placed it on the workbench. "Oh, Jasper," he said, his voice strangled. "Oh, what have you done? What did you let him do to you?"

"Didn't have a choice," Jazz whispered. His voice, raw from screaming, was nearly useless.

"Always a choice," Billy reprimanded. "We're masters of our own destinies." He crouched down by Jazz, his cool blue eyes scanning up and down Jazz's body. Jazz shivered; he hadn't been this close to Billy in years. They'd been separated by a table at Wammaket State Penitentiary. Now it was just inches. And there were no shackles. No guards.

Billy craned his neck to peer closely at the bullet wound and its attendant lateral cut. "You've butchered yourself, boy. Didn't you learn nothin' from listening to Dear Old Dad?"

"I..." Jazz stopped. He was exhausted. Too tired to speak, much less to engage in the psychological thrust and parry of a conversation with Billy Dent.

Billy took a moment to drag Morales into the unit—*unit 83F!* Jazz thought deliriously. *Population fifty-fifty, dead to alive!*—and then closed the door again, plunging them back into darkness until he produced a powerful lantern from the leather satchel. The unit lit up; shadows leapt and pranced along the walls. Jazz went dizzy. Again. Stared off into the dark.

"That's right. Nothin' worth seein'."

Clucking his tongue, Billy—with a gentleness that would have surprised anyone but Jazz, who now, quite involuntarily, experienced a sudden memory of his father tucking him into bed one night—took hold of Jazz's left ankle. Supporting Jazz's leg under the knee as well, he slowly rotated the leg down and settled Jazz's heel on Billy's own thigh, keeping it elevated a bit.

"You go after that bullet? That what you did? Damn, boy. You got guts, that's for sure. Could have made it worse."

"Cleaned it," Jazz whispered. "Bleach."

Billy sighed expansively. "Just when you had me all impressed...Bleach don't clean out infection. Waste of time."

Whistling a tuneless little ditty that Jazz didn't recognize, Billy pawed around in the satchel and began laying out instruments. Jazz couldn't stand to look at them.

"This Morales..." Billy mused, as if chatting about the weather over tea and cake. "She wanted me dead, didn't she? Tracked me halfway across Kansas and through part of Oklahoma, back in the day."

"Hand-in-Glove."

"Yep. She came close, too. Real close. But I was closer. Walked right past her in a 7-Eleven outside Wichita. Tipped my hat to her and held the door, all gentlemanlike."

Well, that was mighty nice of you, Jazz thought, but did not have the energy to say.

"She was…" Billy shivered with a tiny frisson of delight. "I can't tell you how much I had to fight myself not to take her, Jasper. Good thing I'm a man of strong will and good character."

The instruments clinked. Billy was organizing things, humming under his breath now. Jazz wet his lips and took a deep breath.

"Who did you make me cut?" he whispered.

Billy leaned in close. "What? Can't hear you."

Jazz licked his lips again. "Who. Did you. Make me. Cut?"

Billy's expression went blank.

"Don't pull that on me," Jazz told him. "When I was a kid. I have memories of it. Of you telling me to cut someone. And I did it, didn't I? Which of your victims was it? Which one?"

"Never made you do nothin'," Billy said. "Now, did I— let's see—*guide* you in the proper technique, once you started the cuttin'? I surely did. I care, see? But I never suggested it. Never put that knife in your hand."

"I wouldn't have done it without—"

"Hush, boy. Dear Old Dad's gotta think."

Despite himself, Jazz went quiet. Right now, his only hope for surviving was Billy. Strangely enough—or maybe not so strangely—Jazz felt safe. Secure. He knew that Billy wouldn't hurt him, knew that Billy would do everything in his power to keep him alive.

Just like any other father. God, that's bizarre.

Billy probed the wound with a clinical air that did nothing to blunt the pain his touch caused. Jazz tried holding his breath against it, but he had to exhale eventually. With the exhalation came fiery threads crawling up his leg.

He craned his neck. "Holy shit, Billy—"

Billy slapped him once across the face. "Language, boy!"

His father returned to examining the wound, separating the edges with a hemostat. Jazz watched in sick fascination as his thigh opened. Blood welled up.

"Nothing major hit. Lotta little bleeders in there, though. Hell." Billy grabbed one of the plastic jugs of water from the storage unit and splashed some water on Jazz's leg. The blood cleared away, and he pried open the hole a bit more. If not for the look of studied concentration on Billy's face, Jazz might have thought his father was enjoying this.

"How bad is it?" he asked.

"Hush. Daddy's thinkin'."

More blood welled up, obscuring the wound again.

"No way to get to that bullet," Billy announced. "Not with what we got here. Not without a proper irrigation setup and more clamps than I got in that kit and maybe some extra hands."

Great.

"Just gonna have to sew you up. Stop the bleeding."

"Leave the bullet *in*?"

"Don't go panicking," Billy said. "I'm gonna sew you up good and tight. That bullet ain't gonna do any more harm just sittin' there." He rummaged in his bag and came up with a curved needle trailing thin blue filament, which he held using something that looked like a pair of blunt-nosed scissors. With the water bottle, he cleaned the wound again.

"Why didn't you teach me *this*?" Jazz managed to ask. "Something useful?"

"Never had the chance," Billy said with real regret. "I was planning on starting this stuff soon, but then I got taken away from you." He paused for a moment. "This is probably gonna hurt like hell, by the by."

And then, without another word, he drove the hooked needle into Jazz's thigh. Earlier, Jazz'd imagined the pain as fiery threads; now he saw just how impoverished his imagination had been. *This* was fire. This was white-hot cables of sheer agony unspooling from the wound site, racing up and down his leg, filling even his lungs with pain.

Billy flipped his wrist, spinning the hook under the skin, popping it out on the other side of the cut. Jazz screamed.

Hardly taking his eyes off the suturing before him, Billy used his free hand to find and then shove Jazz's belt at him. Jazz took it and stuck it between his teeth, biting down in groaning torment. Against his own will, he sat up partially and thrashed, trying to escape the awful bite of Billy's needle, but his father simply sat on Jazz's lower leg, holding him in place.

"Rest your damn head on the floor!" Billy snapped. "If you pass out, I don't want you splittin' your skull open. I ain't got the equipment for that."

Somehow, through the endless stabbing at and in his thigh, he understood and managed to lie back.

"It's for your own good," Billy said with casual kindness as he executed the sutures quickly, with no regard for the pain. He made six individual sutures, each one knotted neatly and precisely, the knots pulled to one side. "So it won't irritate the injury," Billy explained.

When it was over, Jazz lay exhausted on the floor, his forehead shiny with sweat, his body soaked in it. He was wrung out, spent, drained even of thought.

"That'll hold you, keep the blood loss down," Billy said. "I used a simple interrupted suture. There's gonna be infection, so this way they can just pop one of 'em to drain it. Soon as I'm clear of this place and somewhere safe, I'm calling an ambulance for you, boy."

"Look who's bucking for Father of the Year," Jazz whispered.

Billy chuckled. "You know what most parents don't get, Jasper?"

"Enlighten me."

"Most parents, they're all—what do you call it—narcissists. Is that the right word? I think it is. Parents get all focused on themselves, and then they see their little babies start walkin' and talkin', and since they kinda look like them and sound like them, they start thinkin' of those little babies as extensions of themselves. And so they do everything in the world for them, Jasper. Everything." Here, Billy rocked back on his heels, pensive. "And then somethin' funny happens. Those babies grow up to be kids and teenagers and grown-ups in their own right. And they stop bein' little extensions of the parents, but the parents can't let go of that. They can't deal with it, because it's like a part of their body—like a leg or an

49

arm—just up and decided to act on its own. So everything the kids do, everything, is a betrayal. It's a mark of ingratitude, Jasper. That's how those parents see it."

Billy began wrapping a clean bandage around Jazz's leg.

"But not Dear Old Dad, Jasper. No way, no how. I ain't like that. Father of the Year? Maybe not. But a damn sight better than most."

"You're crazier than the shrinks say if you believe that crap," Jazz managed. "You've spent your whole life trying to turn me into you."

Billy pursed his lips and regarded Jazz with a look that was pure wounded puppy. Jazz wouldn't countenance it; sociopaths didn't have real emotions.

Still. If anyone could hurt Billy, it would be his son, right?

"Now, that hurts, Jasper. It hurts like, well, like a bullet. Truly. I ain't never treated you as nothin' but your own person. Never made you do anything you didn't want to do. Let you find your own path. Didn't tell you who to kill or how or why or when. Left that up to you. Even now, you see me takin' advantage of your situation to make you do anything you don't want to do?" He shrugged. "I just want you to be true to yourself, boy. Be who you're destined to be."

"I know Mom's alive," Jazz said, struggling into a sitting position. Maybe it was just psychological, but with the sewing of his wound and the stanching of the bleeding, he felt a little stronger. Probably all in his head.

Billy nodded distractedly as he wound the bandage. Every time he lifted Jazz's leg to get under it, a little burst of pain raced up Jazz's left side.

"Nothing to say about that?" Jazz asked.

"What's there to say?"

"What are you going to do to her? Now that you've found her?"

Billy shrugged. "I guess that'll be up to her."

Jazz lay back down again. Billy would happily talk all day without actually saying anything. He tried another tack:

"What's the deal with the Crows, Billy?"

"The Crows? Same as the deal's always been, I suspect."

"Don't play me for a fool. There's something, isn't there? I always knew you had fans out there, but I didn't think they would actually kill for you. Is that what your idiot followers call themselves? Crows? Because of that fairy tale you told me as a kid?"

Billy frowned. "Weren't no fairy tale, Jasper. It was allegory, you see? And the Crows ain't followin' *me*; they're followin' a dream. Pursuin' it, you might say. Tell you what: Next time we meet face-to-face like this, when I ain't all concerned about some bastard cop wanderin' in on us, I'll sit you down and tell you all about the Crows. Deal?"

"I expect nothing less from the Crow King."

Billy chortled. "The Crow King? Me?"

"New name for yourself, right? Green Jack, Hand-in-Glove, the Artist, Satan's Eye. And now, the Crow King."

Billy didn't so much smile as he seemed to suffer some kind of lip spasm. The delight crossed his face so quickly that it was gone in the same instant that Jazz noticed it.

"You flatter me, boy."

"Will you give a straight answer? Just once in your life?"

Billy sighed and sat back, eyes lifted to the ceiling as though thinking, *Lord, give me strength.* It was a pose and an expression familiar to any parent of a teenager, and seeing it on Billy Dent's face was one more reminder of how good a job Billy did blending in with human beings.

"Ain't got too much time, Jasper. Can't really spend it chitchatting with you about your mom and the Crows and whatever else pops into your head."

"Are you trying to convince me that you're not the Crow King?"

"I'm not trying to convince you of anything. I'm *not* the Crow King, and that's the plain truth. Whether you believe it is up to you." He started packing his satchel.

"I—"

"Here's the thing, Jasper." Billy leaned in close, his eyes shining. "Here's the thing: Once upon a time, we were *all* kings. You understand? Once upon a time, the commoners were there for us, for our pleasure."

"I don't understand."

"I'll be happy to explain it to you when the time comes. When we ain't in such...constrained circumstances. In the meantime, think about, oh, let's say Caligula. Think about Gilles de Rais. You know more than you think. You've got the beginnings of it, boy. Told you as much back at Wammaket. Told you where it started. The genesis of it. 'And Cain went out from the presence of the Lord.'"

Jazz's head spun. Billy hadn't said anything at all about the Crows at Wammaket.

Before he could say anything, though, Billy finished packing up his things. He left out the lantern.

"Now, here. Take this." He held out two pills: one pink, one white.

"What is it? Are they, I mean."

"A little painkiller and something to knock down the fever you're buildin'. Nothing too strong. Want you awake enough to tell the EMTs what happened to you when they get here."

Reluctantly, Jazz took the pills from Billy's outstretched hand. As he did so, he noticed something on his father's wrist. Like a bracelet, almost, but tied, like one of those braided—

Wait.

There was a bead at one end of it. A shiny red bead. Just like the beads—

"That's Connie's," he whispered, staring at it. He knew it. Knew that braid.

Sick terror and rage swelled in his gut. He choked back the urge to vomit.

"That's from *Connie*," he said, finally tearing his gaze away from Billy's wrist and looking up at Billy's face.

In the bright white light of the lantern, Billy's eyes danced merrily.

"Was wonderin' how long it'd be before you noticed."

From Connie. It was from *Connie*. It was her *hair*. Billy had been knife-close to her and oh my God oh my *God*.

With a choking cry, Jazz rolled onto his side, ignoring the flare from his thigh, and reached out for Billy's throat with both hands. Billy nimbly fell back just far enough to avoid Jazz's grasp.

"What have you done?" Jazz demanded. "Tell me what you did!"

"Is this the part where you threaten me? Where you tell me I better not touch a hair on her head?" He held up his wrist, Connie's braid loosely draped around it. "Oops."

"I'll kill you," Jazz told him through clenched teeth. He clawed at the concrete floor, and if rage meant strength, he would have torn great gray chunks from it. "If she's hurt, I will *kill* you."

"Well now, like I said last time we talked: You go on and do that."

Billy picked up his satchel and then snagged a knife from Dog's workbench. He tossed the knife on the floor near Jazz, who immediately snatched it up and lunged for his father's leg.

Billy laughed and took a step back, then another, letting Jazz get a little closer, then evading him easily as Jazz flopped and struggled to move close enough to cut him. They played their father-and-son, cat-and-mouse game for as long as it took for Billy to back to the door.

Jazz lay in an exhausted pool of sweat as Billy raised the door and stepped into the corridor.

"Thing I can't decide," Billy said pensively, "is whether I'm gonna kill her or I'm gonna watch you kill her. Can't make up my mind about that one."

"You're a dead man!" Jazz thrashed on the floor, helpless and enraged and too full of anger to do anything but scream. "I will make you feel every last thing you do to her! I will rip your body to shreds and feed you to the rats! Do you hear me?"

"Of course I hear you," Billy said quietly, and lowered the door.

"I! Will! Kill! You!" Jazz raged with the last of his energy, and collapsed in a heap.

CHAPTER 7

Connie averted her eyes immediately after flipping the light switch, but she needn't have bothered; the overhead light was weak, forty watts at best, and even her dark-adjusted eyes could handle it.

She had managed to serpentine her way over to the bed, where her fellow captive had—after many failed attempts—untied one hand. Then, using her free arm to pull herself along and with the guidance of the other prisoner, she'd gotten to the proper wall, braced herself, levered herself upright, and found the light switch, nestled in a cutout rectangle of the soundproofing material.

There had been many—*many*—failed attempts there, too. Connie's entire body ached and throbbed with her efforts. But at least now there was light.

She wondered if the light was visible under the doorway from the other room. Connie tried not to envision what Billy would do if he walked in at that moment, but her imagination wasn't taking orders. The grisly tableau unspooled in her head over and over, until finally, as a distraction, she forced herself to examine the room instead.

Not much to examine. The room was just as she remembered it from her panicked look around: small, soundproofed with rubbery egg crates on the walls.

And there was the bed, of course. The blankets had been kicked off, and Connie could finally see her fellow prisoner, who was handcuffed to the bedpost by her right wrist. Otherwise, she was unshackled, but that one chain was enough to keep her imprisoned. With a bit of struggle, the woman managed to sit up on the edge of the bed. She pushed her brownish, gray-threaded hair back from her face. She looked younger than the gray would indicate, with an unlined forehead and only a few subtle wrinkles at the corners of her eyes. Her eyes—a shade of hazel Connie knew well—were familiar.

Her whole *face* was familiar.

"Oh my God," Connie breathed, forgetting Billy's imminent return for a moment. "You're Jazz's mother!"

The woman on the bed blinked at her. "Who's Jazz?" she asked.

"Your son. Jasper. We call him Jazz."

Jazz's mother stared at her for a long, long moment. Then a tear spilled from her eye and rolled down her cheek. "You know Jasper?" she asked in a whisper laden with disbelief. She strained to the utmost limit of her chain, lunging at Connie with a ferocity Connie had never before witnessed. It was every maternal instinct, hurtling itself toward freedom for her child. Connie thought she'd never seen something so pitiable, so powerful. "You know him? Is he okay?" Her voice gathered strength, urgency. "Where is he? Does he know I'm alive? Is he—"

Connie had to wave her free hand to stop the barrage, give herself time to think. She was in the same room as Jazz's mother. The mother they had just buried in absentia before coming to New York. She was alive and she was healthy and...

And she was shackled in Billy Dent's Apartment of Doom.

"Jazz's fine," Connie said. "He's here in New York, with the police, actually."

"The police?" She went rigid with fear. "Did he do something?"

"It's a really, really long story, Mrs. Dent." Connie winced as she said it but couldn't keep the name from spilling out.

The other woman smiled sadly. "Given the circumstances, I think it's okay for you to call me Jan. How did you get here?"

"I got a phone call. A few, really. Followed some clues."

"And they led you to Billy."

At that name, Connie froze. She had almost allowed herself to forget, despite being still tied to the chair. But Billy would be back. That much was certain.

"Yeah," she said, trying to fight off the images her imagination insisted on feeding her. Billy would cut off more than a braid next time, she was certain. "But he said he wasn't the one who talked to me on the phone."

"And you believed him?"

Connie sighed. "I don't know what I believe anymore. I came here...Look, in hindsight I realize it was sort of impulsive and stupid. But you have to understand—he sent me a picture of Jazz. Recent. And close. He could get to Jazz so easily, and if I didn't do what he said, he would hurt him. If I went to the police, he would hurt him. I didn't have a choice. I had to come here. And honestly, I really thought I was just gathering clues. Getting info for the police. And, yeah, that was stupid, but I didn't think I would actually run into Billy Dent." She shook her head. "Things that look stupid on the outside...They might actually *be* stupid, but they don't seem like it when you think you're protecting someone you love."

Connie gnawed at her lip. She hadn't meant to let that last bit slip out. She knew Billy and Gramma were both racists. She had to at least consider the possibility....

"You weren't stupid, Connie. You thought you were helping."

"I guess after we caught the Impressionist, I thought it would be okay. I figured we knew what we were doing—*I* knew what I was doing—and it wouldn't do any harm. But instead, I ended up here."

"Don't be too hard on yourself," Jan said quietly. "I was married to Billy. I knew him like no one else, and he still managed to catch up to me, all these years later."

They thought about that for a moment.

There was so much to ask. So much to tell. But Connie didn't have the time. *They* didn't have the time. What would this do to Jazz? What would it mean for the *us* they'd become? How could she—

And she was drifting off again, thinking again, when what she needed right now was action.

"We don't have time for this," Connie said, her voice pitched low and steady. "He could be back soon."

"Come back over here," Jan told her, "and I'll try to get that other knot untied."

It had taken too long for Jan to untie the first one in the dark. Connie began to thump her way over. She fell a few times but eventually made it there. Crossing the six feet to Jan's bedside was like running hurdles. But every time the room fell silent, she thought she heard a door open somewhere, and that just spurred her on even more, until she was at the bed; by the time she got there, she was winded and sweating.

Jan started working at the knot. "It's a little tighter than the last one," she said apologetically.

"Take your time."

They both laughed—short, frightened laughter. Time was the one thing they didn't have.

"Maybe don't take your time."

"Going as fast as I can. You said 'we' call him Jazz," Jan said as she worked. "Who's we?"

Connie found herself welcoming the distraction. Better to talk than to think right now. "Mostly Howie and me. Howie's his best friend."

"There was a boy named Howie Gersten in the Nod. I remember him. He was sick. Anemia or something."

"That's him. And it's hemophilia."

"That's right." Jan sighed. "Jasper has a friend. That's good."

"And, uh, a girlfriend."

"Of course." Jan smiled. "That's good. That's normal, right? I was always so worried that he would, well…" She sniffed back tears and nodded. "Good. I'm glad, Connie. Good for you. And him."

Connie grinned, despite her situation. A moment later, she yelped in pain.

"I'm sorry!" Jan rushed to say. "So sorry! That was my nail. I was digging under the rope and jabbed you."

"Is it bad? It feels bad." And it did. It felt worse than just a little jab. "Is it bleeding?"

"Just a little. It's all right. Not so bad. Not, uh, like…" Jan's eyes flicked upward.

Oh, right. In all the confusion since she'd been dragged into the room, Connie had forgotten about the cut along her neck. She probed it gently with her free hand. The blood was still oozing, but it had thickened, gone slightly tacky. She figured it was clotting and left it alone, no matter how badly she wanted to pick and prod at it.

"Okay, no worries. Just get me out of this and I'll get you out of there and then…"

"One step at a time, Connie." Jan grunted as she tugged at the rope.

One step at a time. I bet that's what Billy thinks when he's dismembering—

Bad idea to go down that route. She distracted herself again: Connie told Jan about the box she'd unearthed in Billy Dent's backyard, the bell engraved in it, the Auto-Tuned voice that might or might not have been Billy that used a combination of goading and threat to bring her back

61

to New York. The trip to the luggage pickup, where she'd received the toy gun and the picture of Eliot Ness that had brought her here.

"The whole thing," she summed up, "seems crazy."

They exchanged a knowing look. Jan smiled wryly. "Do you think?"

"I just mean..." She remembered her drive to the airport with Howie. *Sammy J.* Jazz's aunt. They had wondered if maybe Billy's sister possessed his same madness.

"Do you know Billy's sister?"

"Samantha? Not *well*; she wasn't around a lot."

"Did they keep in touch?"

"Maybe. Turns out there's a lot that was going on when I was with Billy that—ah! There!"

The knot finally pulled apart. Connie's hand tingled with the sudden rush of blood and sensation. She flexed the fingers, wincing at the pain but also glad for it. Pain meant life.

Yeah, keep thinking like that, Connie. I bet Billy loves that kind of crap.

She bent and found that she could just barely reach the rope around her ankle.

"There's something else," Connie said, working on her left leg's knot while Jan worked on the right. "Something we need to talk about."

"What's that?"

"I found things in the lockbox. Pictures of Jazz when he was a baby. A toy crow."

"So?" Still working on the rope.

"Jazz's birth certificate."

Jan stopped tugging at the loops of rope but stayed bent over, not looking up. She said nothing.

"Jan."

Still nothing.

"Jan, the space for father was—"

"I'm not ready to talk about that yet."

"But it could mean—"

"I said," she snarled, pulling savagely at the rope, "that I'm not ready to talk about that yet!"

Connie counted to five in her head. Was this really the time or the place to have this conversation? Probably not. But they weren't leaving anytime soon. "I just think it's important," she said. "If Jazz isn't—"

"Stop calling him that!" Jan snapped. "'Jazz.' It's ridiculous. It's a girl's nickname. His name is *Jasper*."

"All due respect, you don't know a whole lot about him these days."

Jan stopped her ministrations at Connie's ankle and pulled back, withdrawing bodily onto the bed. Connie felt terrible. Who knew how long this poor woman had been Billy's captive? And before that, what had she seen and endured during their marriage? Hell, what had it been like for her at first, on the run, terrified that Billy could be around every corner, waiting in every car, loitering in every elevator?

And then Connie reminded herself that Jan had left an eight-year-old boy alone in the house with Billy Dent, and her sympathy dried up.

"I guess I deserved that," Jan said.

"You left him," Connie retorted, more coldly than she'd thought herself capable.

"You don't know what it was like. You can't understand."

"I understand you were his mother."

Jan nodded. Connie liberated her left ankle and got to work on the right.

"Are you good for him, Connie?"

"For Jazz?" She thought of their hotel room here in New York. Of the night Jazz had woken up from a dream and clutched at her, only to fall off the bed and then snap at her. She thought of her yearning for him, of what they'd endured together.

"I think I'm really good for him."

"I bet you are."

The last loop of rope gave, and Connie prized it loose. She rubbed some feeling back into her feet, then chanced standing. The world went wobbly for a moment, but she controlled her breathing until the sensation subsided.

Jan gazed at her from the bed.

"Now," Connie said, grimacing as she stared at the handcuff, "we work on *you*."

CHAPTER 8

Howie tried his best, most dashing smile on G. William, but the sheriff was having none of it. He planted himself with a solid thud on a chair next to Howie's bed and glared intimidatingly enough that Howie forgot the joke he was about to crack.

"It's one thing for Jasper to go gallivanting all over God's creation like some kind of idiot, but it's gonna get you killed one of these days, Howie."

"Probably when my parents get here."

G. William snorted an unamused blast of air from that misshapen nose of his. "You think your parents are what you have to worry about? Your biggest concern is sitting right in front of you."

"What do you mean? I didn't do anything!"

"You have a funny definition of 'didn't do anything.' Since I saw you last, you went to see a person who you claimed could be a serial killer. You got a senior citizen in the hospital. And, oh, yeah, you warned Connie that I was onto her.

That's right, Howie—I dumped your phone records, including your texts, right after you left my office. Was 'go ghosty' supposed to be some kind of clever code that a dumb hick like me couldn't break?"

Ah, man. G. William was onto them. "Pretty sure you violated my right to privacy or something by doing that," he said, but his heart wasn't in it.

"Don't act as stupid as you look, Howie. It doesn't suit you." G. William leaned in close. "And now—because of you—Connie's gone missing. We can't find her. She took your advice and vanished."

Howie grunted and turned away from G. William. "I don't know what you're talking about."

"Where did she go, Howie? This isn't a game. She could be in a lot of trouble. If she gets hurt, it's on your head."

Great. Just what I need. Already have Gramma on my conscience, so now we have to add Connie, too?

"I don't know anything," he said quietly, pretending to be captivated by the drip-drop of the IV fluids in his line. "I don't know where she went, other than to New York."

"Look me in the eye, Howie."

Reluctantly, Howie returned his attention to the sheriff. "I really don't know, G. William. All I know is that the guy on the phone told her to go to terminal four at JFK. We don't know why."

G. William nodded thoughtfully for a moment, then fiddled with his smartphone, texting. "That's a bit more than we had before. I'll let the NYPD and JFK security folks know."

"What's the deal with Gramma?" Howie asked. "And Sam. Where's she?"

"Jazz's grandmother is in the ICU. She's in rough shape, Howie. I'm not gonna lie to you. She had a scare, and with a heart as weak as hers, that's bad, but the blow to the head..." He shrugged. "They're doing their best. They think she'll pull through, but when you're that old and frail, even the best doctor's opinion is just a guess."

"What about Sam?" Howie asked quietly, absorbing the news about Gramma.

"The one you think is Billy Dent's partner? The woman none of us knows a damn thing about? That one?"

"Get out. Now."

The new voice was familiar—too familiar. Howie groaned at the sound of his mother, brittle and strong at the same time.

"Mrs. Gersten," G. William said politely, rising from the chair and tipping his hat. "Sorry we have to meet under these circumstances again."

"I said, 'Get out,' Sheriff. Howie is a minor."

"You can't question him without us present," Dad said. "And we're not consenting."

"Your son is a material witness to a—"

"Get out!" Mom shrieked at the top of her lungs, and Howie winced.

"Mom, be cool."

"I will not 'be cool.' And if you ever go near that Dent boy again, I will—"

"I'm almost eighteen. You can't—"

"We're not talking about this in front of the sheriff," Dad interrupted, then turned to G. William. "If you have more questions, you can wait until I get a lawyer in here."

G. William shuffled to the door, stepping aside to let Howie's parents move past him to the bed. "I guess I have enough for now. Thanks for your help, Howie."

Just outside the door, he paused, holding it open long enough to peer back into the room. "By the way, Howie—that person you were asking about?"

Howie nodded.

"Well, she's gone," G. William said. "Wasn't at the house when the EMTs got there. She just up and vanished."

A chill ran down Howie's spine as the door slowly swung shut and he was left alone with his parents.

CHAPTER 9

Duncan Hershey did not anticipate taking any pleasure in killing his wife and children. It was just something he would have to do. Now that he had won the game and ascended past the pathetic Dog to the ranks of the Crows, the Hat Killer was ready to take his next step.

There would be a new name. A new town. Fresh new women to take, to possess, to reduce to nothing.

But first he had to erase his old life. That was the plan. His wife and children had, for a time, served their purpose. They had made him appear human and, therefore, less suspicious. But now they dragged at him, like a parachute caught in the wind. They held him back.

The sooner done, the better. While he longed to take his time and give each of them the personal touch, he knew that a horribly murdered wife and children would only cast suspicion on the missing, surviving father. It was always the way. The world always blamed men, when it was truly the women who were at fault. The women, who held themselves back and above. The women, who tempted and taunted.

So Hershey planned a meticulous tragedy involving the apartment's gas stove. It was possible that people in the apartment below might meet their end as well—he was unsure exactly how big the explosion would be—but the collateral damage would make the "accident" more believable.

And how sad for the father, who happened to be out at the moment of the explosion. Oh, the media would fete him for his stoicism afterward. And when he chose to leave town, to disappear, well... Who could blame him? *Poor man. To lose his whole family like that... I would leave town, too.*

Hershey would vanish. Then reappear where least expected, like the best of magicians.

And then the killing. The sweet, sweet killing!

The plan was perfect. Hershey's new life as a Crow would be perfect. Only one thing stood in his way.

Billy Dent.

Hershey sat at his kitchen table, staring at the knobs on the stove, the unturned knobs. His plan had been devised months ago and took little to put into action. But he'd been told not to. He'd been told to do nothing, to kill no one.

By Billy Dent.

It was past midnight. Down the hall, his wife slept. His children slept. Sleep and death were cousins, after a fashion, and it galled the Hat Killer that his family cozied up to one and not the other this night. Who was Billy Dent to tell him not to kill? Billy Dent had come late to the game, which had begun the previous summer, run by Ugly J. The Hat Killer had not liked Ugly J, of course. Ugly J was too lax. And there was a lilting, laughing tone to Ugly J's voice that Hershey despised. It made him want to reach through the telephone and pull Ugly J to him and begin sloughing off flesh with a sharp knife, whittling down through the muscle, all the way down to the bone, his work's soundtrack the sweet and innocent screams of someone being tortured. Such music.

But at least Ugly J had made some sort of sense. Roll of the dice and a number, and then "Bring proof" and "Now we accelerate." Sensible. Rules.

Then, suddenly, Billy Dent had begun calling in the dice rolls. Arrogant and commanding. Demanding. Insisting on side games.

WELCOME TO THE GAME, JASPER.

Hat had added that sentence to the woman left on the S line at Billy Dent's decree, writing it in lipstick across her dead and sagging breasts. Written it. *Written it.* Leaving a handwriting sample for the police. An insidious and stupid order, but Hat had followed, had played the game to its conclusion.

It wasn't his fault that Dent's son had showed up with the FBI agent.

A fog had come over Hat in the storage unit. He'd lusted for Jasper Dent's death. Yearned for it.

He did not care for killing men. Men meant nothing to him. They were worthless since they allowed themselves to be controlled by women.

But Jasper Dent...

To kill the son of Billy Dent. To kill the child of the man

who had taken over the game and made Hat's victory riskier and more difficult...

Had Ugly J still been his usual contact, he would have killed the Dent boy without a second thought. But Billy Dent was not to be trusted. He was mercurial.

And so he'd done the best he could—left the Dent boy alive but where he could not alert the police. Then he'd contacted Billy, and Billy had...

Hat gritted his teeth and stared down. He realized that he was standing, no longer at the table, but now looming over the stove, his right hand already on one of the knobs.

Billy had told him to kill no one.

To kill no one!

Didn't Billy know how impossible that was? Might as well tell the lion not to eat the gazelle! Tell the Venus flytrap to let the bug go.

Hershey bristled. One Crow should not tell another not to kill! And Hershey was a Crow now. He'd won the game. He'd ascended. Billy Dent was not the Crow King, and even the Crow King should not—

There was a knock at the door.

🐾

Billy grinned as the door opened and he beheld, for the first time, Duncan Hershey, one-half of the Hat-Dog Killer.

"Evenin', Duncan," he said.

Hershey scowled as he ushered Billy inside. "It's technically morning," he said with an air of annoyed officiousness.

"It's past midnight. Long past midnight." A pause. Then, whispered: "They should have been dead already."

They were in a short, narrow vestibule. No room for maneuvering. Hat blocked the way farther into the apartment, which was just fine by Billy.

Billy clapped a hand on Hat's shoulder. "I understand your dilemma. But I'm here to resolve it for you."

"I don't need your help. I have a plan."

"I'm sure you do. But then you shot my son and left him bleeding where no one could help him. So your plan comes after mine, you see?"

"Ugly J said—"

"Yeah, well, I'm the one here."

"I'm not afraid of you."

"Course not. You're not smart enough to be afraid of me."

And then Hat did exactly what Billy knew he would do, exactly what Billy had been waiting for: He pulled a big kitchen knife from behind his back and lunged at Billy with it.

It was a laughable attempt. Billy had seen it coming at least ten seconds before it happened. Hat had come to the door with both hands in full view, so as soon as he reached back with one, Billy knew what he was in for. It would have to be a knife, of course, because Hat wouldn't want the noise of a gun.

Knives were easy. In the confined space of the vestibule, Hat couldn't get in a good swing, so he had no choice but to jab at Billy's midsection.

Billy was ready.

He didn't even try to sidestep the blade. He chopped down hard with the edge of his hand, smashing into Hat's knife hand with bone-shaking force. Hat yelped in pain; Billy, prepared for it, was silent.

The knife, propelled down, missed Billy's gut, catching on his belt instead, cutting partially through before the blow to Hat's hand numbed his fingers enough that he let go of it. Billy had a scratch on his belly, but no big deal.

The knife clattered to the floor. Billy's hand was going numb, too, from the hit, but he didn't need that hand. Not right now.

Before Hat could react, Billy threw up his forearm, lodging it at Hat's throat, driving the man back a step until he fetched up against the wall. At the same moment, he drove his knee into Hat's groin. Hat would have wailed in pain had Billy not been cutting off his air supply.

Hat's one hand was useless. His other Billy met with his own good hand, pinning it to the wall. With his weight pressing against Hat, Billy had him completely off-balance and immobilized, all for the price of a belt.

"Hell, now, Duncan—you sure that's your best play? You maybe want a do-over? Take another shot at old Billy?"

Hershey struggled against Billy. Billy jammed his knee a little higher against his balls. Hat's face began turning purple.

"I only kill for, well, for pure reasons. I kill them what don't matter, them what call to me, what summon me with their need for dyin'. I don't kill for petty reasons. I don't kill for hate. Or revenge. Nothing like that. You hearin' me, Duncan?"

Hershey said nothing. His eyes had gone panicked. His lips burbled as Billy leaned harder on his windpipe.

"I guess what I'm trying to explain to you, Duncan, is that this ain't bringin' me no joy. This is like a football player runnin' for the subway train, got it? A person doin' what he's good at for a really pedestrian reason. A really *insulting* reason."

Hat's eyes began to roll back. His nostrils flared, desperate for breath.

"And I suppose if I thought you cared for them, I would do your wife and your kids next. But I know you were lookin' forward to that, so I'll tell you what, high-and-mighty Hat Killer, high-and-mighty Crow: I'm gonna leave 'em alive. Just to piss you off. They're gonna outlive you. How do you like that?"

Hat shuffled his feet, trying to get an angle that would allow him to push back. But he couldn't find the right purchase. And he didn't have any strength left, anyway, as his cells and muscles pleaded for more oxygen.

Billy wiggled a finger. "Hey, look at that! My hand's comin' back to life. Well, good. That means maybe this *will* be a little bit of fun after all."

CHAPTER 10

It was three in the morning when the cell phone at his bedside blasted just enough of an old Eric B. and Rakim song to wake Detective Louis Hughes from a sound sleep. He flailed around in the dark for a moment, still half-waterlogged by dreams, then finally slapped at the phone to shut it up. The caller ID showed the dispatch desk at the 76th Precinct.

"Hughes," he said. "I'm not catching tonight, so who the hell—"

"Captain Montgomery said to call you," the dispatcher said apologetically. "We caught a call about Duncan Hershey, and Montgomery said you're the guy to talk to."

Duncan Hershey. It took a moment for the name to bleed through the layers of dissipating sleep fog. Hershey. One of the men they'd interrogated about the Hat-Dog killings.

Oh, Jasper, you sick son of a bitch. Were you right? Were there two of them?

"What did he do?" Hughes demanded, vaulting out of bed, halfway into his pants already.

"He didn't do anything," the dispatcher said, and then kept talking as Hughes, now fully awake but numb with both fascination and dread, kept getting dressed.

Less than twenty minutes later, Hughes stood in the entrance vestibule to Hershey's apartment. Farther inside and out in the corridor, cops and crime-scene techs milled about.

Hughes stood over the body, careful to keep his shoes from disturbing the pool of blood.

Who knew the old man had so much blood in him?

Shakespeare, right? Not quite a hundred percent, but close enough for government work.

Sometimes Hughes's mind did this trick at crime scenes, at the really bad ones. He started dredging up random bits of trivia, quotations from books read back in college....The brain's way of coping with horror, maybe.

In the apartment, he could hear a child crying, wailing over and over. And a woman—Hershey's wife, no doubt—sobbing as she told a uniformed officer, "...and I thought maybe I dreamed the noise, but Duncan wasn't in bed, so I went looking and that's when I saw..."

Duncan Hershey—according to Jasper's theory, the "Hat" in Hat-Dog—wouldn't be killing anyone ever again. He wasn't just dead; he was *severely* dead. He was one of the deadest people Hughes had ever seen, and Hughes had seen quite a few.

The eye sockets were pools of blood and glistening jelly

that Hughes suspected the ME would confirm to be Hershey's own vitreous humor. One ear lay nearby against the baseboard, as if tossed or — Hughes's gut seized — spat there. The nose was busted, and a crust of blood fanned out from both nostrils like a half mask, covering almost his entire lower face.

The neck had been clawed open at one side. Enormous gout of blood there.

Stomach cut to ribbons. More blood. Blood everywhere. Splashed up the walls. Running in rivulets along the floorboards.

At Hershey's crotch, there were what appeared to be stab wounds, as well as more bloodstains. Hughes did not relish the moment when the dead man's pants were pulled down. Hughes had seen and experienced a hell of a lot as a New York homicide detective and had become inured to most of it over the years, but genital trauma still skeeved him out.

"Yet who would have thought the old man to have had so much blood in him?" That's what it was. Macbeth, *right?*

"*Macbeth* had the bit about 'who would have thought the old man,' et cetera, right?" he asked a crime-scene photographer crouched down near the body.

The photog's expression clearly revealed that she thought Hughes had been to one too many crime scenes. "How the hell am I supposed to know?" she asked.

"Well-rounded education?" Hughes suggested.

Maybe it was a falling out. If the Dent kid's theory held, then Hershey had been working in concert with Oliver

Belsamo. Maybe they disagreed about something. Maybe Dog decided to eliminate Hat from the Monopoly board.

But here? In the man's own home, with witnesses right down the hall?

Hughes remembered Jasper saying, *It's probably the only thing in the world that makes sense to him, actually.*

"Done here," the photog said, standing up. "You can take a look."

Hughes hunkered down, careful to keep the long train of his overcoat from dragging in any stray blood. There was now a complete photographic and video record of the crime scene, but no point messing things up.

No point getting blood on his clothes, either.

The widow Hershey was still sobbing in the other room. The kid was pitching a fit, too. And now a third voice— another kid—joined the chorus.

You people are better off, Hughes thought. *You have no friggin' idea.*

Next to the body, he focused on two playing dice. He'd noticed them immediately upon entering the apartment, but he hadn't touched or disturbed them yet. They were translucent red, with white pips. Boxcars. Nothing exceptional about them.

But now that he was closer to them, he noticed that they held down a slip of paper that was beginning to sop up some of Hershey's blood.

"You get a picture of this?" Hughes called to the photog, who had just gotten out the door. She turned around, saw where he was pointing, and rolled her eyes.

"Yes, Detective. I pointed my camera at the paper and made clicky noises with the buttons."

Hughes hated the world.

With a pair of tweezers, he prized the now-sticky paper out from under the dice.

There was a bit of writing on it:

YOU'RE WELCOME. — Wm. C. Dent

"Oh, in the name of all that is holy," Hughes whispered. A headache sprung full formed behind his left eye, pulsating so badly that his eyelid began to twitch.

"Shut down the block!" he screamed, rising from his crouch. "Shut down a five-block radius! Do it now!" he roared when the uni next to him only blinked in surprise. At the roar, the uni rushed into the hall, barking instructions into his shoulder mic.

"I need every available unit and man in this area, and I need it ten minutes ago!" Hughes went on. "We are going to personally search every unit and every room in every building in this area. I don't care how long it takes. Billy Dent was here no more than twenty minutes ago — move it!"

He watched for a moment as the chaos around him shuffled and shimmied into some kind of order. There could be no doubt in his mind that this was half of the Hat-Dog Killer, just as Jasper had suspected. Then, looking down at the body, another thought occurred to him.

"And get me Jennifer Morales! Now!"

CHAPTER 11

Howie's phone reported the time as well past three in the morning when he decided to creep forth and surveil. The hospital was quiet, and Howie's parents were long gone, having been somewhat mollified by the usual lies and half-truths. Howie had slept most of the evening, thanks to whatever Dr. Mogelof had shot into him, so he was wide-awake now.

Perfect time for some snooping.

"I am the best sidekick in the history of sidekicks," Howie muttered to himself as he swung his legs out of bed. "I will be promoted to bona fide action hero any day now. It's a lock."

They had turned off his monitors once his vitals stabilized, so he didn't have to worry about any sort of alarm going off. His IV stand—miracle of miracles!—was well greased and didn't squeak as he pushed it along the floor. He made a quick pit stop in the bathroom and checked himself in the mirror. Yikes. It was pretty bad. He could see why

Mom had been spazzing. There was a massive bandage strapped to his forehead, and his face was puffy and more black-and-blue than its usual pasty white. He looked as though he'd gone several rounds with a heavyweight champion, and he decided instantly that that would be the story he'd tell at school. Followed by "You should see the *other* guy!"

I conveniently will not mention that the other guy is a middle-aged woman.

Thinking of Samantha brought him back to the present. He had to figure out what had happened to her. The best way to do that was to find Jazz's grandmother. Sam would be with her, no doubt, and Howie decided that—as long as she didn't actually turn out to be a serial killer—he would forgive her for hewing to her mother's side and not his. G. William claimed she'd disappeared, but that could just mean she was off on a Starbucks run somewhere. If she brought Howie a latte, he'd forgive a lot.

But if she's a serial killer, all bets are off. Unless...conjugal visits? Hmm...

The only problem immediately before him was actually right behind him. His bony ass was hanging out of the hospital gown. He rummaged around in the room's dresser and closet, finding nothing, then spied a plastic bag under his bed. It contained his clothing, minus his shirt, which he imagined had been soaked in blood.

I lose more shirts that way...

He slipped into his jeans and left the gown on, then stealthily opened the door to his room, creeping along with

infinite patience. He couldn't be caught. This was too important. Too big.

Cracking the door just enough to slide through, he eased
into the silent corridor.

"Going for a little walk?" a nurse asked as she breezed by.
"Great! Just watch your IV line on the door handles!"

Howie watched her recede down the hallway. *I totally
saw that coming. Totally.*

He made his way to the nurses' station, where a tired-
looking woman in her fifties (or nineties—Howie couldn't
tell once people hit forty) barely glanced at him. He had to
clear his throat several times before she finally looked up
from her phone screen, where she was fiercely texting what
looked to be roughly fifty percent emoji.

"I need to find a patient," Howie told her.

The nurse's eyes flicked from Howie's battered face to his
IV pole.

"A patient *besides* me." *Smart-ass*, he added mentally.

"Patient confidentiality—"

"You can tell me if someone is *here*, right? I'm not asking
for a diagnosis and a copy of her X-rays."

Howie could tell that the nurse was about to say something like, *I don't have time for this* or *I'm busy*, but she
caught herself, realizing that her now-chirping phone put the
lie to those notions.

"Patient name?" she asked, resigned.

Howie had an awful moment where he couldn't remember
Mrs. Dent's first name. He almost blurted out "Gramma."

"Uh, she was admitted today. Old white lady." The nurse

herself was kind of an old white lady; Howie hoped she wouldn't be offended. "Last name: Dent." Helpfully, he spelled it out.

She paused in her typing at the computer. "First name?"

"Oh, come on. How many Dents are there in this town? For real."

"Too damn many," the nurse muttered under her breath. "She was admitted earlier to—well, late yesterday, technically. Room two-zero-zero-seven. She's in a step-down unit from ICU. But she's on the no-visitors list."

"That's fine. I just want to send flowers," Howie said, backing away, giving her his best, most flirtatious smile. She grimaced at it. Must have been the bruising.

Room 2007 was one floor up. Howie sought out the elevator and spent the brief ascent practicing his seduction rap on a cute doctor with uncute bags under her eyes. As he got off the elevator, she stayed on and told him, "Psych is *down* two floors." Which was random, but helpful, he supposed.

Even if he hadn't been given the room number for Gramma Dent, Howie would have found it easily. He was fairly certain that only the mother of Billy Dent would have a uniformed Lobo's Nod deputy parked outside her room.

And oh, lucky day! It was Howie's favorite: Deputy Erickson. Howie's wrists still ached from Erickson handcuffing him to a bench in the sheriff's office last October, all for the minor, minor sin of breaking into the morgue. And examining a murder victim. And photocopying a confidential medical examiner's report.

"Hello, Erickson." Howie sniffed.

The deputy sat on a folding chair, scrolling through something or other on his cell. "Howie. Glad to see you're up and about."

"I bet you are."

"Come on, Howie. Bygones and all that."

Howie knew there was some kind of kick-ass rejoinder involving "bygones" and flipping it to "gone by," but he couldn't manage to wrap his brain around it at the moment.

"I'm not here for you, Erickson. I'm here to see Jazz's grandmother."

Erickson slipped his phone into his pocket and stood, folding his arms across his chest. Howie towered over the deputy by a good three inches, but what Erickson lacked in Howie's height, he more than made up for in sheer muscle mass. And in not being a hemophiliac.

"Can't let you in. No visitors. G. William is worried about press wanting pictures of Billy Dent's mom in a hospital bed."

"I'm not press."

"He's also worried about victims' families looking for a little revenge."

"I'm also not—"

"Come on, Howie! No visitors means no visitors. I'm not messing around here. Go back to your room and get some rest. You look like hell."

"I just want to check up on her."

"She's resting. There. You've checked up."

"And I need to talk to Sam."

"Sam who?"

Howie sighed. "Man, I lost a lot of blood today. I'm in no

mood. Samantha. Jazz's aunt. She's in there, right?" He jerked his head toward room 2007.

Erickson seemed genuinely baffled. "There's no one in there but the old lady."

That didn't sound right. Sam had been extremely protective of Gramma every time Howie'd seen them together. He couldn't imagine Sam abandoning her mother like this, despite G. William saying she'd disappeared. *Disappeared* didn't have to be sinister—it could be as simple as being in the hospital john when the cops checked your mom's room for you.

"You're playing with me. Sam *was* there, right? When did she leave? Where did she go?"

The deputy shook his head, frowning. "I have no idea what you're talking about. Other than doctors and nurses, no one has gone in there. *No* one."

But Sam would stay with her mom. At least check in with her, right? Unless...

"According to G. William, the nine-one-one call came in from the Dent house landline. By the time the ambo got there, all they found was you on the floor, bleeding, and the old woman nearby. That's it. No one else."

Unless Sam turns out to have more in common with her brother than just hair color. Crap.

"If that's true, then there's a good chance Samantha is working with Billy. You gotta let me see Gramma. There might be some kind of clue—"

"No visitors, Howie."

"Look," Howie begged, "just let me go in and—"

86

"No. Absolutely not." Erickson refolded his arms across his chest, as if that made some kind of point.

"Fine." Howie shuffled away down the hall. After a moment, he turned back.

"I'm still pretty sure you're some kind of serial killer, Erickson." It was the best insult he had in him at the moment.

"You've got serial killers on the brain, Howie. You're seeing them everywhere."

Howie snorted. "Well, yeah. That's only because they *are* everywhere."

CHAPTER 12

Nothing Connie tried could budge either the handcuff around Jan's wrist or the one encircling the bed's metal frame. She was keenly aware that Billy could return at any second. Every moment that passed, her adrenaline seemed to come more and more alive, as though it were a second being living inside her, one that ran through her every cell, screaming one thing over and over at the top of its lungs:

RUN.

The first thing Connie had done was go to the door, thinking that she might be able to find a key or at least something to pick the lock with, out in one of the other rooms. Barring those possibilities, she figured her cell might still be out there and she could at least call the police.

But the door refused to budge, even when Connie threw all her weight at it. Too sturdy for just a mere door. Maybe Billy had a police bar on the other side, or a bracketed barricade. Either way, that was it for the door.

Connie remembered an old movie she'd seen once, where

a guy handcuffed to a bed had used one of the mattress springs to pick the lock. With Jan's help, she managed to tear open an edge of the mattress and pick open one of the coils, at the cost of abrading her fingers until they bled.

But no matter how much she poked and prodded the keyhole with her little makeshift lockpick, she couldn't get the cuffs open. It was much harder than it appeared in the movies.

"I don't know what to do," she said, trying to fight off the *RUN* that still coursed through her. Her fingers were trembling, and her blood smeared the handcuff. "Can we take apart the bed? Unscrew the pole where you're cuffed?"

Jan shook her head. "It's a welded joint. Billy's not an amateur."

Connie stood up and paced the room, jittery as though overcaffeinated. She couldn't stop herself from touching the side of her neck, tracing the line of the laceration Billy had made there. The new blood from her fingers slicked the tacky, drying blood on her neck.

"What do we do?" she asked. Some rational part of her understood that she was skirting the line of complete panic; some rational part of her knew that it wouldn't be long before she began screaming and pulling at her own hair and bouncing off the goddamn soundproofed walls.

But with every second that ticked by, she grew less and less rational.

"What do we do, Jan?" she asked again. It was idiotic, but somehow she felt like Jan should have all the answers. Jan was an adult, right? Jan had been married to Billy, for God's sake. She should know *something*, right? Right?

Connie tried to slow her breathing and—for the first time since she'd started yoga at twelve—realized that she couldn't. Which made her breathe even faster.

I'm gonna hyperventilate right into unconsciousness and Billy's gonna come back and find me on the floor and then—

"Connie," Jan said quietly.

"What?"

Jan raised a finger to her lips in the universal sign for *Shut up*. Connie realized she'd been breathing so rapidly that it was audible. She held her breath for a second.

A door.

A door, closing.

Nearby.

Her eyes met Jan's. Connie was shocked to find no panic in the older woman's eyes.

Just resignation.

They didn't say it out loud. They didn't need to.

Billy's back.

Connie spun in a circle, as though she could somehow magically manifest another room or a weapon or *something* if she just kept looking hard enough. Her eyes fell on the chair. That was all she had. A plan began to form.

She would hear him disengage the police bar. She would stand by the door with the chair held high. The door opened out, so she couldn't hide behind it, but as soon as he came through, she would bash him with the chair and—

And he would recover and kill her because he was tougher than her.

Connie spun around again. The room was four walls of

soundproofing and the door. Nothing more. In a blind panic, she started pounding on the walls, desperate. Her blows were muffled, the pain muted, the resounding thumps solid.

Until.

Until she slammed a fist against the far wall. It felt different there, somehow. She tried it again.

Definitely different.

"What are you doing?" Jan whispered.

Without a second thought, Connie began clawing at the soundproofing. Her bloody fingers found a seam, and she dug in, raking her nails down until she had enough purchase to get a grip and pull.

An industrial staple popped out of the wall, and a corner of the soundproofing came up. She saw the edge of a window, lower down than she was used to, at waist height.

"Dear Old Dad is home, ladies!" Billy's voice boomed from the other room. He sounded happy, and that terrified Connie. "Just let me wash up and make a call, and I'll be right in!" It was the jovial Billy the town of Lobo's Nod had lived with for years, the popular Billy, everyone's friend. If you didn't know what Billy Dent was, that voice would be the signal for good times.

But Connie did know. And the voice, while terrifying, also somehow grounded her. Connie stopped clawing at the soundproofing for a moment and turned back to Jan, who had drawn her knees up to her chest on the bed.

"What about you?" Connie whispered. "I can't leave without you."

"He'll kill *both* of us, if you don't get out."

"I can't leave—"

Footsteps. Close.

"I'm the adult, Connie. The parent. I'm doing for you what I should have done for Jasper—protecting you. Now *go*."

Connie reapplied herself to the soundproofing, snagging a corner. She peeled away a great swatch of it. Sure enough, there was a window there. She fumbled with the lock; it wouldn't move.

He welded the lock shut. He. Welded. The. Lock.

Panic rode her like a horse. She tore down the remainder of the soundproofing. At the same time, she heard—through the door—the police bar drop.

"Hurry!" Jan nearly shouted.

Connie grabbed up the chair, and just as the door opened, she slammed the chair against the window with all her might. The window shivered and cracked. The chair was sturdy and withstood the blow.

She cast a panicked glance over her shoulder and saw that Billy had frozen for a moment in the doorway. Was that a delighted smile she detected playing at his lips? Yeah, she thought it was.

Delight this, she thought, and crashed the chair into the window again. This time, the glass broke into dozens of pieces, forming a jagged opening.

"You little witch!" Billy marveled, and some part of Connie found it amusing that Billy Dent didn't drop the B word on her.

And then Billy roared like a bull moose in full mating throes and launched himself across the room at her, arms wide. Connie shrieked in abject terror and swung the chair around, putting every last ounce of her body weight into it. The chair smashed into Billy, who threw his arms to one side to shield himself. It sounded like someone dropping an armload of firewood, mingled with Billy's shout of surprised pain.

Connie's arms were numb with exertion, but she somehow found the strength to swing the chair again. This time, though, her swing was weak, and Billy caught the chair, wrestling it from her grasp. He hurled it across the room. His seething face came into uncomfortably close view, his nose bleeding, a scratch high up on his cheek where the chair had managed to get through.

He grabbed her and jerked her close.

"You can't—" he began.

And Connie didn't know where it came from, but she hooked her knee straight up, catching him squarely in the crotch, just like they taught in self-defense class. *Eyes and groin. Go for the balls, whichever one you can.*

Billy howled but didn't lose his grip. His fingers did slacken a bit, however, just enough for Connie to twist out of his grasp.

"Run!" Jan screamed, her voice high and on the edge of panicked laughter. Connie realized she'd been screaming the whole time. Her adrenaline had whited out all sound until now. "Run, Connie!"

Billy showed impressive fortitude for a man who'd just had his balls mashed against her knee—he was gasping for breath, but he single-mindedly, doggedly, reached out for her again. Connie spun back to the window. The opening beckoned her, lined with sharp glass teeth.

No choice. No time. She couldn't think, couldn't even pause.

She covered her face with her arms and launched herself through the window headfirst. The shards scraped and tore at her, slicing furrows along her arms and snapping off as they caught on and ripped her clothes. But she was through the window. Through the window and onto a fire escape and—

And Billy's hand was locked around her ankle.

Connie lay half in, half out the window, glass studding her along her arms and torso. As she twisted to turn her gaze to Billy, her weight drove glass deeper into her. She barely even noticed. All her senses were filled with Billy, with the gleam in his eye as he leaned toward her through the window. That gleam—that glow he seemed to exude—filled her sight and even her hearing and touch and smell. She could *taste* it.

She kicked with her free foot. A piece of glass slashed up her calf, but she didn't care. She cared only that she managed to land a blow against Billy, just enough that he relaxed his grip on her ankle. She jerked away from him, spilling onto the fire escape, tumbling. She saw the sky through the fire escape above, then the filthy alley floor one story below.

Barely able to move, shaking with adrenaline, she pulled herself to the ladder. Billy knocked the remaining shards of glass out of the window frame and started to climb through.

Footsteps behind her. So near. She didn't dare take the moment to look back. She flung herself at the ladder.

The opening was there, but the ladder was retracted all the way up. She couldn't figure out how to lower it, so without thinking, she just dragged herself to the lip—

Only one story really only one story only about ten feet or so that's all it is that's all

—and dropped through feetfirst.

A dizzying moment of breathless descent. A cry from Billy, above.

She landed on her left foot a half second before her right touched down. Something very much like a shot of electricity blasted up her left leg, pins and needles along every inch of flesh, sunk deep into every muscle. She exhaled a *WHOOF!* and stumbled forward, nearly falling down but somehow managing to keep her feet under her, where they belonged.

run run run run run run

When her left foot came down, that electricity sizzled again, and she nearly screamed in pain, but she needed her breath for running. She hissed into the agony and forced herself to run, hobbling as quickly as she could, not caring which direction she went, not paying attention to where she was, just propelling herself forward as fast as she could go, each step a mad, hurtful rush.

Each step taking her farther from Billy Dent.

CHAPTER 13

Hughes didn't want to coordinate his efforts to catch Billy Dent from the kitchen of the Hat Killer's apartment, but right now he had no choice. He had uniforms rushing to him constantly, giving him updates every minute or so, and he wasn't about to take the time to drive back to the precinct. He'd had someone get Hershey's family to a hotel for the night about an hour ago and had set up camp at the table where—he was keenly aware—the Hat Killer had eaten dinner every night.

Currently, he was on the phone with his captain, Niles Montgomery, trying to get through the man's head that they needed to shut down Brooklyn entirely.

"I'm talking buses, subways, tunnels," Hughes went on. "Close the bridges...."

"Lou, I'm not closing down the entire borough just because you have—"

"Captain, look—we've never been closer to Billy Dent

than we are right now. He was here. Right here. If we don't close off the borough, he'll slip away—"

"You don't even know if it's him," Montgomery said.

"He signed a—"

"For all we know, this was a falling-out between Hat and Dog, and Dog's trying to throw us off the scent. Keep up your house to house and report back to me. I'll put out the word to the media, and we'll see if we get lucky. But I'm not telling the mayor and the commissioner that we have to declare martial law in Brooklyn because you *think* Billy Dent might be here!"

Hughes hung up, grimacing. He had a map spread out on the table before him and had been marking with a Sharpie where his uniforms had confirmed no Billy Dent. So far, they'd tackled only three buildings in the immediate vicinity. It was past four in the morning, and it had taken time just to muster manpower at that hour, to say nothing of knocking on all those doors and then explaining to the groggy, angry inhabitants what was going on.

An officer in civvies approached Hughes. Most of his cops had been roused from home and hadn't had time for uniforms before reporting.

"Detective Hughes?"

"Yeah?"

"I just wanted to let you know: still no answer on Special Agent Morales's cell or at her hotel. Do you want me to send a unit over there?"

Hughes gnawed on the end of the Sharpie. He didn't want to spare the manpower. "Keep trying."

The cop didn't budge.

"Something else?" Hughes asked.

"Well, yeah. Nine-one-one just recorded a call about Jasper Dent."

Hughes grunted and drew a circle around an abandoned bakery just up the street. Not a bad place for Billy Dent to hole up. "What's he gotten into?"

"Not sure. Anonymous call says that he's, well, that he's been shot in a storage unit somewhere in—"

Hughes snapped to attention. A storage unit. He remembered the information Jasper had given him, the stolen info from Oliver Belsamo's apartment.

"A U-STORE-IT-ALL building?" Hughes asked.

The cop stared at Hughes as though he'd just turned water into wine. "How did you know that?"

"Never mind. What else did it say?"

"Just that the kid was injured. Nine-one-one sent an ambo, but when they arrived, the security guard on duty was dead. Units are on the way."

A ball of molten steel settled deep into Hughes's stomach and began leeching into his guts. *Jasper, what have you done?*

He handed the Sharpie to the cop. "Grudzinski'll be here in ten minutes; tell him he's in charge and fill him in. Until then, you're boss."

"Me?"

But Hughes was already out the door, barking for a car.

It had rained the evening before, then paused. As Hughes pulled up to U-STORE-IT-ALL, the rain—of course—decided to pick up again.

There was an ambulance parked near the gate into the facility, as well as several NYPD cruisers. A uniformed cop in an NYPD poncho hustled over to Hughes as soon as he got out of the car and introduced herself.

"Finley. Natalie Finley. Ambo arrived about a half hour ago. When the EMTs got to the security desk, they saw the dead guard and called it in." Officer Finley chewed at her bottom lip. "Detective, I know there's supposed to be a hurt kid in there, but I didn't think—given the circumstances and all—that I should let the EMTs inside. I don't—"

"You did the right thing, Finley. Show me the guard."

Finley walked him over to the glassed-in guard booth.

Within, the guard was slumped over toward the speaking grille set in his window. His tie dangled through the little slot where patrons could pass money or keys. Hughes could imagine it step-by-step, after years of homicide work—someone had goaded or tricked the guard into leaning forward. Just enough. And then that someone reached through, grabbed the tie...

Pulled hard enough and long enough to cut off the oxygen to the brain. To knock the guy out. And then kept it up.

He went over to the gate and ordered the assembled uniforms to man a perimeter and secure any other exits.

"Open the gate," he ordered, and it rumbled open.

Jasper, what have *you done?*

Before he could enter, Finley came to his side. "I'm going with you," she said.

Hughes shrugged and unholstered his sidearm. Finley, after a moment, did the same, and they stepped into U-STORE-IT-ALL.

A map on the wall just inside identified each building and its attendant units. They had no trouble making their way to unit 83F. They took their time, though, padding quietly through the corridors, weapons drawn, guiding each other around corners and through shadowy spots.

In the corridor outside unit 83F, Hughes spotted blood on the floor. The padlock to the unit was unlocked, hooked through the loop that held the door shut.

Finley gestured and Hughes nodded. He stood off to one side, his weapon up. Finley grasped the padlock.

Hughes nodded again.

Finley lifted the lock out of the loop silently, then placed it on the floor. Her weapon steady in one hand, she crouched down and used her free hand to fling the door upward into the ceiling. It rattled and screeched all the way.

Over the noise, Hughes boomed, "NYPD! POLICE! DON'T MOVE!"

The storage unit was lit from within by a lantern. A stench rolled out and Finley—not as accustomed to the smell of death—gagged, but (Hughes noted) she never let her weapon waver.

"Jesus Christ!" Hughes exclaimed. It was a bloodbath in there. Three bodies that he could see, with bloody drag tracks leading in and out and across the breadth of the unit.

He absorbed it all in an instant, with the practiced eye of a longtime homicide cop. There was Oliver Belsamo, propped up against a workbench, quite dead, his face and mouth a blasted eruption of gore.

And there. Ah, God. Poor Jennifer Morales. No wonder she hadn't answered the calls. Damn it. Dead as dead could be, her life snuffed out in a crappy, filthy storage unit.

She deserved better.

Under Finley's watchful eye, Hughes edged into the storage unit. The third body.

Jasper Dent.

Hughes stared for a long moment, and then Dent's eyes fluttered open.

Rage flooded every muscle, every vessel, every cell of Hughes's body. He had *told* Dent! He had *warned* him about taking the law into his own hands! Damn it, he had warned him in no uncertain terms, and here was Dent with a dead serial killer and a dead FBI agent.

Yeah. She deserved much, much better.

"However you want to play it," Finley said quietly.

Hughes's weapon was still up, aimed between Jasper Dent's eyes. Those same eyes flickered to Morales's body and then back to the barrel of the gun.

"Give me one good reason," Hughes said, "why I shouldn't put a bullet in you."

Jasper said nothing. He licked his lips.

When he spoke, his voice was a dead croak, ripped from his throat.

"I can't," he said.

They stared at each other over the gun. The rest of the world—the storage unit, Finley, the bodies—went away. It was just the two of them. And the gun.

At last, Hughes said, "Goddamn it. That's the one thing you could say to save your life." And lowered his gun.

Part Two

Escape Routes

CHAPTER 14

Jazz opened his eyes to a hospital room. He swallowed and suffered a sensation not unlike gravel going down.

In movies and on TV shows, there was always a doctor or a nurse conveniently standing nearby when a patient woke up, but Jazz was alone. He considered getting up, but even the thought of it exhausted him. Sunlight streamed through the window. The rain had passed. Jazz wondered what day it was. How long he'd been asleep. Had they put him under?

His leg no longer hurt. He lifted the sheet covering him and peered down there. Billy's sutures were gone, replaced by a similar, neat row of new ones. A tube jutted from his leg. A drain for infection, no doubt. Jazz also realized that he was hooked up to not one but two IV bags. Fluids and antibiotics, he guessed.

How long would he be laid up? Connie was in Billy's hands. Mom was out there, somewhere. He couldn't waste time in a hospital bed.

"He's awake!"

Jazz hadn't even heard the door open. A youngish man in a white lab coat who looked like he needed two or three nights of good sleep sauntered to the bedside, consulting an iPad. "How do you feel?"

"How long have I been out?" Jazz rasped, surprised by the grit in his voice.

"Someone's got a pond's worth of frogs in his throat!" the doctor exclaimed. Dr. Meskovich, according to the embroidery on his lapel. Jazz figured he wasn't going to like Dr. Meskovich. He had little use for bedside manner.

Meskovich poured Jazz a glass of water from a jug on the bed's rollaway tray. Jazz gulped it, then tried again.

"How long have I been out? Have the police caught Billy? Is—"

"Ease off, weary warrior." Meskovich grinned in what Jazz found to be a thoroughly annoying fashion. "You had a hell of a night. Nice sutures, though. Do 'em yourself? If so, props to you. But you were just chock-full of infection, so we're pumping you up with antibiotics, and you'll need a script for them when you leave. You allergic to anything? Penicillin, maybe? Because we didn't have any information when you came in, so we went safe and didn't use any of the cillins, but I'd prefer to give you—"

Hell of a night. So maybe ten or twelve hours, then, since Hughes rescued him. Jazz figured the doctor would blather for a while and started tuning him out. He tried bending his left leg, and it seemed to work. Of course, he was probably pumped full of narcotics. If he'd been out only since the previous night, then Billy had had Connie for only a few hours.

Which meant nothing—in a few hours, Billy could do things to Connie that could never be repaired. And how had he gotten ahold of her, anyway? The last time Jazz had spoken to her, she'd been in the Nod. And where was his mother? Billy had a picture of her, so *he* knew where she was. Oh, God—both of them in Billy's hands. In ten or twelve hours, the things Billy could do to the two of them...

"—only in the OR for about an hour. Fortunately for you, the bullet missed the femur and the big blood vessels, so at the end of the day it was easier just to leave it in—"

That got his attention. "Wait a second. Did you say you left it in? It's still in there?"

Dr. Meskovich nodded. "Sure. It's not hurting anything. The body forms a protective cyst around it. You're a young guy—there'll be some pain for a little while, but we can manage that. You'll limp a bit, but that'll go away, too, after some time."

Jazz stared. He couldn't believe it. "You're *never* taking it out?"

"Trust me—there's a better chance we'd do *more* damage poking around in there for it. It's a little tiny thing, and it's nestled close to stuff you don't want me mangling. You'll be fine. You have no idea how many bullets I've left in people, and they're all still walking around. Makes for a fun story at airport security."

It was official: Jazz *hated* Dr. Meskovich.

"How long am I going to be here?" Jazz asked. "I have things I need to do."

"I hope one of them isn't running a marathon."

Jazz winced as he forced himself into a sitting position.

"Look, I'm sure most of your patients appreciate this whole ironic-but-brutally-honest-smart-ass thing you've got going here, but I don't have time for it. I need to talk to the cops. I need to make some phone calls. And I need to know how quickly I can get out of this place because it's literally a matter of life and death."

Dr. Meskovich pursed his lips and narrowed his sagging, baggy eyes. Jazz had miscalculated; he'd thought the blunt approach would cow the doctor, but instead it had just made him retreat into his own ego. Sleep-deprived people were tough to manipulate. You could never count on their reactions. "We need to keep you under observation for a while. You can probably leave tomorrow, but I advise against it."

"Tomorrow's too late. I need to go, like, ten minutes ago."

"No." As if Jazz didn't understand the word, the doctor also shook his head firmly. "Not a chance. You need more IV fluids and antibiotics, and we're not done draining the leg. Tomorrow. Not a second sooner."

"Then at least let me talk to the police. The cop who brought me in — Hughes."

Meskovich snorted and tucked his iPad under his arm. "I'm not your butler. I'm your doctor, and I saved your leg a few hours ago. You need to talk to people? Use the damn phone." He spun and marched out of the room without a backward glance.

Good job, Jazz. You've alienated the guy who signs you out of this place.

He managed to rotate the bedside tray over his waist. In addition to the water jug and pitcher, there was a plastic bag containing his cell phone, wallet, and key chain. He fumbled the bag open and thumbed on the phone. A small part of him expected a message from Connie, even though he knew that wouldn't be true, couldn't be true.

Stay calm, Jazz. You're no help to her if you get emotional and miss something.

It was true. But deep down, he knew a darker truth, that Connie was most likely beyond his ability to help. He had only one tiny glimmer of hope in that darkness: Billy's history of never having killed a black woman. As his phone booted up, Jazz found himself silently praying that Billy had some kind of fetish about not murdering black women. That he *couldn't* do it. As opposed to an equally likely possibility: His father had just been saving his first African American for someone truly special.

The phone's screen lit up. His battery power was almost nil. A single text message floated on-screen.

Howie: *in hospital. again. ok, though. call me*

What the *hell* was going on? Connie was somehow in New York, and Howie was in the hospital again? Jazz had thought that by keeping Howie and Connie in the Nod he was protecting them, shielding them from Hershey and Belsamo and Billy. But he'd failed.

He'd failed everyone.

Everyone was right. Everyone who told me I was just a kid and shouldn't be doing this stuff. Hughes tried to warn me off. G. William tried to warn me off. And I didn't listen. I didn't listen, and now Howie's in the hospital and Connie probably—

He did not allow himself to finish the thought. He couldn't.

He texted Howie back: *hospital? you ok? you still there? what's going on?*

And then—even though he knew it was useless—he tried calling Connie. No text for her. He needed to hear her voice, even if it was just the outgoing message on her voice mail.

But before the phone even rang, a sound outside his door caught his attention. He canceled the call and tucked his phone under his pillow.

The door opened. Louis Hughes strode in, his mouth set in an unyielding line. Jazz thought of Hughes's gun pointed at him. Of the murderous anguish in the homicide detective's eyes.

I didn't kill Morales, but I might as well have. I need to get Hughes back on my side. I need his resources to save Connie. And Mom. And when I find them, I'll find Billy, too.

But while Jazz was thinking, Hughes snatched away the plastic bag of Jazz's belongings. Before Jazz could protest, Hughes leaned over and snapped a handcuff around Jazz's wrist and then around the bed's railing.

"What the hell!" Jazz blurted out.

"You're under arrest," Hughes said, his lips turning up in a mirthless, satisfied smile.

Connie opened her eyes and saw—she couldn't believe this, really truly couldn't—her father nearby, slumped in a chair as if he'd been punched in the gut so many times he couldn't even contemplate standing. He was unshaven, and his eyes were bloodshot and sunken deep into his face. But as her eyes fluttered open, he gasped and bolted upright.

"Oh, thank God!" He leaned over to her and took her hand, swallowing it up in both of his massive paws. "Thank God, thank God, thank God." He was near tears, fighting them back with whatever energy remained from thanking God.

Connie's voice sounded like a rough wind over a rocky beach to her. "You look terrible," she told him.

He gaped at her. "*I* look terrible?" He bit his lip in regret as soon as it was out. With infinite slowness and tenderness, he stroked her forehead. Her cheek. Careful. As if avoiding something.

Something.

Oh. Oh. She remembered now.

Billy Dent. Cutting off her braid. Jan. Crashing through the window. Glass. Blood. The fall. The run.

"You're in the hospital, baby. In New York." The tears threatened again. She'd never seen her father on the brink of such emotion. "I came here as soon as the sheriff told me you disappeared from the plane. Your mother's been beside herself, and Whiz is—"

"Dad, you're crushing me."

He eased off but wouldn't let her go. "Oh, baby. We were so scared. I was a basket case on the flight. And then when I landed, they told me they'd found you. The doctors say you're going to be okay. Your leg and your foot will get better, and after a while, you won't even be able to see the scars."

Connie pulled away from him and ran a fingertip over her face and neck. She felt padding, bandages, several intersecting rows of butterfly bandages.

I'm ugly. How am I going to be an actress when my face is cut to shreds?

"The scars will fade," her father said, reading her thoughts. She suddenly felt incredibly close to him, suddenly needed him more than she'd needed him in the past several years. All their fights—about what she wanted to wear, the music she listened to, the white boy she dated—dissolved into meaninglessness. Her father was here. That was what mattered.

"What happened?" she asked him.

"That's what we're all wondering. You were found in some place called Clinton Hill. You were cut up and screaming and running. And someone saw you and called the police, but you'd passed out by the time they arrived." He shivered. It was an almost frightening and violent spasm in such a big man. "Let me get the doctor; she can tell you more."

He disentangled himself from her and left her alone. She probed her face some more, trying to assess the level of damage she'd done crashing through the window. Reminding herself that she was lucky to be alive and in possession of all her parts.

Still, she couldn't help running her fingers along the bandages. There wasn't a lot of demand for disfigured actresses in Hollywood or on Broadway. It was a tough enough road to walk as a black girl; now she had to be deformed, too?

He said it'll heal. And maybe he wasn't lying to you to spare your feelings.

She wanted to get out of bed and look in the bathroom mirror, but she couldn't move. She realized that her left leg was suspended several inches above the bed. Multiple IV lines ran into her, and she was wired up to a monitor as well. She wasn't going anywhere, not even to the bathroom. The thought of the bathroom made her wonder how she was supposed to relieve herself; an instant later, she discovered that she'd been catheterized. She felt a hot rush of shame for some reason she couldn't identify, followed immediately by a sense of relief.

Dad returned just then with a spookily tall woman in a white coat. As she did with all tall women, Connie dipped her eyes down to check out the heels, only to find the woman wore flats. She was a million feet tall.

"This is Dr. Cullins," Dad said. "She's been taking care of you."

"Hello, Conscience." The words sent a spike into Connie's heart, and all eyes in the room went to the monitor as the line leapt and beeped, then settled.

Hello, Conscience. The words spray-painted over the door to Billy Dent's Apartment of Doom.

"Connie, please," Connie whispered.

"Of course. I'm sorry. Your dad tells me you have some questions? Concerns?" Cullins was all business. She had a slight accent that Connie couldn't identify, and for some reason, this was driving her nuts.

"The scars..." Dad said.

"Right." Cullins sounded as though she couldn't be bothered discussing something as trivial as Connie's face. "The facial and neck lacerations were significant and numerous, but mostly superficial. We used butterflies instead of sutures, and I imagine within a few months, you won't even see the scars. Anything that's left over will be easily concealed with some base."

Connie suddenly felt enormously superficial and enormously relieved at the same time.

"What about my leg?"

Cullins nodded approvingly, as though happy they'd moved on to something of substance. "You did some damage there, for sure." She consulted her clipboard.

"I jumped off a fire escape."

Dad gasped. Cullins shrugged as if to say, *Sounds about right.* "You have some ligament damage and pulled muscles in the right leg. It's going to hurt for a while, but you'll be fine soon enough. The left leg, though... You have a fractured femur, and you've broken your left foot in six places. Including," she said with something like a flourish, "the absolute *worst* place to break a foot. It looks like you continued ambulating after the damage, too."

"I was running from a serial killer," Connie said coldly. Who was this woman to judge her?

"Conscience!" Her dad was both angry and terrified at once.

"I'll tell you all about it later," she promised·him.

"Well," Cullins said, "we've stabilized everything and put some pins in your foot. Had to rebreak one of the mets, but that's the worst we had to do. You'll be on crutches for a few months, then in physical therapy after that."

Connie absorbed this. Okay, it wasn't quite as bad as she'd

thought. Unless Cullins was lying to spare her patient's feelings, Connie would get through this. It would take time, but she would be able to say she'd stared down Billy Dent and lived to tell the tale.

Cullins cleared her throat. "There is one more thing.... We ran a tox panel and found Rohypnol in your system." She glanced at Connie's dad, who sat impassive and motionless.

"Darkene," Connie said, remembering. "He shot me up with it."

"I thought you'd like to know that, well, given your condition when you came in and the presence of Rohypnol, we ran a rape kit. We found nothing." The doctor hesitated. "That doesn't... What I'm saying..." She looked over at Connie's father again before turning back to Connie. "Would you prefer we discuss this in private?"

"I wasn't raped," Connie said. "He didn't rape me."

The doctor breathed out heavily. "Okay. I'm sorry to ask about it, but the rape kit looks for certain signs, but you were so bruised and cut up all over that there's always the chance that—"

"Nothing sexual happened. I would tell you if it had. Really."

"Good. I'm glad to hear it. Get some rest, Connie. It's the best thing for you right now." Cullins nodded curtly and left.

Connie settled back on the pillow. She was missing her sleeping bonnet, and her hair was probably as big a wreck as her face and leg, but she couldn't summon the energy to care. Jazz loomed large in her mind; where was he? Hadn't the police notified him that she'd been found? There was too much happening, and it was too overwhelming. She'd been able to stave it off with the dry medical facts from Cullins, but now that the doctor was gone, she could do nothing but relive what had happened, then jump to the mystery of Jazz's location, and then back to her time with Billy, and over and over, in a loop that spun around her like glittering confetti in a whirlwind, each sparkling bit a memory or a worry that she could glimpse but never capture.

Her father took her hand. "What happened, Connie?" he asked, his voice gentle. He already knew about the Auto-Tuned voice, he told her, the dig at the Dent house, and the birth certificate. "Sheriff Tanner told me all that, but what happened *here*?"

As she remembered it, recounted it to him, the fear and the helplessness came over her again. It was as though she was back in the claustrophobic room with Jazz's mother, bound, trussed for the slaughter. She was safe now; she was with her father, and even though they fought and even though she was far past the age when his mere presence could offer shelter, none of that mattered. In that moment, in that hospital room, she had her father, and she told him all of it, everything Billy had said, everything he'd done. About Jan and the handcuffs and the chair and the window and the fire escape and the jump. Her father said absolutely nothing, just squeezed her tighter at certain moments. When she was finished, he murmured at her, lips against her forehead, and she couldn't understand him, but that, too, didn't matter.

The painkillers were still in her blood. She fell asleep in his arms.

She woke later to find her father still sitting by her bedside, texting. Mom, no doubt. When he saw she was awake, he smiled gently. "Hungry? It's been a while."

How much time had passed since she'd fallen asleep? How much time had passed since she'd crashed through that window? Since the snack she'd eaten on the plane to New York? She didn't know and didn't want to know. Her stomach tightened at the thought of food.

"I don't know if I can handle it."

"The doctor said you could have something if you wanted, but if you're not up to it..."

"I just don't—"

The door swung open, and Detective Hughes walked in. He looked haggard and exhausted, more so than her dad, more so than Connie herself felt at that moment.

"Ms. Hall," he said, clearly restraining himself. The last time Connie had seen him, he'd been friendly. Now he was on edge, ready to snap, and Connie figured she had played a part in that. He glanced at her dad. "Mr. Hall, I assume?"

"You are...?"

Connie quickly explained who Hughes was; her dad nodded along, keeping a wary eye on the detective.

"You have something to tell us, I imagine?" Hughes cut her off as she was in the middle of her explanation. He brandished a notepad and pen. "Found running like a crazy person through Clinton Hill...You're not even supposed to be in New York, right?"

Connie started with the Auto-Tuned voice in the Nod and brought him up to date as quickly as she could. It felt like it took forever, especially given that Hughes's expression evolved from exhausted annoyance to aggressive disgust as she went on.

"Ness Paper?" he asked her at one point.

"Kitty-corner to there, yeah."

Hughes stepped outside for a moment. She could hear him on a phone or walkie-talkie, barking orders. She heard him say "BOLO" and "close a four-block radius."

"Am I in trouble?" she asked her dad.

"I don't think you did anything illegal," he told her. "Stupid, yes."

"I know. I was—"

"You were trying to help Jazz. You didn't realize you were being led right into a trap. I know."

"It was still stupid, though," Connie admitted.

Her father nodded slowly, reluctantly. "We all do stupid things, Conscience. If they don't kill us, they weren't stupid enough, I guess."

Hughes came back in, practically shaking in anger. Connie had the sense that if her father hadn't been present, Hughes might have started yelling. As it was, his voice strained and shook as he spoke. "So let me get this straight: You wandered into the lair of the world's worst serial killer. You evaded airport security to do this. You specifically flew to New York to do this. You didn't bother telling anyone what you were doing. Am I right so far?"

"I told Howie," Connie said.

118

"Who the hell is Howie? Never mind; I don't want to know. You—"

"Detective," Dad said, "I'm going to ask you to watch your tone. My daughter has been through hell."

And whose fault is that? Hughes clearly wanted to say, but he didn't. "You didn't think to tell anyone until *just now* that you were with Billy Dent last night?"

"I've only been conscious for—"

"She's been through a lot—"

"Sir, I'm sorry, but I'm talking to your daughter because I *need* to talk to your daughter. I've got two dead suspects from a serial killer investigation, as well as a dead FBI agent on my hands. And I've got Billy Dent on the loose in my town, and your daughter is the last person to see him. Now that she's awake and lucid, I *will* speak to her."

Dad pursed his lips for a moment. He and Hughes glared at each other, but Dad turned to Connie and nodded.

"I didn't know the clues would lead to Billy," Connie explained. "The voice on the phone said it wasn't Billy." She had liked Hughes when she'd first come to New York, but now she couldn't stand him. "You know, this is all *your* fault. You're the one who brought Jazz here in the first place."

She'd expected that to shut him down, but no luck. "I brought him here as a consultant. To sit in a room and look at some files. Check out some crime scenes. Not to go off on his own and get people killed."

"Get who killed?"

Hughes's phone rang. He answered and listened for a moment, then swore with words that would have had Connie grounded until graduation. "They went to Billy's apartment," he told them when he'd hung up. "No one was there. Just the bed you described, the room in disarray as you described it. Oh, but they *did* find your phone there, so I guess it's all good, huh?" Barely able to contain himself, he spun around to leave.

"Get *who* killed?" Connie demanded. "You said Jazz got someone killed. What did you mean? Where is he?"

For a moment, she thought he would ignore her and keep walking, but he paused with his hand on the doorknob. Without turning to her, he said, "We found him in a storage unit. We think he was involved in the murder of a suspect in the Hat-Dog killings. A dead FBI agent was at the scene, too."

That couldn't be true. There had to be an explanation. "Jazz wouldn't kill anyone," she said.

Now Hughes turned around. His face seemed too small for the rage it expressed. "I'm glad you think so. But there were two dead bodies there...and your boyfriend. That makes him a suspect. And apparently, his father just happened to show up to sew up his bullet wound. Very convenient."

"Bullet wound?" Connie heard her heart monitor ping in alarm, but she ignored it. "He was shot?"

Dad put a calming hand on her arm. "Detective, maybe you could just tell us exactly what's going on, instead of making us pull it out of you."

Hughes laughed mirthlessly. "Oh, sure. Let me help you out, put your fears to rest. After you went barreling through my city without a care in the world. You want an update?

Here it is: The Hat-Dog Killer turned out to be the Hat-Dog Killers, and they're both dead, along with an FBI agent. And Billy Dent is loose somewhere in my city, and if you think I'm letting your boyfriend go anywhere, you're nuts."

"What exactly is he accused of doing?" Dad asked very, very calmly.

"He's accused of killing an FBI agent," Hughes said, "and I'm sure I'll have something else by the time I'm through. In any event, I don't want him going anywhere for the time being."

Connie opened her mouth, but her father tightened his grip on her arm, silencing her. "Detective," he said, "where exactly *is* he right now?"

"One floor up."

Connie bolted upright in bed, then whimpered in pain as her leg jostled. "I have to see him!" she said. "I have to—"

"No one's seeing him."

"Except for his lawyer, you mean," Dad said.

Hughes shrugged. "I'm sure at some point Legal Aid will get someone down here."

Connie saw the struggle as it flitted past her father's face. It took only an instant, and then it was gone. Her father stood up, shoulders back, and cleared his throat.

"Well, I *am* his lawyer, Detective. Jerome Hall, at your service."

Hughes's face fell. A classic *Oh, crap* moment if ever there was one. Connie couldn't help grinning, even though it hurt.

After Hughes left them, Connie's dad took a moment in her little en suite bathroom to splash water on his face. He looked like anything but a lawyer in his jeans and golf shirt; more like a bored, tired suburban dad headed to a cookout.

"I'll be quick," he promised her. "I'm just going to check in on him, and then I'll be right back."

"I'll be fine, Dad. I'm sure not going anywhere." She hesitated, not wanting to ask the next question, fearful it would prompt him to change his mind. But her curiosity outweighed her dread. "Why are you doing this? You don't even like Jazz."

Dad shrugged. "*Like* doesn't enter into it. When you become a lawyer, you swear an oath to uphold the law. Doesn't matter who you're upholding it for."

"You're sort of like Superman," Connie said.

Her father laughed for the first time in what seemed to Connie to have been a very, very long time. "I *am* Superman!" he said, and briefly struck the classic fists-on-hips pose before bestowing a soft kiss on her forehead and leaving the room.

🖤

Howie opened his eyes to the stark realization that he had inadvertently lied to G. William.

"Oh, man," he muttered to himself, "I'm a dummy, I'm a dummy, I'm such a dummy...." He grabbed his cell phone. There was a text from Jazz—hallelujah!—but he skipped it for now to call the sheriff's office.

"Hey, G-Dub!" he said as brightly as he could muster. "Totes forgot to tell you something when you were here. You dumped my texts after I left your office, but Connie texted me hours later. An address in New York and the words *bell, guns, Eliot Ness.*"

He held the phone away from his ear as G. William screamed and cursed.

"I totally hear you, Sheriff, but you were busy yelling at me and then my parents got here and then—"

Held the phone away again. For a fat guy, G. William sure could sustain a *long* burst of screaming and yelling.

"Well, I hope this helps. Later!" He hung up and held his phone at arm's length, squinting at the screen, waiting for it to light up with the sheriff's office phone number. When that didn't happen, he finally relaxed and checked Jazz's text.

hospital? you ok? you still there? what's going on?

What's going on? Ha! Not enough texts in the world could explain that. He decided to keep it simple:

yeah still in hospital but leaving soon. where you at?

A moment later: *Believe it or not, in the hospital, too.*

Howie boggled at his phone. Didn't Jazz know that *he* was the one who was supposed to end up in hospitals? Jazz was horning in on his jam. Not cool.

Joking, he texted back, *what happened, you get shot or something?*

Yeah. By an FBI agent. It's a long story.

What the hell?

you ok?

Technically, yes. They say I'll be fine. But I'm also under arrest and I don't think they know I have my phone, so I don't know how long I'll be able to talk to you.

Howie stared at the screen. Just when he thought his life couldn't get weirder, more dangerous, or more complicated, trust Jazz to throw bullets and bedpans into the mix.

dude you owe me many many tattoos at this point

CHAPTER 15

dude you owe me many many tattoos at this point

Jazz fumbled with his phone as the door to his room opened.

Connie's father.

Connie's *father*.

What the hell was *he* doing in New York—

Oh, God. If they found Connie's body, they would have called him. That's why...

"What are you doing here? What's going on? Is Connie—" He sat up too quickly. The handcuff tugged him back, cutting into his wrist and his words.

The door swung shut, and Mr. Hall stood far back from the bed, his arms crossed over his chest. "I'm going to pretend I didn't see that phone," he said, "but if the police ask me if you have one, I'll have to tell them, even though I'm your lawyer."

"My lawyer?" Jazz tucked the phone under his sheet. He still didn't know what Mr. Hall was here for, but the fact that

Connie's father hadn't begun strangling him indicated that he wasn't in New York to identify her body. He didn't know which was worse—Connie found dead or Connie still in Billy's clutches. If the former, her torment was over. If the latter, she could still be saved. Maybe.

"You're in a lot of trouble," Mr. Hall said. "The NYPD thinks you killed an FBI agent and a serial killer suspect."

"Trust me, forensics will bear me out on this. My fingerprints are nowhere on any of the murder weapons. And I was shot."

"Which could have happened while you were killing someone else. And the lack of evidence will actually be used *against* you—they'll point out that your father taught you how to throw off the police. All a jury will see is a kid, raised by a monster, who finally snapped."

Good point. Wasn't that exactly why Jazz had begun looking for the Impressionist back in Lobo's Nod? To prove to the world that it wasn't him? And you only need to prove that if people already think it's you in the first place. For the son of Billy Dent, "guilty until proven innocent" was more likely than not. He had no witnesses to speak for him— only complicated forensic evidence that a jury of twelve morons would overlook in favor of kicking the apple that didn't fall far from the tree. He also had no money to speak of, certainly not enough to hire the kind of lawyer he would need to defend himself. He would be stuck with an overworked legal aid attorney.

"What do we do?" he asked quietly. "Don't I have to pay you if you're my lawyer?"

"I can't lie to you—I don't usually litigate. And I'm not licensed to practice in New York, so there's not much I can do right now. But I can keep the cops from hassling you until we get you a New York lawyer. Don't talk to them, okay?"

Not a problem. One thing about being Billy Dent's son— you learned not to talk to cops.

"I'm one floor down with Connie," Mr. Hall said, "but I'll check in on you as much as I can."

Jazz shot up in bed, handcuff be damned. "*What* did you say? Connie's *here*? Is she okay? I need to see her." It was entirely possible that she was all right physically, but that Billy had done something to her psychologically that no one would notice. "I need to see her right now."

Mr. Hall harrumphed and shook his head. "Jasper, understand me and believe me when I tell you this: You will never, ever see my daughter again."

***

Eventually, Jazz dozed. As the light outside his window turned to twilight and as the relief of hearing Connie was alive eroded his adrenaline rush, the boredom of being stuck in this room alone swaddled him with sleep, and he drifted off.

—touch—

This time, it was the sex dream.

—his hand runs up—

The cutting dream was on hiatus. He didn't need it anymore. He knew now that it wasn't merely a dream—it was a memory. As a child, he had taken a knife and he had sliced into the flesh of another human being. The sensation of trying to cut his own leg open to dig out the bullet had confirmed it.

Oh, yes, you know —

Then what did the sex dream mean? If the cutting dream turned out to be real, then what did the sex dream mean and who had —

The vibration of his phone startled him from his slumber. He jerked as he woke, once again yanking hard against the handcuff that held him fast to the bed. The pain shivered up his arm.

It was nearly eight o'clock at night. Caller ID showed HOWIE.

"You alone?" Howie asked, his voice low.

"Yeah. You?"

"Yeah. My parents are gonna be here soon to take me home, so I figured we better do this now because once I'm in the house, they're gonna be on me like the fifty tattoos you owe me."

"Fifty's a little much." Jazz glanced at the door. He was certain there was a cop stationed there; Hughes wouldn't be stupid enough not to have a guard posted. He dropped his voice to a whisper and turned as best the handcuff would allow, showing his back to the door.

"I want a tattoo that just says 'tattoo,'" Howie went on. "It's a meta thing. Very postmodern. Avant-garde. I don't expect you to understand. Anyway, hang on a sec." Jazz heard a clicking sound. A moment later: "You still there, Jazz?"

"Yeah."

"We're all in the hospital at the same time. What are the odds? Okay, I'm conferencing in—"

"Jazz!"

It was Connie's voice. It was the sweetest, sweetest thing Jazz had ever heard in his life. Until that moment, he had imagined her in an ICU or on an operating table, fighting for her life after the depredations Billy had unleashed upon her. Tears surprised him, and he dabbed at his eyes with the corner of the sheet.

He wanted to shout. He longed to scream his joy at her voice until his elation filled every last cubic inch of space in the hospital.

Instead, he forced himself to keep his voice to a whisper: "Are you okay? What did he do to you?"

"Nothing. Well, not nothing, but I got away."

"You fought off Billy?" He didn't mean to sound disbelieving, but he actually couldn't believe it. Couldn't believe that Billy would let Connie go, no matter what it took.

"I messed up, Jazz." Connie's voice broke into sobs. "I was stupid. I was trying to help you and I came to New York and—"

"Hey, look, guys," Howie interrupted, "Connie's dad could come back soon. We don't have much time. Let's figure out what's going on, and keep it quick."

They tried, but it proved impossible. Too much had happened since the last time they spoke to one another.

Jazz explained to them about the Hat-Dog Killer and the game of serial killer Monopoly. About tracing Belsamo to the storage unit and everything that had happened there.

About his mother being alive.

"I know," Connie said. "I met her."

Jazz could not have been more surprised had Connie announced she was pregnant with Howie's love child.

"I can't believe this," Jazz said. "Howie? You still on?"

"Yeah, sorry, I was just trying to figure out the actual odds of us all being in the hospital at the same time."

"Howie!"

"What? It's weird!"

"What's going on down there in the Nod? With Gramma and Aunt Sam?"

"Yeah, about that... Your grandmother's doing okay in the hospital. Sam is gone."

"Gone?"

He listened as Howie recounted his night at Gramma's house. Then, with a little backtracking and some help from Howie, Connie recounted what she'd been up to in Lobo's Nod and her trip back to New York. Jazz's relief at her safety flopped in and out of his heart, alternating with his terror at what she'd endured at Billy's hands and his complete outrage at the danger she'd blithely walked into.

"It was so stupid," she said, "and I know it was. But there was the picture of you, Jazz. And I couldn't bear the idea of him hurting you. You get it, right?" There was a thick cast of concern and love and self-recrimination in her voice, and not for the first time, Jazz knew exactly how undeservedly lucky he was. "After the Impressionist and after helping out in New York, I just thought... I don't know. I thought I could contribute and it was *you* and..." She trailed off, and the three of them said nothing for a while.

"I'm so glad you're going to be okay," Jazz whispered at last.

"Tell him the rest of it," Howie said. "What you found when you dug up his old backyard."

"Oh, right. What was in the box?" Jazz asked.

And Connie told him. The childhood photos. The plastic toy. The birth certificate.

Jazz couldn't breathe for a moment. His mouth opened and closed like a fish lacking water. "It's not true," he managed at last. "It's a fake."

"Howie can text it to you. It looks real, Jazz."

"It doesn't matter," Jazz said. The moment the words came out, he knew they were true. He had been raised by Billy. Taught. Indoctrinated.

But what if it's not in my DNA? What if I'm not damned by my own blood?

Yeah, what if? Then all that means is that Billy was able to conquer nature. He opened up my head and dumped his crazy in there. I'm not sure which is worse—being born to it or learning it.

"It makes no difference," he said again. "We're not talking about it anymore. It doesn't matter."

Connie and Howie gave him a moment. "Jazz..." Connie began.

"Seriously. Not talking about it. Tell me about this bell and the stuff you found at JFK."

With his eyes closed, he could see Connie pursing her lips and nodding in studied, resigned frustration at his obstinance. "It was some kind of code," she said. "There was the

131

bell and the gun at JFK. And then this picture of Kevin Cost-
ner, believe it or not, as an FBI agent, and the place where he
was hiding was near this place called Ness—"

Jazz nearly choked. "Dude, you all right?" Howie asked,
panicked. Connie chimed in, just as concerned: "Jazz? Jazz,
are you still there?"

"You're sure about all that?" he asked. "A bell, a gun, and
Ness?"

"Yeah. But what—"

Jazz leaned back on the pillow. It was just the kind of sick
joke Billy would play. "Bell. Gun. Ness," he said.

"Right," Connie said slowly. "Does it mean something?"

"It's a name. Not *bell* and *gun* and *Ness*. A name. Belle
Gunness."

"I don't get it," Howie said. "Was she a friend of your
dad's or—"

"She was a serial killer," Jazz told them. "One of history's
rare female serial killers. Over a hundred years ago."

Silence on the line again. Jazz didn't want to say the next
thing, the obvious thing.

"Then that means your aunt Samantha..."

"There's a reason she's disappeared," Jazz said. He didn't
want to say what came next, because somehow saying it
made it real. But he had no choice: "Aunt Sam is Ugly J."

❧

The antibiotic IV was nearly empty. The saline drip was a
newer bag.

Jazz pulled the antibiotic first, easing the needle out of his arm with care. The millimeters of metal slipping through his flesh felt like yards. But after Billy's suturing of his leg, he could handle it.

A couple of hours ago, a nurse had come by to remove the drain in his leg. He could bend it, and the pain was much, much less than he'd feared. He sensed he would have a limp, but all that mattered right now was that the leg worked.

He had to get out of here, handcuff notwithstanding.

Hughes thought he'd killed Morales. Or had at least been involved somehow. And who could blame him? Hughes had known Jazz a total of four days, and in those days Jazz had nonchalantly broken into someone's apartment, stolen private property, and disobeyed any number of requests from the police. Top that off with a couple of bodies in a storage unit, and *of course* Hughes thought he was responsible for Morales's death.

Then there was the more disturbing fact of the matter: Namely, that Jazz *was* responsible for Morales's death.

You're gonna be the death of that FBI agent, Jasper. I promise you that.

Just as Billy had predicted.

You'll watch her die.

Hughes had told Jazz to back off on his Hat-Dog theory. He'd expressly and explicitly told Jazz to do nothing, in effect sending him to his (hotel) room while Hughes himself tried to figure out what to do with the illegally obtained evidence Jazz had procured. But Jazz had ignored that command, had gone to the FBI agent with a towering hard-on for Billy Dent, and had persuaded her to join him on a jaunt to unit 83F.

Persuaded might be too strong a word. It hadn't been difficult to lure Morales into going. Like so many of those who'd stalked Billy, she had more vengeance and rage pumping through her veins than blood. Billy had humiliated her as Hand-in-Glove, leading her on a merry chase through Kansas and Oklahoma, teasing her with false evidence and fruitless leads. It wasn't personal, Jazz knew. Billy didn't care about individual pursuers. They were—despite their rank, position, title, or agency—"bastard cops," one and all. Morales, though, had taken it personally. She'd sacrificed her marriage in pursuit of Billy Dent, a law enforcement cliché if ever there was one, but that would have been little comfort to Morales and her ex-husband.

Charlie. She called him Charlie, and she packed a framed picture of him that she took on assignments.

Yeah, his days of getting assistance from law enforcement were over. Hughes would probably insist on throwing the switch himself if Jazz were given the death penalty. No one was going to help him.

He had to rely on himself.

That's the way it's s'posed to be, Jazz heard Billy say in his head.

He hated it when his father told the truth.

Aunt Samantha was Ugly J. She fit. Using the name Belle Gunness was the final piece of evidence Jazz needed.

A brother-sister pair of serial killers. And I sat right

across from her at my kitchen table, and she Billy'd me like a pro. I can't believe I fell for it.

Billy was on the loose. Sam had disappeared from the Nod. They were reuniting, Jazz was certain.

They had his mother.

It made sick sense. Jazz remembered telling Hughes how the Hat-Dog Killer's crimes made perfect sense to the murderer. The same held true for Billy and Sam. Billy was obsessed with Jazz becoming the next generation of killer.

Thing I can't decide, Billy had said as he left unit 83F, *is whether I'm gonna kill her or I'm gonna watch you kill her.*

At the time, he'd meant Connie. Connie's death—whether by Jazz's hand or before his very eyes—would push him over the edge into Billyland.

The antibiotic IV was out. Jazz took a deep breath and reached for the saline needle. This one was in a little deeper.

With Connie out of his grasp, though, Billy would move on to the next best thing: Mom. Jazz was positive that Billy would keep his mother alive for now. Until he could murder her in front of Jazz.

That was the original plan, I bet. That's why he came to New York. Sam was here looking for her all along. And she was using Hat and Dog, playing with them. Then Billy got to town, and we stupidly called Sam for help. They must have been laughing their asses off at us. I let her right into the house. I left her with Howie, of all people, the most fragile person I know.

Tears blurred his vision. He rubbed them away savagely,

focusing on removing the needle without tearing the skin or slashing open a blood vessel.

Don't lose it, Jazz. Not now. Howie's safe. Connie's safe. Gramma's safe. Mom is only safe for now. You have to find her. You have to save her, and you can't do that from a hospital bed.

At the name Belle Gunness, he'd remembered more than that she was a serial killer. He'd also remembered what Billy had said in the storage unit. About Gilles de Rais. About Caligula. About "where it started."

The needle came out. He was now completely free.

Except for the handcuffs.

You've got the beginnings of it, boy. Told you as much back at Wammaket. Told you where it started.

Yes. He understood now. Where it all began. It would lead him to Billy, he was certain.

Carefully, lest he stab himself through a finger, he bent one of the IV needles, giving it a ninety-degree hook at the end. He inserted this into the handcuff's keyhole and used the edge of the hole for leverage to bend the needle again.

It broke.

Damn it!

Well, that was why it was a good thing he had two needles.

He was more careful with the second needle. The second bend took. Exhaling a breath he hadn't realized he was holding, Jazz wiggled the needle into place and heard the *click* of the cuff as it opened.

CHAPTER 16

Hughes slumped at a table in the hospital cafeteria, nursing his third Red Bull of the day. He wondered exactly how many cans of the noxious swill he would need to drink before his heart exploded. It seemed, at the moment, an experiment worth conducting. Less than twenty hours since the phone call about Duncan Hershey had awoken him from a deep slumber, the world had turned topsy-turvy in ways he never could have predicted, right down to Jennifer Morales already leaving the morgue for a flight to . . . to wherever the hell she was from. With Grudzinski handling the logistics of the Billy Dent manhunt for now, Hughes could — in theory — head home and grab some shut-eye.

Truth be told, he didn't want to shut his eyes. He knew what he would see — the abattoir of unit 83F. And were there scents in dreams? He didn't know, but he was certain he would smell its noisome human reek, too, with undertones of bleach and preservative.

Hughes scrubbed his face with both hands. Goddamn it. He didn't even know where Morales was from. Didn't know if she had family. Didn't know a damn thing about her, despite them working ass-to-nuts God knows how many months on the Hat-Dog case. And then along came Jasper Dent, killing the ant colony with a grenade.

My fault, Hughes thought. *My damn fault.*

He had disobeyed orders and gone to Lobo's Nod to entice the Dent kid to Brooklyn out of sheer desperation, nothing more.

Well, there *was* something more. Hubris.

Pride went before, ambition follows him. More Shakespeare. One of the Henrys, he thought. Sure, okay. Cards on the table? It was pride, and it was ambition. But they'd been stymied for *months*! People were abjectly terrified. Hughes hadn't seen fear like that in his city since the days after 9/11, when the streets were damn near empty, the subways echoing, hollow tubes. What few people braved the outdoors had the haunted, shell-shocked looks of soldiers going into battle. Brooklyn had a similar savor to it these past few months. Something had to be done. They were days away from vigilante justice. Mobs in the streets.

And so Hughes had reached out to Jasper Dent, desperate for something—anything—that would bring sanity back to the borough.

It's not like I turned the investigation over to him. I just showed him the facts. I asked him to draw some conclusions.

He took another swig of the Red Bull. It burned his throat. Who was he kidding? He'd screwed up. Monumentally.

Bringing the Dent kid to New York had been like dropping napalm on an oil spill.

If only I knew then what I know now....

His phone buzzed for his attention. An unfamiliar number. He answered it, only to hear a drawling, booming voice:

"Is this Detective Louis Hughes, NYPD? This here's G. William Tanner, sheriff of Lobo's Nod."

Hughes turned down the volume on his phone. "Sheriff Tanner? What can I do for you?"

"I've been doing a little digging on my end of things here in Lobo's Nod. I understand you've got a couple of my kids in the hospital there."

Hughes weighed what he knew of Tanner from conversations with Dent and from the media. "That's true, Sheriff. And I have to tell you—the Dent kid is currently under arrest for a whole slew of things."

He could almost hear the gears ticking over in the sheriff's head before that booming voice came back again. "I'm sure you've done what you think is right, Detective. Ain't gonna try to convince you otherwise. But look here—I've been talking to a boy here in town name of Howard Gersten. Wanted to fill you in on what he told me."

Ah, the mysterious Howie reared his head. Leave it to Dent to figure out how to cause trouble in two places at once. "Shoot."

Tanner spoke for a few minutes, rattling off information, most of which Hughes didn't care about. Lockboxes buried in backyards and toy birds and baby pictures. Secret flights to New York. Dent's racist grandmother and something about a missing aunt and blah blah blah.

The only thing he *did* care about was the birth certificate. *That* was interesting. Hughes had interrogated any number of criminals, and he knew that one way to break them was to yank some fundamental underpinnings away. Tilt their world askew, force them to see it from a new angle, and sometimes something shook loose.

Hughes was convinced that the Dent kid knew more than he was telling. He couldn't believe that Billy Dent would show up in the storage unit to sew up his kid's leg and not let something drop, some important bit of information that Jasper now held tight like a baby blanket.

"Thanks for that information, Sheriff," Hughes told him, downing the last of the Red Bull. The day wasn't over yet. "Hey, I have a question for you."

"Go 'head."

"Do you mind me asking what the *G* stands for?"

"Don't mind you askin' at all. Do mind telling, though."

Hughes chuckled and signed off. He crumpled the Red Bull can into a ball and surprised himself with a perfect three-pointer into the trash can. A nearby nurse applauded.

Hughes had put Finley on guard duty at Jasper Dent's hospital room door. She seemed like a good cop; when he'd had that moment in the storage unit where he wanted to put a bullet in Jasper, she'd said nothing. Probably would have backed him up on it, too. That was Hughes's measure of a good cop—someone who will back you up if you do something stupid. It was on him not to do the stupid thing, of course. It was just nice to know he had backup, if necessary.

"Anything go down since the lawyer came by?" Hughes asked Finley, who had—almost adorably—stood at attention when he approached.

"Nothing. Couple of nurses. Doctor stopped by. They removed the drain from his leg. Said they're taking him off the IVs soon."

Hughes grunted. Dent's health mattered to him only insofar as he couldn't indict a dead body.

"How long have you been on?"

Finley shrugged. Hughes knew it had been about ten hours of sitting in front of Dent's room.

"Go stretch your legs. Get some coffee. Smoke a cigarette."

"I don't smoke."

"You will."

Finley took a few steps toward the elevator, then hesitated. "How long should I—"

"I'm not leaving him until you're back, Finley. Take your time."

He took a deep breath, hand on the doorknob. How best to play this? Dent had lawyered up, and the kid was no dummy—he would refuse to talk unless Hughes could prod him into it. Such prodding would have to be done carefully; anything Dent said at this point would be inadmissible in court...unless Hughes could get him to waive his right to counsel. He'd done it before. There were ways of convincing a suspect of what Hughes thought of as the Great Lie: *It'll be easier for you later if you talk to me now.* Many, many, many idiot scumbags had fallen for it in the past.

Jasper Dent wasn't an idiot, but he wasn't superhuman, either. He could be broken and twisted into a new shape just like anyone else.

Hughes knocked once and entered. The overhead light was off, as was the TV. The only light came from the dim little reading lamp over the bed. Dent had the sheet drawn up to his chest. In bed, enervated, he looked like any other kid, and Hughes had to suppress a momentary spasm of pity. Serial killer's son. Bastard never had a chance.

"Evening, Jasper." Hughes removed his overcoat and hung it on a peg. It was a casual move, designed to communicate how comfortable he was in this situation. And that he planned to be here for a while. He stood near the door. Dent didn't respond, staring straight ahead.

"I said, evening," Hughes repeated, more loudly. This time, Dent turned his head, moving as though his neck had rusted. His eyes were heavy, lidded.

Drugged. The painkillers. Or whatever the docs had given him.

Tricky legal ground. Later, Dent's lawyer could claim that he'd been under the influence when talking to the cops and couldn't competently waive his rights. Risky.

Screw it. There was a dead FBI agent, and the kid was the son of a serial killer, and Hughes was amped up on an absurd amount of caffeine. He would take his chances.

"I've been talking to Sheriff Tanner. Down in Lobo's Nod."

Dent stared at him dully.

Hughes groaned. If the kid was too out of it to talk, then this was useless. He came closer to the bed. "The sheriff," he said loudly and slowly. "In Lobo's Nod. You know him, right?"

Dent slurred something that Hughes realized was "G. William."

"Right. Him. Hey," Hughes said, trying to get the kid to respond, "you know what the *G* stands for?"

More dull staring.

"Believe it or not, I'm trying to help you, Jasper." Making a connection to the suspect was crucial. "I have some information that could maybe exonerate you. Or at least make a jury see things differently. Maybe I tell you something and you tell me something in return. That's how it works."

Jasper cleared his throat. It took forever. A streamer of sputum trailed from his lips to the pillowcase.

"I know I was pretty pissed before, but you have to understand. You have to see it through my eyes, you know? You get me?"

Jasper nodded weakly and whispered something. Exasperated, Hughes dragged a chair over and sat next to the bed. "What was that? What did you say?"

"I'm sorry," Jasper managed.

Hughes's toe began tapping on the linoleum, but he succeeded in keeping his face impassive and contemplative. *I'm sorry* sounded a lot like the beginning of a confession. Time to dig a little more, get the kid talking, get him to the point where he couldn't stop, then pull back. *Can't talk to you any more unless you waive your right to remain silent....*

"Sorry for what?" Hughes asked.

"This," said Jasper Dent, and before Hughes knew what was happening, the Dent kid was going for his throat.

✦

A good choke hold, Dear Old Dad had once told Jazz, *is all about geometry.*

Jazz had been maybe ten years old at the time. Geometry wasn't yet in any of his textbooks, but it was part of the special father-son tutoring that went on every day at the Dent house. Geometry helped you figure out the angle of view of security cameras. Geometry told you where to stand and in which shadows. How to position the knife or the saw.

Geometry also guaranteed that your choke hold blocked the blood vessels on both sides of the neck, crucial placement if you wanted your victim unconscious and not merely pissed off and thrashing.

Pretend your elbow is a point, Billy said, *and that her chin* (for it was always and ever *her* with Billy) *is another. You want to be able to draw a line between 'em. A perfect line.*

Jazz had punched Hughes in the throat first. Not enough to break his windpipe—just enough to silence him and catch him off guard. Then, much to Hughes's shock, he'd rolled out of bed, his right arm—the one that was allegedly handcuffed—outstretched so that when he finished his roll he was standing behind Hughes, the crook of his arm lined up with the detective's Adam's apple.

He bent his arm. His forearm compressed one side of the

neck, his biceps the other. His elbow and Hughes's chin made a line so straight that surveyors could have used it.

Jazz's left leg throbbed, but he ignored it. As soon as he'd popped the cuff, he had risked pacing the room, testing his leg. True to Dr. Meskovich's promise, he could walk. He limped and it hurt, but he could stand and walk, even with the bullet still lodged in the meat of his leg.

He tightened his arm. Hughes gagged and flailed and made sounds and movements that would have eked pity out of almost anyone else. But Jazz knew how to tamp down his pity. How to shove it in a box without any airholes and let it suffocate.

No matter what his birth certificate said or didn't say, he was Billy Dent's son.

A rush filled his ears. The ocean. His own blood. Maybe the roar of Hughes's rage and surprise, psychically transmitted. Or maybe the ghosts of Billy's victims, howling in betrayal.

Hughes passed out, slumping in the chair. Jazz held him tight for a few more seconds, just in case the cop was playing possum.

As soon as Jazz released Hughes, his hearing returned to normal and the timpani of pain in his leg jumped a degree. He took a deep breath and denied himself the weakness, the pleasure, of worrying about his leg.

Sometimes, Billy said, *you'll be hurt. And that's when you gotta make a decision: Is it a big pain, the kind that'll kill you? In that case, deal with it. Otherwise, shut it away. Lock it in the closet. Stuff it in a bag and throw it in the river 'cause if it ain't gonna kill you, you don't need it.*

145

Meskovich had told Jazz the leg would eventually be fine. So he gagged it, bound it, and rolled it into a mental trunk, then slammed the lid. .

Gagging. Binding. Right. Back to work.

Hughes wouldn't be out for long. Jazz had been prepared for this moment, though he'd thought he would be choking out a doctor or nurse, not Hughes. Under his pillow, he'd stashed some things he needed. Like torn strips of sheet, which he stuffed into Hughes's mouth and then taped down with some medical tape he'd found in a drawer. Not as good as duct tape, but he couldn't afford to be picky.

Just as Hughes began to rouse, Jazz snapped the handcuffs on him, threading the chain through the bed's far railing first. Hughes was helpless, and he knew it. His grunts through the gag were pathetic.

"I'm not going to lie to you," Jazz said. "This is going to suck. You're gonna be a laughingstock around the precinct for a century or two." He couldn't really crouch down with his leg the way it was, but he was able to bend at the waist and look right into Hughes's eyes. "I want you to remember something for me, Detective. I actually sort of like you. I guess I have a thing for people who break the rules. I want you to remember that I could have killed you very, very easily, but I didn't. When it comes to my trial—assuming I live that long—you better tell the jury that."

He pulled the chair away from Hughes, forcing the man into the uncomfortable and maximally helpless position of half leaning over the railing, half crouching on the floor. A quick frisk turned up Hughes's wallet, badge, phone, and gun. The gun tempted him. It seemed to communicate with him telepathically. *Take me with you, Jazz*, it said, speaking in a sexy female voice for some reason. *You know you want to. You're afraid you'll use me, but that's what makes me so much fun, Jazz. All the possibilities.*

He settled for releasing the magazine and tossing the bullets in the toilet. The gun itself he left on the bed. Everything else he would take.

"Don't worry." He cast one look back at Hughes, who was trying to thrash violently, trying to make some noise. But the angle of his bent body over the railing made it impossible — every move punched him in the gut.

Angles.

You done well, Billy said, and for the first time in his life, Jazz didn't mind it. He thought he felt something bordering on pride.

"Someone will come along soon enough," Jazz said. "This is gonna hurt your reputation more than anything else."

He took Hughes's overcoat from the peg. Unfortunately, Jazz's clothes were long gone, vanished into an NYPD evidence lockup somewhere, no doubt. All he had right now were a couple of hospital gowns. The overcoat was better than nothing. He filled its pockets with his phone, Hughes's phone and wallet, and the cop's badge. Anyone looking at his bare feet would realize he didn't belong, so he paused a moment to steal Hughes's shoes, too. They were too big, but when he stuffed some gauze in them, they worked.

With a deep breath, he cracked the door. The original plan had been to knock out the next nurse or doctor in his room and create a commotion to draw in the guard at his door. Then overpower the guard, too, and escape. When he'd heard Hughes dismiss the cop outside, though, he'd known that this plan was even better.

He slipped into the corridor and quickly checked left and right. There was some activity to his right, but only empty hallway and a bank of elevators to his left. Bingo.

Forcing himself to walk calmly, he strode to the left. He found that as long as he took careful, deliberate steps, his left leg didn't bother him so much and his limp was barely noticeable. He grudgingly admitted that the surgical tag team of Billy Dent and Dr. Meskovich had done a good job.

At the end of the corridor, he paused. Elevator, or the emergency stairs off to one side? Elevator was faster, but there would be a camera in there, and if something happened, he'd be trapped in a box. Stairs were slower, but probably empty, probably not monitored, and he could exit on different floors in an emergency.

Fate or chance—he had no opinion on which—took the choice out of his hands. With a *BING!* that seemed unnecessarily loud, the doors in front of him slid open.

And Jazz found himself staring right at Officer Natalie Finley.

CHAPTER 17

Finley had a cup of coffee in one hand, a bag of food in the other. She was alone in the elevator, and the instant she saw Jazz standing there, a spurt of recognition widened her eyes and parted her lips. She froze for just a second.

One second too long.

She wore a bulletproof vest, he could tell. Made sense. Most of them did these days. So he went for the coffee cup, knocking the lid off as he smacked it toward her exposed face. No matter how good her training, her basic instincts took over and all her attention went to the hot coffee spattering into the air for just a moment. She dropped the bag of food, but she should have dropped the coffee, too. Jazz reached into the elevator, grabbed her by her collar, and yanked her into the hall, spinning her around as he did so.

She yelped in total surprise and finally let go of the coffee. Hot droplets pebbled Jazz's cheek and neck, but he ignored them, focused only on the woman before him.

Bet she's got somethin' special under that vest, Billy

teased, and Jazz shouted back, *Shut up! I'm working!* with a ferocity he'd never have dared face-to-face.

The bank of elevators was centered on the short branch where two hallways met in a T. Jazz kept his momentum and spun Finley around, careful to pivot on his right leg. She dizzily clawed at her holster, but at the last moment, he released her and she staggered backward with violent speed, stumbling and tripping against an abandoned cart of electronic equipment. With a cry of shock, she lost her balance and went down, banging her head against the cart along the way.

She clunked to the floor like a dropped sack of flour, hitting her head a second time on the floor. She lay very, very still.

No one seemed to have seen or heard. The elevator bank was empty, and they were now shielded from the folks down on the long stem of the T by the corner where the two hallways met. Jazz checked Finley's pulse and breathing. She seemed okay. Just unconscious.

That wouldn't last long.

A buzzing in his ears deafened him. His heart raced. He'd barely walked ten yards and already he'd had to fight two armed cops, with a healthy dollop of sheer dumb luck partially responsible for his continued freedom. Luck, though, as Billy had said so many times, was like lightning—it struck sinners and saints in equal measure, and it did so on its timetable, not yours. At some point, someone would get the drop on him.

Have to get out of here. Have to get moving. Mom needs me.

And Billy. Where Mom was, Billy would be, too.

Next time you see me, you go right ahead and kill me.

That was the plan. For Connie. For Mom. For everyone else. For the one hundred and twenty-three and counting.

And Sam? What about her?

He shook if off. Finley wouldn't stay unconscious forever, and he couldn't just stand over her out in the open like this. He swiped her handcuffs and tossed her service revolver into a nearby trash can. One less gun coming after him later.

After a moment of thought — a plan beginning to form — he took her shoulder mic and radio. There was a schematic of the hospital layout mounted on the wall opposite the elevators. Jazz studied it for a moment. Yes. Yes, this might work.

It was crazy, but then again, so was Billy. And look at how long *he'd* managed to stay one step ahead.

Jazz ducked into the stairwell. It was freezing in there. The hospital's heating system could not penetrate the concrete box that ran between floors; he shivered, nearly naked under the overcoat.

Ascending the stairs proved difficult with his leg. Walking on a level floor was one thing, but bending his leg and putting pressure on it to go up was quite another. By the time he'd made it up one floor, he was drenched with sweat. But he also understood why people in horror movies always ran upstairs, even though everyone in the audience screamed at them to go down.

Because people expect *you to go down. They assume you're trying to get out, so they're waiting for you downstairs. Upstairs gives you some breathing room.*

He went up only one floor. That was all he needed, fortunately, as he didn't think his leg could take him up another flight. Pressed against the wall next to the stairwell door, he risked a glance through the glass slit that revealed the elevator bank on this floor. There were some doctors and nurses milling about. No cops or security that he could tell.

Am I really going to do this?

Well, yeah. What other choice do you have? Are you gonna take hostages? That never works.

He switched on Finley's radio and raised the mic to his lips. Thumbed the Send button.

"Attention, all units," he announced. "Attention! Attention! We have sighted suspect Billy Dent! He is converging on the back entrance to the hospital! Repeat: back entrance to the hospital! All units, please respond!"

The radio immediately exploded into a flurry of calls and countercalls. One voice demanded—repeatedly—"Who is this? What's your call sign?" But it was swiftly drowned out by an overlapping cacophony of calls and responses from a multitude of officers. There were rules and procedures and protocols, but Jazz knew the NYPD was on edge right now. Morales was dead. Hat-Dog was dead, by mysterious means. No one was thinking straight. Everyone was on hyperalert.

And then Jazz had tossed Billy like a grenade.

He exited the stairwell and with a smooth, unhurried action, produced Hughes's badge, holding it aloft. "NYPD!" he shouted in his most authoritative tone. "EVERYONE, PLEASE CONFINE YOURSELVES TO THE NEAREST

ROOM! CLOSE THE DOOR, AND DO NOT OPEN IT UNLESS TOLD TO BY A MEMBER OF THE NYPD!"

He marched straight into the cluster of doctors and nurses, the badge before him like a torch. His left leg throbbed, but his slow, confident stride ameliorated the pain.

"What's going on?" a doctor asked.

Jazz didn't speed up and he didn't slow down. He knew he looked just barely old enough to pass for an adult, but he didn't want anyone taking the time to notice how young an adult. "Sir," he snapped, "please get into a room and close the door. Billy Dent has been seen in the area."

Kablam! Another Dear Old Dad grenade. The doctors and nurses obediently scattered. Jazz made his way down the hall, the badge his standard, barking out instructions.

See how they run? Billy whispered. *See how they obey? That's 'cause they're not real, Jasper. They hew to you; they hearken. Because you are one of the only things in the world that matter.*

People are real, Jazz told himself. *People matter.*

No, they aren't. No, they don't.

"Back in the room!" Jazz barked to a nurse who was just emerging through a door. "Now! Do it now!" She scampered back comically, and if he could have afforded to, Jazz would have laughed.

He made his way across to the other side of the hospital. His radio still squawked and bleated with pandemonium. He imagined the panic throughout the hospital itself, on the streets outside, as cops told one another to stand down or to move into position or whatever. Occasionally, he chimed in on the radio, contributing something garbled or cut off, something easily interpreted ten different ways. Even a well-trained force like the NYPD could be thrown into disarray. Who, after all, would expect Jazz to do this?

From the hospital map, he'd memorized a side exit on the opposite end of the building. There was a bank of elevators here, too, but he eschewed them for the stairs after donning a cloak of panic over his voice and shouting into the mic: "Oh, crap! Trip wire in north stairs! Repeat, trip wire in north stairs! Keep *out* of the stairwells! This son of a bitch is playing with us!"

Someone commed back: "Bomb squad is en route. Stay frosty." Jazz shook his head and chuckled. For the first time in his life, Billy's reputation as a superhuman murder machine was working for him, not against him.

Going down the stairs was easier than going up. He could lean on the railing and take most of the weight off his bad leg. He hop-ran down the stairs, taking the corners at dangerous speeds. He couldn't afford to linger. Eventually, someone would realize that there was no Billy Dent, no trip wires. Or someone would find Finley or Hughes. He had to get out of the hospital as quickly as possible. Disappear into the jungle of New York. He'd hated New York almost from the moment he'd landed at JFK—days ago, years ago, lifetimes ago—for its crowds, its unconscionably cramped streets, its temptingly expendable population. But now he could use that to his advantage, vanish against the backdrop of humanity. Gather his wits. Figure out Billy's next move.

He's probably already out of the city. He wouldn't stick around after Connie escaped. He would know the heat would come down. Fast. So he'd get the hell out.

The police probably thought they could blockade Billy, keep him contained in the city. What they didn't understand was that Billy always had an exit plan. More than one, usually.

You never go into a place, Jasper, Billy had said so many times, *without knowing how you'll get out. And don't never assume you can come out the same way you went in. You make that assumption, you'll end up pig-stuck in the weight room at Wammaket or bleedin' out of your ass in some local jail somewhere.*

Billy himself had ended up in Wammaket and had managed to get stuck nowhere. Billy always survived. Like a cockroach.

The world's smartest, meanest, craziest cockroach.

He'll scurry away. But this time he's not alone. He'll take Mom with him. She escaped, and he'll want to punish her for that. And me.

He paused at the stairwell door. He'd made his way down to the first floor. If the map he'd memorized was right, there was a side entrance not ten yards from here. Ten yards and he would be outside, with all the cops in the world at the *back* of the building, looking for Billy.

I'm coming, Mom. As fast as I can.

Before he could open the door, it opened for him. A hospital security guard—young, vaguely Middle Eastern, pudgy—gawked at him for a moment before fumbling for his radio.

There was no time to finesse it; it was the guard or Mom, and that particular coin came up in Mom's favor every single time Jazz flipped it.

He punched the guard in the face. Pretty sure nothing broke, but the guard staggered back, his nose gushing blood. Jazz grabbed him by the lapels and jerked him into the stairwell. No gun, but the guy had a Taser holstered at his hip, so Jazz yanked it free and gave him a good jolt right in the neck. There was a sizzling sound, and the man danced comically for a moment before collapsing to the floor.

Jazz ripped loose the radio and stuffed it in his pocket along with the Taser. Out in the corridor, he spied two cops— not security, actual NYPD—standing by the exit he needed.

He ducked back into the stairwell. Damn it! He'd thought this plan couldn't fail. Draw the cops to one door, then leave through the other. Simple, right? But the NYPD wasn't so easily fooled. They were probably focused on "Billy's" location, but they clearly were willing to divert a portion of their forces to guard the other entrances, just in case.

Bastard cops ain't all that smart, Billy said, *but they're smart enough, you hear? And for the times when their brains aren't working, they got all kinds of protocols and procedures and rules and guidelines that substitute for their thinking. Keeps 'em dangerous.*

But predictable, Jazz realized. And no matter how well trained, no matter how smart, cops were still human beings. Human beings with emotions.

Which meant vulnerabilities.

Jazz raised his stolen mic to his lips. He spared a second to prepare himself, and then hit the Send button and screamed into the mic.

"Officer down! Officer down! North side! Oh, Jesus!"

Then, into the security guard's radio, he raised his voice an octave and shouted, "Copy that! Copy that! Officer down! Repeat: officer down!"

Quite involuntarily, he grinned at his ruse. Both Billy *and* Connie would have been proud of his performance.

As expected, the two cops at the door dashed down the corridor, weapons drawn, barking into their shoulder mics. Jazz gave them a moment to round a corner, then slipped into the hallway and out the door, into the frigid, free Brooklyn night air.

Billy Dent's face was on every channel in Connie's hospital room. She vacillated between CNN and a local station. Both covered Billy's presence in New York with breathless excitement. She could almost see the ratings charts reflected in the eyes of the reporters.

One corner of the screen was given over to a photo of Billy from his days at Wammaket. Next to it was a police-artist sketch of Billy as he appeared now. The NYPD had sent in an artist to get a description of Billy's disguise from Connie. The words ARMED & EXTREMELY DANGEROUS scrolled over and over again.

"If you see this man," the reporter said, "do not approach him or otherwise engage him. Contact NYPD immediately...."

The sketch didn't matter. By now, she figured, Billy had changed his appearance yet again. Probably as soon as she had escaped. He wasn't stupid. You didn't kill more than a hundred people over a twenty-year period by being stupid. Billy Dent knew exactly what he was doing. He'd most likely worked out the details of a new disguise before Connie even got to New York. As soon as it was necessary, he would just pull it on like a snake in reverse, slipping into a new skin.

"...now being told that Dent may be converging on Maimonides Medical Center in Brooklyn," the reporter said, holding a hand to her ear. "Rumor has it that Dent's son, Jasper, is a patient there, and there is some speculation that Dent is perhaps trying to retrieve his son. The hospital has been placed on lockdown, with patients confined to rooms, and medical personnel..."

Connie's throat locked, as though a metal claw had snapped shut around it. She couldn't swallow. Couldn't cough or even breathe.

Billy Dent. Billy Dent was headed this way. And maybe he was coming for Jazz, but would he even consider leaving without settling accounts with the girl who'd escaped him?

Temporarily escaped. No one ever really escaped Billy, she realized. Not his son. Not his wife. Certainly not Connie.

He's coming back. He's going to get me this time.

Her father had gone down to the cafeteria for something to eat. She was stuck here, alone. Helpless. Shattered foot.

Broken leg. She cast about for any kind of weapon, something she could use to defend herself when Billy came through the door. There was nothing. Even the food tray was cheap plastic, and her utensils were gone, having been taken by an orderly.

Her phone buzzed. The NYPD had returned it to her in a plastic bag, grimy with fingerprint dust. A uniformed cop had handed it over with a shrug and mumbled, "Nothing on it," without so much as a note of apology in his voice. She had left it on the nightstand, forgotten as she dozed in and out of a drug-aided sleep.

Now she tilted it out of the bag and wiped the screen with the edge of her pillowcase. It was a text from her dad.

Stuck in the caf. They're going to bring me up with a police escort soon. Sit tight.

A police escort. She was a target.

She wondered if there was still a cop positioned outside her door. There had been when she'd woken up, but that was almost a day ago now. How long would they keep an eye on her?

Still, if they were sending Dad back with cops, that meant they must assume she was in danger. How quickly could they get here? What if Billy got here first?

The other phone—the room's landline—rang. Connie stared at it as though it had grown tentacles.

It rang again.

Half expecting the Auto-Tuned voice of Samantha Dent as Ugly J, she answered and nearly sobbed with relief when she heard Jazz's voice.

"How did you…" Connie paused and looked around, even though she was alone in her room. She lowered her voice to a hoarse whisper. "How did you know this number?"

"I just asked the hospital operator for you. Easy. I figured they're already tracking your phone, but I went through the switchboard to the landline, so that might buy us some time."

"Jazz, your father is here. He's—"

"No, he's not."

Connie looked over at the TV. She had muted it when she realized Jazz was on the phone, and now the screen showed what she assumed to be the exterior of the hospital she was in, swarming with NYPD SWAT units in full tactical gear. Fat snowflakes had just begun to drift into frame; in a nice, warm hospital, it was easy to forget that outside, the January cold lurked with Billy Dent.

"The police have the hospital totally surrounded. They're probably on their way to your room right now to protect you."

"Well, that's nice of them, but I'm not there anymore."

"Where did they take you?"

"Let's just say I checked myself out."

Connie could have sworn she heard—through the phone—something like a garbage truck or a big city bus. "Are you *outside*? Did you leave the hospital?"

"Yes, and yes."

As Jazz related his tale, beginning with choking Hughes into unconsciousness, Connie felt the room begin to rotate around her, as though her bed had been mounted on a lazy

Susan spun by a bored child. It started slowly, but as Jazz's story lengthened and turned more and more horrifying, the speed picked up until she had to shut her eyes against it. Even then, she still felt dizzy and nauseated with truth.

"Jazz, you have to turn yourself in."

"Yeah, that's not happening. Not until I'm done."

"You're not thinking straight." Now that she was no longer petrified of Billy Dent slipping into her room with a grin and a knife, she could start to sort her thoughts into some kind of order, as opposed to heaping them into a single unruly pile of panic. Jazz's refusal threatened to send the room into its own sick revolution again. For the sanity of them both, she needed to talk him down.

"You've been through hell," she said. "Come back. You have to take care of yourself. You've been *shot*."

"It's not that bad. Well, okay, it's actually pretty bad. But I'm getting around all right."

"Where are you?"

"I don't know. Somewhere in Brooklyn." He laughed at himself, and she could see the quirk of his lips, the dance in his eyes when he laughed like that. She loved him and hated him in that moment.

"I just wanted to call you because...because it'll probably be a while before we talk again. I'm using Hughes's phone, but I'll have to ditch it soon. They can track it. Mine, too, now that I think of it. Battery's almost dead, anyway."

He sounded cold. She glanced at the TV again. The snow-flakes weren't any thicker in the air than before, but they weren't thinning, either. It was literally freezing out there.

"What are you wearing?" she asked. "Are you warm enough?"

"There might a little charge left in there, though?" he said, ignoring her. "I don't trust it. I'm going to have to ditch it. I can't let them follow me."

"Why? Where are you going?" But she knew before he answered.

"I'm going after Billy."

"You're not serious."

"I need to do this."

"Let the police—"

"The police can't handle him. They've proven that. They had him in a maximum-security prison, and they couldn't hold him."

"You're going to get yourself hurt—"

"Already did that. And it didn't stop me. I'm going after him. He has my mom, Connie. I can't let him hurt her."

"Look, I get it. You're in pain. A couple of different kinds. And you've had a bunch of shocks: the birth certificate. Finding out about your mom. But it's over now. The cops know where he held me, and they're tracking him, and they'll get him and save your mom. It's not all on you anymore. We can rest now. Let them do what they—"

"Connie! Listen to me!" It was the first time she could think of that he'd raised his voice to her. Once, months ago, when hunting the Impressionist, he'd tried to scare her with his creepy Billy skills. What she thought of—in her most private thoughts, not even for recording in her diary—as his "wannabe sociopath" persona. He'd thought he was doing it for her own good, of course. She hadn't bought it then, because she was always on guard for the sudden reappearance of those walls he could erect at a moment's notice. She'd spent their first year together knocking them down, then scaling the ones she couldn't bash through. She knew them intimately. Knew when he was acting out in order to push people away so that he could keep from hurting them. And she also knew that much of the time, his shields powered on not to protect someone else, but to protect himself *from* himself.

But this wasn't typical Jazz. This wasn't a ploy calculated to frighten her or shut her up. He was legitimately out of control. His emotions had finally smashed through those walls from the inside.

"The police can't stop Billy," he ranted, his voice hot. "The FBI can't stop Billy. Cops and feds across the country had twenty years to hunt him, Connie. Do you get that? They had two *decades*. That's longer than we've been alive. He hunted prospects, and he raped and murdered his way around America. And G. William got lucky. He'd be the first to tell you that. He got lucky and Billy got stupid, and the two things happened at the same time, and that's the only reason Billy ended up in Wammaket."

"Jazz—"

"No, I'm not finished yet. Listen. The only person who can stop Billy is Billy. And I'm the closest thing we've got. He spent my whole life trying to turn me into him. Well, now I get to turn that back around on him. He wants me to be a new version of him? Fine."

"Stop it." Connie squeezed her eyes shut even tighter, tears swelling against her lids, pressing at the corners. With her free hand, she gripped the edge of the bed, her world tilting and whirling until she felt that she could be hurled from the bed by the sheer force of their argument.

But he was relentless. Like his father. He couldn't stop.

"And let me tell you something about that birth certificate: I owe you and Howie for finding that. For showing it to me. Because it made some things really, really clear to me."

What things? she wondered but did not ask. She knew he wouldn't answer. "You're right—you owe me. I'm calling in the debt, and what I want in return is for you to go to the first cop you see and turn yourself in. Come back to me."

"If I turn myself in, I'll never see you again. Your dad made that abundantly clear. And besides, I assaulted two NYPD cops and made a slew of them look like idiots. I'll be lucky to get out of a squad room alive."

"The police aren't going to hurt you." The irony of an African American defending the cops was not lost on her; it cut her to her heart. But she had to believe that the police wouldn't hurt him too badly when they caught up to him. And certainly a lot less if he came in voluntarily than if they had to hunt him down. "Just turn yourself in. Pick a public place, if you want. I can help coordinate something with the press—"

"It's not happening, Connie. I'm the only one who can do what needs to be done."

What needs to be done. Five simple words. Monosyllables. Nothing exceptional or special about them. But when

Jazz strung them together, polychromatic spatters erupted behind Connie's closed eyelids.

"You can't kill him." She hated herself for saying it. Days ago, before she'd ever met the man, she had fantasized Billy Dent's death. She lusted for it even more deeply now. But not at the expense of Jazz. Not with the risk of him spending the rest of his life in jail. It was selfish and self-absorbed of her, but even for the betterment of the world, she wasn't willing to sacrifice Jazz. Let Hughes put a bullet in Billy. Let Jan break free and rip his throat out with her bare hands. It was the least she could do to make up for the years of jealous freedom she'd enjoyed while Jazz lived under the thumb and tutelage of a lunatic.

Anyone. Anyone but her Jazz.

"He won't stop," Jazz said. "He'll never stop. Unless he is stopped."

She had only one more card to play. It wasn't an ace or a king—it was the meanest, most unpredictable card in the deck. She was dead serious as she threw down her trump card, the joker:

"I'm trying to understand, Jazz. I really am. I'm trying to get past it. But I need you. I need you in my life."

"I need you in mine, too."

"My father can't keep us apart forever. But I can't be with a killer. I can't do that. If you go—if you kill him—we're over."

Silence. She longed to let it stretch out, to force him to respond, but she found that she couldn't bear the mute emptiness from the other end of the line.

"Remember what I told you before? If you kill him, he wins."

"And I told you: If I kill him, he's dead."

She was openly sobbing now, grief at war with rage, pissed at his stoicism, at his control. They were right at the cliff's edge. They'd come this far, survived four different madmen to get to this very moment, and he couldn't back down, couldn't join her on the solid ground. He should be crying, too. He should be a wreck.

"He wants you to do this." She sniffled and felt the heat rise within her. The anger. "You're being stupid and selfish and blind. He wants you to lose yourself by killing him. Or by trying."

"I know." His voice was hushed. She imagined his breath at her ear. "I know, Connie. I've told myself the same thing over and over. It's the only thing he wants from me. And I have to give it to him."

And then he was gone, the connection severed. Connie didn't even try to call him back.

CHAPTER 18

Jazz needed clothes. Hustling past people on a cold night, he'd been lucky enough that no one noticed his bare ankles under Hughes's overcoat, but the lightning of luck would fry him sooner or later. He also needed to give his leg some time to recover. Once out of the hospital, he'd run as best he could for several blocks, turning down alleyways, climbing over the occasional fence or low wall. If he didn't have a destination in mind, then he figured the cops couldn't predict his moves. Crazy thinking, he knew, but it was all he had.

Calling Connie had been equally crazy. He should have known she wouldn't understand. She knew him better than almost anyone else, but life as Billy Dent's son stretched the most elastic tolerance far beyond the breaking point. What would come next wasn't a matter of intellect or reason or even mere emotion. It was as basic as biology. It was blood and sinew and brain matter. Raw.

He couldn't turn himself in. Couldn't give up the pursuit

of Billy. Any more than Howie could wish away his hemophilia.

He'd escaped the hospital. Now, escaping the cold was his top priority. Then he could figure out how to escape the city.

At this time of night, most places were closed. Light, warmth, and frivolity leaked out onto the street from a variety of restaurants, sorely tempting him. But restaurants were too well-lit. And wearing the overcoat at a table would make him dangerously conspicuous.

And there was the need for clothes.

A bar was a better bet. There was one at the end of the block, dark and noisy. Perfect for his purposes.

The bouncer at the door, a titanic mountain eroded and sculpted into human form, imprisoned by a black turtleneck three sizes too small, sneered at Jazz. "ID," he grunted.

Jazz knew he looked older than seventeen, but it was too much to hope that he looked old enough not to be carded. In any event, his ID was in an evidence lockup somewhere, and he was pretty sure that even a bouncer with a neck as wide as his head wouldn't believe it if Jazz showed him Hughes's ID instead.

"Designated driver," Jazz told him, and feigned a yawn, just to prove how unconcerned he was.

The bouncer paused, clearly caught off guard. He peered around.

"Assholes are always late," Jazz complained, shivering a little. That much wasn't faked. "And I had to park all the way over on Hoyt." He jerked his thumb in that direction. *Always notice street names*, Billy had instructed. *Makes it seem like you belong when you can rattle 'em off.* He stamped his feet for effect. "C'mon, man. I'm freezing my nuts off."

The bouncer shrugged and gestured with a hand stamp. "Gotta stamp you so the bartender knows not to serve you."

"No problem." Jazz offered his left hand—the knuckles on the right one were scraped raw from when he'd punched the security guard.

With a bright blue DD stamped on his hand, Jazz stepped inside. The place was crowded, which was good. Made it easier to disappear. He fought through the crowd and found an open spot at the bar. He needed to sit for a moment. Rest his leg. Gather his thoughts.

"Just water," he told the bartender when she looked his way. She sighed, then noticed his stamp and nodded.

Sipping the water, he considered his options. A part of him wanted to follow Connie's advice—turn around and walk out of the bar, straight to the closest cop he could find. Turn himself in and get the cops to rescue Mom. They were cops—that's what they did, right?

But he couldn't rely on the police now. They weren't his allies anymore. He didn't necessarily blame Hughes for pinning Morales's death on him. If he'd kept his nose out of the investigation and let Hughes take things at his own pace, Dog would have been caught nonetheless. Morales would still be alive.

But Dog probably would have killed someone else in the meantime. And Hat would probably still be out there.

Another thought occurred to him, chilling him colder than the frigid January night air could ever hope to: *If I didn't get shot in that storage unit, Billy wouldn't have come to help me. And Connie never could have escaped.*

He would deal with the police another day. Right now, what mattered was rescuing Mom. No one else could do it. Like it or not, he was a fugitive. He hadn't killed Dog or Morales, but now he could add multiple counts of assault (on police officers, no less) to his future rap sheet, along with the initial breaking-and-entering and theft charges from his inspection of Belsamo's apartment. The NYPD wouldn't listen to him. They had their dragnet, their moves, their rule book, and they were going to chase Billy their way.

What they refused to understand was that "their way" had failed spectacularly and gruesomely for twenty years as Billy crisscrossed America, writing his name in the history books in the blood of one hundred and twenty-three innocents. "Their way" wouldn't work. He was willing to bet that Billy was already out of New York, already on the way to his next safe house.

Somewhere, there would be a Crow willing to help him. Because that, Jazz knew now, was what Crows did. They were the Billy fanatics, the Dent worshippers, the ones who'd congregated to protest his imprisonment, wrote the fan letters, the people like the Impressionist. Anything Billy needed, they would provide, and getting Billy out of New York would be just one more favor.

Jazz scanned the crowd with a practiced eye. Billy's advice over the years had most often slanted in the direction of plucking from a group the most vulnerable woman, isolating her effectively, and then removing her from the world. A woman was no good to Jazz right at the moment. He needed clothes, which meant he needed a man. Fortunately, Billy's lessons were adaptable.

Look for the one who's alone in the crowd. The one not fully engaged. The one moving from group to group or person to person. It'll take longer for that one to be missed.

Altered states are good, too, Billy went on. *You get yourself a drunk or a little girlie on X, and you're halfway home.*

Someone distracted. And distractible.

Most important of all: Just like a carpenter, you measure twice and cut once. You don't get do-overs. You don't get to rewind the clock and start from scratch. Once you commit, you're in. You do it. So make damn sure the one you pick is the right one. See yourself taking her in your mind over and over. Watch the angles. Figure the possibilities. Do it all with precision until you know you can do it. Then wander it in your mind again, just to be sure.

There was a drunk guy who was about the right size, in a cluster of people at the other end of the bar. The guy kept forcibly inserting himself into conversations, clearly a beat or two behind the thread. The indulgent shoulder shrugs and occasional eye rolls of those around him made it obvious he didn't belong with the group, but that no one was willing to confront him. Which meant no one would ever miss him. Perfect.

Jazz lingered, nursing his water. Sitting at the bar took the weight off his leg; the relief was almost as palpable as the pain.

This would be a waiting game. Jazz kept tabs on the guy he'd begun to think of as Ryan. He didn't know why Ryan. But he knew that he had to give the guy a name. Thinking of him as *Drunk Guy* was one step removed from thinking of him as *Victim #1*. Which was one step from thinking of him as something less than human.

People matter. People are real. Even Ryan.

He ordered a Coke when the bartender raised her eyebrow at him, managing to indicate both his near-empty water glass and the actual paying customers who would kill for his spot at the bar. The last thing he needed was to be kicked loose. Or to have her paying attention to him. Better to buy something. Fortunately, there was a sheaf of bills in Hughes's wallet. As she sprayed the Coke into a fresh glass, he tipped her noticeably, but not extravagantly. He didn't want to be memorable.

In the next instant, he had no choice but to be memorable. His picture was on the TV over the bar.

❧

JASPER DENT ON THE RUN! exploded from the screen like fireworks to Jazz's dark-adjusted sight, along with a gigantic logo reading SPECIAL REPORT. They had pulled his driver's license photo, which—sadly—was an extremely good likeness. He'd sweet-talked Lana, the sheriff's office assistant who also handled the local DMV, into retaking the picture until he had one that didn't look as though he'd just woken up from a bad dream. If he could, he would kick Past Jazz in the nuts. The damn photo was perfect. He felt eyes on him, vision crawling over his body like spiders. Everyone in the bar was looking at him.

Stop it. No one's looking at you. No one is even paying attention to the TV. The sound is off, so no one can hear what I'm sure are blaring trumpets announcing the manhunt for yours truly.

No one at the bar had looked at him, so he kept his head down, sipping his Coke. He just had to wait for the report to end. The bar had been playing some kind of soccer match before. Not the kind of channel to linger overlong on a local crime issue. Soon enough, they'd wrap up their socially conscientious reportage and get back to men in knee socks preventing one another from scoring.

He risked a glimpse at the TV, only to realize that the bartender was staring at him.

Don't react. That was the most important thing. He couldn't let her know that he'd noticed her looking at him. The recognition in her eyes presaged an imminent cry of *Holy crap! It's the guy on TV!* There was only one way to preempt that moment, and he acted instantly:

"Holy crap!" he said in a self-consciously loud voice. "That guy looks just like me!" And pointed to himself on TV.

The guy next to him, deep in a mug of beer, goggled at him and then at the TV. The bartender blinked and turned from Jazz to the TV, then back again, and back once more.

"Isn't that crazy?" Jazz punched the shoulder of the man next to him and adopted a tone of bemused disbelief. "Just like me! Can you believe it?"

The drunk shrugged. "Lotta people look alike," he mumbled.

The bartender approached him. "You *do* look like him," she said.

"Like?" Jazz sneered. "That guy could be my twin! That's creepy as hell!" He shuddered in deep revulsion at the depredations scrolling on the screen under his own name. His New York accent—liberally borrowed from the cops he'd been around over the past few days—seemed to be working. "I wouldn't want to be whoever the hell tonight, that's for sure! I better stick around here until they catch him, huh?"

The bartender considered, then nodded. "That might not be a bad idea," she said, and topped off Jazz's Coke with her beverage gun. Jazz nodded his thanks and reached for Hughes's wallet, but she shook her head. "On the house. I do it for all the fugitives." She grinned at him.

Jazz flashed his most winning smile. His megawatt Charmer. The bartender was the only person in the room. The only woman in the world. She actually blushed, barely visible under the bar's red-black lighting.

"I get off at three," she mentioned.

Jazz nodded. "Like I said—I'm not going anywhere tonight."

He watched her as she walked away, an alternate plan forming. If Ryan never went to the bathroom, he would need another way to get some clothes and get out of Brooklyn. Maybe it made sense to stick around and let the bartender— he decided her name was Doreen—take him home. The police wouldn't look twice at a couple walking home together, hunting as they were for the desperate loner known as Jasper Francis Dent.

174

That could work....

Just then, though, Ryan broke away from his cluster of sort-of friends and made an unsteady, weaving, lurching path for the bathroom. Jazz casually slid out of his position at the bar and pushed through the crowd, timing his arrival just after Ryan's. Ryan stopped, hand on the knob, sensing Jazz there. With the goggle-eyed, jelly-necked courtesy of the abjectly drunk, he essayed a little bow and gestured to Jazz, offering him the first use of the john.

Jazz declined, and Ryan, with a shrug, went into the bathroom.

Once you get her alone, Jasper, you got any number of ways to make her yours. Quick and quiet's best. Most women, you show 'em a weapon or even just your intent, they'll clam up real quick. They know they're weaker. They all been taught: Give him what he wants and he'll let you live. So you let 'em think it's a robbery or such, and by the time they realize what they're really in for, you've already got her trussed up or gagged or both.

Course, if she looks like she'll put up a fight, you just blitz her. Overwhelming strength. Overpower her right away. Shock and awe. Shocking and awesome.

Ryan was drunk, but he was Jazz's size and he was a man. Jazz decided on blitz attack.

Before Ryan had the chance to lock the bathroom door behind him, Jazz shoved it open and stepped inside, shutting it quickly. The bathroom was tiny, barely big enough for a toilet and a sink, lit with the same hell-on-the-eyes crimson bulbs as the bar. Ryan moved as though in slo-mo, lidded eyes registering Jazz's presence, even as his brain attempted to process that same presence. His fly was already down.

"Sorry," he slurred. "Thought this was the men's—"

He didn't get to finish, because Jazz jabbed at him with the Taser, hoping that Ryan wouldn't piss his pants when the voltage hit. Ryan's whole body seized, and he went down in a satisfying heap.

Jazz locked the door and removed Hughes's overcoat, then the hospital gown, standing naked over Ryan, who, groggy, now panicked and tried to move his frozen limbs.

"Don't worry," Jazz promised him, "I'm not going to take your virtue or anything."

Moving swiftly, he tore the gown into strips and used them to gag Ryan. Then he used Finley's handcuffs to fasten him to the pipe under the sink, maneuvering carefully in the confines of the restroom.

Once Ryan was secured, Jazz stripped off his clothes, leaving the poor guy the dignity of his skivvies at least. Ryan had, thankfully, not pissed himself—maybe the electricity clamped down on his urethra. Whatever the reason, Jazz was grateful that he wouldn't have to explain away urine stains on the pants he'd already begun thinking of as his.

The clothes were a bit too big, but better too big than too small. He dressed in Ryan's socks, shoes, pants, and shirt, then threw the overcoat back on over it all. He added Ryan's cell to his collection and rummaged in his wallet for cash, discovering nearly a hundred bucks as well as learning that Ryan's name was actually Mark.

"Sorry to do this," Jazz said. "I would explain, but you're

pretty drunk. Someone will eventually find you in here, so just hang tight."

He paused, about to leave, when a thought occurred to him. Kneeling down, he set his cell phone on Ryan/Mark's heaving, terrified chest. "You hold on to this, and I'll trade it back for yours someday. Assuming I get out of this alive. If I don't, well, keep it to make up for me stealing yours."

Since the bathroom door opened inward, Jazz hooked his hand inside as he left, knocking the trash can over. It would make it harder for someone on the outside to open the door and give him a little more time.

He made sure that the bartender wasn't looking his way. The TV was back to soccer already.

He threaded through the bar and slipped outside.

CHAPTER 19

There was a ridiculously hot blond on Fox News blaming Congress and the mayor of New York for Billy Dent's reign of terror. Those exact words—BILLY DENT'S REIGN OF TERROR!—flashed in a migraine-red box under her as she ranted.

Home from the hospital but confined by the Parental Annoying Authority Act to his bed for the time being, Howie couldn't quite follow the logic. Still, the blond was hot, and when Howie muted the TV it was easy to pretend that he could lip-read her saying, *Howie, you are so dashing, what with your bruises and your stitches. I can feel my panties sliding right off me.*

Then again, Howie thought, maybe he shouldn't bother checking out the talent. The last woman he'd wanted to give his heart and (more importantly) his loins to had turned out to be a serial killer.

She could have killed me as I lay on the floor, unconscious. I got lucky. Maybe she doesn't kill men, just women.

I don't know. I can't figure out serial killers or women. Combine them and I got nothin'.

He blinked as he realized that Jazz was on TV. Unmuting the TV, he heard:

"...after assaulting members of the NYPD. The younger Dent is believed to be armed and almost as dangerous as his father...."

As he watched and realized that Jazz was on the run and wanted for a string of crimes, he decided that fame was a double-edged sword that probably shouldn't be handled by hemophiliacs or their best friends.

"And let me just say this," the commentator went on. "If New York City let its citizens carry firearms, we'd see the Dents either locked up or—better yet—dead already."

Howie imagined the city of New York armed to the teeth, terrified neighbors blowing one another's heads off as fear set imaginations afire and itchy trigger fingers on the highest alert. Sounded like the most moronic idea ever, and that was coming from a guy who'd put the moves on a serial killer.

He switched around the channels until he found one not in talking-heads mode, this one with a live feed from the hospital where Jazz and Connie had been admitted. A very pissed-off cop was giving what looked like an impromptu press conference.

"—including assault, robbery, battery, impersonating a police officer. And that's just to start—"

Jazz was in big-time trouble. No question about it. Which could mean only one thing.

Howie sat up in bed and grabbed his phone from the nightstand. 3...2...1...

The phone rang. Caller ID said MARK CULPEPPER, but Howie wasn't surprised at all to hear Jazz say, "We don't have much time, Howie."

"Mark Culpepper? Nice alias, Rambo."

"Am I all over the news still?"

"You could say that."

"Have they shut down the city yet?"

"Not so far as I can tell. Looks like mostly Brooklyn is on high alert." As if on demand, a list of bullet points appeared on the TV, among them: DENT WOUNDED, ON FOOT and BELIEVED TO BE CONFINED TO BROOKLYN.

"Okay, that's good. I managed to get to Manhattan. Let them look in Brooklyn all they want."

"Do you even know the difference? What if they're the same place?"

"We drove over a bridge. I recognized it from when Hughes took me to Manhattan."

"Who's we?" Howie was beginning to worry now—had Jazz gotten mixed up with Billy? Was he on the run with his dad for some reason?

"Gypsy cab. I think that's what they call them. He was on duty all night. Hadn't seen the news. I paid the guy a hundred bucks to get me to Manhattan, hidden under a blanket in the backseat. Told him it was a fraternity prank. Nice guy. Chatted with him. Passed the time. Got out right before the blockades went up."

"So, now what?"

"Can't tell you."

"You wound me."

"Well, you wound easily."

"This is true. But come on—give me a clue. Let me help."

"No. The cops will come to you eventually. It's better if you can't tell them anything."

"I wouldn't squeal on you." Howie pouted, even though Jazz couldn't see him.

"Yes, you would."

"I totally would," Howie admitted. "I'm weak. I lack character, Jazz. That's my problem. That's always been my problem. I blame my mother. For coddling me." He thought for a second. "And I guess for carrying the hemophilia gene in the first place, too."

"Save it for your shrink. I need you to do something for me. I'm going to call you later from a different phone."

"So I am part of the plan?"

"Of course, you idiot. Do I ever do anything crazy or illegal without you?"

"I feel so much better now."

"And Howie—whatever you do, you can't tell Connie anything. Got it?"

"Scout's honor."

"You better not have your fingers crossed."

Howie stared down at his free hand. He did, indeed, have his fingers crossed.

"Totally don't," he promised.

Now Jazz needed a woman.

Preferably, one old enough to have kids of her own. That meant the optimum level of maternal pity.

He watched several walk by from his position in a graffiti-stained doorway. Most were close to his age, college girls, traveling in clusters and pairs. Smart and safe. Good for them. He wasn't interested in them, but maybe someone else was. Someone like his father. Safety in numbers was never a bad idea.

Even at this late hour, he spied one or two with children. Heading home after a late dinner with family, maybe. They were no good to him. He wanted someone old enough to have kids, but not actually with them. Women in the presence of their children were the deadliest of the species.

He knew he would need to compensate for his appearance. He was a male (bad), young (even worse), and tall and fit (worst of all). He needed to look as helpless and pathetic as possible.

And hope that anyone on the street at this hour hadn't seen the news yet.

He spotted her at the end of the block, headed his way. Midthirties, from the look of her. Well dressed. A professional, coming home from a late night at the office. Perfect.

Jazz took a deep breath, reran his plan in his mind—*Measure twice*—and then dashed out into the street as though in a panic, looking behind him. Certain to emphasize his limp, he ran toward her, always checking over his shoulder. He made sure to "accidentally" trip and fall long before he got to her.

Sprawled on the sidewalk, he panted and heaved, then pushed himself up on his good knee and both hands, scanning around himself, a fox desperate to elude the hounds.

He was wondering if he would need to amp up the melodrama when he heard her:

"Are you all right?" she asked. She stood a good ways off, well out of his reach. Best possible decision on her part. She had one hand in her purse already. Cell phone? Maybe. Pepper spray? Possibly. Was pepper spray legal in New York? Jazz didn't know, but he did know that he wanted to avoid a face full of the stuff. His day sucked enough already.

With a great show of agony, Jazz dragged his bad leg around and managed to sit up against a trash can. He scrubbed his face with both hands, as if wiping away tears.

"I need help," he said as plaintively as he knew how. Still, she didn't approach. Which was fine. He didn't actually need her close to him.

"I'll call an ambulance—"

"No!" Jazz said. He wanted to shout it but was afraid his raised voice would frighten her away. "Please. No ambulance. No cops. I just need to get away from him."

Him. The magic word. Jazz and the woman were now bound together by their mutual terror of an amorphous, unidentified, but very real male threat.

"Who?" she asked.

"It's my father." And that was the last true thing Jazz said to the woman.

CHAPTER 20

With the press reporting rumors that Hat-Dog was dead or in custody, the already-cramped street around Brooklyn's 76th Precinct was jammed with news vans, reporters, and citizens just desperate to know what the hell was going on. Even though it was nearly midnight by the time he returned to the precinct—having been interrogated and examined at the hospital like a victim—Hughes still discovered a sizable crowd on the street.

I'm with you, Hughes thought as he pushed through. *I want to know what's going on, too.*

Hat-Dog was dead. Hughes was certain of that, but proving it would be the work of many weeks. Knowing that Belsamo and Hershey had conspired to execute Hat-Dog's victims was one thing; proving it to the satisfaction of the law was another. *Because Jasper Dent says so* wasn't valid evidence in a court of law.

He finally bulled his way through the crowd to the door of the precinct, which was guarded by a uniform who nodded and let him in. The din of the crowd abated only slightly once he was inside. He headed for the captain's office.

Niles Montgomery wasn't the sort to lose his temper— very calmly and with no bombast, he handed out orders to his lieutenants: Ramp up the bridge and tunnel patrols, widen the Billy Dent search parameters, stay alert. Hughes waited until the lieutenants had scampered off to do their captain's bidding before clearing his throat.

"Don't say a word." Montgomery slid into his chair and sighed for what seemed to be an entire minute. "Just tell me you're ready to announce the Hat-Dog stuff is over. It'll take a little of the heat off."

"I'm not ready to announce that yet."

"Come on!" Montgomery slapped his desk blotter, the first sign of the toll the past couple of days had taken on him. "The kid predicted two killers, right? You've got two dead suspects, both of whom had access to the storage unit. Done deal."

"Right. So I announce Hat-Dog is dead, and then another body shows up, and we look like we can't take a dump without out a map to the crapper."

Montgomery chuckled, but it was hollow and grim. "Lou, do you honestly believe the Hat-Dog Killer is still alive and active?"

Hughes had to admit that he didn't.

"Then put together a statement, and let's turn down the heat the tiniest bit, okay? We have enough on our plates now with the Dents."

"We've already missed the boat on that," Hughes said

with all the confidence he could muster. "Trust me on that. I'm telling you, Jasper's already out of the borough. We need to shut down Port Authority and the bridges out of Manhattan—"

"You think he has magic powers or something? He's wounded. I thought this kid was a bumpkin from the sticks. What makes you think he even knows how to get *to* the city, much less get out?"

"He's a bumpkin with the smarts of his dad. We need to use the Patriot Act to get access to the kid's phone and e-mails, as well as the phones and e-mails of everyone he knows. The girlfriend. The people back in Lobo's Nod. Maybe something leads us to a safe house."

"Lou, this kid isn't Osama bin Laden. He's seventeen years old, and he's injured and alone."

"The Patriot Act is for terrorism. This kid's got people terrified. We don't know if he's in cahoots with his dad or not, but it sure looks like it to me. I shouldn't have to remind you that Morales is dead. We have multiple crime scenes and all kinds of craziness going on, and we can't tell the good guys from the bad guys. Hell, maybe Belsamo and Hershey were innocent in all this. Maybe the Dents framed them." He held up a hand to keep Montgomery from interrupting him again. "I don't really believe that. But someone will put it out there. All I'm saying is this: We don't know enough to feel confident that the Dent kid is innocent. I'm not saying we put him down like a dog, Cap. I'm saying we get him and hold him and sweat him for information. Meanwhile, CSI and the labs do what they do. And when we have some actual information, then we can start seeing who we kick loose. Anything else is irresponsible. And dangerous."

Montgomery sighed heavily and steepled his fingers before him, elbows on the desk.

Hughes pressed on: "At the very least, start tracking *my* phone. He took it with him. I'm giving you permission; you don't need a warrant or anything."

"Okay, yeah, let's do that." Montgomery picked up the phone on his desk, and just then a uniform barged in, breathless.

"Captain!" she shouted, completely unnecessarily. "We have a lead on Dent!"

·•·

The lead was on Jasper Dent, not Billy, but Hughes would take it.

The guy's name was Mark Culpepper, and he'd been found unconscious, bound, gagged, and in his birthday suit plus skivvies in a bar bathroom in Boerum Hill. Jasper's cell phone, nearly dead, had been found on him. Stunned and still slightly drunk, Culpepper sipped bad precinct coffee in one of the interrogation rooms as Hughes and Montgomery watched through the one-way mirror. He'd had little to say, but a canvass of the bar turned up a bartender who claimed to have seen Dent.

The bar was pretty far from the hospital where Jasper had

escaped. He'd made it much farther on foot than anyone could have anticipated.

"Well?" Hughes said.

Montgomery's eyes narrowed as he looked through the glass. "I can't say we need to shut down the whole city, but I can say this: It's time to start talking about it."

CHAPTER 21

"Thanks, Miranda!" Jazz said, climbing out of the cab. The sight of Port Authority thrilled and terrified him all at once, but he managed to keep his voice nervous and tentative, as he had during the cab ride uptown from the place Miranda had called SoHo.

"Be careful, Mark," she told him. "And reconsider calling the police, okay?"

He'd told her a lie. Several of them, actually, layered on top of one another and configured to maximize her pity. A physically abusive father. A mother addicted to drugs. A final straw, drawn when Dad "nearly broke my leg." A kid trying to get away, to leave the city for the safety of a friend's house in New Jersey.

Playing the abused, terrified kid to perfection, Jazz had hoped for nothing more than instructions on how to get the hell out of New York. The city was a bewildering array of streets, alleys, avenues, subways, tunnels, bridges. . . . He felt as though he could wander its byways for a century and keep doubling back on himself, never breaking free of its confines. But while the police thought he was in Brooklyn, he'd made it to Manhattan. Now, before they realized where he actually was, he had to get out of New York entirely. Once beyond its endless concrete and glass chasms and canyons, he could disappear into the relative wilderness. They could cordon off bridges and stop subways, but they couldn't blockade every road in the world.

So, still slumped against that trash can, he'd asked the woman he soon knew as Miranda for the best, cheapest way to get out of town, and she'd told him a bus from Port Authority. And then, after a few more pathetic moments, she'd offered to go there with him in a cab.

It was more than he could have hoped for. In a cab they wouldn't be alone, so she felt safe and didn't mind accompanying him. And a couple in a cab wouldn't draw the same scrutiny from a police force and citizenry looking for a single man.

There was a little TV screen in the cab, but fortunately, it was running sports scores when they got in. Jazz couldn't figure out how to turn it off entirely, but he muted it and positioned his "nearly broken" leg so that Miranda couldn't see the screen.

And now she dropped him off at Port Authority. He waved to her as her cab pulled away. On the trip from downtown, he hadn't been able to devise a way to persuade her to walk him into the building and to his bus, so he had to do this alone.

He'd never been to Port Authority before, so he had no idea if the cops milling about represented the usual force or an amped-up, "looking for Jasper Dent" force. In any event, he had to avoid their notice at all costs.

If you're on the run, you got two choices, Billy had said. *You can go balls out and hope to outrun whatever's behind you, or you can go nice and slow, easy as you please. Let whatever's chasing you start to wonder if you're the thing it's really after. Don't work like that in the wild. A gazelle can't try reverse psychology on a lion. But it works a treat on humans, Jasper. It truly does.*

Fortunately, Jazz's limp was much less pronounced when he walked slowly. He ambled along the sidewalk, surreptitiously glancing at the doors into Port Authority, taking in the police presence, looking for patterns in their patrols. A food cart was parked against the sidewalk on the corner, and even though Jazz wasn't hungry, he paused to buy some kind of kebab. Fugitives on the run didn't stop at food carts.

See? See how normal and unthreatening and totally not fleeing the jurisdiction I am?

He meandered up the steps to the phalanx of glass doors, stuffing his face with the kebab as he went. He chewed with obnoxiously huge bites, stretching out his face as much as he could. Anything to look even a tiny bit different.

No one approached him as he reached out for the door handle, and a moment later he was inside, though no less worried. One hurdle leapt, but there were many more to go.

More cops inside. Again, he couldn't tell if this was the usual complement or a beefed-up patrol. He had to assume the worst-case scenario.

He risked kleptoing a Yankees cap from a nearby stall. He

didn't want to stand still long enough to buy it and give the vendor a good look at his face. His shoplifting skills were rusty but good enough for this. He didn't pull the cap down low over his face; that would be as good as screaming, *Come and get me, coppers!* at the top of his lungs. Instead, he swept back his hair and trapped it under the cap, tilting the brim up high. The result made his forehead seem several inches higher, changing the look of his face just slightly. It also concealed his hair, giving the cops one less marker to identify.

Port Authority was as bewildering and as complex as the city itself; New York in miniature. Jazz had expected something like the bus station in the Nod, only bigger. What he had gotten was a mini shopping mall choked with cops and no buses in sight.

At an information kiosk, he grabbed a handful of touristy brochures, a map of the city, and a bunch of bus schedules. He merged with a cluster of college-age kids who were laughing and giggling at one another in a way Jazz knew he would never experience. He didn't even try to mimic them, just fell into step behind them and buried his nose in the map, the geeky outcast who had insisted on joining the cool kids in New York.

When his "friends" passed a men's room, Jazz peeled off and slipped inside. His heart thudded nearly to a stop in his chest, though, when he saw a sign mounted above the sink:

RESTROOMS ARE PATROLLED BY PLAINCLOTHES OFFICERS

There was a man at one sink. Jazz froze for the first time since his escape from the hospital, paralyzed. Of *course* the police would patrol the restrooms. This was a big city. People went into restrooms and did all kinds of nasty things. To themselves, to one another.

Maybe I can use that, he thought.

The sign continued, offering numbers to call from the pay phones or house phones in the building. Before the man at the sink could finish and turn around, Jazz locked himself in a stall that smelled as though hoboes had been living in it for a month. For all he knew, they had. He was one of them now, in a way. Homeless, helpless, friendless.

That's not true. None of it. Stop feeling sorry for yourself.

He gnawed at his bottom lip as he shuffled through the bus schedules. With Mark Culpepper's phone, he went online to fill in the gaps of his plan.

Yes.

Yes, this would work.

I'm coming, Mom. Intentionally or not, Billy gave me the clues, and I'm following them. Hold tight. I'm coming to get you.

He spied the house phone as soon as he left the bathroom. Hoping that no one would take notice, he went straight to it, picked it up, and dialed the code from the bathroom sign.

When a voice answered, he reported—in his highest falsetto—that a "bad man" in the bathroom had "touched me where Mommy says no one is supposed to touch me." Before the voice could ask any questions, he dropped the receiver and walked calmly away.

At the first pay phone he saw, he did it again, this time in a slightly different tone of voice, and this time reporting a man shooting up heroin in a stall.

He didn't want to generate too suspicious a level of criminal bathroom activity, but he wanted some general disarray. With his brochures and the map of Port Authority on Culpepper's cell, he made his way to the ticket kiosk, detouring twice for more calls. The cops on the floor were starting to move a bit differently. Maybe they suspected something. More likely, they were adjusting their patrols as some of them went to inspect the reported men's rooms. Either way, they were slightly off now, and Jazz would take every little bit of help he could get.

Between Hughes's wallet and Culpepper's, he had only thirty bucks left. Cash was precious; he needed to hoard it now. He used Hughes's credit card at the kiosk, buying four different bus tickets to four different destinations. Three of them went into the trash. If the cops had a trace on Hughes's cards, they wouldn't learn anything at all, other than that he was at Port Authority.

And he wasn't going to be there for very long. His remaining ticket was for a bus to Albany, leaving in five minutes. Jazz mingled with the last few people to board and found a seat as close to the back as possible. Now he tugged his ball cap low over his face, turned up the collar of Hughes's overcoat, and crossed his arms over his chest, pretending to sleep.

But sleep—though craved—was the last thing on his mind.

Stay strong, Mom. Stay alive. I'm coming.

CHAPTER 22

They were searching Brooklyn and paying extra-special attention to the tunnels and bridges, but it didn't matter. Billy had a secret weapon, and between that and his new look (ditched the damn glasses, applied a theater-quality beard and a deliberately bad hairpiece), he cruised right on through a checkpoint in his rented car. Smiled straight at an NYPD officer in her winter weather gear. Said, "God bless, Officer!" in a tone he knew from previous experience to be calming and eminently forgettable.

Same way he'd said "You're welcome" back in Wichita when that tit-heavy FBI agent had walked out the door he held for her at the 7-Eleven. She hadn't even said "Thank you," the self-involved bitch. If she had—if she had taken a moment to look up at the man holding the door for her, a courteous man, a gentleman—then maybe that liberated, enlightened, feminist, woman-power-believing lady cop might have recognized the man—the *man*—she was hunting, standing right there.

But she hadn't, so she hadn't. And Billy had made a point of saying "You're welcome." Remind her of her manners, not that it helped.

And now she was dead. Dead by Hat's hand, and that was fine by Billy. Let the trash take out the trash. It was fitting. Almost poetic.

Bastard cops thought they could catch Billy. That was nothing new. The bastard cops *always* thought they could catch ol' Billy.

Hadn't done yet. Except for that fat prick in the Nod. G. William Tanner. Good ol' boy done good. But that weren't good police work or any kind of *deduction*. No, the sheriff had just gotten lucky was all. And sure, Billy had helped him along. Killing those two Nod girls had been foolish. Foolish and wrongheaded and just plain dumb. Billy knew that. He'd known it all along, and yet he'd been unable to help himself.

He had *needed one*.

When the urges came and the fantasies and the trophies of past kills weren't enough, he *needed one*, and Billy was not the kind of man to deny himself. He hadn't lived and studied and trained at his craft for so many years—he hadn't ascended to the Crows—all so that he could sit at home with a beer and ESPN like a prospect, wishing he could do things to the cute little blond up the street.

No, sir. Not Billy Dent.

He was not a man of *whims*, Billy Dent. He was a man of *passions*. A man of *convictions*. He knew what he believed, and he knew what he deserved. When there were things to be done to the cute little blond up the street, Billy Dent *damn well went and did them.*

Because no one else would, and Billy couldn't live in that world.

There were some of his persuasion who felt guilt at their urges, their actions. Those sad sons of bitches ended up in jail for life, each and every time. Or dead by their own hands.

Billy knew that he was the most important man in the world. That his needs were, therefore, the most important in the world.

All men were like Billy, he mused. Well, except possibly the faggots. Billy had no hate in his heart for men who lusted for other men—they were as nature made them, just as Billy was as nature made him. Still, they were faggots, and it was ridiculous to call them anything else.

"Everything has a proper name," Billy said aloud.

Janice said nothing. He expected such.

All men had the urges. They all wanted to possess, to dominate. They were triggered by a stolen glimpse of cleavage, by a daring hint of thigh. They dreamed and they wallowed in fantasy, but they never acted. They pilfered moments of pornography when their wives weren't looking, masturbated relentlessly over their longings, then felt shame and relief in equal measure.

Only men who were real, men who mattered, men who were important—men like Billy—could rise above the base mud of morality and take charge, assume the mantle. Capture the prospects and do as nature intended.

Men like Billy were whole. Living in a world of sad, unfulfilled fractions.

Billy drove along through the night. His wife was with him again, after so many years. As was appropriate. Man and wife should be together, not separated by distance and deceptions.

All was good.

Except for one thing.

It was time, Billy knew, for the reckoning. Time to tie up loose ends. Jasper was almost a man. Long past time to stop treating him like a boy.

"When I was a child, I spake as a child, I understood as a child, I thought as a child: but when I became a man, I put away childish things."

That was from the Good Book. Billy didn't quite believe in God — not quite — but the Bible was surely a useful source of wisdom. Good writing was good writing, no matter what you believed in, prayed to, or jerked off over.

Yes. It was time for Jasper to put away childish things. Jasper would take the next step toward becoming a Crow.

Or suffer the consequences.

CHAPTER 23

And now they had a driver.

Hughes figured he'd had less than four hours of sleep over the last forty-eight, but he didn't care. He'd gone longer when on a case, when on a hunt, and this was the biggest, best hunt of his career. A few more Red Bulls and a cup of the terrible swill the Seven-Six dared call coffee and he was right as rain, his mind buzzing along like nothing had gone wrong.

The noose was draped over Jasper Dent's neck. Soon, he could tighten it.

He was alone, watching through the glass as Detective Miller interrogated the hack, who'd come forward after seeing the news. The Dent kid had flagged him on the street, or so the hack—one Khosrow Abbasi—claimed. Hughes didn't buy it. Dent wasn't familiar with the city. He wouldn't have known to flag down Abbasi's unmarked black Lincoln any more than he'd've known to switch to the uptown 6 at Broadway-Lafayette to get to Grand Central. So Abbasi probably saw the kid on a street corner and pulled over, thinking he could grab a quick fare. Happened all the time. Abbasi was vigorously protesting that he'd not done anything wrong, probably more concerned about his fate in front of the Taxi & Limousine Commission than by the fact that he'd shuttled a wanted fugitive over the bridge into Manhattan.

Hughes tapped twice on the window, lightly—the precinct's code for "hurry the hell up." Time was wasting. They needed whatever information Abbasi had, and they needed it now.

New York City wasn't a speedboat; it was a tanker. It couldn't turn on a dime. It took time—hours—to execute a lockdown, to shut down certain routes, to do it right. And along the way, there were any number of opportunities for a bad guy to slip through the sieve. Deep down, Hughes knew that it *should* be this way; you couldn't just shut down a city of eight million people on a whim—the ensuing chaos would be catastrophic. But a part of him wished it were possible. That there could be a button somewhere he could press that would close the bridges and tunnels and stop the subways and kill the buses and ground the planes out at JFK and LaGuardia all in the same instant.

Keep dreaming.

A brief tableau flashed before Hughes's eyes: Morales, dead on the floor of the storage unit. Then her body loaded onto a stretcher by the medical examiner's team, the way her head had lolled, one arm trailing off the stretcher as though she were drifting on an inflatable pool raft on a warm summer day...

Damn. He pinched the bridge of his nose. That wasn't like him. Victims didn't haunt him like that. They were cases, not ghosts. All his years as a homicide cop, and he'd had scanty nightmares. Partly because he was good at seeing the murder as a puzzle to be solved. But also, mostly, because he was good at what he did. He cleared cases. Period. That absolved him of a lot of sleepless nights.

But usually you have a grasp on it. And usually you don't know the victim.

There was a light tap at the door, and then a uniform stepped in.

"Captain Montgomery wanted me to let you know: We have that trace on your phone up and running. And we got a hit on one of your credit cards. Four tickets bought at an automated kiosk at Port Authority."

The need for sleep receded into the furthest recesses of Hughes's mind. "Tickets where?"

The uniform handed him a printout. "And the cell trace indicates he's northbound on 495. From the rate of movement, it looks like he hitched a ride."

Hughes pondered the printout. "Or he hopped a bus to Albany."

"We shut down all the buses."

"Yeah, but he could have gotten out before then. He's been one step ahead the whole time." Hughes massaged his temples. The headache that had flared at the sight of Billy Dent's note near Hat's body had never really gone away—it just ebbed and flowed with the levels of caffeine in his system. "Get me a cup of coffee. And tell Captain Montgomery to have all northbound buses stopped and searched. I'll call the state police myself to coordinate."

The uniform about-faced and headed out. Hughes closed his eyes and enjoyed the quiet of the observation room for a single, lingering moment.

And then his face split with a wide, satisfied grin.

Gotcha.

Part Three

Killers Hunt Me

CHAPTER 24

Jazz opened his eyes, but the dream followed him into wakefulness.

Touch me

says the voice

like that

it goes on

And he does.

His fingers glide over warm, supple flesh.

Touch me like that

And his legs, the friction of them—

And so warm

So warm

like that

The woman was in shadows and the hands on her were his own, his own small, childish hands, which had yet to learn how to dismember, how to hack, how to strangle. Innocent hands, they should have been. Young, soft, small hands roaming the endless fields of her. "Her," the mystery *she* of his dreams for months now, the woman he now realized—in a lightning-fast, thunder-loud burst of epiphany—could be no one but his father's partner in crime, Billy Dent's hidden, secret weapon: Samantha Dent.

Aunt Sam. My own aunt. I—

Oh, God.

He lurched upward in his seat, gagging.

"Not in the truck!" Marta yelled. "Roll down the window!"

Jazz fumbled to his right for the window controls. A blast of cold air hit him as the glass slid down, the shock of it forestalling the moment of regurgitation. Straining against the seat belt, he leaned his head out the window and let go, unselfconsciously vomiting in an impressive stream that wicked back along the side of the truck, spattering the paint job and flicking away into the still dark.

When he was done, he struggled back inside and lay back against the worn seat, gasping for breath.

"You okay?" Marta asked. "Water at your feet."

Jazz's mind churned like his now-empty gut. Marta's voice was familiar, and the smells around him reminded him of something, but he was still thrashing against the dream, his stomach-sick body fighting itself.

Sure enough, there was a half-full bottle of water at his feet. Jazz managed to pluck it up and rinsed his mouth, spitting the befouled water out the window.

He remembered. Marta. The truck driver.

He knew the NYPD could track him via cell phone GPS, so he'd taken a calculated risk. Billy always said, *Cop toys are just like a little baby's toys: They love 'em so much that they just have to play with them, even when it's not good for them.*

The cops (he managed to stop himself from thinking of them as "the bastard cops," but only just) wouldn't be able to help themselves—they knew he had Hughes's phone, so they would track him with it. So he'd left it on the bus to Albany, wedged between the seat and the wall, and then gotten off at the first stop, an unscheduled "convenience break" at a New Jersey rest station. The bus driver had loitered near the bus, smoking and guzzling coffee, while most of Jazz's fellow passengers had made for the vending machines.

Jazz, though, had immediately headed for the gas pumps, where massive semitrucks hissed and belched like dragons lined up at a buffet. Concealed in the shadows, he'd watched each truck. He knew he was in bad shape. His leg pulsated like an alien egg sac in a horror movie. He couldn't remember the last time he'd slept. He needed to be on the road and needed to be safe.

So once again, men were out. He needed a woman trucker, and he'd been pleasantly surprised that it didn't take long for him to find one.

Marta's rig had blue flames emblazoned on the hood, with a slit-eyed green girl dancing among them, naked, her naughty bits strategically concealed by licks of flame. The words TRUCK IT UP, spelled out in cursive, wafted above her. The joke—if there was one—was lost on Jazz. The trucker herself was slighter than he'd anticipated, his prejudice predicting a mannish, bulky half woman. Marta didn't resemble the fetching alien creature prancing on her rig's hood, but she also was not some buzz-cut caricature from a homophobe's nightmares.

He'd approached her tentatively when she left the restroom and had barely begun the rollout of his sad, sad cover story—repeated sexual molestation by stepdad, mom a useless junkie and part-time whore—when she'd shaken her head and welcomed him into the passenger seat. "Details make me depressed. Just don't get carsick, okay?"

Now, as Jazz finished rinsing, she glanced over at him. "You okay?" she asked again.

"I think so."

"You're hosing that shit off my rig at the next stop," she said, her tone not unkind.

"Of course."

The sun peeked above the hills and treetops. The NYPD thought he was headed north, following the reliable signal of Hughes's GPS. But Jazz—thanks to Marta—was going south. South and west. Marta's route wouldn't get him exactly where he needed to go, but she would get him close enough. How would he make it the rest of the way?

He'd improvise. It had worked so far.

He knew where he was going, though. That much was critical.

He'd figured it out in the hour he'd spent on the bus.

Where would Billy go, once leaving New York? His father had the whole world open to him.

I'll be happy to explain it to you when the time comes. When we ain't in such...constrained circumstances.

That's what Billy had said, before leaving unit 83F. So he wanted to see Jazz again. To explain. That meant he would leave clues. A map, written in a language only Jazz could understand.

In the meantime, think about Caligula. Think about Gilles de Rais.

Caligula and Gilles de Rais. Both murderers from ancient times.

You know more than you think.

Flattering, but useless. The Caligula/de Rais bit made Jazz think Billy referred to the beginning of something. *You've got the beginnings of it, boy.* That confirmed it. *Told you as much back at Wammaket. Told you where it started. The genesis.* "*And Cain went out from the presence of the Lord.*"

And Jazz had figured it out. When the bus had stopped soon thereafter, he'd left Hughes's phone and sought out a truck heading south.

South.

Home.

And Cain went out from the presence of the Lord. Genesis, chapter 4.

And Cain went out from the presence of the Lord, Jazz recalled, *and dwelt in the land of Nod.*

The land of Nod.

Billy was returning to Lobo's Nod.

CHAPTER 25

Connie opened her eyes to the light of a new day, the sun streaming in through the open hospital room window blinds. She couldn't greet the day with hope or even a smile, though. She'd told her father to wake her if there was news of or from Jazz during the night, so the fact that she'd actually slept eight hours meant that Jazz was still missing.

Maybe that's a good thing, she thought. *Maybe it means he's safe.*

But even Connie's natural optimism couldn't crumble the ramparts of fear that had risen up around Jazz. Jazz was wounded and on the run, with every cop in New York looking for him. If there was no news, he was probably —

No. No.

Dad was standing over by the door to her room, huddled in the corner, murmuring into his cell phone. Trying not to wake her. Connie smiled, and the smile hurt, reminding her of the long road to recovery before her.

"Dad?"

Her father glanced over at her. "She's up now. Yeah, I'll tell her. Love you, too." He slipped the phone into his pocket and came to her bedside, taking her hand. "Mom sends her love."

Her mother would be looking after Whiz. Pulling him out of school and bringing him to New York would be a headache none of them needed. "I bet you had to have someone tie her down to keep her from getting on the first plane here."

"Pretty close. How do you feel? Should I get the nurse—"

"No. No, I'm okay." She winced as she adjusted herself into a sitting position, putting the lie to her words. But the pain—while significant—wasn't overwhelming. "Has there been any—"

Dad's frown told her everything she needed to know, but she pressed, anyway. He told her what he knew from the news: that the police believed Billy Dent had escaped the city. The FBI had once again placed Billy at the top of its vaunted most-wanted list. He was considered armed and dangerous; there was a nationwide 1-800 number for information about him, and every news story emphasized that, if seen, he was not to be approached.

As for Jazz: They were circulating photos of him, too. He was considered "potentially armed and dangerous" but also "wounded and scared." Once again, no one was to approach him.

Connie wanted nothing more than to approach him. To hold him. To be the anchor she knew she was and could be for him. She replayed their last conversation over and over. She had given him an ultimatum, a recklessly stupid thing to do in this situation. Jazz wasn't thinking straight. Threatening him with the end of their relationship was supposed to shock him back to reality, make him see how dangerous his current course was. Instead, it had sent him scurrying into that same dark, safe, lonely bolt-hole he'd been living in when she'd first met him. He'd withdrawn completely. Gone dark.

He always thought he knew best. He was so confident of it that he would risk his life over and over, supremely assured that, in the final analysis, he would be proven right.

She fisted tears away. Her dad pulled a chair over and put a gentle hand on her arm, away from any of the bruised or slashed exposed flesh. "Is the pain that bad? I can call the nurse and get some more painkillers."

"No. No, it's not that." How could she explain it to her father? It wasn't just that he hated and feared Jazz. Even if it hadn't been Jazz—if it had been a quiet, shy, respectful black guy—her father still wouldn't understand. He would tell her that no boy her age was worth crying over. He would tell her that true love doesn't start in high school. *When I was your age*, he'd said many times, *I had no idea what I wanted or needed. You know why? Because I didn't even know who I was yet. If I'd met your mother when I was seventeen, I wouldn't have even spoken to her.*

Usually, at this point, Mom interjected: *Don't flatter yourself, honey. I wouldn't have given you a second look if you were on fire.*

"When can I get out of here?" Connie asked. A mighty and all-consuming urgency bubbled up from the same place as the tears. She had to get out of this hospital bed, out of the hospital itself. She needed to *do* something. The rest of the world was hunting Jazz and Billy; Connie knew Jazz better than anyone else in the world—she should be out there, too. On crutches or in a wheelchair, if that's what it took, but she knew she could contribute. Yes, Billy had tormented her, terrified her, but she would hunt him now, if she could. If that would finally resolve Jazz's torture, then that's what she'd do. Billy scared the living hell out of her, but for Jazz, she would happily confront him again.

If I kill him, Jazz had said, all too calmly, *he's dead.*

I have to do something.

"I want to go home," she said.

"What?"

She favored her father with the most piercing stare she could muster; she'd practiced it for months in a mirror, teaching herself how to lock eyes with someone and not blink for minutes at a time. It was very unnerving, she knew—Jazz had used it on her in the past.

"Home," she said. "I want to go. Today." It had come to her along with the resolve: Jazz was headed back to Lobo's Nod. It had to be. There was no other option. It was his only strategy. He knew the Nod, and he had the Hideout there, his ramshackle, run-down sanctum in the woods, where he could recuperate and make plans. He would feel safe there. Surrounded by a building of his own design, he would be able to start over and figure out how to mount a rescue mission for his mother.

Only Connie knew about the Hideout. Not even Howie knew.

"Honey…" Her dad had that look he got when he was about to tell her how "impractical" or "capricious" something was. "Baby, you need some more time before we go gallivanting off on an airplane. You can't just—"

"I'm not in any danger. Dr. Cullins said so. I have some broken bones. So what? People travel with broken bones all the time. I can use crutches. I'll be fine."

He shook his head, and she knew the volley of excuses and rebuttals was about to accelerate; it was a game she was too familiar with, living in her father's house. But before he could speak, her cell phone rang.

BLOCKED, said the screen.

Jazz, Connie thought, and swiped to answer.

"Hello, Conscience," said Mr. Auto-Tune.

She stared at her father, for a moment unable to understand why his expression was one of confusion and irritation, not shock, but then she realized: Of course. He couldn't hear Mr.—or, possibly, *Ms.*—Auto-Tune. He was annoyed at Connie for answering her phone in the middle of their conversation. If only he knew.

He *had* to know.

Get the police, she mouthed to him.

"Conscience?" Mr. Auto-Tune said. Connie thought maybe there was a touch of bemusement in the voice, but it was difficult to tell. "Are you so beaten up you can't talk?"

"I'm here," she told the voice, then hit Mute. "Dad, go get

the cops." When he raised his eyebrows and moved not an inch, she growled, "Go! Seriously, Dad!" He paused as though he didn't believe her for a moment, then hopped up and darted out the door.

Mr. Auto-Tune had been talking the whole time, but Connie had caught only pieces of it. *Have to keep the call going so the cops can trace it.* She unmuted her phone and just flat-out interrupted:

"Why the Auto-Tuning?" she asked. "I already know who you are. You're either Billy or Samantha."

The voice was silent for a time. Then: "You're a very smart girl, Connie. And lucky, too, to survive your recent...travails. When you dropped off the fire escape, did you think you would survive, or were you just so desperate to get away that even falling to your death seemed preferable?"

"What's the difference? It worked."

"There are entire oceans of difference between the two." Even through the flat inflection of Auto-Tuning, she caught a note of disapproval. "If the former, you're optimistic. Hopeful. If the latter, you just surrendered to the inevitable."

Keep the conversation going. Keep it going. Dad, where are you? "Why don't you turn off this stupid Auto-Tuning thing? I want to know if I'm talking to Billy or Sam. Did you feel it when I kicked you in the balls, or did Billy just tell you about it later?"

"Bravado lacks a certain element of verisimilitude when it comes from someone who, not long ago, was pleading for her life."

"I'm ready for round two," Connie said with a bravery

that surprised her. The only way she ever wanted to see Billy or his twisted sister was on a morgue slab.

"I'm sure you think you are, but you're one step behind, Connie. That game is over."

"Too bad. I was just getting good at it." *Dad! Come on!*

"All games end, Connie. Hat and Dog have concluded their business in New York. And so have you. So has Jasper. It's time for everyone to come home, don't you think?"

"So you can use me for a hostage? I don't think so."

That tinny, reverberating laughter. It had given her a headache before, and it was no better now. "Your days as a hostage are quite over, Connie. You've fulfilled your service. Your utility is at an end. Pawns are always sacrificed before game's end. When next we meet, you will witness your last vista, hear your last cry, weep your last tears. You will take your last breath."

Connie shivered and closed her eyes, pressing herself back against the pillow. For a moment, she'd been back in that horrible little apartment, bound to that chair, Billy Dent looming over her. The threats weren't idle. She knew that. Billy had cut open her neck and would have done worse if he hadn't gone off to rescue Jazz. She'd been a blade's width from death already, and only luck had saved her.

"If I'm not important anymore," she heard herself say, "then why are you even bothering to call me?" There. It was out there now.

"Because I find you interesting, Connie. I admit a certain weakness toward you. You fascinate me. Outsider. New. Black girl. Forcing yourself into the inner circles of popularity in a town like Lobo's Nod. Dating the local outcast, but still maintaining your clique status."

"Need lessons in social interaction?"

"When you die, Connie, it will be ugly. I promise you that. And I also promise you that I will be a little sad at that moment. But only a little bit.

"Good-bye, Conscience."

She bolted upright in bed, hissing in pain. "No! Wait! Don't go!"

But the line was dead already.

Her dad chose that moment—that useless moment—to push breathlessly through her door with Detective Hughes in tow.

CHAPTER 26

Howie opened his eyes to the familiar, glorious sight of the delectable Uma Thurman, gazing saucily down at him from his ceiling. It was his own personal collage of Ms. Thurman, culled from photos discovered online, strategically covering most of the space above his bed.

Uma was tall. Howie, being of basketball-ish mien himself, adored tall women. Especially tall women with lots of pictures online. Especially tall women who, in pursuit of their art, had gone nude in something like a half dozen movies.

Howie loved women who pursued their art. It was a small thing, sure, but it made Howie happy.

Howie's head throbbed as he swung his ridiculously long legs out of bed. The painkillers were wearing off, as was the nice dose of lidocaine Dr. Mogelof had injected into his scalp. He would have a scar, he was sure. Maybe more than one. To go with the scar on his midsection after the Impressionist had cut him open a few months back.

Maybe Mom was right. Maybe hanging around with "that Dent boy" would kill him.

Oh, well. Everyone had to go sometime, right?

For now, though, he had one more in an endless string of favors to execute for Jazz. Howie wrapped himself in a megasized robe and crept into the hallway. He called out for a parental unit—just in case—and received no reply. Good. He was home alone.

Mom and Dad's bed was unmade when he stole into their room. He tried their en suite bathroom first. Medicine cabinet. Duh. Where else do you look for medicine? But other than Mom's Xanax—the extra-large, economy-sized prescription—and Dad's blood pressure meds, he came up empty. So he rummaged around in the cabinet under the sink, pretending not to see the boxes of tampons and maxipads and failing. *Great Zeus, how many of these things does one woman* need? *It's like her own personal feminine hygiene aisle under here.*

He recovered some old cold medicine and a half bottle of cough syrup, but not what Jazz needed.

I'm going to need some stuff, Jazz had said the night before.

Of course you are. You always need something.

Painkillers would be nice—

Got 'em. In spades. Dr. Mogelof was very generous with my prescription. She underestimates my manly ability to shrug off pain that would kill lesser mortals.

But what I really need are antibiotics.

And I'm supposed to procure these how? My street dealer only has meth and crack.

Don't be an idiot. Your mother hoards meds. You know it. I know it. She's been doing it since we were kids. "Just in case." I'm willing to bet she has a course of penicillin or a Z-pak stashed away somewhere. And I'm gonna need it, or my leg is going to blow up like a microwaved sausage.

With that disgusting image fully implanted in his psyche, Howie scrounged deeper into the darkest, cobwebbiest corners under the sink. He found an old blister pack of allergy medicine and several used-up toilet paper tubes, but nothing else.

Great.

Jazz was right, though. Duh. When it came to reading people and remembering things and drawing inferences from those two data points, Jazz was pretty much unparalleled. He knew when the pop quizzes were coming in school, based on how tired a teacher looked the day before. He knew how to avoid getting caught in the halls based on the bell schedule. And he knew that Howie's mom worried obsessively about a medical emergency striking her genetic freak of a son at any moment, so she often talked Howie's doctors into writing an extra script or two here and there.

Where did she keep the stuff, though?

As distasteful as it was, Howie realized he would need to prowl the dark and nameless tracts of his parents' nightstands.

"Here there be dragons," he muttered as he went back into the bedroom. Dad's side of the bed was closest, so Howie cursorily examined the disarrayed jumble atop the nightstand—mystery novel, *Sports Illustrated*, iPad, iPhone dock—then delved into the drawers themselves.

To his massive, undying chagrin, he found a tube of

"personal lubricant" that was a little less than half-full. Howie tried not to imagine how many parental sex sessions that meant. He pawed around, finding only stray business cards, some more paperback novels, and Dad's collection of eyedrops. The man was petrified of dry eyes, apparently.

Mom's nightstand was neat and orderly, with a stack of magazines squared to the perpendicular edges of the surface. Her alarm clock stood at a perfect right angle to the stack, positioned precisely in the cone of light thrown by her reading lamp. She needed to unclench something fierce.

Exploring within, he groaned at the sight of a pack of birth control pills. *Come* on! he mentally upbraided the universe. *Stop throwing this stuff in my face! Parentals shouldn't be going at it. Especially when I can't.*

Another tube of "personal lubricant," this one a bright purple that somehow made it worse. But underneath a copy of *Women's Running*, he hit pay dirt: a neatly organized (of course) tray, with a variety of amber prescription bottles, all made out in Howie's name. Howie grinned and began pawing through them.

CHAPTER 27

Erickson had been standing guard outside Clara Dent's hospital room off and on ever since the old lady had been brought in. When he'd moved to Lobo's Nod back in October, he'd never imagined himself getting caught up in any of the Dent family nonsense. "That stuff ended years ago," he'd confidently told family and friends. Lobo's Nod had returned to its status quo ante, just another sleepy little burg in a sleepy little county, with the benefit of a terrific sheriff to learn from, a sheriff most likely ready to retire in a few years. The perfect place for a guy like Erickson to spend a couple of years, learning from and impressing the boss at the same time. And then, when the big man retired, well, who knew? Sheriff Erickson? Why not? Sheriff of a sleepy little burg in a sleepy little county.

Ha! Within days of signing on at the Nod, Erickson had witnessed a naked dead girl in a field, fingers chopped off. He'd caught Jasper Dent skulking around the morgue, slapped cuffs on the kid *twice*, been suspected of being a serial killer, and gotten caught up in the hunt for the real killer.... If Lobo's Nod was sleepy, it was the fitful sleep of a colicky baby.

And now he was guarding the mother of the most notorious serial killer in the world. The hits, as Erickson's mom loved to say, just kept a-comin'.

The guard duty wasn't that bad, honestly. It was just boring. He relieved the previous guard, radioed to the office that he was on-site, and then commenced eight hours of sitting on his ass, playing with his phone. Food was brought to him, and when he had to take a piss, a hospital security guard would spell him for five minutes.

Did G. William *really* think Billy Dent would try to contact his mother? Erickson had enormous respect for the big man, but he thought in this instance, the sheriff might be a few clams short of a chowder. Crazy was crazy, sure, but walking into a hospital in the town where everyone knew your face was just idiotic.

Shortly after he settled in for his latest shift, a nurse came by for the old lady's usual vitals check. They did this every couple of hours. As best Erickson could glean, Mrs. Dent was in a "light coma" due to the twin traumas of a mild heart attack and a serious concussion. Separately, either one would have laid her up for a while—coming one right after the other as they had, she wouldn't be waking up anytime soon. The docs were pretty confident she would recover; they just weren't sure exactly when.

The nurse grinned at Erickson. He tipped his hat and said, "Evenin', ma'am," just like a cowboy hero. She ate it up, her grin widening. "I thought you were a deputy," she teased, "but you sound more like a marshal."

She was young—midtwenties maybe, a little younger than Erickson—and pretty, even in her shapeless scrubs. Glossy black hair and pale green eyes that made Erickson think of sour green-apple Life Savers. In the best, sexiest way possible, of course. Erickson surreptitiously admired the toss of her hips and the sway of her ass as she went into Mrs. Dent's room.

If life were a movie, Erickson realized this would be the moment when he would turn back to the hallway and— violin sting!—Billy Dent would be standing there, bigger than life and ten times as crazy.

But life was life, not a movie, and the hallway was empty but for a couple of doctors.

When the nurse emerged, Erickson flashed her a smile. He considered the hat tip again but figured it would seem tired already. He settled on asking, "How is she?"

The nurse glanced around. "I'm really not supposed to tell you. But..." She bit her bottom lip very fetchingly. "She's stable. BP isn't bad. About as good as can be expected. She came in breathing on her own, so that's good. And I've been monitoring her from the nurses' station. She's pretty stable. The doctors will know more later."

"I guess that's the best news we can expect, huh?"

With a nod, the nurse headed off, but not before flashing a very winning, very welcoming smile at Erickson. He basked in the glow of that smile for a few minutes, calculating his chances and his next reasonable move. Soon his curiosity got the better of him. He'd been guarding this woman for days, and he had no idea what she even looked like. He stood and stretched. No one was around, so he opened the door and poked his head in. A little peek wouldn't hurt.

From his vantage point at the door, he could barely make out the shape of her on the bed. The lights were out, except for a dim bar mounted above her. Tubes, wires, and cables ran to her from machines and IV stands arrayed around her. It was like watching a car in the shop, hooked up to all manner of monitoring gear. The heart monitor beeped steadily along, and her chest rose and fell in a shallow but reliable rhythm.

If I ever get that old and that bad, Erickson thought, *someone pull the plug.*

＊＊＊

About a half hour later, a second nurse stopped by. This one was older, midforties, with her hair tied back in a severe bun and bright red, chunky glasses that he couldn't stop staring at. Nice enough–looking woman, but Erickson wasn't interested in cougars. Still, he stopped her before she could go in—not for conversation, but just to let her know that Mrs. Dent had already been looked in on, just a half hour ago.

"Young pretty thing?" The nurse rolled her eyes when Erickson nodded. "God, these girls right out of school...She used the wrong solution." She held up an IV bag. "Maybe someday she'll learn the difference between point zero five percent and five percent."

Erickson wanted to leap to the nameless young nurse's defense, but he really had nothing to say. He shrugged and let her through.

　　　　　　　　　　🐾

In the hospital room, the nurse paused for a moment at the door, waiting to see if the deputy would look in. She gave him only a few seconds. Any longer would be foolish.

Dropping the IV bag in the trash, she went to the bedside and looked down at the patient. She had always been withered and wasted, but in the hospital bed, she took on the appearance of a cadaver, one that hadn't realized it was time to stop breathing.

"Hello, Mom," the nurse whispered.

She didn't expect a response and, indeed, got none.

"Good-bye, Mom," she said, and withdrew a needle from her pocket. She emptied its contents into the IV line through the port, slid the needle through the slot on the sharps container, and walked out of the room, not bothering to speak to or even look at the deputy as she went.

CHAPTER 28

They stopped somewhere in southwestern Pennsylvania for fuel, both for the rig and for themselves. Jazz delved into Hughes's wallet and treated Marta to lunch—it was the least he could do, even though it reduced his funds to the depressingly low level of a single twenty and two ones. He couldn't risk using Culpepper's or Hughes's credit cards or debit cards; they would be monitored and give away his location. He cursed himself for not maxing out the ATM cards in New York. There'd been a machine at the bar where he'd met Culpepper. NYPD wouldn't have known about Culpepper until hours later, so it would have been a risk worth taking. Stupid. Stupid, amateur mistake.

There was no TV in the tiny diner where they'd stopped. Tiny miracles, making life just a wee bit easier every day. He hoped his luck would hold out.

While Marta used the restroom, he—as promised—hosed his vomit off the truck. It wasn't the most pleasant task, but it had the advantage of being repetitive and brainless, allowing his mind to wander.

He kept coming back to the birth certificate.

Howie had texted it to him before he'd broken out of the hospital, and he'd looked at it several times before dropping his phone on Mark Culpepper in that bar bathroom. It looked legit to him. It had to be legit, right? Why would anyone bury a fake birth certificate in his backyard?

Anyone meaning Billy, of course. He was the only one who could have done it, would have done it. After Mom had escaped the Dent house, Billy had sent her straight into the memory hole, scouring the house for anything reminiscent of her—clothes, books, magazines, photos, the box of tampons under the sink, everything. Jazz had come from school one day, and Mom was just *gone*. Eradicated from the Dent house. No matter what he asked Billy or how he asked, no matter how he begged, pleaded, or importuned, Billy would not speak of her, and soon enough Jazz learned to go about his day as Billy did, pretending Mom had never existed. If not for the wallet-sized photo of her he'd luckily had in his backpack that day, he might have come to believe that, in fact, she never had existed, that he had been born of no woman, had sprung fully formed from Billy's fevered brow like a prepubescent Athena.

Billy must have buried the birth certificate, the crow toy, and the pictures at the same time. Why? Why not destroy it all?

The birth certificate had haunted Jazz at first. Initially, he'd been obsessed with—maybe "possessed by" was more accurate—the notion that he might not be Billy's son. He'd pondered the multitudinous possibilities of his parenthood. If Billy wasn't his father, then who was? One of Billy's victims? Some boyfriend or one-night stand of Mom's?

The more he thought about the birth certificate, the more he came to understand that while it held many potentialities, in the end only one mattered. He knew exactly what the birth certificate meant.

"Looks good," Marta said, coming up behind him. "You ready?"

Jazz throttled the hose and beheld his handiwork. Marta's rig glistened, nary a trace of puke to be found.

"Yep. Let's go."

Driving straight through from the New Jersey rest stop to Lobo's Nod would have taken less than fifteen hours, by Jazz's calculations. Marta was by all accounts addicted to a particular brand of energy booster that came in tiny, shot glass–sized bottles. She slammed them back with a ferocity and frequency that made Jazz fear for the disposition of her heart. Still, even she wasn't about to drive straight through.

Her route, as best he could tell, would take him to within a couple of hours of the Nod, along I-40. He wouldn't ask her to take him straight to the Nod; he couldn't. It was risky enough having her see his face. He couldn't further risk having her remember by name the one place in the world irrevocably associated with the Dent family. He could picture the interrogation already: *The kid who hitched? Yeah, I guess he looked like this Jasper Dent kid. Dropped him off at a place called Lobo's Nod.* And boom. The police, the FBI, the press—they all instantly knew everything they need to know.

Near the Kentucky border, Marta finally hit her limit. Either that, or she ran out of energy shots. One way or the other, she pulled over on the highway and announced that she needed a few hours' shut-eye. She climbed into the berth behind the seat and curled up, but not before showing Jazz the pistol under her pillow. "You seem like a nice kid and I hate to do this, but if you try something, you should know that I'm a crack shot."

Jazz had merely nodded. The gun didn't scare him. Taking a gun away from a sleeping or half-asleep woman was child's play. He had no intention of harming Marta, anyway, so it was a moot point. He huddled in the passenger seat, nearly vibrating with anticipation and annoyance. Why couldn't she have bought more energy shots when they'd stopped? Why did they have to stop? He was a fugitive. By definition, he was on the run. "On the run" did not include parking on the side of the highway, waiting for some distressingly dedicated Kentucky state trooper to decide to take a look-see inside the cab of the big rig resting on the shoulder. Peering through the window and—hey, that's the kid on TV!

Then Jasper would have no choice but to fight again. And now he knew that Marta had a gun. It would be difficult *not* to go for it, when cornered.

I won't let it get that far.

It's already gone that far, Billy said. *You choked Hughes. You knocked out that girl cop. You beat up a drunk man in a bathroom. Violence suits you.*

Exigent circumstances.

Life is an exigent circumstance, Jasper.

Shut up.

He couldn't help remembering what Billy had said to him back at Wammaket: *Want to know the difference between good and evil, Jasper?* And then Billy had snapped his fingers. *That's it, kid. That's the difference. You won't even know you've crossed the line until it's way back in your rearview mirror.*

And now: *You crossed a whole lot of lines today. Got some momentum going. Not many more to cross. Pretty much just the big one.*

You're right, Billy. I'm a violent thug. Always have been. Held back until now. But you've proven yourself right. You told me back at Wammaket: I'm a killer who hasn't killed yet. But that will change when I see you.

I look forward to it. Who knows? Maybe you actually will kill me. That would be sad for me, but good, too. Because then the beast is loose. The god within you is loose. And your next victim is your mother. And then your girlfriend. And then you and Ugly J can walk this world together. Crows.

He slapped himself, both to silence the voices and to keep himself awake. No matter what happened, he did *not* want to sleep. Not again. No matter how tired he got. Sleep meant dreams and the dream....His stomach turned in on itself at the thought of the sex dream. Now that he knew his tango partner, he had no desire to relive the dance. He feared dreaming further details, and he didn't want to know how far he'd gone with his aunt as a child.

Female serial killers rarely committed sexual homicide. Their motivations were typically fear or compassion or greed. Black widows and angels of mercy. They preyed on the weak, the elderly, children. Lacking the physical strength of men, most of them worked in teams. Support staff for a male murderer. Billy's personal, handpicked handmaiden of slaughter. His own sister.

Best of all, they avoided capture for so long because no one ever suspected them. Jazz himself had never even considered the possibility that Sammy J and Billy were a team.

Fernandez and Beck...She pretended to be *his* sister in order to lure women to him for the slaughter. They died in dual electric chairs, still proclaiming their love for each other. Hindley and Brady...Two Brits in love with the Nazis. And with killing children.

How many people had Sam killed? When you added her total to Billy's, what was the final reckoning?

And worst of all: How much of it had she *wanted* to do? Jazz knew the force of Billy's charisma firsthand. Was Sam a willing participant in the murders?

In the things she'd done with Jazz?

Was it consensual on her part? Did Billy make *her do it with me?*

Necessary questions. Reasonable questions.

He didn't want to come within a mile of the answers.

He wanted only two things: His mother safe. And Billy's neck in his hands.

It was a comforting brace of thoughts. Despite himself, he drifted off to sleep.

CHAPTER 29

Things were finally looking up, Hughes figured.

While state units were stopping buses all along 495, he had returned to the hospital to sweat the girlfriend for more info, figuring he'd be in for a rough time with the father—goddamn lawyer—but then he'd actually bumped into the guy in the corridor, babbling about his daughter and a phone call. Hughes knew all about the girlfriend and phone calls; the trace on his own stolen phone had revealed that Jasper Dent had called her the previous day, and she hadn't told anyone.

Hughes didn't relish the prospect of interrogating a broken-up, terrorized teenage girl in her hospital bed, but she'd been holding out on him, and he was sick of people holding out on him. No matter their age, sex, or medical status. He was prepared to use every trick in the book to break open that girl's head and scoop out the secrets stored in there.

But then the father had grabbed him and dragged him to the room, and the girl was more than willing to crack her own skull and spill. Miracle of miracles, the lawyer-dad (surely the most frightening combination of words *ever*) kept his yap shut and let the daughter talk. Her bruises were fading, and much of the swelling on her face had gone down. She was starting to look again like the pretty girl who'd surprised him at JFK.

Hughes pulled up a chair to listen as she recounted the conversation with one of the Dent siblings. No way to know at this point if it was Billy or Samantha, but Connie's suspicion—which she wasn't shy about offering—was that it had to have been Samantha.

"She used words like 'verisimilitude.' Her whole way of talking was distinct from Billy's."

More Patriot Act requests were in his immediate future. The phone on the other end was probably a burner, probably already smashed on the side of the highway somewhere, but he would make the effort. He might be able to pull some location data.

Not that he thought he needed it. *It's time for everyone to come home, don't you think?* That's what the voice had said. That could mean only one thing: Billy Dent was heading back to Lobo's Nod.

It's the last place in the world anyone would think to look for him. No one would think he would be stupid enough to go where the people know him best. So of course, he makes a beeline for it, while we're searching the rest of the goddamn planet for him. The guy's a social-engineering savant.

He made a mental note to put out a BOLO for Samantha Dent and to check all the usual law enforcement databases for her.

But first, he needed something else from the girlfriend.

"Connie, we need to talk about Jasper."

She nodded contritely.

"He's in a lot of trouble. And I know you think I want to put him down like a dog, but I swear to you: I just want to catch him before he hurts anyone else. Get the truth out of him, whatever it is."

"He wouldn't normally hurt anyone," she said. "But it's his mom. He's convinced Billy's going to kill her."

"I get that. But that's what I'm here for. The FBI. He needs to let us handle this."

Connie's lips quirked. "With all due respect, it took twenty years to catch him last time. And even then, it wasn't you guys or the FBI. It was G. William."

Hughes's jaw tightened. "Yeah, well, I wasn't a homicide cop twenty years ago, and Billy hadn't come to New York yet." He hated to admit that she was right—Billy had stood right in Hughes's palm, right in his precinct, and then vanished before Hughes could clench his fist.

"We know Jasper called you here. We have a record of a call from my cell to this hospital, and the attendant at the switchboard says that call was routed to this room. What did you talk about?"

To his surprise, she told him, and he didn't think she was leaving anything out.

"You think he's going to kill his father?"

Clearly struggling, Connie eventually settled on a lopsided shrug that made her grimace. "I don't know. I think he wants to. I think he thinks it's his only option." She wiped a tear away. Hughes knew she was an actress, but he didn't think she was *that* accomplished. "Can you help him? At all?"

"I have to find him first."

On his way out of the hospital, Hughes used his borrowed cell phone to call the precinct. He caught Miller at his desk.

"I've got good news and bad news," Miller said in such a way that Hughes knew even the good news wasn't that good. He rubbed his temple.

"Tell me."

"Well, we got your cell phone back."

Hughes groaned. "He ditched it?"

"Yeah, that's the bad news. Left it on the bus, got out at a rest stop, and never got back on."

"And we *fell* for that?" Hughes roared. "We fell for that eighth-grade crap?"

"Hey, don't blame me. I'm not the one who let the kid escape in the first place."

Hughes allowed himself a brief, beautiful moment of fantasizing Miller covered with honey and fire ants.

"He went north to lure us that way. He's really heading south."

"That's a big assumption," Miller said. "He could have just dumped the phone and kept going."

"No." If Hughes could figure out that Billy was headed home, so could Jasper. Assuming they weren't in cahoots all along. "Daddy's heading home and so is Junior. It's the only thing he knows. The only thing he understands. He's hurt and he's going home. Montgomery was right—I've been overestimating him. He's running home, like all scared kids do."

"Well," Miller said doubtfully, "okay. We're canvassing the rest stop."

"Don't forget to pull video and credit card receipts."

"Gosh, thanks for the reminder." Miller's voice overflowed with sarcasm.

Hughes ignored it. It was best for everyone that way. "And while you're at it, run every possible database and trace for information on Samantha Dent."

"And what are you doing while those of us who still have badges are running your errands?" Miller snarked.

Hughes ignored the jibe. Partly because he outranked Miller, but mostly because it still stung. "I'm headed out of town. I'll clear it with Montgomery on my way to the airport."

"Helluva time for a vacation, Lou. You gonna send me the paperwork I need for the Patriot Act?"

"Just tell the telecoms and credit card companies this is an ongoing terrorism investigation. Dent killed over a hundred people and his sister probably helped, so it's no lie. They'll help you without the paperwork. I'll e-mail something over when I land."

"Yessir." Miller managed to inject several cc's of sinister disrespect into the nominally respectful sign-off, but Hughes knew he would get the job done, anyway. Miller was a so-so detective, but a world-class paper pusher.

In the cab on the way to JFK, Hughes managed to book his flight. The idea of flying to Lobo's Nod in the middle of Pennsyltuckessee or whatever the hell they called states down south wasn't on his top-ten list of things to repeat, but even Montgomery agreed, when Hughes called him, that one or more Dents were most likely headed to Lobo's Nod and that "someone on our side needs to be on the ground down there." The last thing they wanted was for the feds to swoop in and snatch up the Dents. And like all good city cops, Hughes and Montgomery shared a mutual distrust of the competence of their rural brethren. That Tanner guy had caught Billy once, sure, but dumb luck bought you only so much respect.

Still, Hughes rationalized, he was going to be on the sheriff's turf. It was only fair—and protocol—to let him know. Hughes was well within his rights and powers as a New York City detective to chase Billy Dent and Jasper Dent over state lines, but it was only polite to let the folks in South Bumweasel know he was coming.

He scrolled through his phone until he found the number Tanner had called him from before he'd been throttled by Jasper Dent. A woman answered far too perkily, "Lobo's Nod Sheriff's Office! Lana speaking. How may I help you?"

"I'd like to speak to Sheriff Tanner. This is Detective Louis Hughes calling from the NYPD."

To her credit, the perky woman had Tanner on the phone almost immediately. From the static and background thrum, Hughes surmised that she'd patched the call through to Tanner's car radio.

Quick reintroductions dealt with, Hughes dropped the

bomb: "We have reason to believe that Billy and his sister and/or Jasper may be headed back to Lobo's Nod. So I'm on a flight out of New York in about an hour, and I plan on being in your town this evening."

"I see." Tanner spoke with a placid equability that no doubt belied his outrage. "Billy, I get. But Jasper... You sure about this? He's still a suspect?"

"More than a suspect, Sheriff."

"You got a warrant and all?"

"Sure do. Breaking and entering. Robbery. Assault. Battery. Assaulting a police officer, multiple counts." He paused to let the big one sink in. "Wanted for questioning in connection with the murder of a federal agent."

"You don't think Jasper had anything to do with *that*, do you?"

"I'd like to ask him myself."

"I've known that boy a long time, Detective."

"Are you going to tell me that you don't think it's possible he did these things?"

To Tanner's credit, he didn't answer right away. "Let's just say I think it's unlikely."

"I don't want us to be at loggerheads, Sheriff. But the NYPD wants the son in addition to the father. If it makes you feel any better, I'm not happy about it, either."

Skipping the issue of whether he felt better, Tanner said, "And I suppose the FBI will be joining us, too?"

"Depends on how persuasive they find the Hall girl's testimony. But one of their agents is dead, so I imagine they're going to want to cover all the bases."

Tanner sighed a long, staticky sigh. "Hell. Just got those boys out of my town, now they're comin' back in."

Hughes checked the time and the traffic flow. "Sheriff, I'm almost at the airport. Of course, once I land and get a rental car, I'll check in at your office—"

"Don't bother," Tanner said. "Text me your flight info, and I'll pick you up at the airport myself."

After Hughes left, Connie sent her dad to scrounge something from the hospital vending machines, claiming a sudden jones for dark chocolate. Alone, she wondered if the tear had been too much. If she'd overdone it.

But she didn't wonder long. Hughes, she knew, was her best hope to help Jazz. Hughes was the only tool she had at her disposal to catch him before he caught up to Billy.

Because if Jazz caught up to Billy, Connie knew only one of two outcomes would follow: Either Billy would kill his obstinate son for refusing to follow in his footsteps...

Or Jazz would kill Billy, thus cementing his transition to "the Crow King."

Both were unacceptable. Better to have Jazz caught. Even if he ended up in jail. At least he would be safe.

At least he would still be whole.

"I'm so sorry, Jazz," she whispered, and this time the tear wasn't faked. "But even if you never want to speak to me again, at least you'll be alive to hate me."

CHAPTER 30

When the hospital alarm went off, Erickson fumbled his phone into his pocket and was on his feet in seconds, one hand to his sidearm. The idea of drawing his weapon in a hospital, where it would be too easy to hit someone innocent or blow a hole in some crucial piece of lifesaving equipment, made him uneasy. But he was prepared to do it.

Billy Dent. They were right. He's coming.

Just then, two white-coated doctors and a trio of nurses burst into his vision from around a corner. One of them was the cute young nurse from before, but this time she wasn't even looking at Erickson.

"Out of the way!" one of the doctors shouted. Erickson realized he was interposed between the doctor and the door to Mrs. Dent's room. At the same time, he realized this wasn't a security alarm.

He stepped aside, and the doctors and nurses rushed in. Erickson—one hand still on his gun's grip; you never know—peered inside. Mrs. Dent's EKG trembled a sine wave for a moment before flatlining, its death whistle audible over the alarm from the nurses' station. "Shut that down!" one of the doctors snapped, and Erickson's favorite nurse flipped a switch. The room fell into a loud silence for a moment.

"What the hell?" someone complained. "Cardiac arrest?"

"She was *fine*—" the young nurse protested.

"Start CPR," a doctor ordered. "Get a crash cart in here and intubate her."

As Erickson watched, they fed a plastic tube down her throat. A doctor and nurse tag-teamed CPR: one performing chest compressions, the other breathing into Mrs. Dent with a handheld pump. Seconds stretched into protracted minutes, and Erickson was frozen at the door, his hand still poised at his gun, as though he could shoot and kill whatever threatened Mrs. Dent.

"Do we have her?" a nurse asked.

"I don't know," said a doctor. "She's breathing again, but I don't know. Let's get her back to ICU."

The young nurse headed to the door. Erickson grabbed her by the arm. He didn't want to be rough, but he had to speak to her.

"Look," he said, his voice low, "I'm going to have to tell them."

She glared at him and shook his arm off. "I don't have time for—wait, tell them *what*?"

He grimaced. He didn't want to have to do this. But it would be unethical and probably illegal for him not to reveal what he knew. "I know you screwed up her IV. The other nurse told me."

"I don't know what you're talking about." She moved aside as the other medical professionals came through the door, pushing Mrs. Dent's bed, shouting at one another. Before Erickson could say anything more, they were all gone, the cute nurse included.

Erickson stepped into the room after they left. It had been quiet the last time he'd been in here, but it was somehow even quieter now. Maybe if the old woman didn't die, he could keep his mouth shut. It would be a shame for someone to get in trouble so young, so early in her career....

On the way out, someone had knocked over the trash can. Erickson bent to right it. As he did so, he noticed something inside.

It was an IV bag.

He plucked it from the trash can and hefted it in his hand. It was full.

Oh, no.

Yeah, someone was going to get in trouble. And it wasn't going to be the cute nurse.

Erickson triggered his shoulder mic. "Erickson to dispatch. Lana, we got a problem at the hospital...."

CHAPTER 31

MSNBC had already moved on from the Billy Dent story. Oh, sure, they ran a crawl in the lower third with occasional updates, but Doug Weathers didn't think much of crawls. No context. No real opportunity to *expound*.

CNN was updating the story once an hour. Fox was doing the same, but had also announced a rushed-into-production hour-long special with the baroquely lurid title *Dent & Son: The Bloody Saga of Butcher Billy*.

Weathers had offered his expertise to all three, but they'd declined.

Well, screw them, he thought, sitting on his sofa with a bowl of cereal in his lap. He had been glued to the TV since waking, occasionally dashing to the kitchen for a refill of the cereal bowl during commercials.

Weathers knew that he could do a better job than any of the press hacks in New York. Or any of the gibbering morons on TV. He was a *real* reporter. Old school. He wasn't afraid to get his hands dirty in pursuit of a story, and he didn't care whom he pissed off. When Billy Dent had been arrested years ago, Weathers didn't hesitate to put himself right there in the story. And why not? He'd been covering the deaths of the two girls from the Nod whom Billy had killed from the get-go, keeping Sheriff Tanner's feet held firmly to the fire. He fulminated from the front page of his paper, and when his editor claimed the story had "cooled" and moved updates below the fold and then inside, Weathers had fired up his old blog and started a series of scathing attacks on the Lobo's Nod police force. He'd gotten the attention of the national media—*finally*—and become a darling of the major cable news networks.

But when Billy had been caught, all the attention had gone to Tanner, who prissily and steadfastly refused offers of interviews and book deals and all the other sundry trappings of fame. Suddenly, the man who'd kept the story alive and kicking and in the limelight was thrown over for the man who'd finally gotten off his fat ass and done his job at Weathers's constant prodding.

It was more than insulting. More than infuriating.

It was *wrong*.

And no matter what he did, he couldn't force himself back into the story.

He shook his head. He had to focus. He'd been trying everything for the past few years. But even Billy Dent's sister had stonewalled him, speaking to him only through the closed door of the mother's house. All she would tell him was that her nephew was in New York.

The CNN hourly update came up. Pictures of both Dents,

then a screen showing the various disguises Billy could be wearing. Weathers grimaced. They needed someone on who *knew* Billy. He knew a producer at CNN—Dhuti, her name was. Or Dharti. He couldn't keep them straight. But he remembered that it started with *Dh* and that she'd worn a small ruby in her nose and had spoken with a delightfully unexpected southern accent. Pure Georgia, that one.

Would she return his call? He thought maybe she might. She'd been an assistant five years ago, and her work with Weathers had propelled her up the ladder to producer. She owed him one.

He fumbled with his phone to look up her number, but before he could scroll to the *D*s, the phone vibrated.

BLOCKED.

"Yeah?" He wasn't expecting any calls. He *deserved* them, but he wasn't expecting them.

"Mr. Weathers? Mr. Douglas Weathers?"

It was a woman's voice. Unconsciously, Weathers gathered his robe around himself, covering his nudity.

"Speaking." Deep down, he knew that this would be a telemarketer. Or maybe another aggressive repo caller hired by his ex-wife.

But maybe it wasn't.

"Mr. Weathers, I have an opportunity I'd like to offer you."

"Oh?" Definitely telemarketer. Weathers was already refocused on the TV, where the NYPD's disastrous press conference was being replayed.

"How would you like some exclusive information about Billy Dent?" the woman asked.

Doug Weathers stared at the TV. As though by magic, as she'd said the name, CNN had decided to flash another photo of the man himself.

Weathers cleared his throat. "*What* did you say?"

。。。

Doug Weathers belted his overcoat tightly and turned his collar up against the cold. He lingered near his car for a moment, gazing up the short driveway to a ramshackle old Victorian, shutter eyed and board mouthed. Shingles hung from the rooftop, and thick curlicues of paint peeled from the columns holding up the porch roof. The house couldn't be described as on "the edge of town"—it was actually just past the town line, in what was technically unincorporated territory. County land, not town land. It sat roughly a football field's length back from the main road, partly concealed by spindly white pines and near-dead American beeches.

The mailbox was rusted shut. The word DAWES could be made out in faint, sun-faded black paint.

The woman on the phone had given him explicit instructions—he was to tell no one about this visit. He would be allowed a notepad and pen, but no laptop or tape recorder. Yes, he could bring his cell phone, but it would be surrendered when he arrived and given back before he left.

"Who *are* you?" he'd asked. Natural question, even for someone who wasn't a reporter. Weathers had had enough bad leads in his life to retain a healthy level of skepticism, especially in the face of an open treasure chest.

"Someone who knows Billy Dent very well," the woman answered. "Maybe too well. Are you interested?"

He'd hesitated. Of course he'd hesitated. Crackpots and lunatics overflowed the world's borders.

"Maybe you need proof of my bona fides?" she asked. "Let me give you a scoop: Billy Dent's mother recently passed away at the hospital in Lobo's Nod. Confirm with your sources, if you'd like. I'll call back in ten minutes."

The line went dead, and Weathers could almost hear a stopwatch's rhythmic, near cricket-like clicks as he stabbed at his phone with a now-sweaty finger. He still had a source at the hospital—the perfect one, in fact. Dale Carbonaro, one of the attendants in the morgue. Dale had given Weathers access to the body of one of Billy's victims from the Nod back in the day, allowing Weathers to scoop other news sources with illicit details held back by the cops.

"You on duty?" Weathers asked as soon as Dale answered his phone.

"Weathers? This you?" Dale hawked and spat. "You still owe me fifty bucks from last year. Slipping you the report on the Myerson chick."

Myerson. Ellen. Or Helen. He couldn't remember now. One of the Impressionist's victims. He'd forgotten all about the money he owed Dale.

"Do I? I could have sworn I paid you."

"You've been avoiding me for months, you prick. You know you owe me."

"I need to know about a new body."

"Screw you, Weathers."

"Dent's mother!" Weathers screamed into the phone.

The other end of the line was silent for so long that Weathers checked to make sure he was still connected. Sure enough.

"How did you know about that?" Dale asked in wonder. "Sheriff's department has locked us down on that and we—"

"Thanks, Dale! Drinks on me soon!" He hung up and let the phone lie across his palms, the screen facing him.

What ensued were the slowest, most painful three and a half minutes of Doug Weathers's life, but the phone finally vibrated again, and he had to force himself not to kiss it before answering.

"Do you believe me now?" No preamble.

"I do."

"Are you ready to meet?"

"Absolutely."

And so he had been given the name Jack Dawes and told to go where it led him. He begged for more information, but received none.

A quick check of the county property records had brought him here. A house so nondescript and decrepit that Weathers had probably driven past it a hundred times in the past six months and never once noticed it. Property owned for twenty-odd years by a Mr. Jack Dawes, though from the look of it, Mr. Dawes was no longer an upstanding member of the community.

Before Billy Dent had been unmasked as Green Jack and Satan's Eye and the Artist and the others, he had masqueraded as a solid citizen. This looked like the kind of place

Billy Dent would go to hang out. A beer. A ball game. And maybe, just maybe, a bull session with his good buddy Jack Dawes, reliving murder and mayhem and torture and rape, the two of them howling over it like schoolboys zapping ants with a magnifying glass.

Had Dawes known what Dent was? Maybe even serial killers had best friends. Weathers didn't know.

He grinned.

Sure, he didn't know. But he would. Soon. That was his specialty. His gift.

He learned. Eventually, he learned everything.

He patted his pockets, feeling for his pad and pen. His cell was in one, and he was ready to surrender it. There was also a tape recorder in the other. He would pretend to forget it until the last minute and then hand it over sheepishly — "It's just reflex; I take it everywhere." — which would keep Jack Dawes or the mystery woman from looking for the second recorder, the tiny digital job he had tucked into his waistband.

No one told Doug Weathers when to go off the record. *Off the record* was for people who didn't really want the story.

The steps to the porch didn't so much creak as whine when he put his weight on them. The porch itself made dangerous cracking noises as he walked across it. A storm door was loose on its hinges, vibrating slightly in the cold January breeze. He wrestled it aside, fearing it would blow off entirely, then rapped at the front door with a rust-spotted knocker.

Waited.

Nothing.

He knocked again.

He shouted, "Hello!"

With a shrug, he tried the doorknob and it turned easily, more easily, perhaps, than it should have for such an old house.

"Ms. Dawes?" he asked, stepping inside. He didn't know if she was a Mrs. or a Miss, so Ms. seemed safe. Not that it mattered to him. She could call herself empress for all he cared—as long as her information bore out. She could have been Jack Dawes's mother, sister, wife, daughter.... Who knew?

"Ms. Dawes? It's Doug Weathers." He closed the door behind him. The corridor before him was lit by a Coleman lantern placed on the floor, about five feet from the entrance to the house. A set of surprisingly sturdy stairs ascended to his right, its terminus doused in murk. The hallway straight ahead shivered with shadows.

All in all, the house was neat and clean inside, if empty. Nothing on the walls. No knickknacks or furniture just inside the door. There was a layer of dust on the floor, disturbed into tracks, but no actual filth.

He took a step forward and almost jumped out of his own skin when the woman appeared before him, emerging—he realized with relief—from a side door on his left, just past the lantern.

"Mr. Weathers," she said.

Weathers was in his late thirties and would stumble his way into the big four-oh soon enough, but he still thought of the woman—clearly in her forties—as "older," and not merely in the relative sense. Attractive, though. For an "older" woman. An easy smile. She was relaxed and glad to see him, which made him all the more certain he would be able to pull the tape recorder gambit on her. She was off guard.

His favorite kind of woman.

"Ms. Dawes." He squared his shoulders and offered his hand. "Doug Weathers. Pleased to meet you."

Still smiling, she declined his hand. "You followed the instructions?"

"Of course!" He produced the pad and pen, as well as his cell phone, which she took. It wasn't his real cell phone, anyway—just a burner he used on occasion. His real cell was in the car. He wasn't about to hand over something like that to a stranger.

"Oh, wait!" Feigning chagrin, he probed in the left-hand pocket of his jeans and came up with the old microcassette recorder he never used anymore. "I'm so sorry. I—"

She shrugged indulgently and held out her hand for it. "I'm sure you put it in your pocket reflexively. I understand. You can have it back when we're done."

Weathers bit at the inside of his cheek to keep from grinning. At the small of his back, the digital recorder—voice activated—was already doing its job.

"This way," she said, gesturing to the door she'd just come through. "He's eager to speak with you."

Weathers nodded politely to her and stepped through the entryway into what had once been, perhaps, a parlor or dayroom. It was just as barren as the hallway, though the dust on the floor had been swept away. From the flickering lantern light out in the hall, he could barely make out a single piece of furniture—a chair, steeped in shadows.

"Hello," Weathers said, and the man in the chair leaned forward.

"I just want you to know something, Dougie," Billy Dent said. "This here what's about to happen to you? It ain't business at all. It's entirely personal."

Weathers didn't think or gasp or stammer. He turned to run, but the woman was standing there. She was still smiling, and Weathers realized—to his gut-choking horror—that she was still very, very glad to see him.

CHAPTER 32

Some indeterminate time later, Jazz awoke, feeling eyes on him. Bleary-eyed and groggy, he looked over and realized Marta was staring at him from the sleeping berth. She had a laptop back there, its lid open, and a small antenna jutting out of one end. No Wi-Fi, of course, but she must have had a cellular modem in there.

Jazz figured he was pretty unavoidable on the Internet right about now.

He lunged for the gun a microsecond before she did, her shock and realization paralyzing her for that crucial instant. His leg screamed at the lurching movement, but he ignored it, focused on nothing but the feel of the gun in his hand.

Credit to Marta: It wasn't a tiny little thing. She had a nice, big Desert Eagle, with a modified grip. He lay there, across the divide between the front seat and the berth, and made a point of aiming the gun at the ceiling.

"Let's not do anything crazy," he said. "We can both come out of this just fine."

Her eyes darted back and forth, from the gun to Jazz's eyes to his leg and back again. She was trying to figure out if she could smash his leg, use the pain there to make him lose the gun.

"Think about it, Marta: Is my leg really hurt? Or is that just something I told you to play on your sympathy?"

The notion itself wasn't all that persuasive, but the fact that he'd so obviously and easily read her intent made her think twice. She shrugged and said nothing—just glared at him.

"What are they saying about me? If they're telling the truth, then you know I haven't killed anyone. Did I hurt some people? Yeah, I did. I'm being honest with you. None of them permanently. Or even badly. I did what I had to do. My father has my mother. Hostage. I'm the only one who can help her."

"The cops—"

"The cops took twenty years to catch Billy last time. My mother doesn't have the luxury of that kind of time."

"Where are you headed?"

He couldn't tell her the truth. He mimicked her shrug. "Just a little farther down the road. And then you're done with me."

Something had to break the tension or else they'd be here all day. Jazz popped the ammo clip from the gun and ejected the round in the chamber. He tucked the clip and the stray round into his pocket and then, without fanfare, reversed the gun and handed it to Marta by the handle.

She took it without hesitation and with overt disgust. "Useless."

"Well, now neither one of us can use it."

"Get out of my rig."

He shook his head. "I'm sorry. I can't do that. I need you to take me farther. I promise not to try anything or to hurt you. Honest."

"And what's that worth to me?"

"Think about it: I've only hurt people in my way. You're not in my way."

She snorted. Jazz hauled himself back over the divide into the passenger seat. His leg protested, but he tamped down the pain, not allowing his expression to betray him.

Marta crawled out into the driver's seat, the gun jammed into her waistband. She settled her hands on the steering wheel and stared straight ahead.

"You seemed like such a nice kid," she said at last.

"I am a nice kid. Usually. Or I try, at least."

She gunned the engine. "How long?"

"Few more hours. I'll pick a spot to get out."

They drove in silence for a long time. Jazz figured they were probably well suited to that. Marta had to be used to hours of quiet from her long hauls, and Jazz had been trained by Billy to sit without making a sound for hours at a time. Stalking, after all, was by and large a noiseless activity.

At one point, a police car pulled up beside them. No lights. No siren. It was just pacing them.

Not necessarily a problem. Could just be a coincidence.

But when Marta noticed the cruiser, her eyes visibly widened and Jazz imagined the sparks in her brain right now, most of them screaming *RESCUE*.

"Don't do it," he told her. "Keep driving, and let me out when I say, and you'll be fine. I don't want to have to take you hostage. That doesn't end well for anyone."

"Tough to take me hostage with just bullets."

"You think I can't take away that gun from you?" In truth, he wasn't one hundred percent sure he could. His leg had been throbbing terribly for the past hour or so, and it required most of his concentration not to let that show. But he didn't have to tell the truth — he only had to sound like he was telling the truth. And in this case, the harsher the truth, the better.

"Maybe you think you can get the drop on me," he went on. "Maybe you're willing to risk me getting the gun. I get that. I do. But here's the thing, Marta. I know your license plate numbers. I know the DOT number on your rig. When we stopped for gas, I went through the glove box and learned what I could from that stuff. I just escaped an entire city of cops looking for me. You turn me in now, and I'll just escape again.

"But listen closely, Marta—if you turn me in, when I escape, I promise you one thing: I won't kill you. I'll leave you alive. You have my word on that. But everyone you love? Everyone you care for? *Them*, I'll kill. Horribly. Slowly. And I'll be sure to record their final moments, as they curse you with their last breaths because I'll make sure they know that *you* are the reason why they're dying. So make your decision, Marta. Make it now. Be sure about it."

He meant it. Until he'd spoken the words, he didn't realize how far he was willing to go to rescue his mother. But the endless crashing waves of pain from his leg and the lack of more than a few hours' sleep had sent him into a sweaty, desperate zone of near hysteria. It took all he had in him to keep from exploding at Marta, from yelling, *For God's sake, just drive the goddamn truck and get me home so I can kill my father! I don't want to kill you! I want* him *dead, but if I have to kill you to get to him, I will!*

Such displays of emotion, though, were counterproductive. *You go screamin' and they start screamin'. Only natural. Stay nice and calm, icy, and they listen real good. They believe you.*

Marta clenched her jaw and eased off the gas slightly. The rig fell back a bit and the cop kept on his course.

Jazz exhaled slowly through his nose so that she couldn't tell, his gaze rigidly fixed straight ahead, masking the terror that blazed through him.

That last voice in his head.

It hadn't been Billy's.

It was his own.

CHAPTER 33

Dr. Cullins had not appreciated the announcement that Connie would be checking out of the Blood-n-Bones Hotel and had registered her disapproval with clipped, no-nonsense medicalese, delivered in that unidentifiable accent of hers. Connie put her acting chops to good use, gazing levelly at the doctor, pretending to listen and absorb everything she said.

"Thanks for your concern," she said when Dr. Cullins paused for breath. "But I'm really ready to go home."

"We'll make sure she follows up with our family doctor," her dad added, a comforting parental insert that elicited only an eye roll from Cullins.

And now Dad was off organizing things, something he excelled at, and Connie was staggering around her hospital room, practicing with her new crutches. She made her way to the bathroom, where she allowed herself to sit down and pee like a human being for the first time since being admitted to the hospital. The catheter had been removed (and *that* was a sensation she had precisely zero desire to relive), and she felt like she'd recovered some of her dignity. Such a simple thing. Then again, for a while there, she'd thought she would never get to do even the simplest things ever again.

She thought of Jazz's mom, still in Billy's clutches. Jazz was convinced that his mother had to be alive, that Billy's pathology wouldn't allow him to kill her because he wanted to save that dark honor for his son. Connie wasn't so sure. She wasn't deluded enough to think that she knew Billy Dent better than Jazz did, but she thought she had a pretty good handle on the lunatic. Certainly better than most of his victims, at least, none of whom could report in on their observations, being dead and all.

Maybe Jan was still alive. Connie certainly hoped so. But Billy could keep her alive and still make her life hell. Psychologically, emotionally, and physically, his torments could make Jan beg for death.

That could even be Billy's plan. She closed her eyes, and she saw a battered, bloody, part amputee on a dirty floor in some anonymous wreck of a building somewhere: Jazz's mother, begging her son to kill her.

Yes. That tracked. That made perfect Billy-sense, and Connie's gorge rose and swelled at the knowledge that she could think like Billy now. How had Jazz lived his whole life like this?

Back out in the room, she turned on the TV and slumped in

a chair. More local news about Jazz and Billy. People calling for the head of the captain Jazz had met—Montgomery—as well as the commissioner's and the mayor's.

There was nothing she could do from her chair, and even changing the scenery from a Brooklyn hospital room to her own bedroom in the Nod would accomplish little. She was sidelined, down for the count. As Dr. Cullins had said, it would be months before she was truly mobile again. In the meantime, all she had to offer was her brain. And maybe that could help.

She called Howie, surprised when he answered immediately. In the time since her escape from Billy, winter break had ended and school had started again in the Nod. According to texts from Mom, there was talk of temporarily closing it down again if the FBI confirmed rumors that Billy Dent was headed back to town. Connie wasn't sure where she would feel safer—at school, surrounded by a thousand kids, where an unfamiliar adult would stick out, or at home, with her parents and absolutely no weapons.

"Playing hooky?" she asked Howie.

"I was injured in the line of duty. Parents want me home. How you doing?" Howie's voice was clipped, lacking its usual bounce. No joviality. No faux urban patois. No lurid, inappropriate comments.

Something was up.

"Jazz and Billy are all over the TV here. What about down there?" she asked.

"The usual."

"The cops here think Billy is headed back to Lobo's Nod. Jazz, too."

"Oh, really?"

There was no such thing as a "poker voice," but if there had been, Howie would have the absolute worst in the world.

"What are you up to, Howie?"

"These days? About six seven, six eight. Depends on the state of my hair erection."

That was the Howie she knew. But there was a worried tone to his joking; he couldn't hide it.

"Howie, tell me what's going on. Have you heard from Jazz?"

"From Jazz?" Stalling. God, the boy was so obvious. "From *Jazz*?"

She heard something *thump/thunk*. A car trunk closing? Probably.

"Tell me what's going on. Right now. If you've heard from Jazz, then we need to talk. Remember what we said at Billy's house? That we can't stop Billy, but we can ruin him?"

"I really have to go."

"Howie! We agreed! We can save Jazz and that destroys Billy. Don't shut me out now. We're supposed to be a team."

"Sorry, Connie. I'm about to get in the car, and you know my parents hate it when I talk and drive."

"You have Bluetooth! Don't pull that crap on me!"

"Gotta go now," Howie said. "I bet you're sexy as hell with your leg in a cast. See ya."

She stabbed at his number on her phone, fuming. But he

sent her to voice mail, no matter how many times she called and re-called.

you are an idiot and I'm onto you!!! she texted, knowing she would receive nothing in response.

She struggled up from the chair, leaning on her crutches, her armpits already chafing. Howie knew something. He'd been in touch with Jazz. She was certain of it.

The only question now was: Would she tell anyone?

CHAPTER 34

Howie knew that his parents would totally, completely lose their fecal matter when they realized he'd sneaked out of the house. Again. While injured. Again. He thought there was a good chance of them taking his car away from him this time. They threatened it often enough, on the slimmest of pretexts and for the slightest of crimes against parental sensibility.

On his way out of town, he drove past the Coff-E-Shop. Which naturally made him think of poor Helen Myerson. She'd been their usual waitress and had good-naturedly whipped up any number of outright bizarre concoctions Howie demanded. And then the Impressionist had killed her, and that was the end of Helen, and now that Howie thought about it, he hadn't been back to the Coff-E-Shop since.

I am way too young, he thought, *to have so many dead people in my life.*

He drove along the main road through the Nod until he was outside town, then gunned it when the speed limit jumped. His phone's maps app showed him the way.

In the trunk was a brand-new pickax and shovel. Connie had lost his slightly-less-than-brand-new ones when she punked out and ran from an irate neighbor after digging up Billy Dent's backyard. She still owed him twenty bucks.

"All we do is dig around here," Howie muttered, one eye on the road and one on the phone's screen. "You'd think it could wait until the ground *isn't* frozen."

He caught an entrance ramp to the highway and drove east. In a small bag on the passenger seat, prescription bottles clicked against one another and pills rattled within. Soon he'd arrived at his destination, a run-down gas station near the state line. Total number of ignored calls from Connie during his drive: four. Plus a text. She'd left him three short voice mails, none of which he bothered to listen to. If this wasn't bros-before-hos territory, then there was no such thing. Times like this, crises like these, forged the bonds of best-friend-dom or broke them irrevocably. An old joke says that a good friend won't tell anyone if you show up with a dead body in your trunk, but a *best* friend will help you bury the body.

He thought of the pickax and shovel. He really, really hoped there wasn't a body to bury.

🐾

He parked away from the pumps and let the car idle for a bit, reluctant to get out. The cold had the heartbreaking ability to reach inside his injuries and make them pulsate with new life. The warm interior of the car was much better.

He turned off the car. Hours passed. He began to worry that his parents would be getting home from work soon and find Howie convalescing in absentia, which, to their minds, didn't really count. He occasionally fired up the engine long enough to heat the car a bit, then killed it again.

And he waited.

And waited.

He decided to see how Gramma was doing, so he called the hospital and asked for the nurses' station on her floor. But when he asked if there had been any change in Gramma's condition, the nurse paused, said, "Hold on," and then clicked him over to a Muzak version of Justin Bieber, which was sort of like adding Tabasco to a bullet. After several moments, the line opened again, this time with a gruff voice saying, "Who is this?"

"G. William!" Howie cried. "We meet again, telephonically speaking! Are you part-timing it at the hospital these days? Does the sheriffing gig not —"

"Shut up, Howie." G. William sounded weary, annoyed, and relieved all at once. Howie made the connection instantly — the cops were monitoring calls to Gramma. Of course. They thought it might be Jazz. Or maybe even Billy. "Don't have the time to humor you. Did Jazz put you up to making this call?"

"Hells to the *N-O*, G-Dub. You forget — I'm a regular at Casa de Crazy. Just wanted to see how the old lady's doing. She's missing most of the cards in her deck, but there are times she can remember how to make a mean snickerdoodle. You don't just give up on that shizz, Sheriff."

Tanner's sigh wound through the phone connection and filled the car. "Howie, I might as well... We've been holding this back, but the hospital's about to make an announcement, so I might as well tell you: Mrs. Dent passed away a little while ago."

Somehow, from the moment of G. William's sigh, Howie had known what was coming, but even prepared, the news struck him like a semi running down roadkill. A clot blocked his throat, and he struggled to swallow past it.

It was his fault. All his fault. She'd be alive if he hadn't gone stomping into her house with that damn useless shotgun, Bruce Willis-ing up the place in an effort to figure out whether or not Sam was Ugly J. He should have just brought a real gun and pulled the trigger on her; it would have been faster and more humane.

"Howie? You still there?"

Speaking past the clot: "Uh-huh."

"I don't want you blamin' yourself, you hear me, son? She was an old woman. Her health was not good, not at all. It was her time, okay?"

"Sure, Sheriff."

"I mean it, Howie. Anything—absolutely anything—could have startled her like that."

I killed my best friend's grandmother. I can't believe it. "I gotta go, G-Dub," he said with forced brightness. "My Xbox isn't gonna play itself, you know, and someone has to save the universe. Might as well be me."

Once he broke the connection, he stared at the phone in

his hand, resisting the urge to hurl it as far as he could. Or to smash it against the dashboard.

Dead. She's dead. Oh, man. Oh, man, Jazz is gonna kill me. Or, hell, Billy is gonna really *kill me. Like, for a long, long time.*

He wiped tears from his cheeks. *Damn it. Damn it. Damn. It.*

CHAPTER 35

Jazz and Marta drove through hours of frosty silence.

He didn't think she was actually scared. More like wary. She didn't know what to think or what to believe, and that was just fine with Jazz. Off-kilter people generally chose the safest courses of action, and at that moment in time, the safest thing for Marta to do was to keep piloting her rig.

He munched on a granola bar he'd bought at their last rest stop, back before the Nap That Changed Everything. Marta hadn't stopped since then, as though she believed the gas pedal was some kind of antimurder lever and if she could just keep up the pressure, no harm would come to her.

Billy had called him a killer who hadn't killed yet. Jazz hadn't believed him, but Billy had also scoffed at Jazz's claims of being a virgin; Billy had been proven right about that, as Jazz's stomach proved every time he thought about Sam. Which meant maybe Billy was right about the other thing, too. Jazz had to admit—the thought of killing Billy warmed his insides, like hot apple cider. It suffused him, body and soul.

Consequences would arise. Of course. He wasn't so stupid or so foolish or so obsessed that he thought he could kill Billy and walk away without the world taking its requisite pound of flesh from him. But—and maybe this was naive—he imagined that the consequences might not be quite so dire as imagined at first blush. Removing the Artist, Green Jack, Satan's Eye, and all the others from the world with one swift blow would most likely make Jazz something of a folk hero to some. The families of his father's victims would no doubt rally to his side. Jurors would look sympathetically at his upbringing, his father's depredations. His defense attorneys would invoke battered-person syndrome and the theory of "learned helplessness."

What kind of defense attorneys do you think you're going to have? How much money does that kind of expert testimony cost?

It could go either way. He could end up in maximum security or he could end up doing time in a mental-health facility somewhere until he was determined to no longer be a danger to others. Good luck with that.

And, of course, in every formulation, he would lose Connie. If he hadn't already. That made sense. She could handle only so much. He couldn't blame her. But this was bigger than her happiness, and certainly bigger than his own.

"Take this exit," Jazz said, breaking the silence. He directed Marta into two or three turns from the off-ramp, and the rig belched and groaned to a stop at a run-down gas station that squatted, isolated, on the side of the road. Jazz spotted Howie's car parked across the way but pretended not to notice it. They were a good hour away from the Nod.

Hand on the door lever, he glanced over at Marta, who stared at her own knuckles, tight on the steering wheel.

"I'm leaving now," he told her. "I'm letting you go." The words tasted both magnanimous and filthy. Yes, she would live. But who was he to be making that decision?

He didn't know. And it no longer mattered. Nothing mattered except for catching Billy.

"I want to ask you something," she said.

"No. Just go."

"But my family..."

The toughness, the power in her—it all melted away in that instant, and she lay naked and terrified before him. Jazz ground his teeth. She was, he realized, his Lisa McVey, the girl Bobby Joe Long had let go, even though he knew she would lead the police back to him.

People are real. People matter.

It couldn't be that simple. Billy mattered, but Billy had to die. Jazz was real, but he knew he didn't matter. His life and his dreams were nothing compared with Billy's machinations.

Marta is real. Marta matters.

Maybe that's all he could rely on right now.

"All that stuff I said before? I think..." He hesitated, unsure of the words until they actually came out, hearing them for the first time and recognizing them not by his voice or by their sounds, but by their truth. "I think it was bull. Maybe. I don't know. I really don't. But I think you and your family are safe. I'm pretty sure. I'm looking for my mother, and I have to kill my father because it's the only way, and I think maybe I'm losing it, but I don't know for sure. It's been a rough few days. But I'm pretty sure you'll never see or hear from me again."

Before she could say anything more, he opened the door and hopped out of her life.

Howie watched Jazz head to the ramshackle gas station building and cut around the far side. Bathroom break?

After long moments, the rig Jazz had arrived in wheezed into gear. Its brakes farted, and it groaned back onto the main road. Still, Jazz remained in the bathroom. Howie found himself nervously strumming the steering wheel. He seriously considered—only for a minute, but still—gunning the engine and peeling out of the parking space, hauling ass back to the Nod. Abandoning his best friend in a moment of desperate need? Yeah, that was pretty high on the "instant karma's gonna get you" scale, but it still seemed a vastly superior alternative to telling Jazz about Gramma.

Who are you kidding, Howie? You're not going anywhere.

Soon after the big rig disappeared down the road, Jazz came around the side of the building, walking quickly, a stutter to his step. Howie wanted to hop out and give Jazz a shoulder to lean on, but the instructions had been explicit: Start the car, stay in the driver's seat, unlock all the doors, be ready to take off.

Jazz eventually made his way to the car and flopped into the backseat.

"Constipated? Shy bladder?" The jokes tumbled out of Howie reflexively but didn't sound funny even to him. Gramma was dead.

"Had to wait until she left," Jazz said. The sound of his friend's voice startled him—it was flat and completely disaffected. Sure, Jazz had been through three or four kinds of hell recently, but he sounded like someone who'd died.

Or, more accurately, like someone who'd given up living.

"What are—"

"Drive," Jazz said. He was crouched in the backseat, even though the requisite contortions must have hurt his leg. He pulled Howie's old raincoat over himself.

Howie backed out of the spot and pulled away. "Where to?"

"The Nod."

"Oh, sure, that's a great idea. No one thinks you're going there."

"I'm not asking you to take me home or to the middle of town. We're actually headed to the end of Danvers Street."

Making the turn onto the road, he scoured the rearview mirror for a glimpse of Jazz but could see nothing, so he reached back and dangled the bag of meds.

"Stop that," Jazz ordered, snatching them. "Just drive like there's nothing wrong and no one back here."

Howie heard a prescription bottle open, then the sound of

274

Jazz crunching through a pill. The longer he went without telling Jazz about Gramma, the worse it would be when he finally did. The impact would be heavier, the guilt stronger. But he couldn't do it like this. Not while cruising down the road, Jazz tucked and hidden away like a toddler who thought that if he couldn't see you, you couldn't see him.

So they drove in silence. They were back on the highway, bound for the Nod, when it clicked for him. Danvers Street. Danvers...

Oh. Right. Of course. Because who wouldn't want to go to the town cemetery?

CHAPTER 36

By the time they arrived at the cemetery, a winter's early night had fallen around them. Jazz had not spoken at all for the rest of the drive; Howie thought maybe he'd fallen asleep back there on the floor. When he pulled up to the cemetery, he cleared his throat, about to say, "Hey, wake up, Jazz," but before he could speak, Jazz's voice floated up from behind him, still dead:

"Is there anyone around?"

"No. Just us."

"Look at the big fir tree on the north corner, kitty-corner to the gate. One of G. William's deputies likes to take smoke breaks there when he's on this shift."

Howie didn't want to know how Jazz knew this. He squinted through the windshield and saw nothing. He told Jazz so.

"Good." Jazz popped up from the backseat. "You brought the stuff I asked for?"

"Yeah, of course." As soon as he said it, Howie flashed to

the shovel and pickax in the trunk. Feeling like an idiot, he added the tools to the location and found something gross on the right-hand side of the equal sign. "No way, Jazz. We're not digging up a body. Not happening."

Jazz shrugged as he slid across the seat and opened the door. "'We' don't have to do anything at all. I can do it alone."

Of all the things Jazz could have said in that moment, that was the one thing guaranteed to prompt Howie to get his skinny butt out of the car. Jazz *never* said he could do things alone; he almost had a mania for bringing Howie along on his quests. Howie didn't flatter himself that Jazz just craved his inimitable company — it was most likely because he knew the loner streak that ran through serial killers like his father. Almost as though having Howie along acted as a breaker switch, a kill switch, really, that would trip when too much crazy juice ran through the wiring. Howie's eternal (and internal, for that matter) fragility forced Jazz to be more careful than he might otherwise be.

Which made Howie join Jazz at the trunk. "You're not going in there alone."

Jazz shrugged again. For the first time, Howie could actually see his best friend. He tried to tell himself it was just an artifact of the wan, dull lighting of a gibbous moon and the feeble bulb from the trunk, but the fact was this: Jazz looked awful. His face was sallow, his eyes sunken and bloodshot. His hands trembled just slightly as he reached for the pickax and shovel.

"Jazz," Howie said quietly. Jazz didn't listen, bracing

himself against the lip of the open trunk in order to lever out the tools.

"Jasper." It was the first time in forever that Howie had used Jazz's real name, and it didn't have the effect Howie hoped for. Jazz hauled the tools out with a soft grunt, slung them over his shoulder, and turned to the cemetery.

So Howie fired the last arrow in his quiver.

"Dude, your grandmother is dead." He winced as he said it, both for himself and for Jazz.

Jazz paused and looked back at Howie. "Are you kidding?"

Shaking his head, Howie said, "I wish, man. Really, I do. But she died in the hospital today." He held out his hands, arms outstretched, ready for the bro hug that would come.

Instead, Jazz laughed.

The laughter was quick, unexpected, and bright. Jazz dropped the pickax and shovel with an ill-considered clang and leaned against the car as he caught his breath.

Oh, holy hell. He's lost it. He's seriously lost it.

"You okay?" he asked as Jazz stooped to pick up the tools.

"I've never been okay," Jazz told him, and walked away.

Howie froze for a moment as his best friend disappeared into the darkness. Then, without thinking further, he dashed off after Jazz.

Inside the cemetery, Howie loped along beside Jazz as they maneuvered through rank-and-file headstones and the occasional ostentatious piece of statuary. The people of Lobo's Nod were not given to overbearing displays of remembrance for their dead; a simple gravestone sufficed in lieu of the ornate statues and vaults Howie had seen in movies. The Nod's cemetery was flat and dull and the same in most directions. A million jokes floated through his head, but he somehow managed to keep them from gusting out of his mouth.

Once he'd caught up to Jazz, it was no trick to keep up— his best friend's leg was clearly bothering him. When Jazz walked slowly, like now, he could maintain a steady gait. When he sped up, his left leg dragged.

Howie couldn't bear the silence any longer. He usually hated quiet, but quiet in a cemetery was the absolute worst. "What was the deal with that truck that dropped you off?" he asked.

"Nothing. She probably called the cops as soon as she left. That's why I had to hide in the backseat. Would take too long to hitch from there."

And you're not exactly walking at your best....

"What exactly are we doing?" Howie asked, even though the tools made their task obvious.

"Looking for what Billy left behind," Jazz said, and put on a little speed.

Useless. Even on his best day, Jazz couldn't outpace Howie's ten-foot-long legs, and this was so not Jazz's best day.

"Billy left something here? In the cemetery? With a victim or what?"

Two of Billy's victims, as best Howie could remember,

were buried in the Nod. His last two, in fact, before his arrest. He couldn't imagine how or why Billy would leave something in their caskets, though.

"No," Jazz said, and they stopped. "He left it here."

Howie followed Jazz's pointing finger. The moon's light was just enough that he could make out the engraving on the stone.

JONATHAN WALTER DENT

And two dates.

Howie did the math. "Your grandfather?"

"Yeah. Died something like twenty years ago."

"We weren't even alive twenty years ago. Billy wouldn't know to leave something for you."

Normally, a comment like that would have jostled loose some kind of snarky retort from Jazz, but he only shrugged, a gesture Howie was quickly tiring of.

"I didn't say he left it for me. I said he left it. Period." Jazz dropped the shovel and took an experimental swing with the pickax, stretching out his muscles. "When he came to me in the storage unit, Billy told me he'd already explained how this all began."

"I don't get it."

Silent and then with a painful grunt, Jazz swung the ax. It bit into the frozen ground just below his grandfather's headstone, chewing out a depressingly small amount of turf.

"I read in a book once," Howie said, "that if you roll a trash can full of fire over the frozen ground, it makes it easier to dig."

Jazz took another swing. "Where would we get a trash

can of fire?" In that same lifeless voice. Matter-of-fact. Not the genially combative voice Howie had become accustomed to. "And how would we keep the light from being seen?"

"I don't know."

Then shut up floated, unsaid but understood, in the cold January air.

Jazz attacked the ground again. And again. After a while, he paused to wipe sweat from his brow and leaned on the ax handle, catching his breath.

"Billy told me that he'd given me a clue when I talked to him at Wammaket," he said, unbidden. "And I couldn't figure out what he meant, but then I did."

Silent again. Howie wanted to prod for more, but Jazz had vanished into the zone. More chopping at the ground. Rhythmic and sustained. Howie surreptitiously checked his phone. Both parents would be home from work soon. How long could he stay here with Jazz? Until he froze as solid as the ground? Jazz was working up a sweat, but Howie was shivering already.

"I have something else I need you to do," Jazz said in a tone that revealed no apology and brooked no dissent.

"What?"

Jazz told him.

CHAPTER 37

Before releasing Howie back into the real world beyond the walls of the cemetery, Jazz had him bring the prescriptions he'd filched from his mother. Waiting until Howie left, Jazz greedily gobbled down another painkiller—he was now at twice the recommended dose—and one of the antibiotics, then slumped against a tombstone for a break. The cold ground burned his ass through Mark Culpepper's pants. Sweaty from his labors, he'd stripped off Hughes's overcoat, so he folded it up and sat on it.

Before him, his grandfather's grave looked chewed. He'd broken through the hardest layer of earth in a ragged oval measuring about three feet through its major axis. Now dark, rich dirt welcomed him. Less frozen, sure, but he would need to shovel it out rather than just use momentum and gravity and his own weight to break through it.

He thought—briefly—of Howie. And of his grandmother. He hadn't believed Howie at first, but it took only moments for him to understand her death to be true and immutable.

Jazz didn't believe in ghosts or magic or the supernatural; he didn't cotton to ESP or psychic powers or any of that crap. But he somehow *knew* she was dead, knew beyond and more deeply than Howie's simple reportage. Something fundamental had shifted. In the universe. Or in him. Maybe in both.

She was gone. He'd fantasized her death, and now it was reality. Just as Billy had dreamed so many murders and then sketched them into the real world by sheer force of will and by dint of his exceptional, lethal prowess.

I didn't kill her, he told himself. *I didn't kill her.*

He wondered: If there was a God or some other sort of figure controlling the universe, was it his/her/its idea of a joke that Jazz would come to exhume his grandfather right after his grandmother's death?

If so, it was a lousy joke.

Maybe I should dig another hole right next to him for Gramma.

He hauled himself to his feet. The painkillers made him dizzy and dreamy for a moment, but his leg's complaints had gone silent, which was welcome. With a small groan, he began digging.

You know more than you think, Billy had claimed. *You've got the beginnings of it, boy.*

He'd invoked Gilles de Rais. But not Belle Gunness. Belle Gunness, one of the first black widows of the modern age, maybe. Late 1800s. Came to America. Killed the men who courted her, lived off their leavings. Killed her own two daughters.

And, in her crowning achievement, vanished from history. Never brought to justice. It was believed she'd faked her own death. Disappeared into some other life.

Like Aunt Samantha, leaving the Nod, disappearing into a new identity.

He should have seen it. Should have recognized her for what she was. Aunt Sam was Ugly J and she was Belle Gunness. Using multiple names, like Billy.

He wondered: Had Billy taught his sister how to evade capture? Or had she taught him?

It had to be the former. Women just didn't seem to have the constellation of psychological disorders necessary for prolonged strings of murder. Most typical was for them to work with a male partner, like Fred and Rosemary West in England, a couple who had murdered boarders at their house, as well as their own daughter.

Rosemary had claimed Fred forced her into it. Pleaded her innocence.

To their credit, the Brits didn't buy it, and she was still in prison.

How many had Ugly J killed, wandering the world, utterly free, unsuspected? How many were dead because no one would ever think to point the finger at a woman?

Billy said it all started in the Nod. And it did. This is where he and Sam grew up. Where they learned how to prospect. Maybe over the years they teamed up on occasion. Maybe they gave each other tips. It was a game to them, just like the murder Monopoly Hat and Dog were playing. I bet they stayed in touch, one-upping each other over the years.

Until Billy ended up in jail. And Sam just couldn't bear that, could she? Her partner in crime, her brother, locked up? Penned in like a common criminal? Not a chance.

It had taken her years, but she'd been able to get to the Impressionist. Set him on his way, sent him to the Nod. Put Jazz in a position where he would have to seek out Billy's help.

And then, when Billy was ready, he broke out. By having me send a signal to Sam without even knowing it.

He remembered that time with Billy in the penitentiary. He'd thought that he was safe from Billy, what with the chains and the guards. But Billy had been in control the whole time. It was like playing checkers, only to learn that your opponent was playing chess all along.

And he told me…

Told you as much back at Wammaket. Told you where it started.

Yes. Yes, he had. Jazz just hadn't realized it at the time. What it meant. It had sounded like more of the verbal chaff Billy vomited into their air, aurally toxic nonsense designed to keep the listener off guard and one step behind.

But not this time. No, this time he had flat out told Jazz where to go and what to do. And Jazz hadn't listened. He'd been too impressed with himself for bearding Billy in his den, for not only daring to defy his father but also to go to him cloaked in that defiance and ask Billy to help—through Jazz—the police.

And Billy had played him masterfully.

I don't think you'd be wanting me dead, anyway, his

father had said. *Know what set me off on my prospecting? My own daddy died.*

It was bull. Jazz's grandfather had died twenty years ago, and Billy's first confirmed kill—Cassie Overton—dated to a little more than a year before that. And knowing Billy's meticulous and conservative nature, that meant he'd been planning and plotting murder for at least a few years before that.

Know what set me off on my prospecting? My own daddy died.

Not true. Many serial killers were set off by the death of a father or father figure, but not Billy. Which meant there was something *else* about the late Jon Dent—or, more accurately, his death—that Billy had taunted Jazz with. Idiot that he was, Jazz hadn't even known he was an idiot.

A squirt of pain shot through the barrier of the drugs Howie had delivered, and Jazz realized he was hip deep in dirt, having dug several feet down without pause. He didn't know how long he'd been digging, and the still night sky offered no clues. Only the ache of his shoulders and neck told him it must have been over an hour.

He leaned on his good leg until the bad one sank back into a dull throb, then kept digging. Soon his shovel clunked against something hard.

Failing to keep his excitement in check, he found himself in a renewed flurry of digging. He didn't have time to dig a six-foot-deep trench the length of the casket, so he settled on clearing away the dirt covering the upper third, where the hinged lid was divided into a separate door to reveal the head and upper body for a viewing. His late grandfather, as best he could remember, had died of a stroke. (Gramma, now late herself, had alternated between the stroke story and claiming that her husband had been killed by a bolt of lightning cast by a local witch.) No reason not to have an open casket at the service.

With sharp blows from the pickax, he broke the hinges and clasps on the casket. Took a deep breath and held it. The stench, he knew, would be epically awful. And possibly dangerous—some sort of bacterium or toxin could escape with the uncovering of the body. Jazz figured crossing his fingers would have to pass as disinfectant. And maybe those antibiotics would shield him if Gramps had something to offer from beyond the grave.

Still holding his breath, he wrestled the top section off the casket. An invisible cloud of warm, noisome air wafted up at him, drifting into his nostrils even though he held his breath. Fighting his gag reflex, he set the wooden door aside and then scrambled out of the hole to lay panting on the cold ground. He rolled onto his back and stared up into the night sky. He'd missed the stars while in New York. Too much light pollution there; too few stars. Home in the Nod, the sky fairly exploded with them.

After a few minutes, he ventured back into the hole. The stench of decayed flesh and rotted gas lingered. Jazz tugged his shirt up around the lower half of his face and breathed through his mouth. He didn't know what inhaling this might do to him. A decomposing body didn't just disappear—the decomposed parts had to become something; conservation of matter and energy proved it. So the noxious air swirling around Jazz actually *was* parts of his grandfather, devoured and converted to gases by the population of microorganisms that lived in the intestines.

Jazz remembered the stages of decomposition as Billy had taught them to him the way other kids remembered commercial jingles. "A, P, B, P, F, and DD," he muttered in a singsong tone under his breath.

Jazz's grandfather had been in the grave twenty years. He was in the final stage of decomposition, the mayor of Dry Decaytown, no question about it. In the waning moonlight, Jazz spied white bone and the endless-seeming pits of empty eye sockets and nostrils. The casket was old and cheap, not waterproof. Mildew and mold clung to the bones here and there. Jazz wished he'd asked Howie to bring a flashlight.

Not thinking straight. The damn leg. The truck. Marta. Everything else. Nice job, Jazz.

He crouched down, poised precariously over his grandfather. He didn't relish the idea of having to fish around in the casket. There could be washes of corpse liquor in there—a foul liquid slick of decomposed remains containing all kinds of nasty bugs.

As he adjusted his position, the pale moonlight fell, illuminating the tattered remains of the lapels of his grandfather's burial suit. He spied the very edge of something there, something that most likely lay clasped in the dead man's hand. From the glimmer in the moonlight, it looked like a clear plastic bag.

Reaching into the casket with infinite care, braced cautiously against the side of the pit he'd dug, Jazz brushed his fingertips against the object.

Definitely plastic. A Ziploc bag. With something in it.

It felt like a book.

He tugged at it carefully, not wanting to pull anything other than the book. It stuck fast. He tried a little harder.

Something gave. There was a hollow *snap* and a rattle, and the book came out into his hands.

Fortunately, it was dry. He clambered out of the grave and proceeded to cough until he vomited, steadied against his own grandfather's headstone as his guts recoiled and contracted until he dry heaved the memory of food long-since digested.

Please let this not be my grandfather's beloved Bible or diary. Please let it matter.

He propped himself against the other side of the headstone, avoiding the slick of his puke. The book was black. Or dark green. Or brownish red. It had once been blue. Or gray. Or puce. Who could tell? Protected by the plastic bag, it had suffered less than Grampa himself, but age, decay, and mildew had still taken their respective tolls. Unzipping the bag, he caught a brief whiff of mustiness that was almost pleasant and welcome in comparison to the reek from the grave.

The book was hardcover, its face blank. It looked like a sketchbook of some sort. Jazz cracked it slowly, worrying it would fall apart. Dust filtered down into his lap and the spine split, but the book held together well enough.

No sketches. Not on the first page, at least. Just words. Cramped and diligently scripted from gutter to fore edge.

He recognized his father's handwriting immediately. The page was clotted with text, impossible to read without decent lighting, but one sentence loomed larger than the others.

Today she told me about the Crow King.

CHAPTER 38

Hughes figured he would recognize Sheriff Tanner on sight, and sure enough, he could have picked the guy out of a crowd even without the uniform and ridiculous sheriff's hat. Tanner looked exactly as Hughes had figured—a corpulent, smashed-nose redneck with a comically absurd mustache. You couldn't have gotten a better look from central casting.

The airport closest to Lobo's Nod was two hours from the town itself, in another state, one equally as infamous for its notably lax attitude toward pesky things like civil rights. Hughes had flown into this airport when he'd picked up Jasper—a thousand years ago, that felt like; back when the boy was innocent, it seemed.

He had only his carry-on, so he shrugged through the crowd to Tanner, who actually tipped his hat in greeting, for God's sake.

"Sheriff. Louis Hughes, NYPD." Under normal circumstances, he would have shown his badge at this point, just to make everything official. But he couldn't do that, because the Dent kid was probably using it to 'jack cars right about now.

And the damn sheriff knew it, too. Hughes detected a hint of a smile beneath that ridiculous mustache. "Pleased to meet you," Tanner said, and held out a hand. They shook.

As they headed to the sheriff's car—parked, Hughes noted with grudging respect, in the no-parking zone—Hughes thumbed through his phone, looking for updates from Miller. Nothing yet on Samantha Dent.

"Anything new?" Tanner asked as they pulled away from the airport.

"No. I have my people looking into the sister. All they've found so far for the past few years is that time the media got ahold of her and put her on TV. Nothing outstanding. Everything's boring. Maybe too boring, if you get my drift."

The sheriff adjusted the heat. Hughes was freezing, but a man of Tanner's girth probably ran the AC in December. "Maybe I can have one of my people coordinate with you. I've got a deputy interviewing people who knew her when she lived in town."

Hughes's regard for Tanner almost accidentally slipped up a notch. "Good idea. Anything yet?"

"Not yet. But we have a lot of people to talk to. Folks don't really move away from the Nod. Not the older ones, at least."

"Did you know her?"

"No. She left town young. I never met her. Bumped into Billy all the time. You couldn't live here without bumping into him. Never really spent any time with him until after his wife ran off, though. That's when I got to know him and met

Jazz and..." He hesitated before going on. "I don't suppose you had Wi-Fi on the flight?"

Hughes's internal alerts started flashing. "Why? What happened?" If either Dent had already been found...

"Not sure it'll matter, but Billy Dent's mother passed in the hospital earlier today. FBI is already en route."

Hughes nodded. Of course. Even if Billy weren't on his way to Lobo's Nod, the FBI would suppose that the death of his mother might get him to come home—in disguise, of course—for her funeral. Other killers had been caught in just such a fashion.

"I'm sending deputies to start staking out the cemetery and we're locking down the morgue," Tanner went on. "Just in case."

"How'd the old lady go?"

"Still some debate about that. Looks like heart attack, but might could be something else. Medical examiner's not taking any chances." When Hughes said nothing, Tanner went on: "A nurse went in shortly before she died. No one at the hospital can seem to account for her."

Hughes perked up at that. "A woman. So Dent *does* have a partner."

"Seems like. She matches the description of the sister in terms of age—somewhere in her forties. I've got a sketch artist working with my deputy."

"Why your deputy?"

Tanner shifted his considerable bulk uncomfortably. "Well, it ain't nothing to be proud of, but my deputy was standing guard when all this happened."

Hughes uttered a short bark of laughter and shook his head, then gazed out the window at the complete lack of anything to look at. Endless fields, occasionally broken by a tree. "Nicely done. Small-town police work at its finest." Normally he would be more diplomatic, but he was tired. He was pissed. He was badgeless. And now the Keystone Kops had let an accomplice murder someone literally under their noses.

"Tell me how you really feel," Tanner said.

Hughes grunted. "Trust me, you don't want to know."

"Suit yourself. But you might feel better if you admit your part in this."

Hughes laughed again, without humor. "My part? Are you kidding me?"

Watching the road, Tanner said mildly, "I'm not."

Ready to retort, Hughes instead retreated against the passenger door. Tanner was right, of course. The whole thing (*thing* encompassing too much even to imagine at this point) couldn't be laid at his feet, but he'd played his part. He'd screwed up enough for any ten guys, and even though he'd been well intentioned, it didn't matter. People were dead. Careers were ending, maybe even his own before this was all over with. If it ever *would* be "over with." Billy Dent had avoided the law for decades. His sister had gone radar-invisible for just as long. And a teenage kid was proving to be just as tough to find. At this rate, Hughes had no trouble envisioning a future in which he died in an old-age home somewhere, the TV bleating about the still-at-large Dent clan.

Hughes had brought Jazz to New York in the first place. It had seemed so simple and easy at the time, but then, as bad as things were, they got further out of hand *very* quickly. Which made everything that followed *his* fault. He pinched the bridge of his nose, reliving the moment when Finley had accordioned the door to unit 83F up along the ceiling. The kick of the stench. The blood. Morales's body. Goddamn it.

"I should have kicked him loose the minute he told me about breaking into Belsamo's apartment," Hughes whispered, unable to open his eyes, unable to look over at Tanner. Confessions should always be blind.

"I should have locked him up," he said. "Or at the very least put him on a plane back to Podunktown. But no. No. I gave him the benefit of the doubt. I sent him to his room like a naughty schoolkid, instead of treating him like the jug of nitroglycerin he is. And now Morales is dead and I'm the one on the way to Podunktown and my career's probably over, but I'm goddamn well bringing the Dents down first."

Only the hum of road noise greeted his pronouncement. When he opened his eyes, Tanner was still studying the cone of highway illuminated by his high beams.

"Did you hear me? Does that make you happy? Big-city cop admits he screwed the pooch up, down, and sideways?"

"You feel better?" Tanner asked.

"Oh, sure." The sarcasm dripped thick and bitter. "So much better."

But as much as he hated to admit it, Hughes did feel just a tiny bit better. It wasn't that he'd said it out loud—it was that he'd finally *heard* what he was sure everyone was thinking.

It was out in the world now, those words, those ideas. Not bottled up somewhere, hidden away, waiting to spring on him or to be sprung by someone else. He'd spoken them aloud and made them smaller.

"Seems to me you were doing the best you could with what you had," Tanner said. "But what the hell do I know?"

A lot more than most people—Hughes included—gave him credit for, Hughes suspected.

He sat up straight in the passenger seat and opened the notes app on his phone to go over the checklist he'd made on the plane. He added a few items. "I want to see the Dent house. And the cemetery. And the old lady, for that matter."

"Of course."

"But I should find a hotel first."

"Already got you registered at the one closest to the sheriff's office."

Hughes grinned. When he looked over at Tanner, he realized the big man was grinning, too. From this angle, his mustache didn't look all that ridiculous.

CHAPTER 39

Dad had sprung for first class back to the Nod, so Connie reclined the seat as far back as it would go and closed her eyes. She had just enough room for her broken leg. Perfect. She took one of the painkillers from the prescription they'd filled at the hospital pharmacy, and soon the thrum of the jet engines and the power of the narcotics lulled her to sleep.

When she awoke, they were landing and the flight attendant was telling her to return her seat to its full and upright position. Connie blinked away sleep and groggily did as she was ordered. Next to her, Dad stared out the window at the clouds rolling and crashing like slow-motion waves.

At home, her mother wept over her like she was a returning soldier. Connie murmured assurances and tried not to show how painful it was to be in her mother's tight embrace. She wondered when she would stop hurting. Would it happen all at once, or would some part of her body drop off the roster first, followed by others? At this point, she felt as though even her eyelids and hair hurt; she would be happy with one part of her body not aching.

Whiz feigned indifference, shuffling listlessly off to one side as her mother and father took turns clutching and worrying at her. When Mom said, "Come say something to your sister," he grunted something vaguely audible and hugged her awkwardly with one arm. "Welcome back, I guess," he said.

They rolled her into her room in a wheelchair Mom had bought when Dad called. Her bedroom seemed too big for her, too bright, too loud. The artifacts of her old life stunned her—childish, little-girl baubles. Hair products and cheap jewelry exchanged with friends and pages torn from *Essence* and *Heart & Soul* and the copies of *Cosmo* her friends kept shoving at her. The ruffles at the base of the bed glared at her, almost accusing her of being a frivolous, shallow *girl*. Thank God there was nothing pink—she didn't think she could bear that. She imagined herself screaming for the pink to be stripped from the room, her room denuded if need be.

Managing a taut, convincing smile for her parents, she eased herself out of the chair and onto the bed. Mom had already left extra pillows so that she could elevate her leg while sleeping. Dad put the crutches within arm's reach, and they both asked, "Do you need anything? Are you sure?" multiple times as they slowly backed out of the room.

She didn't need anything. She was sure.

Until they closed the door.

Her heart hammered so fast, so strong, so sudden that she thought it had exploded, that her last thought in this life would be *What just happened in my chest?* But the moment passed. She yoga breathed but had trouble catching her breath.

It was the door. It was closing the damn door with her alone and helpless in her room. It didn't matter that it was her own bedroom; it had become an alien place. It was the soundproof room in Brooklyn, where she had struggled to free herself, where Jazz's poor mother had been unable to escape. It was the fight with Billy Dent, the crash through the window, the drop....

Squeezing her eyes shut, she tried to focus on a meadow. On a field. But there was a body in the field and there was blood in the meadow, and nothing she did could relax her. This wasn't her room anymore. This wasn't her home. This was just a place to live. She had become a new person in New York, and being in her parents' house was like having skin that fit too tightly. She didn't know how she could possibly cope; she would scream, she knew.

The room was the same when she opened her eyes; it hadn't transmogrified through some magic into her prison in Brooklyn. Everything was too bright, too garish. Except for one thing.

Taped to the full-length mirror opposite the bed, a make-shift frame of photos called to her. She groped for the crutches, managed to lurch out of bed, and balanced herself well enough that she could take the four hop-steps to the mirror. There, in the upper-left corner, was the only thing in the room that did not assault her eyes.

A photo. Of her and Jazz. In each other's arms.

It was from the previous summer. The Hat-Dog Killers would have just been on the trailhead of their path through the brambles of murder, but in Lobo's Nod, Connie and Jazz knew nothing of what waited for them in mere months. The Impressionist was still in the future, and Hat-Dog were on their second kill, maybe, and for the moment, Jazz and Connie were just, merely, only, simply happy.

Jazz smiled so rarely. And smiled honestly even less frequently. She adored that smile.

With a trembling hand, she pried the photo from the mirror and held it close. Their closeness. Their becoming indeterminate in each other. Was that even possible now? If he came to her with his father's blood on his hands, could she forgive that? Live with that?

Certainly, she wanted Billy dead. Preferably dead, chopped into little pieces, fed to rats, and then the rats' scat collected and burned. Just to be sure.

But did Jazz have to be the one to pull the trigger?

Maybe it would liberate him. Maybe it would set him free, and with his mother back in his life, maybe...

Maybe maybe maybe.

It was all moot, in any event. Jazz was off, lost in the wind, in some place where she couldn't touch him. Maybe nearby. Probably not. She knew the odds put him in a ditch somewhere, shivering, his leg infected and ballooned up to the size of an elephant's. If anyone could survive on the run, though, it was Jazz.

Where is he, she wondered. *Where is he and what is he doing?*

CHAPTER 40

Surrounded by the Hideout again, Jazz felt as though he'd somehow stepped into the past, back into a world that — in retrospect — was much kinder and easier than he'd thought at the time.

He hadn't been to the Hideout since around the time of the Impressionist. Once the weather turned, even the space heater couldn't keep out the cold, especially given that he had to keep the door cracked when running it, lest the kerosene fumes finish the job Duncan Hershey had failed to complete on his own.

Struggling with the casket, he'd managed to get the removed lid portion back into position, though the lock and hinges were useless now. He had begun refilling the grave — out of common decency, if not a desire to cover his tracks — when he heard wheels on gravel. So Jazz had shoveled one last heap of dirt into the grave and then scampered off into the darkness surrounding the graves.

Finally safe, he spent a few minutes chasing various

bugs, spiders, and other creepy-crawlies out of his sanctum before turning on the heater and settling into the beanbag chair that he usually reserved for make-out sessions with Connie. A sudden, pungent memory smote him—wrapped up with Connie in the Hideout, their breath desperate and ragged as their lips and tongues fought each other for primacy. His hands, explorers, ranged every inch of her; nothing off-limits, nothing left untouched. In those moments, at that time, he'd thought that maybe someday he might be normal, that maybe there might somehow be a happy ending for his story.

He repressed the memory with a savage brutality. There was no time for this. He had a purpose. His mother needed him. His father lurked in the darkness.

If the price of ridding the world of Billy Dent was the loss of his own life, or happiness, or freedom, well, that was the cheapest price imaginable.

And finally—finally!—he had a weapon. One he was not yet sure how to use. But a weapon nonetheless. If Billy had buried the book with his father, it must have contained something important and useful. Something revealing. A chink in Billy's armor, maybe. Some psychological flaw that could be used against him. Or maybe something as simple as a list of safe houses that Jazz could use to harrow his father into the open, where—like a bug skittering away from the baseboards—he would be easier to crush.

Jazz popped another painkiller. The directions on the antibiotics said *Take one per day until finished, as directed*, so he left that bottle closed for now.

He cracked open the book and began reading. Puzzled, he skipped a page. Then another.

He flipped through.

His leg forgotten, he kept reading.

Maybe it was the painkillers, but after paging through and poring over the book for what felt like hours, it still made no sense.

Everything was out of order, for one thing. There was no structure to it, nothing to lend it coherence. The book measured 8" x 10", and every flat white page was crammed full of text, some of it running vertically in the margins, some of it curling in circles, ellipses, or conch-shell-like receding twists. The book spelled out a heady mélange of fantasies, instructions, and bits of doggerel, all connected by nothing but the commonality of Billy's tight, nigh-perfect penmanship. One page would end in the middle of a sentence, only for the next one to start anew with something clearly written years earlier. Where did that sentence end? Did it ever end? Jazz hadn't found out yet. A page would describe in excruciating detail the look of Billy's father's skin at the funeral home, but the next page would be a very-much present-tense discussion of a conversation Billy had clearly *just* had with the man. Time was random, as if the book had been written in chronological order, then unbound, the pages randomly shuffled and rebound.

This, he reasoned, had to be what it was like in Billy's

head. He remembered again telling Hughes how Hat-Dog's murders, while insensible to the police, made perfect sense to the killer. The same truism held here. While the book made little to no sense to Jazz, it obviously meant something to Billy. It obviously *said* something to Billy, and most likely said something *about* him as well.

Two things stood out to Jazz on his first look-through: The first was the name Jack Dawes, repeated throughout, on various pages, always larger than the surrounding text, usually stroked over several times so that it was jagged and bold. The second was a sort of spiral arrow that often connected certain names with other names, sometimes spanning a full spread of two pages to draw a connection between names on opposing leaves.

There was a whole cast of characters, though he was damned if he could figure out who any of them were or what they did. Many of them were mentioned only once, with names like the Surgeon and Honey Trap, the Chef and Respector. Billy wrote as if they were real people, ascribing motivations and physical characteristics ("blue-flecked green eyes," "red wart on finger," "crooked incisor"), so Jazz assumed they actually existed, even though it was possible—he supposed—that they were all figments of Billy's imagination. Still, as crazy as his father was, Jazz didn't think Billy had ever descended into outright hallucination. Delusion? Sure. But seeing or hearing things that weren't there? No. Billy was firmly entrenched in the here and now, obsessively aware of the world around him at all times. Ever alert for motion from the prospects.

Turning forward and back, trying to catch threads that floated away like jellyfish in the tide, he paged the book all night. As soon as he thought he understood some particular aspect or "subplot" (as he'd come to think of them — there seemed to be no main plot at all), he would glimpse some other madness or oddity that wrested his attention away and sent him on another exploratory mission through the text.

Somewhere within the text, he divined an early version — a rough draft? — of the bedtime story Billy had told him as a child, the tale of the Crow King and his harrowing and bleeding of a wayward dove. Jazz couldn't tell if this was something Billy had come up with on his own and written down, or if he'd copied it from somewhere. Seeing it recorded in his father's handwriting set the flesh on his arms crawling.

Without a phone or a watch, he had no idea what time it was as the night wore on. He knew only that even with the kerosene heater pumping away, he was freezing. His fingers routinely went numb as he turned the pages, so he took breaks to blow on them and stuff them into his armpits for warmth.

He'd imagined that the Crows were some sort of collective of Billy Dent hangers-on, a group of Impressionists, as it were, each of them somewhere out there acting independently in honor of their Crow King. But if he had the chronology from the book right, the Crows actually predated Billy. They'd been in existence before he began killing, and he'd learned of them around the time of his father's death. Sam had introduced him to them (*Today she told me about the Crow King.*) and initiated him into their ranks.

As incredible and unbelievable as it seemed, the Crows appeared to be, well...a kind of serial killer social network. Developed and up and running years before Twitter or Facebook or even MySpace. If the Crows were extant in the early nineties, when Billy's father died, then they might even stretch back further. They probably antedated the popularization of the Internet itself, a dark, underground precursor of what was to come. Jazz pictured them gathering in virtual chat rooms—old-style BBSs—or, before that, over ham radio or whatever other technology they had at their disposal. Hell, if the book was any indication, they probably wrote things down and sent stuff through the mail back in the day.

Maybe they still did so. Using the idea of a social network but keeping off the Internet would make it more difficult for some governmental data-sniffing program to identify and isolate them. No one had figured out how to hack paper, so putting a letter in a mailbox was still a safer way to keep things secret, as long as you used multiple addresses and aliases and didn't care about immediacy.

And serial killers could be very, very patient.

Statistically, it was believed that there were roughly three dozen serial killers active and hunting in the U.S. at any point in time. If what Jazz had gleaned from the book was right, that figure was probably low by a factor of three. Assuming, of course, that the names inside weren't different aliases for some of the same people, just as Billy had taken the names Green Jack, Satan's Eye, Hand-in-Glove, and the others.

But what was the point? What was the purpose? Did they just exchange...tips? He had a sudden, comical vision of Billy making careful notes on dismemberment on index cards, placing those cards in an old-fashioned recipe box. Trading them at a serial killer swap meet somewhere like baseball cards.

It was ridiculous. Besides, most serial killers don't play well with others. They are, by their nature, solitary. What on earth could draw them all together?

He closed the book and strummed his fingers against it to keep them moving and limber. His breath frosted the air, despite the heater. A decision loomed: Close the door and shut out the wind, or leave it open so that the heater could stay on?

A check of the heater's fuel reserve answered the question for him: He was low on kerosene, with maybe an hour's worth left. Judgment-call time. He settled on a superficially risky path, shutting the door tightly while leaving the heater on. The Hideout was hardly airtight; long before he could asphyxiate on kerosene fumes, the heater would conk out, but in the meantime, he would store up enough heat—he hoped—to get him through the night.

No closer to catching Billy than he had been when there'd been hundreds of miles between them, Jazz curled into a tight ball on the beanbag chair. He knew he would get no sleep, but that was the last thing he thought before drifting off, the book clutched to his chest like a child's bedtime story.

CHAPTER 41

There was someone in her room, Connie realized.

Even half-asleep and brain-clogged, she sensed the presence. She took it seriously. Right now, her fervent hope was that this was just some leftover dream detritus intruding on her conscious mind and that when she looked, there would be no one in her room but, well, her.

Still, it took her several seconds to work up the courage to open her eyes. It was still dark, the room lit by filaments of streetlight through the slats of the venetian blinds and, she realized, the hall safety light, spilling in through her bedroom door, now slightly ajar.

Her wheelchair had moved closer to the bed, and there was a figure sitting in it.

Connie's throat spasmed; she couldn't scream even if she had to. She twisted reflexively away from that side of the bed, but her broken leg would let her move only so far; it flashed pain at her like a warning sign.

The figure in the wheelchair snorted and twitched, and Connie realized it was her brother.

She turned—gently—back to him, mopping tears with the edge of her pillowcase. Whiz could pretend apathy all he wanted, but sneaking into her room to be with her while she slept spoke more loudly than any whining or eye rolls ever could. The temptation to nudge him awake was strong, but she tamped it down. At least one of them should get a full night's sleep.

It was impossible to relax. Even in her own home. Her own bed.

Pawns are always sacrificed before game's end, the Auto-Tuned voice had told her. She wondered if maybe Billy and Sam both used the Auto-Tuning, so that the listener didn't know which one was which. That was eerily probable, and she hated that she could think that way now.

Jazz thought this way. Jazz had always thought this way, ever since he was a little boy. Wherever he was, whatever he was doing, she thought he had to be dealing with this better than she was.

What was she supposed to do? She hadn't called the police to tell them to talk to Howie, but she could change her mind about that at any time. And maybe she should.

The Girlfriend would call Howie and see what was going on. The Ex-Girlfriend would call the police and tell them to sit on Howie, if they weren't already.

She didn't know which she was anymore. Or even if her status was relevant, if Jazz would eventually be found dead or gibbering and half-starved somewhere along a highway. For some, death came as a comfort, or at least with grace. But for Jazz, she could envision nothing but an ugly death.

When you die, Connie, it will be ugly, the voice had said. *I promise you that. And I also promise you that I will be a little sad at that moment. But only a little bit.*

Nestling against her pillow, she stretched one hand out as far as she could, resting it on the arm of the wheelchair. Close enough to Whiz's hand to feel the heat radiating from him. Whether Jazz's love for her was alive or dead, she would take solace in his courage and his conviction. Even if he killed Billy, he would still be the boy—the man—she'd fallen in love with. And if he never wanted to see her again, that would still be enough. She would not back down. She would not succumb to her fear.

Go ahead and come for me, you bitch, you bastard. Come for me. I won't go quietly, and I promise you this much: I'll take everything from you that I can before I die.

CHAPTER 42

Restlessly pacing his bedroom the next morning, Howie tried to envision the next steps, the world to come. But the portents were murky at best. He'd always relied on his ability to understand Jazz, or at least to predict his movements. Their years of friendship hadn't stripped away all of Jazz's mystery, but they had dragged at least part of the cloak off. Howie had always felt that he could see the line Jazz would walk up to, but never cross. Now, after Jazz's reaction to news of Gramma's death, after watching him dig up his grandfather with manic intensity and in such utter silence, without their usual mordant banter...After all this, Howie wasn't sure how much of Jazz was still inside Jazz.

What happens to the sidekick when the good guy goes off the rails? He didn't know. He had a sudden, disturbingly bright flash of memory from some horror movie he and Jazz had watched as kids, in which the good guys were—one by one—possessed by an alien life force. And at the end, there were only two guys left, and one of them was possessed and with his last conscious thought begged his buddy, "Kill me. Please kill me."

Howie tried to imagine Jazz demanding that of him. Would Jazz recognize the moment when he was about to step over the line he'd drawn for himself years ago? Would he be able to resist? Or maybe he would pause just long enough—murder in his eyes—to turn to his best friend and ask him to perform that one service only a best friend or a mortal enemy could perform.

Stop me, Howie.

And there would be only one way.

Cut it out, Howie. It's not going down that way. Jazz could never kill anyone. And he's smart enough to know not to rely on me to stop him.

Except the words rang hollow even when not spoken aloud. Howie had been Jazz's friend for a long time, half their lives. Howie knew that his friend was perfectly capable of killing someone. That had never been the question. The question—the one Howie had assiduously avoided thinking for years, the one now neon-flashing before him, unavoidable— was *would* Jazz kill?

It could happen. He could cross that line.

What do I do? What am I supposed to do? Do I turn him in? Is that what I do? Turn him in to the cops and see what happens?

It was the most sensible course of action. It savored of *right*, but it also had the sour aftertaste of betrayal. For all of Jazz's faults, he'd never once turned on Howie. Did that buy

Jazz a free pass for the rest of his life? How far was Howie's gratitude for that childhood-bully save supposed to stretch, and did its surface area cover capital crimes? Bros before hos was one thing, but bros before the rest of the world? If Jazz showed up tonight in Howie's backyard, tossing pebbles at his window to lure him out there, and Howie crept down the stairs and out through the garage, only to find Jazz covered in blood and toting Billy's severed head, saying, *Hey, man, things got a little out of control. I need to borrow your car,* well, WWHD? *What would Howie do?*

He was only a tiny bit scared to find that he imagined the theoretical Howie already digging in his pocket for his car keys.

Mom knocked at his door just then, bearing the cordless phone. Howie had been so absorbed in his own morbid morality play that he hadn't even heard the phone ring. "It's your principal. He has assignments from your teachers."

Howie took the phone. You would think helping to catch a serial killer and landing in the hospital after confronting another one would result in the pity scissors being brought out and some substantial amount of slack being cut, but no. The dedicated educators at Lobo's Nod High demanded that their battered and bruised hero still cram their usual wads of useless knowledge into his rattled and shaken skull. He flounced onto the bed and said, "Yeah, hello?"

"Hello there, Howie," said the last and worst voice Howie had ever expected to hear.

Paralyzed on his bed, staring up at Uma Thurman and—for the first time in his life—not enjoying it, Howie could only say, "Hello, Mr. Dent."

"Mr. Dent." Billy chuckled. "So polite. Always did have manners, Howie. When you chose to use 'em, that is. Your parents raised you right. Speakin' of—how *are* Tom and Melinda? Did your dad ever figure out what was wrong with his hip?"

Howie couldn't swallow. His throat had closed over, and no matter how much he tried, he just couldn't.

"Now, Howie, I know it's been a while since we talked, but you can't hold that against me. Them fine folks at Wammaket made it difficult for me to keep in touch, even with my boy's best friend. You gotta forgive me for my rudeness and for being so out of touch."

"Sure," Howie managed at last. He spied his cell phone on the nightstand. He should text someone; that's what he should do. Yeah. Totally. He snatched it.

Billy rambled on, his tone light and conversational. "You keep bein' all silent like that, and I'm gonna think maybe it ain't just rudeness. I'm gonna start thinkin' maybe you're distracted. Maybe by your computer or your cell phone. Maybe you're trying to let someone know who you're talking to. I get that. I really do. But, Howie, I sort of want to chat with you a little bit, and if you go reportin' me, we're gonna have to cut this short. And if we get cut short, well, then I'm gonna have to kill both your parents."

Not a single inflection changed as Billy threatened Howie's folks. Billy could have been ordering eggs over easy from his favorite waitress. The screen of Howie's phone showed the beginning of a text message to his mother: *call sheriff now. not principal. billy dent! be ca*

Be careful, it was supposed to continue. Advice Howie had to apply to himself now.

"Maybe you think I'm bluffing," Billy went on, sounding not in the least bit offended. "I encourage you to rethink that. I'm on a burner cell. By the time they trace me, I'll be long gone. And your parents will never know what hit 'em." Howie could almost see the shrug. "Well, that ain't entirely true. They'll know what hit 'em—they just won't have long to think about it."

Calling Billy Dent's bluff seemed like a very, very stupid way to get his parents off his back. Howie set the cell phone down.

"Are we clear?" Billy asked.

"Yes, sir."

"Sir! Howie! What on earth? You ain't never called me sir in my life! Now tell me," Billy went on, "how's your dad's hip?"

Beyond surreal. "It, uh, it's okay. He changed his golf swing a couple-three years back and—"

"Always told him golf weren't no way for a man to spend his leisure time." Billy tsked. "You be sure to give him my best, you hear? And I hope when they locked me up, he went over to my place and got his rake and leaf blower outta the garage before that sumbitch had the place bulldozed and burned down."

"I...I think he did."

"And tell your mom...Hell, Howie, I ain't got the time. I

315

sure am sorry. We'll have to do this some other time. I gotta admit—at first, I wasn't too pleased with Jasper bringin' home a wounded puppy like yourself. But you grew on me. My boy always seemed...brighter when you were around. Almost like when his momma was still with us."

Billy spoke as though she were dead. Was she, for real now? Howie clenched his teeth and kept himself from asking. As long as Billy wanted to talk, Howie would let him. At some point during the Dent ramble, he'd rolled out of bed and flipped open his chemistry notebook, paging past molecules, formulas, and the obscene doodles with which he populated margins. As quickly as he could and as completely as he could, he was keeping a record of the conversation. Why? He didn't exactly know. But he visualized a near-future sitdown with Jazz, and his best friend groaning as he tugged at his own hair. *You didn't take notes? Billy was talking, and you didn't write anything down?* A very Jazz thing to say.

"You still in touch with my boy?" Billy asked. "Don't bother lying to me, Howie. I got ways of tellin' if you're being truthful or not. Most parents got that sense. Mine's just, well, finer tuned, let's say. It's even better in person 'cause there are certain...let's call 'em *methods*, yeah...certain methods I can use to make sure you ain't being untruthful."

"I don't know where he is." It was sorta-kinda the truth. Last night, before letting Howie leave the cemetery, Jazz had told him about a hidden shack out in the woods. Howie knew it was likely Jazz was there, but he didn't know it for a fact. Technically.

If Billy could tell Howie was splitting hairs, he didn't let

316

on. "You got a way of communicating with him, though, right?"

"Yes." Howie couldn't think of a way to parse that one in any fashion that Billy would find believable.

"Well, good, then. I got a message for him."

"I'll write it down."

"I bet you would." The flesh on Howie's neck and arms curdled into goose bumps. Something about that knowing tone... It made him feel as though Billy were right over his shoulder. He checked just to be sure. Nothing.

"This ain't a written kind of message, though," Billy went on. "It loses a little something in the translation, you catch my meaning? So give me your cell phone number."

Oh, man? Seriously? Do I have to give my phone number to Billy freakin' Dent? For reals?

"What's takin' so long?"

Howie sighed and rattled off the number.

"Good." Billy's voice was a satisfied purr. "Now you just wait a minute or two. Somethin's coming to your phone. You take it to Jasper."

"Does a card go with this present?" Howie's natural inclination to snark would be the death of him, he figured, but at least he'd die with something witty to say.

Billy roared with laughter, dramatically out of proportion to Howie's weak joke. "Ain't no need, Howie. Trust me: Jasper's gonna know exactly who this comes from."

Oh, joy, Howie thought as the line went dead.

He snatched up his cell phone and stared at the screen, waiting.

As soon as his parents were gone for the day, Howie pulled out of the driveway and headed to the Hideout. He had made the mistake of listening to the beginning of the audio file Billy had sent to him, and he wished for a way to scrub through his ears right down into his brain. Maybe some combination of bleach and a wire brush could remove what he'd heard. That voice...Jesus.

He found himself speeding and eased off the gas. The last thing he needed right now was to get pulled over or run himself off the road. His air bag would probably kill him.

The Hideout was back along a deserted dirt road. Howie had lived in the Nod his entire life and never once even noticed the road, much less prowled its length to discover the old abandoned shack back there. Score one for the serial killer gene and its uncanny ability to detect creepy places no one else would ever want to find.

He spied a rough stone structure through the dense cluster of denuded trees. If it had been spring, summer, or even fall—if there'd been any foliage at all—he would have missed it. It was maybe ten feet to a side, crawling with creeper vines and moss. Nature's camouflage.

He climbed out of the car and took in the place, trying not to be hurt by the revelation that Jazz had a special hidden place that only Connie knew about, that his best friend had kept a secret from him.

Well, okay, technically *two* secrets. After all, as kids Jazz had never looked at Howie over a lunch of bologna on white and juice boxes to say, "Hey, man, by the way: My dad totally kills people. A lot."

Howie's nascent jealousy and outrage quelled quite a bit when he actually opened the door and beheld the Hideout. A part of him had been expecting a sort of supervillain lair, another part a true playa's pad, complete with seduction lighting and a glass bowl filled with a variety of condoms.

Instead, the place was a dump. It smelled of dust, mildew, dirt, and that peculiar bloody scent of sheer cold. An undercurrent of kerosene floated beneath it all, no doubt from the space heater just inside the door. There was a single window— if you could call it that—with a milky, almost-opaque sheet of plastic stapled to it; a few rickety barstools clearly scavenged from the curbside on trash days; and a sad-looking beanbag. Sprawled atop the beanbag was an equally sad-looking Jazz, sleeping.

Jazz looked no better than he had last night in the cemetery, but at least he looked no worse. Figuring Jazz would have to avoid stores in the town where everyone knew his face, Howie had sneaked several water bottles, some Gatorade, a few apples, and a fistful of protein bars from the Gersten kitchen before heading out. When he nudged Jazz awake and held a bar out in front of him, his best friend didn't even say "Good morning." He snatched the bar and barely took the time to peel back the wrapper before eating it.

Howie arranged his loose, overlong form on the chair that appeared most capable of providing both support and comfort. He got maybe halfway to each, which he figured was pretty lucky, all things considered. Jazz devoured the protein bar and an apple in an orgy of gnashing teeth and belches, washing the food down with water, chasing it with pills from the prescription bottles, and then more water.

"Good call on the meds," he said. "'Cause when you hear this, you're gonna wish you were stoned out of your mind." Howie held up his cell and waggled it. As Jazz guzzled Gatorade and munched through another apple, Howie set his phone on a chair between them, cranked up the volume, and played the file. Even though he didn't want to.

"...is on now." The voice was familiar. Billy's. It went on: "Brought this little thing here and now we're gonna use it, ain't we? Sound good to you?"

Something muffled in response. Desperate.

"We're gonna get started now," Billy said, and that was the last time he spoke for the remainder of the audio file, which lasted a bit more than twenty-five minutes.

First, there was just that muffled voice again. "Wait," Howie thought he heard. Again: "Wait."

Then the voice jumped suddenly, sharply, turning into a high-pitched *"Nononononononononono."* Cut off just as suddenly and then a scream, a scream unlike any Howie had ever heard before. It was babies in a blender. It was dogs wriggling, still alive and whining to the moon while spiked to the ground with spears. That scream went on for a full minute before breaking off and transforming into thick, heaving, wet sobs.

Howie drew his knees to his chest, as if they were armor.

Jazz chewed his way through another protein bar, staring at the phone. Like a kid watching TV. Rapt, but not disturbed.

Jesus, Jazz.

A rough, rhythmic sound. Firm, but somehow wet.

Howie expected another scream, but heard only a low, guttural groan, interrupted by more sobbing.

Oh, God, he thought. *Is this Jazz's mom? Is Billy torturing her in order to get Jazz to—*

"Jazz, dude, can we—"

"Shh." Jazz stayed focused on the phone, cutting Howie off with a hiss and a chopping movement from one hand. Impossible though it was, he appeared healthier and more vibrant, as though hearing the torment revitalized him.

A solid, *chunk* sound. A slap? A punch? Definitely flesh and bone against flesh and bone. Howie flinched as though struck. Jazz was a marble column, a granite statue. He was *The Thinker* with a half-eaten protein bar and a seriously damaged psyche.

The voice again:

"Pweeeeeeeth."

It took a moment. Howie realized it was *Please,* spoken with lips and a tongue horribly wronged.

It went on. Howie twisted and turned in his seat. What the blue hell was he *doing* here? The message was for Jazz, not for him. He should have left the phone and hightailed it home, or at the very least waited in the car.

At last, it ended. Not with a final scream or another plea for mercy, but rather with the flat *click* of the recorder shutting off.

"Oh, Jesus." The Hideout was cold, but Howie's forehead was dotted with sweat; his armpits were swamped with it. "Double-u tee effing *ef*, man! What *was* that?"

"A message. Instructions."

"Are you kidding me? That was torture porn. For reals. That was beyond—"

"It was for me. Not for you." Jazz blinked and looked over at Howie as though just realizing he was here. "I should have told you to go. I'm sorry."

Howie regarded his best friend for a moment, searching for the old Jazz in there. He thought he detected something way back in those eyes, but he couldn't be sure. Jazz's expression was nearly blank, his speech slow and too deliberate, a robot reading lines.

He's gone over the edge, hasn't he? He's locked down, shutting everything out. He's decided what he's going to do.

"I brought you a blanket," Howie said for absolutely no reason, except that maybe the banal details of life would force Jazz to think of something other than blood and death. "Thought you might—"

"Not necessary. This is ending today." He stood and frowned, then turned to Howie. "That other thing I asked you to do..."

Howie shook his head. "No time last night." He anticipated an outburst from Jazz; the silence was worse. "If my parents take away my keys, I can't—"

"Just do it now, please," Jazz said, far too politely.

"Jazz..."

Jazz reached behind the beanbag and held out a large,

black-gray book in a plastic Ziploc bag. "I need you to take this."

"Is this what you found in, you know, in the grave?" Howie turned the book over in his hands. It was dense with some unknowable mass.

"Yes. It's Billy's. I need you to hide it, and if I end up dead, give it to G. William."

Howie blinked rapidly at the onslaught of tears that assaulted him. Damn sneak attack. Sniffling, he said, "Don't talk like that. You aren't—"

"This is it, Howie. I may not come back. If I do, I'll need that book. If not, G. William can use it to pick up where I left off."

Wiping at his eyes, Howie set his mouth in a firm line. "You're being an idiot. You should take this stuff to G. William and let him handle it."

"It's my job. I have to be the one."

"Why?" Howie hated the note of whining that crept into his voice but could do nothing to excise it. "Why?"

"Because I could have killed Billy. When I was a kid. Or at least turned him in. I didn't. I was afraid."

"You were a kid!" Howie yelled and damn near bashed Jazz over the head with his father's Book of Evil and Crazy. "Stop beating yourself up over this! Go to the cops!"

Jazz shook his head. "I don't expect you to understand. Billy's crazy, and so is Sam. So was my grandmother. And from what I've heard, so was my grandfather. It's genetic, Howie. It's in my blood, inherited, just like you inherited your hemophilia."

"So what? What does that have to do with…" Suddenly it dawned on him. "You *want* to die," Howie whispered. "You don't plan on coming back. You think you deserve it."

Jazz folded his arms over his chest and looked away. "I'm just doing what has to be done. And I'm asking you for these two last favors. And that's it."

"There isn't enough space on your body for the tattoos, man."

Jazz shook his head. "We're not trading here. This isn't *I do something for you, you do something for me*. This is hard-core friendship. Varsity level. This is me asking you to do something for me without getting anything in return. This is friendship, Howie."

More tears. Howie swabbed them away with the heel of his hand. "That's a low blow. You've manipulated me before, but—"

"I'm not manipulating. I think for the first time, I really understand what friendship is. And I have you to thank for that." He rested his hands, gently, on Howie's shoulders, gazing up into his eyes. "You've been the best, most normal thing in my life for the longest time. Before Connie, there was you. And I can never repay you for that. And I can never repay you for what you're doing for me now. You just have to ask yourself, Howie: Do you need to be repaid or not?"

Every piece of him cried out to say *yes*, to demand that in return for what he had done and would do, Jazz would give up now and live.

But.

He knew.

He knew what he didn't know. Which was this: what it was like to grow up with Billy Dent as a father. What it was like to live with that burden hanging over your head, dangling like that sword of that Greek dude they learned about in school and promptly forgot about. What it meant to discover a dead mother still alive but now in the clutches of a lunatic with every reason to kill her an inch at a time.

He couldn't pretend to understand any of that. So his job as best friend was to trust *his* best friend. Trust that Jazz knew what he was doing. And would somehow come out of this alive and whole.

"If you die," Howie said, "I'm going to piss on your grave twice a year. On the solstices."

For the first time in a long time, Jazz favored Howie with a grin. He chucked Howie along the jaw, careful not to do it too hard. "Attaboy," he said.

❧

Howie drove off to the next stop on the Jazz Dent World Tour of Crazy.

In truth, he wanted to be anywhere in the world but Gramma Dent's house. It had always been a creepy, off-putting place. The old lady smell of it. The reality show–level hoarding that rendered certain rooms unusable. And of course, Jazz's grandmother's tendency to erupt at any moment into a fusillade of racist epithets, paranoid delusions, fragmented memories of the past, or some combination of the three. Over the years, he'd gone through different phases during his visits, alternating between finding the house terrifying, hilarious, disturbing, and flat-out weird.

The last time he'd been there, Sammy J had ripped half the skin off his fingers and Gramma had gotten one banana peel closer to the grave. He was just plain damn sick of the place now.

But Jazz insisted and Howie obeyed. He had called the sheriff's office already and blatantly lied, telling a deputy that he'd left his phone charger at the Dent house the night of "the incident" and needed to get it back. The place was technically a crime scene, but the cops were done with it. No reason not to let him in.

They were cagey, though. They insisted he have an escort.

A Lobo's Nod Sheriff's Department car waited for him in the driveway. A deputy he didn't know got out.

"Gersten?" the deputy said. "I'm supposed to be your escort."

"For serious?" Howie climbed out of his car. "An escort? I kinda wanted one with big knockers."

The deputy groaned and gestured Howie to the house.

"Don't get me wrong," Howie went on. "I mean, if you guys are footing the bill, I would have taken an escort with little tiny ones, too, but I'm just expressing a preference, you feel me?" He kept up a constant stream of chatter as he mounted the porch steps and crossed the threshold, hoping that his babble would keep the cop from noticing how nervous he was. Going back into the house...not sure what he would find...

Just inside the door, the floor was strewn with some junk left behind by the EMTs—small pieces of cardboard, torn plastic wrappings, a slim needle cover. There was a brownish stain on the floor that Howie realized had to be his own blood. And the shotgun—the Plugged-Barrel Special Howie had threatened Sam with—lay nearby. His head spun at the sight, and he had to close his eyes for a moment.

"Get a move on," the deputy snapped. "We don't have all day."

Jazz wanted him to check the house for anything left behind by Samantha. Given that Gramma and Howie had both been hauled out on stretchers under mysterious circumstances, the police would have already gone through the house, but—as Jazz put it—*They'd be looking for obvious things. Signs of criminal activity. You were there every day. You'll see what they didn't.*

Howie scoured the downstairs—kitchen, living room, dining room—then went upstairs to the bedrooms. The deputy's eyes widened when he saw Jazz's Wall of Billyness, the photos of Billy's victims painstakingly tacked up in chronological order. *This dude is running straight to TMZ and cashing a big ol' check*, Howie thought sourly. SON OF SERIAL KILLER OBSESSED WITH DAD'S VICTIMS! *The headlines write themselves.*

After checking the entire house, Howie was as annoyed with himself as the deputy was. He'd looked everywhere and found nothing. Even in Jazz's room, where Sam had slept while staying in the Nod, he'd found not so much as a forgotten pair of panties. *Stop thinking about that, Howie!*

With a weak chuckle and shrug of his shoulders — "I guess I lost it somewhere else" — Howie allowed himself to be led back outside and escorted to his car. Trying not to let his annoyance and frustration show, he backed out to the road that made a *T* at the end of Gramma's long, winding dirt driveway and carefully cranked the wheel to turn the car perpendicular. His first time coming here in the car, he'd nearly killed the mailbox on his way out.

Wait.

Wait.

The mailbox?

He hit the brake. In his rearview, Gramma's mailbox leaned halfway out into the road, as it always had. It was dented, appropriately enough, and mounted on a hefty spike of oak. Barely discernible on its sun-faded, pitted exterior were old painted orchids and letters in black reading MR. & MRS. J. DENT. Howie shivered at the memory of the last time he'd seen Jonathan's name. On his gravestone.

Jonathan Dent. Sammy J. Ugly J. What if —

No. Jazz had dug up his grandfather. This was strictly the Billy and Sammy show.

He guided the car back a little ways, coming parallel to the mailbox. Confident that the cop couldn't see him all the way down the driveway, he reached through the window, opened the box, and proceeded to violate federal law by stealing Gramma's and Jazz's mail. Oh, well. Now he and Jazz had even more in common. Maybe they could share a cell at the federal pen together. Roomies at last!

The mail safely inside the car, he got the hell out of there before the cop could meander down the driveway and catch him. Once back on the main drag through the Nod, he pulled into the McDonald's parking lot and riffled through the mail.

Bill. Bill. Catalog. Bill. Junk. Junk.

At the very bottom of the pile was a single plain white business envelope without a stamp or a return address. It said, simply, *JAZZ*.

CHAPTER 43

With two days' worth of antibiotics in his system, Jazz's stomach was complaining regularly, but his leg had finally started to settle down, like a drunk guy in a bar slowly realizing the bouncer was much bigger. Hat's bullet would be with him forever, so it was about time they made their peace with each other. If the leg held out long enough for him to settle things with Billy and Sam, that was all he cared about. Once they were dealt with, the damn thing could wither and die and fall off for all it mattered to him.

He knew the Nod better than most. As a child, he'd explored the town on his own, encouraged by Billy to find "crawly spots," Billy's term for hidden nooks and niches where he could conceal either himself or evidence. To a young boy like Jazz, it had been a parentally sanctioned adventure, and he'd roamed the Nod with a freedom other kids would have envied, had they not been aware of the price of that freedom.

As a result, he knew the town's blind spots, its back alleys, its off-grid pathways. Hughes's overcoat was warm enough as long as he kept moving.

He had no intention of stopping. Not until he arrived at the place Billy had indicated.

Doug Weathers's apartment.

Leave it to Billy to kill a man rather than just send Howie a text with Weathers's address. One more body on the pile. One more name on Billy's roster of death. One more reason for Billy to die.

And damn Billy, anyway, for putting Jazz in the position of avenging the death of a useless pissant like Doug Weathers.

Jazz had recognized Weathers's voice, even through the pain, terror, and mangling of his mouth. That voice had haunted him for years, pestering him with demands for interviews, blaring from TV screens as he bloviated about Billy with the intensity summoned only by the abjectly clueless or the truly desperate.

Both applied in Weathers's case.

A couple of years back, Weathers had been perversely persistent in his attempts to get Gramma to "go on the record" so that "the world knows you're not to blame for your son." He cared nothing for her reputation, of course—he just wanted to grill an old woman with Alzheimer's until he could get her to blurt out something crazy or incriminating. Jazz could barely tolerate Weathers attacking him; he refused to countenance the bastard badgering his grandmother. So he'd gone to the courthouse to swear out a restraining order, and when the time had come to go to court, he'd seen a copy of the subpoena served on Weathers. Complete with the man's home address.

The apartment building Weathers lived in was much nicer than he deserved. Then again, you didn't have to make fat bank to live decently in the Nod. Good thing, too—Weathers hadn't done much since Billy had gone to prison and the desire to put his ugly mug on TV had dried up.

People are real, Jazz reminded himself. *People matter. Even Doug Weathers.*

I suppose.

It seemed a monumental injustice of almost biblical proportions that Jazz had to let himself give a damn about Weathers. Surely even *normal* people hated the guy.

Jazz had waited until almost nightfall—late afternoon at this time of year, really—before setting out, trusting the cold and the darkness to be his shield against recognition. Breaking into Weathers's apartment would be as easy as a baby sticking its thumb in its mouth. He swung around the back of the building. A locked steel door prevented him from getting inside for the roughly ten seconds it took for him to unveil Howie's pickax from under Hughes's coat and knock the doorknob off. Once the inner workings of the lock were exposed, it took him another few seconds to unlock the door.

Within, he found himself in a maintenance room or a janitor's closet of some kind. Tired of carrying the pickax all the way from the Hideout, he left it. It was too heavy to keep carrying, especially with the stairs he was about to climb. Weathers was on the sixth floor. The top. Of course. He would have to be at the top.

His leg surprised him, making the six flights with only a minimum of stiffness and complaint.

Let's hear it for painkillers! And antibiotics! But especially painkillers.

The hallway on Weathers's floor looked empty. Jazz didn't wait around to be sure—he walked swiftly out of the stairwell and strode right up to Weathers's door. He didn't bother knocking—if Billy was in there, there was no point giving him fair warning. Instead, he jimmied the door open with the stiff plastic of Mark Culpepper's Visa card, then stepped inside and immediately closed the door behind him.

Weathers's apartment was dark and cramped. Jazz risked turning on the light, half expecting Billy to leap out at him.

No.

Finding the remains of Doug Weathers spread out around the apartment also wouldn't have surprised him, and he was almost disappointed to find that the place was grungy in that special bachelor-chic way, but otherwise clean.

After being as tortured and carved (and hacked, and bashed, and crushed) as he'd sounded on the audio file, Doug Weathers would have lost enormous amounts of blood, as well as voided both bladder and intestine. The apartment should have stunk of bodily fluids and defecation. That it didn't told Jazz what he'd suspected all along—Weathers had been killed elsewhere.

Of course. Billy never makes it easy. He likes leaving clues. Likes leading me around on a leash.

The idea that this might just be another game floated through his mind. Maybe Billy was long gone from the Nod, a thousand miles away, laughing at Jazz's stupidity with Aunt Sam, while Mom strained against a gag to beg for her life.

But he didn't think that was the case. To have dealt with Weathers meant that Billy had to have been in the Nod recently, and given the timeline of his activities in New York, *recently* had to mean within the past day or so. Even if he'd fled Lobo's Nod, Billy couldn't have gotten far. He wouldn't risk a train or a plane or even a bus. He would have to drive, alternating with Sam, sticking to back roads.

They would still be nearby.

There were two doors, one wide open, one ajar. The open one led to a bathroom, which meant the other had to be a bedroom. Jazz would check them later. For now, though, he spied a laptop on a desk across from the sofa, its lid up. If Weathers wasn't here, he had gone somewhere else, either voluntarily or not. If voluntarily, maybe he'd been goaded along by an e-mail. It was worth a try.

Jazz ran his fingers along the track pad, and the laptop lit up. A Web page came into view, reloading.

A map. A map of the Nod, with a pin somewhere right outside town. Blue lines for driving directions from Weathers's apartment.

Here we go again. More clues. More rolls of the dice.

The weight of it plunged down on him, and he became so tired in that moment that he craved nothing more than to slump onto Weathers's sofa, curl up into a ball, and sleep for a year. Maybe when he woke up, it would all be over: Billy dead, Sam dead, Mom safe.... Yeah, that all sounded about right.

Instead of going to the sofa, though, he sighed and rested his eyes while pinching the bridge of his nose. And that was when it happened. When he heard it.

He wasn't sure if he was supposed to hear it or not. He clamped his eyes even more tightly shut, setting off spirals and whorls of color behind his eyelids.

How had he gotten here? How had he made it to Weathers's apartment? It was as if he'd been on autopilot the whole time, only now totally aware of where he was.

Shaken back into reality by the footstep. Behind him.

Stupid! Stupid! Walked right into it!

Should have checked the bedroom first.

And then Billy said, "Hello, son. Welcome back."

Part Four

The Crow King

CHAPTER 44

Jazz opened his eyes but otherwise did not move, maintaining his frozen position at the desk. Maybe to Billy it looked like he was stunned into inaction.

In truth, he was scanning the desk for weapons, wishing he hadn't left the pickax downstairs. He had the Taser tucked away in the right-hand slash pocket of Hughes's overcoat, but he couldn't be sure Billy would give him the opportunity to go for it.

"Hello, Billy," he said. The desktop was cluttered, sloppy like Weathers himself, but Jazz saw nothing useful. He wished people still used letter openers. Nice and sharp, they were.

"You gonna turn around and say hi to Dear Old Dad?"

Shrugging, Jazz turned, his left leg giving a bit as he did so. He caught a slight wince from Billy, as though in sympathy. Not a chance. Billy felt sympathy for no one.

"Well, lookee here." Billy grinned. He held—of all things—an iPad. He balanced it on the back of Weathers's sofa, which was interposed between them. Billy looked, as always, healthy and vibrant. Killing suited him. He planted his hands on his hips. "Father and son, together again. And this time, no one in handcuffs and no one lyin' on the floor, bleeding. By the by, how's that leg? Dear Old Dad did pretty well, didn't he?"

Jazz's leg trembled, and he staggered a tiny bit. "The doctors said a real butcher must have worked on it before them."

If he was offended, Billy didn't show it. He chuckled. "That you I feel up in my brain, trying to rummage around inside my head, rearrange the furniture? I don't think that'll work. I taught you everything you know, but not everything *I* know."

With a relaxed but confident tilt of his head, Jazz replied, "Maybe I learned some new tricks while you were off in solitary."

Billy laughed again. "That's your weak-ass attempt at psychology? Here's a free tip from the expert: You gotta use something the target *cares* about. Something that *disturbs* 'em. My prison time weren't a big deal to me. Gotta find something that *hurts*."

"Like Mom escaping from the great Billy Dent? That must've been a blow to your ego. No wonder you purged every memory of her from the house."

"Your momma done what she had to do. And I did what I had to do."

"Did Samantha help you get over her?" The question nauseated him, but he had to know: Had father and son both shared in Sam's charms?

"You're asking all the wrong questions." He said it almost plaintively, a child frustrated with the adult who will not play the game properly. "I thought you knew things, Jasper. I thought you'd had time to figure it out."

Static buzzed Jazz's ears. Stars and spots danced before his eyes. Without realizing it, he'd been holding his breath. His fists were clenched. He had come alive, more alive than he'd ever felt before. As though his whole life had been a test run up until now. He wanted to vault the sofa, race to Billy. Wanted his hands around his father's throat. Wanted to feel Billy's last breath wash over his face, wanted those damn blue eyes to roll up inside his head, wanted the trachea in splinters under the force of his grip.

It waits inside you, Billy had said in the visitation room at Wammaket. *It pads around like a big cat, and when you least expect it, it comes up behind you.* Oh, he could feel it now. Exactly as Billy had described. It was a cougar, a tiger, a lion, prowling his innards, softly growling deep in its—and his—throat. It had the taste of blood on its lips and tongue.

It wanted that taste for him. And God help him, he wanted it, too.

"Maybe starting to feel like it's time to do something about me?" Billy asked. "You're welcome to try."

The hospital guard's Taser weighed a thousand pounds in Hughes's pocket. It was his secret weapon, if only he could get to it. It wasn't one of the ranged models—he would have to get within arm's reach of Billy to use it. He would have to get it out of the pocket before Billy could come over Weathers's sofa and take it away from him.

341

Was Billy armed? Jazz couldn't imagine his father being here without a weapon, but there were no telltale bulges or shapes in Billy's pockets. Probably he had a knife tucked into the back of his belt. Billy generally didn't like guns, preferring the quiet and the up close and personal of a blade. Knife versus Taser. Billy was rested and fit. Jazz, less so. But he had youth on his side, and maybe he had justice, too.

"I want to understand things, Billy. I want to know about the Crows. I saw your father."

Billy's eyes lit up. "You did, now! How's my old man?"

"Decomposed. He had some interesting reading material with him, though."

"I bet he did. So, you understand it now."

Whatever *it* was, Jazz sure as hell did *not* understand. Meaning had eluded him like a rabbit in the wild.

"Your writing needs some work," Jazz said.

Billy clucked his tongue, shaking his head. Jazz took the moment to slip his hands into the overcoat pockets, wrapping his fingers around the Taser. It had, as best he could tell, one charge left. One chance to stun Billy.

And then what, Jazz? What do you do with him once he's helpless at your feet?

He knew the answer to that. It *purred*.

"You're disappointing me, boy. Thought you'd get something useful out of your Dear Old Dad's writing. Wasn't much older than you when I wrote that stuff. Figured it'd make sense to you." If Billy noticed the hands in his pockets, he didn't give any indication of it. Jazz had to assume he had and was already making plans.

"Just looked like more garden-variety crazy to me," Jazz said lightly.

Billy lost his temper for the first time. "You watch your mouth, boy. You ain't so old and so big that I can't whup you for being disrespectful."

"Come and get me." He tightened his grip on the Taser. If he could get Billy to make the first move, his chances of getting out of this alive soared.

For a moment, he thought Billy would take the bait, but his father took a deep breath and settled down. "Just thought you'd get it, Jasper. That's all."

"Oh, I get it. I just don't know *why*. You and your socio-path buddies have a little social club, right? The Crows." He larded sarcasm onto his voice, slathering it thick. Adults had an intense allergy to teenage snark, and Jazz was hoping that Billy—who'd gone to prison before Jazz had had the opportunity to launch into teen rebellion—would react blindly and stupidly. "You guys like to kill people, and you help each other out when you can. You identify yourselves with those ridiculous code names you all like so much, but at the end of the day, you know each other by the name Jack Dawes. Because *jackdaw* is another word for crow. You guys are so inventive!"

He'd finally figured out that the repeated references to Jack Dawes in Billy's book weren't about an individual. *Jack Dawes* was a code word, a generic stand-in for a Crow. It was part password, part safe word, part ID. The Crows could shift names and identities as they needed to—Billy had done it repeatedly—but they could always fall back on Jack

Dawes, a name bland and generic enough that if there had been more than one in a community, no one would ever blink at the coincidence. But a Crow would know what it meant. It was, Jazz had to admit, brilliant.

But he wouldn't admit that to Billy.

Billy's lips quirked, and Jazz thought maybe he'd hit home. He struck again: "I mean, what kind of boogeyman plays *Monopoly* to decide who gets to join the club?"

"Ain't always Monopoly." Was that a defensive tone to Billy's words? Jazz hoped so. "What matters is that they compete. Can't have just anyone joining the Crows, you know. Sometimes the game's been chess. Or Scrabble. Or Mother May I? What matters is that one ascends and one dies."

The game is ancient, Hat had said. *The game goes on forever.*

One ascends and one dies.

"Except this time."

Billy grinned wickedly. "No one ever said life was fair."

"So the Crows are down one. You guys are gonna need to do a membership drive. Maybe start letting in the arsonists and the pedophiles."

Another incipient flare from Billy at the mention of pedophiles. *It's not like I hurt kids*, Billy had said at Wammaket. Jazz thought maybe he was whittling away at Billy's reserve.

I can't kill him. Not right away. He has to tell me where Mom is first.

"We're doing just fine," Billy said confidently. "No need to appeal to the riffraff. And that's the *point*, Jasper. Why don't you *get it*? Can't you see?"

"Oh, I see all right. I see a bunch of lunatics telling each other they're okay. A support group for serial killers. Nice."

The mocking tone only made Billy smile broadly. "You think that's what it is? You ain't really seein' the big picture, are you?"

"Well, explain it to me."

"Never thought I'd have to spell it out for you, son. Thought you were smarter than this." Billy sighed, and his stance relaxed, became almost professorial. Jazz inched forward a step, still clutching the Taser.

"You know serial murder used to be relatively rare in this country?" Billy asked. "Relatively. Back in the fifties or so, not a whole lot of it going on. But then something happened. In the eighties, there was a big jump. Almost threefold."

"It was just better reporting," Jazz said dismissively. "You can't—"

"Oh, the reporting got better, but the Crows got better, too. That's when they started. I learned about them years later. Joined right up, too."

"When Sam introduced you to the Crow King." Bang. Jazz didn't know much, but he knew *that* much.

"There's a guy at Penn State," Billy went on, ignoring him, "name of Jenkins. Studies serial killer statistics. Trends. Just like studying baseball or football, ain't that a hoot? Anyway, you go look up his research. He proves that the last three decades have seen a rise in folks like me. That's the Crows. Organizing. Becoming more effective. We're like an epidemic that sweeps across society, see?

"And you'll be at the front of it, Jasper." Billy's face seemed alight with something unholy and powerful. Jazz couldn't help but to be captivated by it. "You'll be the next Crow King, the lord of murder, and you will change *everything*."

His mouth had gone dry, and he could barely feel the Taser in his hand, so numb were his fingers. In spite of himself, despite the need to find his mother, Jazz couldn't prevent his curiosity from thrashing for attention. He had thought Billy wanted him to grow up to be a serial killer, but the truth was more damning and more fascinating: Billy wanted him to *lead* serial killers.

"Why?" he asked, helpless to stop himself. "What's the point? Why don't you guys just do your thing and—"

Billy actually raised his palms skyward and looked up as if begging God for a smarter child. Enthralled, Jazz realized too late that he'd missed his chance to attack.

Keep him talking. Focus, Jazz!

"I gave you all the information you needed!" Billy fumed. "I told you to think about Gilles de Rais, remember?"

In the storage unit. "Yeah."

"And did you?"

"Sure."

"And?"

"He was a lunatic. Murdered people."

Billy snorted. "Crap. Tell me something real."

Dredging up the details from the lessons taught when he was done with his schoolwork each evening, Jazz recited: "He was a French nobleman in the 1400s. He liked going to poor people and pretending to be distraught at the plight of their children. So he would offer to take the young boys back to his manor as servants, giving them a better life. And then he would sodomize them and beat them to death and do horrible things to the bodies, and no one ever knew until he'd killed over a hundred."

"You said a real important word there."

"French?" Jazz taunted.

"No. 'Nobleman.'"

They stared across the sofa at each other, silent. Billy's eyes danced with amusement. Would Jazz figure it out, he was wondering. How bright *was* his boy? In which *bright* meant *crazy* because surely he would *have* to be crazy to understand any of this. Right?

But, Jazz realized, it did all make a sick sort of sense. Why wouldn't people with similar interests come together? The Crows were like...a trade union.

Oh, God. This is starting to sound reasonable to me.

He forced his attention back to Gilles de Rais. But Billy had also told him to think about...

"Think about it," Billy whispered now. "Think about all the lessons I taught you over the years. There's only one more lesson, Jasper. One more, I promise, and then school's out and you can do as you please."

Caligula, the other name from unit 83F, had been an emperor of Rome. Gilles de Rais, a nobleman. Moving though history, stepping through Billy's teachings, there'd been Elizabeth Bathory, a countess and one of history's rare female serial killers. And Lucrezia Borgia, the daughter of a pope, who'd murdered husband after husband. Precursors to Belle Gunness and Ugly J.

"I don't under—"

Billy exploded. "We're supposed to be kings!" he ranted. "You look back through history, and serial killers were the nobility! Jack the Ripper was most likely—"

"—a member of the royal family," Jazz whispered.

"Right! Back in the day, back when our craft was first invented, our guild first formed, we were *rulers*, Jasper! We were nobles and kings and counts and lords. Murder was reserved for the elite, for the cream of society. The Egyptian pharaohs killed who and how they pleased. The Roman emperors. Later, the European and Slavic lords. The myth of Dracula started when a Transylvanian noble drained the blood of his enemies. Vlad Tepes wasn't a vampire—he was a serial killer, boy. We sat at the top of the pyramid, and everyone else was supposed to be here for our pleasure and nothin' else!

"But it's all upside down now." Billy's voice took on an aggrieved, offended tone. "They put the kings in jail, and they let the prospects maunder like lobotomized sheep. And worse than that, worse than that, Jasper—there are killers with no grace, no meaning. They wander the world and make it more difficult for the rest of us."

And Jazz finally understood. The Crows weren't about gathering together serial killers. The Crows were about gathering together the *best* of the serial killers. Using "games" to winnow out the radically unstable ones, the unreliable ones, then pulling up the others, indoctrinating them into the group, coordinating them....

"You want to make a hunting preserve." Jazz realized the

enormity of it in a flash, his mind's eye conjuring the fields of Kansas covered in blood and bodies. He remembered Hat claiming he would fill the Grand Canyon with corpses. "You want to turn...what, the country? You want to make the country safe for your kind. So that you can stalk and kill whoever you want."

"We want what is *ours*," Billy whispered, low and so convincing. "This is the natural order, Jasper. Our history tells us so. The strong and the noble rule over the prospects and use them for our pleasure. It's become perverted over the years. More leisure time. More opportunities for the undeserving—like Dog or even Hat—to muck up the works for everyone, make it harder for the rest of us. Used to be only the upper classes had the time, the discipline, the tools. Everyone else was too damn busy tryin' to stay alive. So it was a naturally self-selecting group. Nowadays, you got too many people with time on their hands, thinkin' they can be the next Bundy or Speck."

"Or Dent?"

"Heh. Don't they wish? I started small, too, Jasper. Ain't gonna deny it. Always had big aspirations, though. Son of Sam was a mailman! A *mailman*! No finesse. No style. Just walk up to a car and shoot 'em. Jesus. You call him kin? 'Cause I sure as hell don't. You and me, Jasper, we're something special. You are one of the strong. You're destined to be a Crow. And as the Crows strengthen, as we take on members across the spectrum of society, we get smarter. Harder to catch. Especially when we have highly placed Crows in government. In law enforcement. You ever wonder 'bout when some intern goes missing in Washington and no one can find her? That's 'cause no one's lookin' too hard. It's tough to catch a killer when another killer has his back."

Or hers.

The thought jolted him. He'd let Billy worm into his head, seducing him with bleak ideas and bloody notions. But at the end of the day, Billy was the man who killed people with his sister at his side. Billy was a father who'd allowed—compelled?—his own child...and...his own sister...

Not now! Not now! Focus!

Where was Sam? Was she waiting in the bedroom, where Billy had skulked? Was she somewhere with Mom, waiting for a signal from Billy to slit her throat?

Worse: If she *didn't* get a signal from Billy at some preapproved time, would she kill Mom then?

His hand went sweaty on the Taser. He feared he would drop it at the worst possible time. He couldn't keep up this verbal sparring with Billy. The Crows didn't matter. None of it did. That was a problem for another day. Right now, his father was before him and his mother was missing, and that was all that mattered.

"You're pathetic, Billy." He wondered if all kids—if normal kids—had this moment of epiphany, this sudden sensation of understanding that their parents weren't gods, weren't even kings. They were just people. Sad, screwed-up people like everyone else. "You think you have some noble cause, but all you do is kill people. And all of your loser friends kill people, too. And you all talk about it. Good for you. You've surrounded yourself with people who think like you do. For comfort and security. You know who else does that? Alcoholics and junkies and sex addicts." He laughed heartily. "Guess what, Billy? You're just like a prospect after all!"

His hand slipped on the Taser. He regripped it.

Billy didn't move. His face was stone.

"You ready to back your words, boy?" he asked slowly.

"Dying to," Jazz said.

"Then you decide, Jasper. You gonna use that gadget you think you're hidin' in your pocket..."

Billy reached around his back and produced a large, wicked knife.

"...or you gonna do this like a Crow?"

And his father held the knife out to him by its blade, the handle perfect and inviting and just within his reach.

CHAPTER 45

Howie opened his eyes. The black sky hung overhead, speckled with stars, the glowing gash of the crescent moon dangling there like a wood shaving. The world was just going on, turning, as if nothing had changed.

The envelope he'd found in Gramma Dent's mailbox — the one addressed simply to *JAZZ* — lay torn open on his passenger seat.

Jazz hadn't said anything about *what* to do with any evidence he found at Gramma's house, so he felt no moral compunction at all about opening the envelope addressed to Jazz.

He read it once.

He told himself it was a lie.

He read it again.

He was convinced it was a lie.

He read it a third time.

It wasn't a lie.

Trade-offs. Life was full of them. Like being basketball tall but blood sick. Like having a best friend who could scare the crap out of anyone...even himself.

Like wanting to help but not knowing how.

He read the letter again. It could so easily be a lie. But it tasted true. Howie didn't have a bulletproof, built-in lie detector like Jazz did, but he had a brain in his head. The letter made sense. It fit.

And if it was true...

If it was true, there was only one outcome for Jazz. One possibility.

He had no way to get in touch with Jazz. He'd driven to the Hideout again only to find his friend gone. Gone where, he couldn't say. Perhaps Jazz had finally wised up and decided to grow a beard, find a cabin in obscurest Alaska somewhere, and settle in for a nice, quiet life as a salmon fisherman. Who occasionally solved minor local crimes. That sounded like one of the ridiculous murder-mystery series Howie's dad devoured, and it would be the best of all possible endings for Jazz.

But Howie knew his best friend too well. If Jazz wasn't at the Hideout, he was off stalking Billy.

At least he took the rest of the food I brought. A growing boy fighting his insane father to the death has to keep the calorie count up there. Fighting to the death is sweaty work.

So what to do when Jazz isn't around and there is Jazz-worthy news to be told? The answer was startlingly obvious, even to the oblivious: Go to the girlfriend.

He called Connie on her cell, expecting to get her in New York, surprised when she told him she was back in the Nod.

"I've got something you should see, then. Can I come over?"

CHAPTER 46

Connie opened her eyes to the sound of her cell phone demanding attention. *"Don't go chasing—"* She grabbed it before it could go any further. She'd chased the waterfall and gotten battered for it.

"Hey, Connie." Howie. Not Jazz. Had she really expected Jazz to call?

"Howie, have you—"

"Not on the phone."

Under ordinary circumstances, she would have found Howie's paranoia either adorable or annoying. But given the forces that had mobilized to look for Jazz, paranoia was probably the most meagerly acceptable level of caution. Billy could kill him. Sam could kill him. The police could shoot him "accidentally." She knew all about the cops and their trigger fingers and their predilection for dealing with those who would attack their brethren. Her father had drummed such stories into her from a young age; more so into Whiz, who bore the burden of being a black boy about to grow into a black teen. *If the police even look at you funny,* Dad had said, *you hit the ground and put your hands over your head. Don't talk back. Don't try to run. Don't try to explain. They're just looking for an excuse to shoot you. Don't give it to them.*

The same would apply to Jazz, she knew, despite his white skin. He'd assaulted cops; bad enough. But he was also suspiciously tied to the death of an FBI agent, and that made Jazz the functional equivalent of a black teenager in a hoodie in a white neighborhood.

If—*when*—the police caught up to Jazz, there was not even the remotest possibility that Jazz would lie flat on the ground with his hands over his head. And the police would, without hesitation, kill him.

She turned her lips away from the phone, struggling with tears. Howie kept talking, and as she told him to come over, she plucked the picture of Jazz and her from last summer from the nightstand. It was the only comfort she had.

🐾

Soon Howie arrived. He almost hit his head on the door-frame coming into her room but ducked at the last possible second.

"Ninja reflexes!" he cackled, and Connie almost burst into tears of gratitude for the familiar comfort of his ironic, overstated confidence. She settled for struggling into a sitting position in bed and holding out her arms so that the big goof could hug her. Wanting to squeeze him hard, she instead held him gingerly, nestling her cheek against his bony, sharp shoulder.

When Howie started crying, it was as though his tears gave hers permission to show up, and soon they were sobbing against each other in intermingled relief and fear, clutching at each other like safety bars on a roller coaster. Connie wept unselfconsciously, dampening Howie's shirt, and his chin vibrated against her hair, but for the first time in her life, she just didn't give a good goddamn about her hair. Let Howie irrigate it with his tears. She didn't care.

Eventually, the tears subsided and she became aware that she was in a deep, desperate clinch with *Howie*, with no idea of how to break loose without hurting his feelings or actually causing him harm. Howie settled it for her when he whispered—in a voice still congested with the detritus of his crying—"I can totally feel your boobs against me."

Oh, thank God. He was Howie again. And she was Connie again, and she released him, pushing him back gently. "Get your face out of my hair, Bleeding Boy."

He grinned at her, and they were good.

"You've seen him?" Connie asked in a low voice, worried about her parents or Whiz overhearing.

Howie laid a too-long index finger over his lips and stood to close the door. Then he returned, slumping into her wheelchair. Despite the several feet of height difference and the too-white skin, he looked for all the world as Whiz had looked, helpless and forlorn and trying so hard to be a man. He nodded.

If she hadn't been cried out after the jag in Howie's arms,

Connie might have fired up the waterworks again. But she was dry and she focused.

"When?" she asked. "Where?"

Howie's lips quirked to the left like they did when he was considering a lie. It made his face look like someone had smeared a finger over a still-wet painting.

"Howie. Tell me."

"Not sure it matters. He isn't where he was. I checked." He leaned forward, spiky elbows on jutting knees. "It's going down, Connie. I think it's happening."

He told her how Billy had called to leave Jazz a message— "And to talk about my dad's golf swing; what *is* it with this guy?"—and how Jazz had disappeared after that. No matter how much she asked, he refused to play the message.

"I'm gonna have nightmares for the rest of my life and then in my next incarnation as the twenty-second century's version of Hugh Hefner. No need to give them to you, too."

"Hefner, eh?"

"Hey, after everything I've suffered in *this* life, I figure I'm due for a lifetime of endless sex. But check it—on orders from you know who, I scoped out Gramma's house and found this." He produced a torn-open envelope from his pocket and handed it over to her.

The letter within was handwritten and brief. Connie read it twice, furrowing her brow as she tried to coax additional meaning out of it. It seemed so simple....

"I don't get it," she admitted.

"What if what it says is true?" Howie asked.

"Well, then…" She trailed off. She wasn't making the connection. Damn painkillers.

"If the letter is legit," Howie said, "then that means we were wrong. You. Me. Jazz. Wrong. We made an assumption, and if it's wrong —"

"Oh, God!" Connie dropped the letter and clapped her hands over her mouth. "Oh, God, Howie! Then —"

"We have to go to the police," Howie said. "No more screwing around. We tell them everything, and if Jazz doesn't like —"

A knock at the door. Her father poked his head in.

"Conscience," he said gravely, "the police are here to see you."

CHAPTER 47

Hughes was expecting Connie Hall, so he was surprised when instead a ridiculously tall, thin white kid emerged from the corridor into the Halls' living room. Hughes hoped that the kid's basketball skills were up to snuff because otherwise all that height was going to go to waste. Damn shame.

He and Tanner had spent the day making the rounds of places in Lobo's Nod where either of the Dents might be holed up, to no avail. "Neither one of them's an idiot," Tanner had confided as they left yet another fruitless spot. "I don't really think we'll find 'em by checking these places, but we have to cross all the *T*s, you know?"

Despite himself, Hughes was growing to like Tanner. Under all that blubber beat the heart of an excellent homicide cop. In New York or San Francisco, Tanner would be a first grade, or maybe running his own unit. His talents and insights seemed wasted in a place like Lobo's Nod, but Hughes couldn't figure out a polite way to say that. Instead, he settled for listening to the sheriff ramble as they drove the

Nod and its environs, occasionally checking run-down hotels and condemned storefronts.

They lunched at a place called—Hughes couldn't believe it—DINNER. He couldn't tell if the joint had begun as a dinner-only restaurant or if someone just didn't know how to spell *diner*. They each checked their phones obsessively as they ate, but there was nothing conclusive. Each Dent had been spotted in pretty much all fifty states at this point, and there were two reports from Mexico and one from Canada. People were seeing the Dents on TV and then projecting.

And Hughes and Tanner had nothing but pure guesswork and the word of a female trucker who claimed that she'd dropped off Jasper Dent an hour away at a gas station. Tanner'd sent deputies to investigate, and they'd found nothing.

Later in the day, Hughes finally asked the question he'd been dying to ask: "Tell me, Sheriff. How'd you catch Billy, all those years ago?"

Tanner cracked a smile, piloting his car past an old railroad track. There were some shacks out that way to check out. "Wish I could tell you it was brilliant police work, but it was just dumb luck."

"I think you're being modest, Sheriff."

"Call me G. William. And my momma used to say modesty is just braggin' that ain't been used in a while."

"What the hell does *that* mean?"

Tanner shrugged. "Not sure. Sounds good, though, right?"

They chuckled together and then swept the shacks with flashlights, guns drawn, and found—again—nothing.

"What now?" Hughes asked as they returned to the car.

Tanner stared off into space. If this had been New York, Hughes would have known the next steps, but out here in Timbuktu, he was at a loss. Were there more ramshackle piles of rubble for the Dents to squirrel away in? God, he hoped not.

"Connie's back in town," Tanner said. "Let's go talk to her. You said Jasper called her while she was in the hospital, right? So let's see if she remembers anything new."

When he said *remembers*, Hughes knew that was his polite, southern way of saying, *Let's see if she's decided to tell us what really happened on that phone call.*

"Sounds good." It actually sounded desperate, but at this point, desperation was the name of the game. Hughes did not want to be standing over another body anytime soon.

And now they were in Connie's living room. The mother had hustled a kid out into the kitchen, and the dad had looked none too pleased to see Hughes again, though he'd been friendly enough with G. William. The gangly white kid loped into the room as if he owned the place and flopped onto the sofa. Hughes expected to hear the rattle of his bones clicking against one another.

"What's the what, G-Dubs?" asked the world's worst gangsta. Hughes had to fight the urge to step over there and smack the wigger out of the kid.

"Howie," Tanner said with the air of a man who had been pushed past every conceivable annoyance and now had attained a Zen-like understanding of them. "Didn't expect to see you here. We—"

Before he could finish, here came Dad down the hallway, pushing Connie in a wheelchair. Hughes winced at the sight of her. In a hospital bed, she'd looked bad enough, but now most of the bandages were off, revealing a patchwork of bruises, abrasions, and cuts on most of her exposed flesh. Her left leg jutted out before her, and her father carefully navigated it around the living-room furniture, positioning her close to the kid named Howie. Hughes couldn't help but notice that Dad had chosen to put her as far away from him and Tanner as possible, with a love seat and a coffee table between them.

Connie reached out and took Howie's hand. How sweet.

"Mr. Hall," Hughes said, nodding. "A pleasure to see you again."

"I'm sure it's all yours."

Lawyers.

"We're here—"

"Aren't you a little out of your jurisdiction, Detective?"

Friggin'. *Lawyers.*

Tanner stepped between them. "Jerry, I know you don't want your girl put through anything more than she's already been through, and Lord knows I don't want to be the one puttin' her through it. We just have a couple of questions, and then I swear y'all can get back to your evening."

That seemed to mollify Hall, who nodded curtly but moved not an inch, arms over his chest, glaring at Hughes.

"Since we have Howie here, though..."

Hughes knew what Tanner was getting at. The sketch artist from the county had finally made her way to the Nod and finished the sketch of the woman Deputy Erickson had seen in the hospital. They were confident the woman was Samantha Dent, but no one in town had seen her in years.

Except for Howie.

"Could you just take a look at these?" Tanner asked, unfolding a sheet of paper and holding it out to Howie. "Upper left is the way she looked to Erickson. Then we have projections without the glasses, without her hair up in the cap. This is the woman we believe may have been involved in the murder of—"

Howie yelped in pain and jerked his hand away from Connie. "What the hell—?"

Connie had blanched. She looked over at Howie, and something passed between them.

"Oh, God," Howie breathed.

"Poor Jazz," Connie whispered. "Oh, Jazz..."

"What?" Hughes demanded. The dad be damned—something was going on here.

"You don't..." Howie shook his head.

Connie fixed him with a tear-filled scowl. "It's hopeless," she said with finality. "There's nothing anyone can do for Jazz now."

CHAPTER 48

The knife was a feint, Jazz knew.

And knowing Billy's sense of justice, irony, and symbolism, he was willing to bet it was the same knife he had used to cut Connie's braid away. It was a beautiful, tempting feint, but a feint nonetheless. If he went for the knife, Billy would all-too-quickly reverse it and Jazz would be staring at the point, not the handle. He wasn't sure if his father would kill him or not; Billy's parental desire to see Jazz slaughtering at his side ran strong and true. But if Billy absolutely believed that Jazz was a lost cause, that he would not become the slaying, torturing godling Billy had envisioned for years... Well, if Billy became convinced of that, there was no telling what he might or might not do.

Jazz wanted that knife so badly that his palms itched.

"I'm not fighting you," he said. "Not until you tell me where Mom is."

"You think that information will mean anything to you?"

"I know that after I kill you, I won't be able to ask you any questions, so I'm asking now."

Eyes widening in excitement, Billy smiled like a child opening birthday gifts. "Now you sound like a Crow, boy!" The knife did not waver, hanging in the air. Jazz tried not to stare at it. Billy was like a magician—one hand distracted you while the other performed bloody tricks.

"I don't know that you're ready to see your mom," Billy went on. "I don't know that you've earned it. Now, whyn't you show Dear Old Dad what you've got in your pocket there."

No choice. Jazz had lost control of the conversation, if he'd ever had it in the first place. Billy held all the cards. Billy had Mom. Until he learned where Mom was, Jazz had to play along with Billy's games.

Blowing out a breath in annoyance, Jazz removed his hand from his pocket and showed Billy . . . Hughes's badge.

"Ha! I bet there's a pissed-off cop gettin' his ass reamed somewhere in New York."

"I'm sure." Jazz had left the badge in the same pocket as the Taser, fortunately. Billy wasn't the only magician in the family. *Watch the shiny badge over here and don't pay attention to what else I might have in my pocket. . . .*

"Pin that on you," Billy said, a tinge of amusement lingering on the edges of his words.

"Why?"

"I don't know. It'll be funny, maybe? I just got a hankering to see you like a cop, and I don't tend to ignore my hankerings."

The overcoat, Jazz thought, would be too thick. He pried aside the lapels and pinned Hughes's badge to the left breast of Mark Culpepper's shirt. "There. Happy?"

Billy smirked. "Nah. Not as funny as I thought it'd be. Oh, well. Don't suppose you had to kill anyone to get your hands on that...." Hopeful note to his voice. A father opening a report card he suspects will be bad but hopes will have at least one B.

"Sorry to disappoint you."

Billy shrugged. "Disappointment is part of parenthood, Jasper. The trick is learnin' to love your kids even when they disappoint you. You know they made me try therapy in Wammaket? Didn't last long, but I did learn that when we're disappointed with someone else, it's actually sort of a mirror bounce. We're actually disappointed at something in ourselves." Billy lowered the knife, clearly convinced Jazz wasn't going to lunge for it. He regarded it for a moment and then, with a one-shoulder shrug, tucked it into his waistband. "I spent a lot of time in solitary. Learned to think real hard about what I done and what I didn't do. And my disappointment in you, Jasper, is really disappointment in me. That I left you so soon. Before I could finish bringing you up right. It ain't your fault you are the way you are. It's mine."

No kidding.

With real remorse in his voice, Billy continued: "If I'd held my...urges in check, that fat prick Tanner never would've caught me. I'd'a been a free man, and I could have finished teaching you."

"You taught me enough," Jazz said quietly. Quite unbidden, he flashed to the knife in his hands, cutting into flesh....

Mom? Was it Mom I cut? Or did Sam let me practice on her?

Billy was still talking, as though Jazz hadn't spoken. Jazz realized he'd gone into a fugue state for a moment, spacing out in front of the most dangerous man he knew. "Instead, you go off and make *friends*." Billy spat the word. "You pollute your flesh with ink."

"Look who's talking." Billy's prison tats still stood out on his knuckles.

"Don't you sass me, boy!" Billy shouted, the cords on his neck standing out. "Don't talk back! These words *mean* something!" He raised both fists. LOVE, spelled the one. FEAR, the other. "This is *philosophy*. Your ink is bullshit. You defile your body for *entertainment*."

And Jazz remembered—with startling clarity—the first needle penetrating his flesh, the day he'd gotten the stylized CP3 tattoo. Howie had stood nearby, the look of sheer joy in his eyes so childlike and innocent in comparison with his lurking, adult frame.

"No. For friendship."

Billy thrust his fists out. The tats were ragged and imprecise. LOVE. FEAR.

"Which one holds your fate, Jasper? Love for your family, for your kin? For the people who made you what you are? Or fear of yourself? Fear of the prospects and the world they want you to live in?"

Leave it to Billy to put it that way. Leave it to Billy to

imagine that you could break down the world into precisely two categories and then to define them thus. *Love* didn't have to mean family. *Fear* didn't have to apply to the rest of the world.

"I think I've had enough of your kind of love," Jazz said, surprising himself that he clenched his jaw tight, tears gathering. "You…you *abused* me," he spluttered. "You did horrible things to me. You made me—"

"I never abused you." Billy dropped his hands to his sides. "I loved—I *love* you, boy. You're my son. My child. I never once—"

"You made me cut her!" Jazz shouted. "You made me cut her and you, and you, and you—" He gulped air. He couldn't speak. Oh, Jesus, what was *wrong* with him! *Can't lose control*, he told himself. *Can't go crazy. You lose it and Billy moves into your head, and then you're done for, one way or the other. You either end up dead or you cave, giving in to the most lethal Father/Son Day ever.*

To his surprise, Billy simply stood there and watched— something like concern spreading over his features—as Jazz composed himself and drew in a deep breath. He wiped his eyes with his sleeve.

"You all right?" Billy asked gently.

"Screw you." Jazz's voice was heated. "You've been manipulating me my whole life, but I won't fall for it anymore. You made me…" He gulped. He had to say it. He had to say it out loud. When he did, it came out in a whisper. "You made me have sex with my own *aunt*. The things you did—"

Billy shook his head and clucked his tongue. "Did no such thing, Jasper. I swear it." He actually raised one hand and put the other over the spot where a human being would have a heart. "Never happened."

"I remember it." Jazz's voice barely worked. He was choking on his own language. He couldn't stop thinking of the dream, the dream that—like the dream of cutting—had turned out to be real. The touches.

"I can't help what you remember," Billy said with a shrug.

Jazz forced himself away from it. He made himself think of something else. The birth certificate. His tear-clotted throat allowed a rueful laugh to escape. That damn birth certificate. That was Billy's first mistake. The mocking, accusatory blank next to *father* had taught Jazz an important lesson.

"If I have to kill you to save Mom," Jazz said, "I will. Without a second thought. Without remorse or regret."

Billy nodded thoughtfully. "And that's one step away from killing *anyone* for *any* reason. Without remorse or regret."

"Stop trying to mess with my head. Stop telling me what I think and feel, what I *will* think and feel. I'm the master of my own mind."

"I'm sure you'd like to think so." Billy withdrew the knife again, and once again held it out, handle toward Jazz. "But you won't really know until you try, hmm?"

Without meaning to, without even being wholly aware of it, Jazz took a step closer to Billy, a step closer to the knife. His right hand jerked upward, and Jazz had to will it back into place.

Billy's eyes twinkled. Blue ice floating on a sea of bloodshot white.

"You can't do this to me," Jazz whispered, but it was already being done. He could see himself taking the knife. Could see himself cutting those damn twinkling eyes from his father's face. Then the tongue, that goddamn tongue that never, ever, *ever* stopped wagging. Yes! Silence the voice forever. Sever the tongue, pull it, still wriggling and longing for speech, from the well of blood that would be Billy's mouth.

And then, when Billy was defenseless and at his most pathetic: the blade. Through the chest. Into the heart. Twist it to be sure. Would he feel the cardiac muscles separating, the sensation transmitted through the blade? Oh, hell yes, he would!

It would be too disappointing otherwise.

He wanted to feel his father's heart as it broke.

His fingers spasmed. They longed for a weapon.

"I think you're ready now," Billy said. They stared at each other, transfixed. His father laid the knife on the back of the sofa. "I think you're ready for the truth. For the Crow King."

"I know the truth," Jazz whispered. "I thought you were the Crow King. But you aren't."

"Never was," Billy agreed. "Tell me what you know."

Yes. Yes, he would. It seemed easier to surrender. The darkness didn't have to be cold. It could be warm. He could settle into it like a down blanket and just...let the world happen. It was what Billy had done, and Billy was so happy.

Why not?

He heard himself spell it out, everything he'd come to understand. How wrong he'd been all along. He'd thought Billy was the Crow King, the ruler, the master boogeyman, but he'd been wrong.

It had been his aunt Samantha all along. The puppeteer. The gender was a ruse. Female serial killers were so rare that no one would ever suspect a woman at the head of the Crows. No one would ever suspect a woman was the Crow King.

Jazz had sat across Gramma's kitchen table from her, drinking coffee. He could have stopped all this back then, if he hadn't been so desperate for some family connection.

Well, he had all the family connections he could ever want now. Father and aunt murder machines. It was in his DNA.

"Sam was older than you," Jazz began. "She made contact first." He thought of the story Sam had told him, of Billy as a child, standing naked in her room one night. He believed that story. She had just ended it too soon, was all. What had happened after what she'd told him?

His own memories of childhood filled in the blanks. And the thought no longer nauseated him. This was just the way of it now. This was what the Dents did. Had his grandfather molested Billy or Sam? Is that how it started? He would never know. His grandparents were dead, and he couldn't imagine Billy answering that question. Sam and Billy had been born bad or they had learned bad. Either way, the results were the same.

For a long time, Sam had said, *I thought there was something wrong with* me *because no one else seemed to notice.* Such an idiot. She'd practically told Jazz who and what she was.

She recognized Billy's madness and propensity for murder early on. And no doubt encouraged it. The doting, adoring older sister, taking her little brother by the hand and teaching him.

"She left the house first. Went out prospecting. Got the attention of the Crows and brought you into the fold. And that's when your career really took off. Maybe she helped you on some of your kills. I'm not sure. But she was out there in the world, working her way up the Crow ladder. Playing their games and winning every single one. Until she became the Crow King and the two of you could reunite. She sent the Impressionist to Lobo's Nod. She arranged your escape from Wammaket."

Billy nodded thoughtfully. "Got it all figured out."

Numb, Jazz shoved his hands into his pockets. Oh, right. The Taser. He didn't even bother with it. There was no point. He could stun and kill Billy, and Aunt Samantha would just come for him.

"You're right about everything," Billy said. "Except for the things you're wrong about. But playtime's over. Are you ready to meet the Crow King?"

Jazz had already met Sam, but he allowed Billy the moment of melodrama as his father picked up the iPad and turned it on.

"This thing? Goddamn miracle, Jasper. Missed out on 'em while I was in prison, but it's so easy...." He fiddled with it for a moment, then propped it up on the sofa so that it faced Jazz. A little light turned on, indicating that the webcam was active, and then FaceTime came up.

"Hello, Jasper," said his mother.

CHAPTER 49

Her voice hadn't changed. Not at all.

"Hello, Jasper."

The first words he'd heard from her in years. They hit him harder than he anticipated, stabbing tears out of his eyes. He dug at them with his fingers, a rage more potent and dangerous than any he'd ever felt before swelling inside him, so fulsome and massive that it overflowed and threatened to explode him.

Had he imagined this was over? Had he really considered surrendering to Billy? Here she was, the woman he'd assaulted and stolen and lied for. Looking so identical to the picture he'd kept all these years that it was as though the time had not passed at all, as though he were a child again. But for the subtle lines around her eyes—those hazel eyes, so like his own, so unlike Billy's—and the slight, silvery tint to her hair, she could be the exact same person he'd last seen before going off to school that day years ago.

His mother. Alive, before him. He could see her. Hear her. Now he only needed to *find* her.

"Where is she?" Jazz demanded. "Where is Sam holding her?"

Billy tsked and sighed a sigh that would have been familiar to any long-suffering parent. "I don't think he's gettin' it, Belle. Want to set the boy straight?"

Jazz's eyes drifted from Billy back to the iPad. His mother, he realized, was smiling wryly, her lips curled in bemusement. There was no fear in her eyes. No worry in her expression.

No.

No. No.

No.

"Jasper," she said, "don't you have anything to say to your momma? It's been so long. I'm sorry I had to go away, but... a Crow King's business is never done."

"No!" This time it erupted from him. He couldn't hold it back. "How did you make her do it?" He turned back to Billy, his fists clenched. "How did you force her to become—"

Billy held his hands up, palms out, his face contorted into a "Don't look at *me!*" expression. "Force her? Boy, I couldn't ever force your momma into anything. This was all her idea. She sure does like her games."

"You're lying," Jazz said, but he knew that wasn't true. He had spent his entire life listening to Billy's lies and Billy's truths. He knew how to tell one from the other.

Billy was—for once—telling the truth. In fact, Jazz

realized, his father had always told him the truth. At least, as well as he could.

"You know that old sayin', son," Billy mused. " 'Behind every great man, there's a great woman.' Well, I, son, am a *magnificent* man." He gestured to the iPad, where Janice Dent, the Crow King, Belle Gunness, Ugly J, gazed out, smiling. "Funny, that, though. Women're so proud when they say it about a doctor or a president or a king. Not so proud when it comes to a fella like me. Now... why is that, do you think?"

"Because my sex is consumed with its own self-righteous victimhood and self-pity," his mother said matter-of-factly.

"I believe you might be right about that." Billy grinned.

Jazz staggered backward a step. The sight of his parents both smiling at him, utterly soulless, their hearts dead as stone — it poleaxed him. He couldn't breathe.

The dreams.

The cutting.

And the...

Oh, God.

He dropped to his knees, gasping for breath. Was this shock? Was he going into shock? He couldn't breathe, and his vision had gone blurry.

He'd touched... He'd *touched*...

Hands pressed to Weathers's cheap carpeting, Jazz tried and failed to draw in a breath. His lungs had turned to stone, the first step in the paralysis when gazing upon the cursed visage of the Gorgons.

Beautiful, the Impressionist had said. *But the way you die is so ugly....*

And beautiful she was, his mother. Ugly, too.

Jazz would choke to death on his own history, here in Doug Weathers's apartment. And it was, he knew, what he deserved. For the hubris of thinking he could possibly conquer his own past and overcome Billy. For the arrogance of thinking he had outwitted his father and deduced the ultimate punch line.

For the weakness of a boy's love for his mother.

Everything he'd believed, everything he'd clung to in his life, had been worse than a lie. It had been a deceit. Deliberate. His safe haven had turned into an ambush.

He stared at his hands, red flushed and wavering, blurring into the carpet pattern. Suddenly everything made sense and nothing made sense. Billy's ability to evade the police wasn't quite so magical when the cops were looking for a single male. Or for a man with a hostage. When Billy and Mom drove out of New York, they must have looked like any other happy married couple, sailing right through checkpoints. Mom leaving had been planned, and Billy's excising her from history was just one more item on the to-do list.

Billy had told the truth. He'd said that Jazz wasn't a virgin. He'd said that he hadn't hurt Mom—

What did you do to Mom? Jazz had demanded.

And Billy had shrugged. *Do? What did I do to your mother? Nothing.*

Lie was truth and truth was a lie. Mom had given him Rusty as a puppy, and Billy had skinned the dog alive in front of him. Was that part of some plan? Had that been *designed* into his life?

377

And of course there was

like that

it's all right

it's not all right

it's right

Jazz threw up. Violently. His stomach contracted over and over, his esophagus rippling savagely. Everything he'd eaten and drunk spewed from him, gushing like a water pipe, a fire hose, an artery. Burning bile scalded his throat, his tongue, and everything that came out of him wasn't enough, as his stomach kept seizing, forcing out nothing more than his own hollow cries.

A slick of puke, streaked with protein-bar chocolate and glow-red Gatorade shimmered inches from his face. His jaw strained, his body tried to force more out of him, but there was nothing left, and he hung poised over his own sick, dry heaving.

"Billy, darling, how's our boy?"

"Pukin' up his guts and then some," Billy said conversationally.

"Sounds pretty rough from here. Maybe you can make sure he's not aspirating anything into his lungs."

Billy came around the sofa and stood over Jazz for a moment. Jazz knew from the sound of his feet and from Billy's Nikes, which came into view to his left, the toes inches away from Jazz's hand.

"Looks okay," Billy said.

"I told you he would have an extreme reaction," Mom said in an *oh, you silly boy* voice.

Jazz hiccupped powerfully, his whole body spasming. He almost lost control of his arms and spilled onto the floor, but Billy stooped down quickly, grabbing Jazz under his arms and keeping him elevated.

"Whoa, there! Looks like he might be a little worse off than we—"

Billy didn't finish the sentence because Jazz jerked his head up. His skull rattled as he connected with Billy's jaw, shutting his father up with a satisfying *Uck!* sound.

"What's going on over there?" Mom demanded from the iPad.

Billy stumbled back, still entangled with Jazz, pulling Jazz over at the same time. Jazz pushed off with his legs, propelling himself bodily at Billy's midsection, knocking his father off-balance. Together, they collapsed onto the floor.

"Billy! What's happening over there?" Mom sounded concerned.

"Nothin' I can't handle, darlin'." Billy shoved at Jazz, who had thrown his full weight on top of his father. From his position lying atop Billy, Jazz was able to pin one arm down. With his free arm, Billy brought a powerful fist down on Jazz's back. Jazz bit back a scream and scrambled to bring his legs around to hold down the other arm.

"You got some fight in you after all!" Billy chortled. "Good for you! Our boy's got spirit, Belle!"

Jazz resisted the temptation to trash-talk. He needed all his breath, all his strength. He'd been faking the tenuousness of his leg before, knowing Billy would note every shake and stutter of it. It actually felt pretty good, thanks to the painkillers and antibiotics. But even with his leg secretly functioning, they were still too evenly matched. Jazz was younger, true, more resilient, but he was also more worn-down. And he'd just puked up his only sustenance. Billy was older but prison buff, his body like a piece of shaped steel.

He blinked away memories, shreds of emotion, vile thoughts. No time for sentiment. Or remembering. He had to be a machine. He had to shove all of it away to deal with later and just focus on Billy. Nothing else mattered.

Holding down one arm with his legs and the other with his hands, Jazz risked using one of those hands to reach back toward his pocket and the Taser. Billy, sensing weakness and incipient freedom, bucked his body and rocked back and forth, trying to shake Jazz loose. Jazz willed himself to be heavier, riding out the thrashing as he got his fingers on the Taser.

Just as he withdrew it from his pocket, Billy managed to find leverage with his feet, arching back and throwing Jazz off just enough that his arms were freed. Jazz brought the Taser up and then arced it down, but before it touched his father, Billy twisted, turned, and heaved Jazz off him, dumping him in a pile on the floor. Jazz's finger twitched on the trigger, and the Taser spat its last electrical charge into the uncaring air.

"How many times did I tell you," Billy asked, now standing, "that you *measure twice*—"

"Cut once!" Mom chorused in from the iPad.

Her voice itself cut. It slashed at him, carving hideous new tattoos into him, whirling arcs and dripping gashes of memory and pain.

Put it away. Put it all away.

Jazz bounced to his feet with a vigor he did not truly feel. He couldn't let Billy know exactly how winded he was, he thought, as he struggled to control his breathing. His heart was pulsating like a drum solo.

"Jasper," Mom said, quite calmly, "the fact that you think you can kill your father should tell you something. It tells you that we trained you well."

"We?" Billy asked.

"Oh, fine. I know, I know—I had to leave before the training began in earnest. It's hard, being a career woman *and* a mother. You have no idea. I didn't want to leave, but I had to. Still, Jasper, consider this: that bloodlust you feel right now? That anger? There are better uses for it. Instead of using it all up, you can embrace it. Nurture it. Let it grow. And use it at our sides. A happy Crow family."

Jazz wiped a gummy residue of vomit from his lips. He was still holding the Taser in his other hand, and at just the moment when someone wiping his lips would have finished and returned the hand to his side, he instead raised the hand holding the Taser and hurled it at Billy. In the split second it took for Billy to react and move to bat the thing out of the air, Jazz leapt.

Billy stood openmouthed for a moment, in shock, and then he realized what was happening.

He'd expected Jazz to leap right at him, using the momentary distraction of the Taser to his advantage.

Instead, he'd hurled himself at the *sofa*, crashing into it so hard that it tipped over, spilling the iPad to the floor, along with Jazz.

Who immediately rolled up onto his feet, crouched low as Billy bolted in that direction.

Only to find Jazz already there, wielding the knife Billy had left on the back of the sofa.

Billy stopped just out of reach, smirking. "Little boy's got himself a pig sticker. You remember how to use one of those, boy? Remember what Dear Old Dad taught you?"

"Yes." Jazz shifted the knife to his right hand. There were different ways to hold a knife. He deliberately used the worst grip for this situation, with the blade pointing down and the edge pointing outward. This grip made for excellent power, but poor defense — you had to raise your arm over your head to strike, meaning your opponent had open access to your chest and belly. It looked badass in the movies, but it was a novice choice.

Billy tut-tutted. "You sure you want to be doin' that, Jasper? I ain't lookin' to check out today, but I want you to have a sporting chance."

"Stop playing with him," Mom said. The iPad now leaned precariously against a table leg, turned on its side. "Take that knife away from him, and let's put an end to this."

"I'll just be a moment, Janice," Billy said. He flexed his fingers. "You ready, boy?"

"Born ready."

Jazz raised his right arm, ready to strike, and Billy charged him, forgetting something important.

Forgetting that Jazz wasn't a prospect.

Prospects were afraid. They squealed and ducked and did

anything to avoid pain. Sometimes they froze up instead, and the pain became inevitable.

Jazz didn't move, but it was a deliberate choice. He knew how Billy would try to blitz him, try to chop at the elbow to make him lose the knife while also shouldering him in the chest to knock him down.

He knew this because he and Billy had practiced it together many, many times.

When Billy collided with him, just before the arm came up to strike his elbow, Jazz quickly dropped his arm back to his side, the knife catching along Billy's shirt as he did so. It parted the fabric and sliced a narrow furrow into Billy's upper arm.

Boom. Billy's weight and momentum smashed into him. Jazz went with it, using his left arm to hook around Billy's neck, dragging his father down to the floor with him. They crashed there like prizefighters, grunting and groaning. Jazz's teeth rattled, and his left leg whined as Billy landed on it.

Billy lay half-on, half-off him. Before his father could exploit his upper hand, Jazz rapidly switched to a fencer's grip on the knife, slashing out with it just as Billy rolled away from him, sensing the arm movement through the contact of their bodies. With a moan he wished he could suppress, Jazz rolled over and managed to shove up onto his knees. Billy was only a few feet away, down on one knee, glaring.

"Not bad," he said. "It's a good knife, ain't it? Your girl-friend sure liked it."

"You gonna talk or you gonna fight?" Jazz sneered. "Always did seem like you couldn't tell the difference."

Billy laughed. "Truce. I can't get in your head, and you can't get in mine."

"No, we're both in each other's heads. There's just nothing worth using in there."

"Might be true."

"Boys," Mom said, bored. "This is all very entertaining but ultimately counterproductive. Jasper, put down the knife, and let's deal with this as a family."

For the space of an instant, Jazz's attention flicked to the iPad, then flicked back just in time to see Billy, suddenly twice as large in his field of vision, springing off that one foot, lunging at Jazz like a linebacker. Jazz fell back and twisted to one side. Billy slammed into his left shoulder, and his knee came down on Jazz's left thigh, setting the bullet wound to howling again. Jazz bit down hard, refusing to reveal the pain, and fumbled to his right, sliding around Billy.

He saw his chance. Billy's back was exposed.

He swung the knife in a wide arc and brought it down on his father's back. A jolt ran up his arm and he almost loosened his grip, but he screamed in that same instant, the sound of his own pain giving strength to his fingers.

He drove the knife in. Billy's shirt folded and ripped under the pressure.

Then his flesh.

Then more.

For a moment, Billy wasn't even aware it had happened.

Then he suddenly yelped, in shock, it seemed, more than anything else.

Jazz drove the knife in deeper. Muscle split. Blood vessels erupted. Jazz felt a crunch, transmitted through the blade, dancing along his fingers.

He twisted the knife once, swiftly.

Billy howled like a dog at its dead master's bedside. He tried to rise up on his hands, his shoulders straining, his neck muscles bulging, his face bright red with exertion.

The scream ended abruptly as Billy collapsed face-first on the floor, silent and still.

Jazz sat on the floor for a moment, his leg trapped under his father. He jerked and shimmied to free himself, then stood, looking down.

Billy lay before him.

Jazz stooped and pulled the knife from Billy's back.

Yes. Very well, then.

He turned to the screen and his mother.

He said: "You're next."

CHAPTER 50

An instant later, the screen shut off and the iPad's camera light winked out. Jazz stared at the black, blank eye for a moment.

Blank.

Sink into the blank and the black.

If you don't feel anything, you can't be hurt. Don't think about it. Don't think about what happened. Don't think about it you're good at that you're good at compartmentalizing don't think don't think don't—

He returned to Weathers's desk and laptop, as if he'd never been interrupted, stepping over Billy on the way.

Weathers had encountered Billy and...

Billy and...

Ugly J. The Crow King. Yes. That's who.

Weathers had encountered them and been tortured to send a message. So there had to be a clue here that led to...

To...

To Ugly J.

Jazz shook his head. He couldn't get the image from the iPad screen out of his mind. It danced and leered from the edges of his vision. He put his palm down on the table and raised the knife. A small pain would do it, he figured. Just something to shock the memory away, to force himself not to think about it, to think of something else, *anything* else. He wouldn't do his best Impressionist and cut off a finger. Or even spear through the whole hand. Just a cut, maybe, across the top of the hand. Avoid the radial nerve and the *opponens digiti minimi* and *opponens pollicis* and there'd be no permanent, lingering damage. Just blood. Just pain. Just what he needed.

touch me

(oh, yes)

like that

His hand trembled as he brought the knife up. The blade passed before the laptop screen, and Jazz once again found himself staring at the map.

A location just beyond the town line.

And in the search field that had led Weathers there, a name: Jack Dawes.

Jazz knew the place. He'd ridden past it on the school bus as a child, or anytime he'd left town on a southwesterly track. It was a big, isolated, dilapidated Victorian that had been old when Gramma was young.

Billy's safe house, Jazz realized. Billy's and his—

Ugly J's.

A place close enough that they could get to it if they needed to. Billy probably would have headed there the day he was arrested, if he'd been able to get away from G. William.

His plan to cut himself forgotten, Jazz scanned the map, plotting out the trip. Walking would take too long and be too visible. He needed a car.

Billy. Billy wouldn't have walked here from the safe house. It's just as risky for him to be seen here as it is for me. He would have driven.

Jazz returned to Billy and knelt down, feeling his father's pockets. He hit pay dirt on the right side and wormed his hand in for the keys.

Just then, Billy coughed and jerked. Jazz pulled back, yanking his hand away. Billy glared, his lips peeled into a vicious snarl.

"Thought Dear Old Dad had gone away?" His voice, clogged with grit and anguish, still managed a sort of sing-song chant: "You didn't have the guts. Didn't have the guts to do it. To kill me. Didn't have the balls to off Dear Old Dad."

Jazz met his father's gaze and did not waver. "Shut up, Billy. You can't goad me into killing you."

"Didn't. Have. The—"

"I had the guts *not* to kill you." He stood, reared back, and kicked Billy in the side, just under the rib cage, not bothering to disguise the sheer glee he felt at the solid contact. "Now shut up."

Billy pressed his palms to the floor and pushed his upper half off the floor, seething, his eyes fixated on Jazz. "Biggest mistake of your life, boy. Not killin' me right. I'm gonna make goddamn sure you got plenty of time to regret it."

Very calmly, Jazz said, "Who says I was trying to kill you?"

Billy hoisted himself higher...and stopped. His expression of rage turned to confusion. Bafflement. He strained to his utmost, pushing with his arms, muscles taut and tense under his shirt, his powerful shoulders flexing.

But try as he might, he couldn't move any farther.

"What the hell—?"

And he realized. Jazz saw the understanding blossom in the sudden widening of his father's eyes, in the slack and horror-stricken rictus of his expression.

"I can't—"

"I cut your spinal cord," Jazz said as neutrally as he could manage. "That was that burst of excruciating pain you felt. The pain that made you pass out. Right at the thoracicolumbar junction, around T-twelve and L-one." He folded his arms over his chest and stared down at Billy with utter satisfaction. "The same way you taught Hat and Dog to do to *their* victims."

"You took my legs!" Billy shouted. "You took my goddamn legs away!" He thrashed on the floor, flailing his arms, desperately seeking some kind of reaction from the lower half of his body, but there was no reaction there. Nothing but the occasional fishtailing caused by the upper body movements. Billy was paralyzed from the waist down. For good.

"You piece of shit!" Billy railed. "I should have strangled you in your crib! I should have ripped you out of your mother's belly! I'm gonna destroy you for this, you hear me? I'm gonna make you wish I never shot my load inside her to make you!"

Jazz crouched down and fished the keys out of Billy's pocket. His father tried to grab his hand, but it was easy enough to avoid him.

"I swear by all that is holy that I will piss in your hollow skull for this," Billy ranted.

"You smell that?" Jazz leaned close and whispered in Billy's ear, his voice trembling not with fear but with barely controllable excitement. "That's your own shit, Billy. You can't control your bowels anymore. You can't walk. You can't ever rape someone again, not with that useless thing between your legs. You're not destroying me. You're not going to destroy anyone ever again. You're going to spend the rest of your life in a wheelchair, getting your diapers changed by a prison nurse."

Billy's bellow of impotent, tormented outrage was beautiful to Jazz's ears.

He recovered the knife he'd used on Billy, the knife Billy had used on Connie. Holding it out as Billy had, handle first, Jazz waited until his father took it, then stepped just out of arm's reach.

"Only one person left you can hurt, Billy," Jazz said, backing away. "So if you get the urge, feel free to put that blade through your eye."

And then, savoring the wailing, doleful cries of rage that filled Doug Weathers's apartment, Jazz left, closing the door behind him.

The car was easy to find. Billy had parked carefully away from any streetlights on the next block over. Jazz kept hitting the remote lock until the headlights glimmered at him. No one was around. He got in the car and started it.

On autopilot. Just keep moving. It's almost over. You don't have to think until it's all over, and then you can look back, but right now just look ahead.

You're next, his own voice said. Over and over.

CHAPTER 51

Tanner drove like a bootlegger or a gangbanger. Hughes braced himself against the dashboard during the sharper turns and prayed like he hadn't since Catholic school that the air bag wouldn't pop at an impromptu moment and drive his forearms up into his shoulders. He'd been in high-speed pursuits before. Several in Brooklyn and a couple in Manhattan. There, traffic made a truly breakneck pace for any length of time nearly impossible.

But out here where men were men and cows were scared, the streets were as empty as a drug corner after five-oh was called. Tanner's siren shoved aside any lingering late-night traffic, and the man took the corners as though he were being paid to test his cruiser's axles to their breaking point.

Just when Hughes was about to ask if Tanner had ever actually hauled ass through his little burg like this before and if no, maybe it was time to slow down?, the sheriff reached over and switched off the siren. Before Hughes could react, Tanner tapped the brakes.

"Don't want him to hear us coming," the sheriff muttered.

Him.

Billy Dent.

Hughes couldn't believe that he was about to encounter the country's number one boogeyman, the guy who'd topped the FBI's most-wanted list under two different aliases, the Master Murderer himself.

The pasty white string-bean kid—Howie—had shown Tanner a letter. Between that and the drawing they'd shown the kids, there seemed to be only one horrifying conclusion.

"Let's not be too sure of that," Tanner had said. Hughes had spent his entire adult life around cops; he knew when one was telling a witness a lie.

Then the kid had pulled out his phone and played a sound file that Hughes truly, deeply wished he'd never heard. A series of sounds he knew he would be hearing again in his dreams and nightmares, and would probably recall with frightening clarity and detail on his deathbed.

As soon as the file ended, Tanner had plopped his hat on his head and hustled the two of them back to the car, then proceeded to fling them into the night, siren blaring.

With the siren now off and the cruiser settling into a reasonable rate of speed, Hughes allowed himself to relax. "You really think Dent is going to be at this guy Weathers's apartment?"

"Best lead we've had all day." Tanner piloted around a corner, then parked illegally against a fire hydrant. Ahead lay their target, a six-story building on the far corner of the block. Relative to the squat buildings around it, it was damn near a skyscraper, and Hughes wondered what it was like to live somewhere with elevators in even the short buildings.

Tanner radioed in for backup. "But keep back a block and don't move until I say so. I don't want to spook him, and if he gets past us, I want y'all ready to close off the roads."

"Copy, Sheriff," a voice came back.

"Best lead all day," Tanner said again. He popped his neck back and forth and drew in a deep breath. Hughes was itching to get out of the car and rush the building, but this was Tanner's town; he would follow the sheriff's lead.

Long seconds ticked by, turning into a minute. "We doing this or not?" Hughes asked gently.

Tanner smiled wanly. "Sorry. Just not lookin' forward to seeing this one again. Memories."

"I hear you. Do you—"

"Let's do it." Tanner slid out of the car with surprising grace for such a fat man. Hughes joined him, and the two of them hustled over to the building, keeping to the shadows. The building was locked up, a buzzer panel the only way in. Tanner produced a ring of keys from his pocket and unlocked the door. At Hughes's raised eyebrows, he said, "This is a small town, Detective. People here actually like having the police able to get inside if necessary."

Hughes tried to imagine the civil-libertarian crap he'd have to put up with if he wanted to walk around Brooklyn with the keys to every building.

They scooted inside, and Hughes drew his weapon an instant after Tanner did so. Nothing in the lobby. Without a word spoken between them, they'd fallen silent the instant they'd entered the building. Hughes's body vibrated with adrenaline. He made sure his safety was on; he didn't want to end up shooting some innocent Lobo's Nod citizen taking her trash out.

Sure enough, there was an elevator. Tanner hit the button and consulted his smartphone quickly. The sheriff flashed a palm-out hand of spread fingers, then a solo index finger.

Right. Sixth floor.

Tanner pointed to Hughes, then the elevator. Hughes tried not to let his expression reveal how absurd the idea was. He gestured for Tanner to take the elevator instead and motioned that he would take the stairs up to six. With a shrug, Tanner shuffled into the elevator as soon as it opened.

Hughes headed to the stairs. Checking up the first flight, gun extended, he realized before he mounted the first step that he was sweating. It was January-freezing outside and the stairwell wasn't heated, and he was his own personal sauna. Pathetic for a man used to a fourth-floor walk-up. *Settle down, Lou. Just another bad guy. Just another bad guy.*

That mantra took him up the stories, easing around the bends, religiously scanning up the stairwell in case Dent decided to bail via the stairs. He strained to hear gunshots, knowing that Tanner would arrive on six before he would.

When he finally got to the top, he'd exerted himself not at all, but sweat still beaded his forehead and trickled between his shoulder blades. He wiped his hands dry before emerging into the hallway.

Tanner waited by an apartment door. Hughes stifled a giggle at the sight of the big man's belly jutting out into the hall as he flattened his back against the wall. Hughes flanked the door, his gun pointed at the floor. Tanner raised three fingers.

Jesus, I hate this part.

Taking the door never got easier. No matter how many times you did it.

Hughes nodded, and together they counted off three head bobs before Tanner flung open the door.

Hughes kicked off the wall and spun around, gun raised and pointed into the apartment. His heart hammered. Nothing.

He flicked off the safety and gestured Tanner into the apartment.

Following the sheriff, he was immediately assaulted by the stench of human excrement, heavy in the air, undercut with the familiar reek of vomit. There was a sofa in the middle of the room, pushed awry and knocked on its back. The smell was thick, and Hughes started breathing through his mouth.

A pool of vomit had half soaked into the carpet in front of where the sofa had been.

And then a shadow moved in the corner of Hughes's eye, and he spun in time to see a figure crawling from behind the sofa.

No, not crawling. Not like a baby, on hands and knees. Pulling itself along on its elbows. And clenched in its teeth—

"Knife!" Hughes shouted, and raised his gun, taking aim at the man's forehead.

He sensed Tanner's bulk beside him.

"Hello, Billy," Tanner said softly, moving into position, his gun raised, too.

Billy. Hughes looked again, squinting. Holy...It *was* Dent. Billy Dent himself. Pulling himself along the floor like a grunt in a bad army flick, a bloody knife held in his mouth.

With the two cops standing over him and aiming at his head, Dent spat out the knife. Blood painted his lips. Even though he and Tanner had the high ground and the advantage, Hughes still found every nerve on screaming high alert. And he was only partly aware of what Billy Dent could do. He couldn't imagine what was going through Tanner's head right now.

If the sheriff was freaking out, he didn't show it, calmly drawing a bead on Billy. "Good to see you again, Billy. You know the drill."

"Outta my way, Tanner." Dent's voice was careworn, his expression haggard. But his growl still sent shivers running from Hughes's head right to his balls. With what seemed to be a preternatural effort, he pushed himself up on his hands, arms ramrod straight. "None of this is about you."

"Only gonna ask you once, Billy. Hands on your head and flat on the ground."

Dent's eyes narrowed in cunning thought. He started inching forward again.

"You deaf, asshole?" Hughes asked.

But Dent merely snorted, glancing Hughes up and down and then pulling himself forward another inch, as though he'd taken Hughes's measure and decided he just didn't count.

"Hey!" Tanner barked. "I said flat on your face and hands behind your head."

"Heard you the first time, you bastard cop."

"The man said freeze, asshole." Hughes tracked Billy's miniscule progress, keeping his head in range.

With an offended and reluctant *whoof,* Billy paused. Ignoring Hughes, he glowered up at Tanner and smirked.

"You thinkin' of puttin' a bullet in ol' Billy? You thinkin' of offin' me?" Billy's voice gathered strength as he spoke, as though he thrived on his own words, took sustenance from his bad attitude. "You better do it *now,* Tanner. You better put that bullet right in there and do it right, you fat piece of shit. I'll dig up your momma and do things to her, Tanner...."

Hughes and Tanner exchanged a look. If Hughes decided to put a bullet into the writhing mass of poisonous snakes Billy Dent called his brain, he was confident Tanner would cover for him. And he *knew* for damn sure that if Tanner decided to off the bastard, his own lips would be sealed.

"Your town," Hughes said with a shrug. "Your call."

Tanner contented himself with kicking Billy in the head. Dent didn't even cry out, just rolled his head with the blow, stiffening his arms.

"We cremated my momma," Tanner said, his tone tight and laden with restraint. "So good luck with that."

For good measure, he kicked Billy in the head again. This time, Dent's skin ripped along his temple and blood gushed. Billy groaned and collapsed on both elbows, but otherwise he didn't move, didn't try to roll away or run.

What in the name of holy Jesus fuck happened here? Why is he so—

And then he thought of Hat and Dog's victims, starting with poor Harry Glidden, the Luxury Tax spot on the Monopoly board.

"He's paralyzed." Hughes's voice resonated too loud and too deep in the confines of the apartment. "From the waist down."

"That so?" Tanner adjusted his stance and nudged Dent in the leg with the tip of his shoe. Then kicked him there. Dent growled and reached out for Tanner's other leg, managing to get his hands on it and—before Hughes could react—heaved himself along the floor and sank his teeth into Tanner's leg, just above the ankle.

Tanner yelped in pain and tugged his leg back, but Dent had a tight clutch with both hands. Hughes couldn't shoot him without risking hitting Tanner, so instead he holstered his gun, grabbed Billy's legs, and yanked at him with all his might. Screaming obscenities and pounding his fists on the floor, Billy came away from Tanner, who hopped back a couple of paces and nearly fell backward onto his ass.

The guy can't move his legs, and he's still making us look like idiots. Hughes straddled Dent and wrestled his arms back one at a time, slapping the cuffs on him. "Try moving now, shit bird," he whispered to Dent, who snapped his teeth at him, making him jump back. Dent laughed.

He kept laughing even though he was completely helpless. He rocked his torso back and forth and cursed at them, trying to shove himself forward with his core muscles. It was the saddest, scariest thing Hughes had ever seen in his life.

"You all right, Sheriff?" He knelt by Tanner, who had balanced on a nearby desk and was rolling up his pant leg.

"You tell me."

Hughes checked the leg. Tanner was red there, but the skin wasn't broken. His pants and sock had blunted the worst of it. "I think this particular vampire didn't get a snack from you."

"Good news. Because we still got a long night ahead of us."

CHAPTER 52

Jazz wondered how many times he had driven or walked past the Dawes house. He wondered how many other people had done so, and how many times, in total.

Lobo's Nod was a small town, true, but even for a small town, multiplied by the years, the number of pass-bys had to be in the hundreds of thousands.

Broken houses, dead homes. They were invisible, Jazz realized. Other than local kids daring one another to skulk the perimeters and throw rocks at the windows, the places sulked and stewed in their own special miasmas of neglect, dust, and mildew, sad mile markers on the road to entropy. He thought of the endless, blank-windowed façades of Brooklyn, only the minutest fraction of them glimpsed during his time there. How many of them were empty but harbored? How many Jack Daweses lived within? In every town, every city across the country—across the world—there were the abandoned and forsaken, the shuttered and barred. Passed into local legend, then myth, then fairy tale, then utter oblivion, as much a part of the landscape as the trees or the hills.

Someone had once said that in plain sight was the best place to hide.

He parked in front of the house. The car he had driven was Doug Weathers's, according to the registration in the glove box.

Waiting in the car as it cooled, pinged, and rattled, he stared up at the Dawes house. It didn't look scary. It wasn't *supposed* to look scary. A house that seemed haunted would have attracted local lore tellers. It would have summoned children to dare one another to spend the night inside.

No, this was just a broken-down, derelict, run-of-the-mill three-story Victorian. It would garner no attention, and that's just how Billy wanted it.

Like a serial killer, the house blended in. It suited its place, and its place suited it.

As best he could tell, there were no lights burning within, but the windows were boarded over, some of them papered from within. He cracked the car door, half expecting the echoing thunder of a gunshot. He knew what it was like to be shot, but he suspected Ugly J wouldn't aim for the leg.

She wouldn't kill me. Not like Billy tried to. She's my mother, *for God's sake.*

He went dizzy and gripped the steering wheel to steady himself.

You're next.

No. It's not what I think. Focus, Jazz.

She's my mother, he told himself again, waiting for the dizziness to go away.

Think about it. Think it through. Think of what you know about female serial killers. They don't do this for pleasure. They partner up with a man, and they get off on the man's enjoyment. Like...

Like that couple in Canada. Homolka. Videotaped her boyfriend raping and killing her own sister. Because it made him happy. That's why women do it—to make their men happy. Or they kill out of fear or necessity. With Billy gone, there was no reason for her to kill Jazz. And no reason for him to kill her.

That was it. That was it for sure.

The mere fact of her—of her existence—bewildered him and made it almost impossible to think. She had been dead and gone, and then she was alive, and then she was Billy's partner, which he still couldn't believe. Not entirely. Billy's protestations to the contrary, what made the most sense was that she was in Billy's thrall. Hybristophilia. Technical term. It happened so often that there was even a snappy, pop-psychish term for it, the kind of thing Doug Weathers would have thrown around on TV and in his articles: *Bonnie and Clyde Syndrome.* Powerful, overbearing man; submissive, eager-to-please woman. The combination was deadlier than the sum of its parts because, left to her own devices, the woman would never kill. Only when under the influence of the male did she become lethal.

Connie had seen her in handcuffs, under Billy's control.

Her devotion to Billy was automatically suspect. His domination of her couldn't possibly be complete. Not if she'd been manacled. Not if she'd helped Connie escape.

I clung to her. My whole life, I've clung to the idea of her, the memory of her. I thought she could have rescued me. But it's the other way around. I have to rescue her.

You're next. No. She's not. It's over. She just doesn't know it yet. I'm going to tell her. This is all going to make sense. I'm going to go in there, and it's all going to make sense.

He swung his legs out of the car. Took a deep, cold breath. Closed the car door behind him and walked to the porch.

The steps creaked and whined in the winter air.

The front door was unlocked. Jazz opened it and went inside.

Inside, the house smelled of parched soil and dust and mold and something else that Jazz recognized but chose not to think about. From the moment he heard Weathers's voice on Howie's phone, he'd known he would smell this particular potpourri of blood, gases, excrement, and urine. He was used to it, inured to it, after helping Billy clean his tools and, on occasion, actual crime scenes.

You gotta get used to the smell, Billy had said. *You get all distracted or all sick or whatnot, and you can't finish the job, see? You try to get out of there too soon and you leave—*

Shut up, Jazz thought fiercely, and was pleased to find that Billy did, for a change.

He imagined his father chasing a pretty young coed in his wheelchair, demanding she come back, and he giggled uncontrollably for a full thirty seconds.

I'm losing it.

He stepped inside and closed the door behind him. A flight of stairs tempted him, but the murk and solid black that ascended from halfway up the stairs stalled him. A narrow hallway before him led into the depths of the house, a flickering light coming from a doorway off to the side.

He realized, with a shock so hard he actually put a hand to his chest as though he could steady his wild heart, that he was unarmed. He'd left the knife with Billy.

Idiot. Idiot!

Still, there was not the slightest chance that he would back down now. Not when he was so close. Not when he could end it now. If he left to get a weapon, he'd come back to find the house empty, he knew.

And you don't need a weapon, Jazz. You're not going to kill her. You're not even going to fight her. She's not Billy.

The floorboards whispered underfoot. Nothing he could do about that. An old house would make noises, and he couldn't anticipate them. He could only acknowledge the sounds, acknowledge that his mother—

Ugly J. Belle. The Crow King.

—would hear him coming and be forewarned.

I was abused. I was molested. I was abused. I was molested.

The thought was too big. He pushed it aside. He would deal with it later. If there was a later.

A lifetime of therapy. And even that probably wouldn't be enough. It would be a start, though.

She doesn't want to hurt me. She just thinks she has to. And if she gets to me before I can tell her Billy's neutralized…

His muscles tightened. His neck tensed. He inched along the wall, his shadow dancing in the flickering light. Creeping along, his breath shallow sips, he flattened himself against the wall and listened, willing himself to hear whatever, whoever, lurked in the other room, the room with the light.

Straining, he heard…

A hiss.

Low and sustained.

There was no other option but to turn into the room. He did it quickly, before he could change his mind.

There was a chair, on which stood a Coleman lantern, hissing in that way lanterns do. In the leaping shadow relief of the lantern's shifting light, he beheld the only other thing in the room of note.

It was Doug Weathers. What was left of him, at least.

Jazz didn't need to approach and search for a pulse to know the man was dead. Weathers was deader than any body or anybody Jazz had ever seen before. His mind raced to catalog the grotesqueries Billy had heaped upon Weathers—

Because it was Billy. It had to be Billy. Billy did this. Billy and only Billy.

—and gave up.

There was an ear nailed to the wall.

Jazz tightened his jaw. He was determined to search this room. For clues. That was the way, right? That was the thing to do.

Avoiding it. You're avoiding it. You're avoiding going upstairs.

He was. She was up there, he knew, and he wasn't ready yet. Not yet. Terrified? Gagging on anticipation? He couldn't tell.

But he wasn't ready.

He sidestepped a slick of blood and something else. The house wasn't heated, so Weathers hadn't begun to rot in earnest. Wintertime. It would take longer for the flies and other bugs to get to him. Lucky Jazz, he had Doug Weathers all to himself.

He tugged Mark Culpepper's shirt over his nose and mouth and looked down at the ruin of Doug Weathers's body. Another involuntary giggle escaped from him.

So, Doug, it turns out you do *have a heart after all! And there it is.*

Stop it, Jazz. Stop it.

There were no fingers on Weathers's left hand, but the palm faced up, cradling a small digital recorder. Jazz stooped down and plucked it away without touching any part of Doug Weathers.

Backing away, closer to the door, he suddenly felt eyes on him and spun around. The hallway was empty.

But *had* it been?

He backed himself into a corner. Now he would see anyone or anything approaching him.

It took him two tries to thumb the recorder to Play.

"Hello, Jasper."

The voice. Her voice. He gazed up at the ceiling, relaxing for the briefest possible moment and he was a child again and he hadn't seen his first body yet and everything was okay and everything would always be okay and then he heard something and he startled and there was nothing there, nothing, nothing.

"If you're hearing this," she went on, "then that means you've killed your father." She paused. "Good for you. The only question, then, is this: Have you learned anything from the experience?"

Had he? He'd had Billy at his mercy. Completely in his control. Helpless. Legless. What had he learned in those soft moments of his father's utter vulnerability?

"I want you to take a little time to think, Jasper." His mother's voice was soothing. It was the lullaby voice, the Band-Aid-on-scrapes voice. He felt tears again. "Think about your past and think about your future. You know the expression 'As the crow flies,' don't you? People use it to mean a straight line. And that's very important. Because the way a capital-C Crow flies *is* in a straight line. It may appear jagged to some, but the Crow flies in a straight line to his goal." Another pause. "Or her goal, as the case may be. It's usually men, though." She laughed. "Mommy broke the glass ceiling, darling. First female Crow King in history. Aren't you proud?

"Anyway, I want you to know two things, Jasper. I want you to know that even though I went away, I never stopped loving you. You are the flesh of my flesh, the blood of my blood. I'm your mother, and it would just be impossible for me not to love you. And the second thing is this: I'm proud of you. I imagine you're harboring some sort of notion that I might be angry with you for taking your father away from me. But he and I both knew that someday it might come to this. That there would come a day when you might rise up against him.

"Back in October, I had to be in Lobo's Nod. As I'm sure you've surmised by now."

Billy's escape. And the Impressionist. Of course. She'd been the one helping him along.

"It wasn't easy. I wanted to come see you. But I had to stay hidden most of the time. It's been years since anyone here has seen me, but small towns have long memories. But I did sneak out one night, disguising myself. That night was the night of your play. *The Crucible*. I stood in the back and watched you, and I was filled with so much love for you. 'There is blood on my head,' you screamed to heaven, and it was true, Jasper, so true, and so glorious, and in that moment you made even me believe that you regretted the blood, that you rejected it. And I knew then, in that moment, that if you could convince me of that, that you could convince the world. I knew that your father was right: You would be the greatest of us all. The new Crow King. For that, the sacrifice of your father is all a part of the greater good."

Jazz moaned deep in his chest, down where the madness had taken root, where his heart had leapt with excitement at the sensation of stabbing his own father. He'd been born and bred for this. For all of it.

"Are you ready to accept this, Jasper? Are you ready to take your rightful place? If so, come upstairs, son. It's been so long. Momma misses her little boy."

The recording ended.

A joist squeaked above him, and he darted his gaze upward, anticipating his mother descending through the ceiling. Another rasp on the floor, then silence.

He dropped the recorder to the floor and returned to the entrance vestibule. The stairs and their darkness beckoned him.

He began to climb.

CHAPTER 53

Hughes and Tanner tried to interrogate Billy, but Dent clammed up, breaking his silence only to mock or insult them. A couple of deputies were staking out positions in the room, marking off the pool of vomit—now more resembling a multicolored scab on the carpet—as well as the spot where Billy Dent still lay on his stomach. A real crime-scene team would be taking more time, called in from the county, according to Tanner.

"We make do with what we've got," the sheriff said without so much as a note of apology in his voice.

They were scrutinizing what had once been Doug Weathers's laptop, its lid propped open where it rested on the desk. A Web map was on the screen, showing driving directions to a spot outside Lobo's Nod.

"I know this place," Tanner mused. "Just an old house there. The Dawes place. Been abandoned for more'n twenty years."

"And they just let it sit there?" Hughes blurted before

reminding himself of all the outmoded, outdated, discarded, and deserted warehouses, bakeries, restaurants, and storefronts in the Seven-Six back home.

"Problem is," Tanner said, "is this a clue left behind by Weathers? By Jasper? Or..." He cast a look over his shoulder at Billy Dent.

Hughes caught on. If Billy wanted them to go to this Dawes place, then that couldn't mean anything good. Booby traps, maybe. Who knew what else?

And if the kid was the one who'd left the clue...What did *that* mean? Billy hadn't been willing to talk, but so far the best possible assumption—the only reasonable inference to make—was that Jasper Dent had, like Tanner and Hughes, followed the audio file hint to Weathers's apartment, where he'd confronted his pops and put a knife in his back. And then...what?

More importantly: Had Jasper intended to kill Billy with that knife blow and botched the job? The precision of the strike made Hughes think not, but there was no way to know for sure. Just as there was no way to know if he'd stabbed his old man in the heat of passion, in self-defense, or in cold blood.

Given Billy's nature, Hughes leaned toward self-defense, but he didn't *know*. It was almost equally likely that the kid had become the father, the acorn grown into an oak, and that they were now in pursuit of not a scared, desperate teen, but a crazed serial killer aborning.

"What's the call, Sheriff? I bet we could get the FBI in here in no time flat."

"No time for it. If Jasper's hurt, we need to move."

"And what if Jasper's the bad guy now?"

To his credit, Tanner didn't protest the idea, though Hughes knew it was anathema to him. "Then it's even more important we move fast." He clicked his shoulder mic. "Lana, this here's G. William. Get those county boys here ASAP, okay, sweetheart? And note that Detective Hughes and I're headed out to the old Dawes place for a look-see."

"Are you psychic or something, Sheriff?" Lana's voice came back startled.

"What do you mean?"

"I was just about to alert you that a call just came in through nine-one-one on the Dawes place. Shots fired."

CHAPTER 54

Jazz stole up the stairs. He braced himself against the railing and the opposing wall, ready for a stair to collapse, whether through age or perfidy.

She wouldn't do that. She wouldn't booby-trap the stairs and kill me. She's my mother.

You're next.

A moment of adrenaline and rage. Of shock and of grief.

Could he talk her back from the ledge of madness? How far gone was she?

He climbed two more steps, probing them each with one foot before mounting them.

You're next.

He'd fallen for Billy's last, desperate act of psychological sabotage: believing that his mother was complicit in his father's horrors.

What had happened to him as a child was beyond monstrous. A part of him knew that he would never truly be able to process the new information, no matter how long he lived. The revelations had made him physically ill, but the truth had done more than prompt up his dinner. It had speared his heart. But—he reminded himself—it had happened to *her*, too. Two victims with one moment of horror, mother and son both damaged together. And that had been Billy's masterstroke. With one depredation, with a single act of depraved sexuality, he had psychically crippled mother and son, the first kneading in the sculptures his diseased mind directed him to mold.

She was as damaged as Jazz was. By the same hand.

Two more steps. Steeped in darkness now. He paused to let his eyes adjust. The murk ahead of him resolved into gray-and-black patterns, swimming in the air.

Depending on how brainwashed Mom was, would she be relieved that Billy wasn't dead? Terrified? Enraged at his paralysis?

He would have to play this carefully. As carefully as his step off the staircase and onto the second-floor landing. It was almost perfectly dark, and then a light snapped on to his right, blinding him. He shielded his eyes with his hand, adjusting. A hallway extended in that direction, an open door at the end. Purling light beckoned him. He walked toward it.

By the time he reached the threshold, his eyes had become accustomed to the light. He paused at the door, then walked in and said hello to his mother.

🐾

The room was surprisingly clean and well kept. Sparse and spare, it had bare, whitewashed walls; peeling hardwood floors; and a single bulb hanging from the ceiling. There were two armchairs, both worn but intact, and a double bed against one wall.

His mother sat in one of the armchairs in the middle of the room, facing him.

"Jasper," she said softly, and her eyes smiled as she bit a knuckle in emotion. "It's been so long."

She was shorter than he remembered. Of course. She'd been a giant to him as a child, but unlike most children, he'd never had the experience of growing up near her, around her, over her. Of that moment Howie's mother had once described, of realizing a child could look her in the eye.

She wore sleek black boots and leggings under a short blue dress. Her hair was long, light brown with scatterings of gray. She was, as the Impressionist promised and as he remembered, beautiful, and his heart lurched at thinking of her that way, at the memory of what his father had compelled him to do with her and to her. His senses told him she was beautiful, his filial devotion told him to be proud of her beauty, and his gut told him never to look at her again.

"Mom." He choked. Ten feet separated them. They'd suffered a distance of a thousand miles and nine years, with the barricade of Billy between them, but these last ten feet seemed insurmountable. They were a marathon and he was exhausted.

"You've grown so much," she whispered.

Neither of them could move.

"You saw my play." It was, bizarrely, the only thing he could think to say.

"Yes. You were very good. I was very proud of you."

He flushed. Parental praise, for something not involving excising clues from a crime scene or memorizing pressure points on the human body? Something new.

"I guess we need to talk," he said slowly. He would need to approach this with great caution. Something deep and primal roared for him to run to her, to embrace her, but he didn't trust it. Didn't trust himself or her reaction, for that matter.

She pursed her lips and nodded. "What would you like to talk about?"

People are real. People matter. Remember Bobby Joe Long.

Bobby Joe Long had released Lisa McVey, even though he knew that doing so would lead to his capture. He'd been unable to stop himself from doing it, compelled by the same dark urges that led him to kill ten previous women.

Maybe that was the way in. The urge to save.

"I want to talk about Connie," he said.

She seemed surprised and even a little annoyed, but she steepled her fingers and nodded. "Well, all right. If that's what you want...."

"I remembered the lockbox in the backyard. I'd buried it years ago, before I left. Things I wanted to be sure were safe. I knew your father would erase me from your life when I left, and I wanted memories there. And when Connie got involved, I just knew that I had to play a game with her, too. So I led

417

her to the lockbox. I'd inscribed it with a bell before I left. For my other name, you understand." She shrugged. "There was that paper company, Ness, right across from where your father and I were hiding out in Brooklyn. It just seemed too tempting, too much fun, to play with her. I bought a toy gun, and the rest was easy. Led her right to us."

"Well, okay, but I sort of had that part figured out." He licked his lips. "I want to talk about what happened when she got to you. When you were locked up together."

She stared at him blankly. "I don't understand."

"You were both Billy's prisoners. You helped her escape."

"I was no one's prisoner."

Denial ain't just a river in Egypt, Howie quipped, and Jazz was inordinately pleased to hear his best friend's voice.

"You were in handcuffs. Chained to a bed."

She continued staring, and then suddenly the light dawned and she threw back her head and laughed, deep and throaty. "Oh, I understand! You *believed* that! Just like she did. I put those handcuffs on *myself*. There was a key tucked under the mattress. The whole thing was a setup. I wanted her to trust me, so that I could learn from her, and the deepest bonds of trust form between those who've suffered similar traumas. I never in a million years thought she would actually *escape*. Believe me, it was a long, quiet drive out of New York after that happened."

"But—"

She shook her head and tut-tutted as though he were a toddler unable to figure out potty training. "Oh, Jasper, we could have killed that silly little bitch anytime we wanted. I was just playing with her. Now that you and I are together, we'll be sure to go get her before we leave the Nod. If you're feeling particularly sentimental, you can take a piece of her with you, but really, don't you think it's time you moved on past this childish, adolescent…jungle fever of yours? Mommy's back, after all. You don't need her when you have me."

Swallowing hard, he pressed on. "Billy isn't a factor anymore. You need to understand that." The final stroke: "You're free now."

She tilted her head and regarded him with an amused smile at play on her lips. "Jasper, what on *earth* are you talking about? Who do you think taught your father everything he knows?"

CHAPTER 55

"The plan was to kill you," she said airily.

"What?" Jazz's lips had gone numb, and he could barely understand himself through the thickness of his own tongue.

His mother made a vaguely maternal groan. "Oh, Jasper. Jasper. Tell me something. Tell Mommy: What is it like to go looking for your soul, only to learn you never had one to begin with?"

Jazz's lips and tongue stubbornly refused to function.

"Did you think Momma was a prospect?" she went on. "Did you think you had a fifty-fifty chance? No, son. You were blessed to be like us from birth. The two greatest killers the world will ever see, united in you.

"But from the first, we planned to birth you, take you home. Then see how long you could survive, neglected. Play with you. Not the way one normally plays with a baby, you understand. The way a Crow plays. That's why we left Billy's name off the birth certificate. He was becoming quite prolific at that point, really just beginning his serial killer career. If the police ever tracked the dead infant back to me, I would be just another postpartum depression mommy to a sympathetic jury. Your father could plausibly deny ever even knowing there'd been a child." She arched an eyebrow. "When Connie"—she spat the name with contempt—"asked about the birth certificate, I had to bite my tongue to keep from laughing. She thought it redeemed you. Thought it meant you weren't your father's son."

"I never thought that," Jazz whispered. "Anyone who thought that was dreaming. I look like him. I sound like him. I'm Billy's son."

"You are. And mine."

"I know who I am and what I am."

"Do you?" She sat up straight, her eyes flashing at him. "Do you really? Because you keep talking like a prospect, Jasper. You sound like one of *them*. Like the men I noticed as a child. The ones who leered and stared at me. From the time I was thirteen on. And it didn't frighten me or even disgust me. It amused me, Jasper. The way all their civility and sociability and intelligence just sluiced away like sand under a hose. My cleavage made them idiots. My legs turned them into morons. I realized then that men did not matter. That they were pathetic, subhuman creatures.

"And that made women even worse. Because everywhere I looked, women painted themselves, dressed themselves, put holes in their flesh to dangle jewelry, all to attract one of these pitiful, abjectly infantile male beasts that could barely control their own urges.

"My own father noticed. My changing body. Stared. Became foolish and stupid until the day I finally killed him."

Her eyes shined as she rhapsodized. "But then I met your daddy. And he was the first real man I ever met. And that changed everything. Billy had only killed a couple before his own father died. But then we met. I knew about the Crows already, but they wouldn't take me. Not a woman on her own. But with your father at my side, with him under my tutelage, we became..." She laughed. "We were the power couple of the serial killer world! Beyoncé and Jay Z! Brad and Angelina! Your grandfather's death was the sign to Billy that it was time to take his calling seriously, that his real life would now begin. And, Jasper, he was more glorious than my wildest fantasies. An imagination more fecund than any I'd ever encountered. Endlessly inventive, endlessly depraved, endlessly wicked. Perfect in every way."

Jazz leaned against the doorjamb for support. His legs quivered and his stomach, though vomit empty, filled with dread.

"This can't be happening," he said, though the denial sounded weak and thready even to his own ears.

"Of course it can. It's already happened." She tapped a long-nailed finger against her chin absently, the same tic he'd seen in Billy. "I wanted the ultimate pleasure, though. Craved it." Her eyes sparkled. "Infanticide. I let myself become pregnant without telling Billy, and then when it was too late, told him. We began planning your death immediately.

"But then your father held you in his arms. And he went

weak, the way men do. Suddenly it was, 'This is my boy. This is my son.' And he became obsessed with the idea of living on through you. So the plans changed. We had so many ways to go. So many options. It was dizzying. We used to sit up nights, watching you sleep in your crib, and talk ourselves drunk with all the possibilities of you. And then we decided. We made up our minds. We would bond you to me. We would isolate you from your father and bond you to me. And the plan was for us to be lovers, and then one day for you to discover your father with me, in bed. Your rival for maternal affection. The Freudian primal scene. Who knows what that would have done to your fragile little brain? I bet it would have been exciting, though.

"But reality intervened. Momma had to go away. The plan changed. And now here we are," she said. "You and I, together again. You're a man now, and it is time for you to fulfill your father's dreams on his behalf. The decks are almost cleared. Once your 'girlfriend' is dealt with, we'll be free."

Decks. Decks almost cleared.

"You killed Gramma." It burned into him like a laser. She hadn't died of natural causes. Ugly J had claimed another victim. He gripped the doorjamb, trying to steady himself, but his legs wouldn't hold out much longer. He retreated from the emotion, locked it away. He was good at that, he thought. He'd been doing it his whole life, retreating from the messy world of feelings to a clean, clinical, antiseptic realm of logic, of facts and details. But now his entire body was shutting down, his mental and emotional denial throwing circuit breakers everywhere. It happened sometimes—psychological shock could traumatize the brain enough to cause unconsciousness. In extreme cases, even heart attack or death.

"Well, yes. It was long past time. Mom had lived a long, full life. You can't tell me you actually miss her. Me, I despised that woman. She hated me from the get-go, from the very moment I came into her house. She thought I was a bad influence on your father. Far from the truth. I liberated him. I did what a good wife is supposed to do, Jasper: I *helped* him. I pushed him to realize his potential. Truly, he should have been the Crow King, not I." She sighed with real regret, the most substantial emotion Jazz had witnessed thus far. "Billy didn't want me to kill her, but I convinced him it would push you along the right path."

Jazz gripped the doorjamb tighter. Then tighter. His fingers cried in pain, but he ignored it. The pain clarified. Gave him strength.

His parents weren't perfect. They'd made a mistake.

Two of them, in fact.

First, the birth certificate. It taught him what didn't matter. That it didn't matter who his biological father was—*I am what I am, regardless. I haven't killed anyone yet and don't even want to. Could I? Sure. Would it be easy? Sure. I even told Connie that once. And it might not even bother me later. But I don't want to. That's their sickness. Mine is that I can imagine it and see it.*

The second mistake was killing Gramma. He'd laughed at the news of her death, but not out of joy or glee. He'd laughed at the notion that she'd been taken away, that the person he'd

424

focused his murderous thoughts on for four years was now gone. He had no target. And that, too, set him free. Free to no longer have to resist killing her, free to realize—now that he couldn't kill her—that he never would have.

Because she was still his blood kin. And as crazy as she was, as spiteful and as mad, she had never, to the best of his knowledge, harmed another human being. Which was more than he could say for his mother or his father. Or even himself. When her Alzheimer's took a turn toward the childlike, she became exasperating and verbally abusive, but also sweet, kind, and funny.

Killing Gramma was *wrong*. It outraged him, and the outrage gave him strength, stiffened his legs, flushed the guilt and shame and pain from his stomach. He pushed off from the doorjamb and stood straight and confident.

My mother killed my grandmother, and that was wrong. It's as simple as that.

I'm human.

She said, "What happened between us was—"

"I didn't want this!" he screamed. "Don't you understand? I didn't ask for this! I just wanted a life!" He didn't even know what he meant by *this*. So many were the depredations piled up in his past that such a small word was too tiny to contain them. From nowhere, tears arose, and he resisted them. He'd made it this far. He could make it through to the end. Whatever that was.

"I'm becoming bored, Jasper," Mom said. "The only question remaining is this: Will you take your father's place, or will you be just another prospect?"

He'd been expecting that question, though he'd thought it would come from Billy or Sam. Not from his mother.

He knew the answer. He'd known for a while maybe, deep down, but certainly since the moment Howie had told him Gramma was dead. At that time, with that news, he'd known instantly who he was. What he was.

"I won't kill for you," he told her.

"Oh."

And then his mother produced a pistol from next to her hip and shot him.

CHAPTER 56

I have to stop getting shot, Jazz thought deliriously.

And collapsed forward, dropping into the room on his hands and knees. He couldn't breathe. His chest was on fire and his mind raced, thoughts flicking by on fast-forward. Not his life flashing before his eyes—not entirely—but random snatches and snippets, intercut with pain and panic. He couldn't catch his breath

—Connie flickered before him—

or focus his vision, gone blurry

—his mother stood from the chair—

The world flooded with black, then red, then glimmered with sparkles before resolving again. Hardwood under his hands. No air in his lungs.

This wasn't like being shot in Brooklyn. This wasn't in his leg. He'd been shot in the chest at point-blank range, and he was dying. His heart jerked and pumped in staccato fits, and his lungs had lost the ignition key.

His mother took her time pacing the few feet between

them, the pistol held casually at her side. He could see her only from midthigh down, lacking the strength to lift his head.

"Killing your daddy and making love to your mommy," she cooed. "We should have named you Oedipus, not Jasper." She crouched down before him and gazed into his eyes. Her brow furrowed. "At least then your pathetic little girlfriend wouldn't call you by that ridiculous nickname. 'Jazz.' I named you!" she ranted. "I gave you your name, your identity. I took your virginity, and I made you mine. Who the hell is she to have a claim on you, Jasper? She's nothing. Nothing!"

He put his head down and gasped, hitching half a breath into his lungs. It felt sweet and bitter at once. He slumped down onto his elbows. *Get the head closer to the floor. Easier for blood to get there. Stay alive. Oh, God, who am I kidding? She's right there with the gun. I can't move. It's over.*

"You are *mine*," she said. "And I am yours. I am for you; she isn't. You signed your work, Jasper. You proved your love."

Her dress rippled into view, dropping away and pooling at her feet as she stood up again. He craned his neck, beholding her in her leggings and bra, glaring down at him.

Her upper arms and torso were a map of scars and puckered, healed wounds.

—like cutting chicken—

—knife in the sink and a hand touches the knife and the hand is his—

428

"Couldn't wear sleeveless blouses or dresses," she said. "Not after you practiced on me."

He groaned and forced air into his lungs. Rested his cheek on the floor and wormed one hand to his chest to feel how bad the shot was.

She'll put a bullet in your head. Doesn't matter. Give up. Probably blood in the lungs already. Dead already. Too dumb to know it.

"You could have been a god with us, Jasper. Could have ruled the Crows and seen us to the glory of a world where we hunt without penalty or fear." She crouched down again, her scars—his scars, his trophies—glimmering in the light. "We have a senator. He's only done three, but that's enough. For now. A man of uncommon needs and uncommon restraint. He'll be president some day, and then...Oh, then things will change, Jasper!

"For a time, we thought of being the police. But we realized: Why be the cops when we can be the ones holding the cops' leash? Politics is such a fine old job for crafty, sociable folks such as us."

He probed his chest, surprised to find that he was breathing much better now. Shallow breaths, but they were coming one after the other, each one a little longer. His heart was still a frog in boiling water, but the fact that it worked at all was a miracle.

His fingers circled the bullet hole in Hughes's overcoat. He hissed in pain at the pressure.

His mother leaned over to whisper in his ear. "And you were to have been the vanguard of that. But now you will die here, in this place, at this time. For your lack of vision. For your pitiable devotion to those who are prospects. Realize, Jasper, that your rebellion has solved nothing, protected no one. Rest assured I will see to the bleeding boy and Connie and the sheriff before I leave. You rescued no one. What do you have to say to that? What do you have to say before you die?"

Jazz muttered something.

"Speak up, son," she said, amused, sounding almost exactly like Billy in that moment.

"I said," he managed, "you shouldn't carry such a girl's gun. Small caliber."

And before she could react, he thrust out his hand, grabbing her ankle and spilling her to the floor on her back.

His heart was fine. His lungs were fine. He was breathing and pumping and alive.

All because his mother was an excellent shot. She'd aimed and hit exactly where a bullet should have at least nicked his aorta.

The precise spot where he'd pinned Hughes's badge earlier.

Another word for *badge* is *shield*.

CHAPTER 57

The pain in his chest was real. He was bruised inside and out, and at least two ribs were cracked.

But he was alive. He wouldn't die. Not yet. Not now.

With an animal growl, he pounced atop her, pinning her right wrist, the gun pointed away. Her finger spasmed and two shots went awry. He leaned hard on her wrist, pounding it until the gun slipped from her nerveless fingers.

As he reached for it, she raked his face with her left hand, nearly clawing out his right eye. Ribbons of pain and blood unspooled from his temple down to his jawline, and he reflexively hauled back, forgetting the gun for a moment. His mother hissed and scratched out again, catching his neck, gouging him there. He straddled her, pinning her down, sitting on her bare stomach, and planted his knee on that free, clawing arm. Then he laid his arm across her, pinning the other arm, and stretched out for the gun. She raised her head and snapped at him with her teeth. The gun was almost in reach. Small caliber, yeah, but he would be shooting her right in the eye. No doubt about what the bullet would do to her.

He flashed momentarily to Morales in the storage unit, as Hat's bullet crashed into her skull. The way her eye had filled with blood.

And his mother heaved, arching her back, throwing him off-balance. His fingers connected with the gun, just enough to send it spinning away from him. It ricocheted off a wall and bounced even farther away.

Jazz elbowed her in the face, then punched her. His ribs grated and kept him from putting his full force behind either blow, but she went still for a moment.

Panicked, he crawled off her and lunged for the gun. It was too far, and his ribs flashed twin bolts at him as he moved. He stopped to catch his breath, and his mother was on him, digging her nails into his shoulders. Before he could react, she sank her teeth into his neck, unspooling fresh threads of shock and blood. He jerked before she could fasten onto him and rip out his carotid, rolling over, throwing her off and onto her back again. Blood ran down his neck.

She stretched out, supine, reaching for the gun, one arm flung out over her head. Jazz fought through the pain and lurched forward, collapsing on top of her. It was enough to stop her from inching closer to the gun. He allowed himself two counts to catch his breath and then put his hands around her throat. Tightened them.

She swatted at him, but he ignored her blows. Let her claw him wide open. Let her shred his flesh. He would not let go of her throat. Not for anything.

Her eyes lit with something known but unfamiliar. She dropped her hands to her sides and then she thrust her hips, grinding against him. Desperate tactic or was she actually into this? He didn't know. Didn't care. The hell with her. And her games. This was how they'd started and this was how they'd end. If they died together, so much the better. She heaved and bucked and she would be dead soon and maybe Billy was right: Maybe it padded behind you like a big cat and maybe that cat was growling and maybe it would pounce on him with her death.

It wasn't until she pulled the knife out of his side that Jazz realized he'd been stabbed. So sharp. So clean going in. Burning eruption of lava blood coming out. Her pelvic thrusts had been so that she could work her hand under her body and have access to a blade.

He gurgled, his side aflame. It was a small blade, but he felt it go in again, this time up to the hilt. She was stabbing blindly, in a panic, and he yearned to keep strangling her, but his self-preservation instinct took over, and he rolled off her. But not before a third knifing.

Coughing and grunting, his mother turned onto her side, facing away from him. Jazz lay on the floor, panting, hands to his flank, trying to stanch the blood. She got up on hands and knees, wheezing, barely able to move. She'd dropped the knife, and she was crawling like an invalid, making her way to the gun.

Jazz kept one hand on his side, rotated on his hip, and reached out, snagging her ankle. She kicked at him but lost her balance and fell over. Jazz caught his breath and pulled her toward him. She wailed with a voice like an asthmatic and thrashed against him.

He used his other hand. It was slick and coated with blood. He grabbed her free ankle and pulled, feeling more blood spurt from his side.

With a burst of energy that he could never have imagined possessing, he managed to come parallel to her. With his hands clapped to her shoulders, he rolled them both over until he was on his back and she lay atop him on her back. They both gasped for breath, their bodies hot, their lungs racing to keep up.

He'd thought before that he didn't want to kill. That had been ten thousand years ago, when he'd been another person. Right now, he didn't care about himself or his own life. He didn't even care about Connie or Howie. He cared about only one thing.

Killing his mother.

It's all about geometry.

He wrapped his arm around her throat. He squeezed, and it was the finest feeling he'd ever experienced in his life.

CHAPTER 58

This time, Hughes didn't so much mind Tanner's driving. Maybe he'd gotten used to barreling through the streets of Lobo's Nod, but more likely it was just that he was aware of how close they were to ending all this. The twenty-plus career of Billy Dent was over. The Hat-Dog Killer was over. And now it was time for the coda to the whole blood-soaked mess.

Outside the town limits, Tanner slowed the cruiser. As he turned onto a dirt-and-gravel drive, he cut the headlights, and they crept along until another car and a house hove into view. The house was dark, save for a slight chink of light escaping through a gap in the boards covering a second-floor window.

Before they'd left Weathers's apartment, Tanner had ordered the deputies to join them at the Dawes house once the county boys arrived to spell them, but the radio remained silent.

"Backup?" Hughes asked, hoping to get the answer he wanted.

"No time to wait," said Tanner. The sheriff did not disappoint.

In the trunk of the cruiser, Tanner had two bulletproof vests. "We do it right this time," he said with an air of gruff self-recrimination. They vested up, and Tanner also plucked from the trunk what was not the world's largest shotgun but was certainly its meanest.

Seeing the look of astonishment on Hughes's face, Tanner shrugged. "Got a fine Nitro in there. Sixty cal. Want it?"

Hughes shook his head at the offered hand cannon. Rednecks and their guns. He was more comfortable with his service weapon. He knew it well.

Weapons out, safeties off, they made their way up the porch. They didn't bother knocking. It was unlocked, and Hughes nudged it open. Tanner followed him through the door into an empty vestibule, covering a staircase with that damn elephant gun as Hughes scanned a barely lit hallway dead ahead.

They exchanged a look. Up or stay here?

A *thump* from upstairs, followed by another, then another, settled it for them. Though his legs urged him to race up the stairs like he was late for the subway transfer, Hughes forced himself to take it one stair at a time, following Tanner. He winced with each creak.

On the second floor, they hung a right toward a light. Tanner led the way; Hughes walked backward, his weapon poised, ready for the ambush from behind.

Then he bumped into Tanner, who'd stopped dead in his tracks. Hughes spun around. The sheriff blocked the door into the room ahead, frozen, saying nothing.

Hughes pushed him to one side just enough to squeeze by. When he stepped into the room, he, too, froze in place.

The floor was a map of blood—spatters, footprints, drag marks. In the middle of the room lay Jasper Dent. Atop him was a woman Hughes recognized from the sketch of the woman Deputy Erickson had seen, the woman who'd killed Clara Dent.

Jasper Dent's own mother. And from the look of it, Jasper was strangling the life out of her.

They were both covered in blood. Jasper's eyes were nearly dead, but he had the look of a man possessed. The mother was half-naked, her expression slack, her tongue lolling from her mouth.

The kid's strength flagged, and he relaxed his grip. The mother gasped, a pathetic hitch, and then Jasper tightened his grip again and she choked and went silent. An instant later, Jasper lost his power again, releasing her for a moment before reapplying his dying muscles to her throat once more.

Hughes's first impulse was to raise his weapon to his own temple and blow his brains out because God oh God oh sweet fucking Jesus Christ, he did *not* want to live in this world.

Years later, he would still wonder: *Would I have done it? Would I have ended myself right then and there if Tanner hadn't done what he did?* And even years later, no answers were forthcoming.

But Tanner *did* do what he did next, which was to shove

Hughes to one side and shout, "Jasper!" at the top of his lungs. When that obviously wasn't going to work, Tanner fired the shotgun at the ceiling. The roar deafened Hughes in the confined space of the room. The overhead bulb swung back and forth, casting the room in a hellscape of churning shadows. The blood on the floor seemed to dance.

Dent lost his grip again. Tanner lumbered forward, and Hughes snapped out of it, rushing to help. He pulled Jasper back as Tanner dragged the mother off her son. As soon as Jasper came free from under her, Hughes noticed a gush of blood from Jasper's side. Kidney hit? He couldn't tell.

"We got a problem," he said, and looked up. Tanner loomed over the mother, who appeared deader than an actual doornail.

"We got two," Tanner said, and was screaming into his shoulder mic for an ambulance before Hughes could respond.

Dent mumbled something. Hughes leaned down to hear.

"...sorry..." the kid said.

Hughes flashed back to the last time Jasper Dent had apologized to him, but this time the kid was clearly in no position to attack.

"I couldn't do it," Jasper groaned. "I couldn't kill them."

"Shh. Ambulance is coming." He glanced up at Tanner, who had started CPR on the mother. "Talk later."

"Couldn't do it," Jasper said, and started weeping. It was an awful sight, the tears streaking the mask of blood on his face. "I'm so sorry. I couldn't. I'm sorry." It tumbled out of him, over and over, a soul-curdling mantra of regret for mercy. Hughes couldn't get him to stop, no matter what he

did, so he rested Dent's head on his knee and held his hand
and listened to him as the first siren sounded in the distance.

Hughes waited with Tanner outside as the EMTs rushed in
and out of the Dawes house. Even outside, he could hear
them shouting at one another, running up and down the
stairs. After a few minutes, they brought out Jasper on a
stretcher. The kid wasn't moving, but an EMT had an oxygen
mask over him and they were racing.

A moment later, they wheeled out Janice Dent. Hughes
caught the eye of one of the EMTs, who simply shook his
head.

The ambulances took off down the dirt driveway, hauling
ass, sirens alive and screeching. Tanner said nothing for a
while. Neither did Hughes.

"You don't have to stick around," the sheriff said at last.
"I'll stay with crime scene. I can get someone to give you a
lift to your hotel."

"I'll stay," Hughes said. His body was still on an epineph-
rine high, and he couldn't imagine being cooped up in a hotel
room right now. He could taste the adrenaline, flooding his
mouth like hot steel.

"Was dark in there," Tanner said after a spell of silence.
"Not quite sure what I saw."

"Yeah." Hughes cleared his throat and craned his neck,
gazing up at the night sky. Damn. He'd never realized how
many stars were up there. He had to get out of the city more

often. "I'll tell you what I saw. I saw that kid defending himself."

"That's what it looked like to me, too." They didn't look at each other. Didn't share a conspiratorial wink. Hughes wondered if the bright flashing thing in the sky was really a star or just a plane. Didn't matter. From down here, it was beautiful.

"You know the ironic thing?" Tanner asked.

"What's that?"

"Best I can tell, Jazz was her only living blood relative. So he'll be the one…"

Tanner drifted off; Hughes got the point.

"Well, hell. It's a funny world, isn't it, Sheriff?"

"Funny like a heart attack."

CHAPTER 59

Jazz opened his eyes.

The world was a dirty windshield.

He left it again.

He woke up again.

A hand held his. Cool and familiar.

He sank back into sleep.

Again.

He thought he caught a flash of Connie's hand.

And a wheelchair.

I did that to her. It's my fault.

He passed out again.

This time, they placed a guard inside his hospital room. He recognized the deputy's uniform, so he was still in the Nod. He didn't know the deputy, though. They didn't want him playing on someone's sympathy.

And just in case, they'd handcuffed him to the bed again.

If he'd thought anyone would believe him, Jazz would have told them that the guard and the cuffs were both over-kill. Sure, he could pick the handcuff lock, but he wouldn't be going anywhere in the near future. His leg actually hurt less than the rest of his body. Between the broken ribs from the bullet, the blood loss, and the multiple stab wounds, he couldn't sit up, much less get out of bed.

He had a lot of time. To think.

It happened.

That was first. He had to start there. Had to acknowledge it.

He rolled it around in his mind for impossibly long minutes. He tasted it.

Everything happened and everything was true. Even the lies were true.

It all happened. It wasn't a dream.

And I'm still alive.

I guess that's something.

Howie was the first to visit him. He'd thought it might be the cops, but it wasn't.

Howie loped into the room as if he did this every day. His face and forehead looked much improved from the last time Jazz had seen him, the scar barely visible. Jazz wondered how long he'd been unconscious.

With a derisive snort and a glare at the deputy, Howie hauled a chair bedside and plopped into it. "I was going to bake you a cake with a hacksaw inside it," he said without preamble, "but—"

"But you realized it wouldn't work."

"Well, no. I realized I don't know how to bake."

Laughing hurt like hell, but Jazz tried to enjoy the pain. Pain meant life. Pain was better than the alternative.

"A man's got to know his limitations," he told Howie.

Howie's head bobbled like a doll's. "True dat, dawg. I'm just so freakin' glad that your aunt turned out not to be a serial killer. That would have said things about my psyche that I'm not ready to explore yet. I'm waiting until I'm on my own health insurance to go into therapy—my parentals have paid out enough, you know?"

Sam. If he'd had the energy, Jazz would have felt guilty for assuming she was Ugly J. "Where is she?" That she'd been cleared as a killer only made it more likely she was a victim.

Howie shrugged and handed over a torn-open envelope that said *JAZZ* on the front. He fumbled out a sheet of paper, unfolded it, and read.

Jazz—

I am so sorry to do this. You can't imagine how sorry. But I have to leave. I can't take it here. I thought that maybe I could help Mom and connect with you and a part of me wants that, but I can't do it. I'm leaving in the morning. Please don't look for me. Please don't come after me. I left the Nod to get away from the Dent crazy, and it reached out and pulled me back.

And then, in a different color ink, clearly scrawled in haste:

So sorry.

Sam

"The, uh, the cops figure she started the letter—"

"And then finished it the night you and Gramma went to the hospital." He could see it, if he tried. Sam, struggling with the decision, starting the letter in order to work out her thoughts and feelings. Figuring she could always finish it when she couldn't stand any more.

And then Howie busts in with a shotgun. Gramma collapses, Sam reacts, Howie's bleeding on the floor....Sam panics. She calls 911, and she realizes she can't handle it. Can't stick around for the aftermath. Can't get sucked back in. So she scribbles a sorry and she leaves town.

Jazz had a hard time being angry with her.

He beckoned Howie closer and, checking to make sure the deputy couldn't hear, whispered, "You still have the book, right?"

Howie made a great show of glowering at the deputy, who didn't even notice. "Yep."

"Where did you hide it?"

"I sort of forgot to. It's sitting on my desk at home."

"Howie!"

"Chillax. No one knows what it is. They can't be looking for something they don't know about."

Jazz supposed that was true.

"So what was your plan? Kill Billy, then get the book, decipher it, and start hunting down Crows?"

"Something like that." I HUNT KILLERS was still emblazoned on his chest, after all.

"Maybe we leave that to the cops, hmm?"

"Sounds good to me." Jazz grabbed Howie's hand. "Thanks, man. For having my back."

"Always."

Connie was there later, when he woke from another impromptu nap. Or maybe he'd slept for days. He rubbed his beard stubble, but he'd never grown it out before, so he didn't know how long it accounted for.

When she rolled herself into the room, he began weeping uncontrollably. She had a cast on her leg, which jutted out before her, and her face was puffy and mottled with bruises and swelling, her scalp covered in butterfly stitches, bandages, and gauze. She rolled to his bedside in her wheelchair and took his hand—cool, slim, *the* hand—and his shame turned his head away from her.

"Jazz, look at me."

He couldn't. She was in pain, she was *damaged* because of him. Because of his quest for redemption, his ego, his self-absorption. How could he look at her?

She raised his hand and kissed it, softly. At her touch, a fresh wave of tears broke out. "I'm so sorry," he sobbed. "I'm sorry."

She held his hand and stroked his arm and sat quietly until the tears could come no more. With a gentle hand, she touched his temple, his ruined cheek, fluttering nimbly around the stitches.

"We're a matching pair," she said.

He laughed again, the pain proving the life. He finally turned to face her, and she was as beautiful as ever. They *were* a matching pair. The world saw a black girl and a white boy, but he knew the truth. Connie was the other half of him.

" 'If you go—if you kill him—we're over,' " he quoted.

"I changed my mind," she said, and leaned over to kiss him. He didn't have much range and she couldn't lean very far, but it was still the sweetest kiss he'd ever had.

"You lied to me," he said.

"No, I changed my mind," she said with some sass. "There's a difference."

"Not then. Last year. During the Impressionist case. We were at the Hideout, and you told me that when you came to the Nod, you knew who I was, but you fell in love with me, anyway." He paused, gathering his strength. Talking for a long stretch hurt his cheeks, his neck, his chest. Pretty much everything. "But you didn't know who I was until you looked me up online after our first date. I forgot all about that until recently."

She shrugged. "Okay, you caught me. But you were in a pretty bad place last year, and it was what you needed."

"Feel free to lie whenever I need it."

"Deal."

"I think that's when I realized I'd fallen in love with you," he said soberly. "But I get it if you—"

"Don't even finish that sentence."

"Don't you wonder, though? It was bad enough when I had Billy weighing on me. But with both parents...How could I possibly—"

"Howie and I talked about that. When we realized your mom was Ugly J, we thought the same thing."

"It's okay; I don't blame you."

"I wasn't asking for forgiveness. We thought it, too. Of course. But you know what? First of all, not everything is passed down. Not everything is genetic."

"But I grew up in—"

"And second of all." She tightened her grip on his hand to silence him. "Second of all, you didn't just have Billy in your life. You had the whole world. TV and movies. Books. Other kids. Other families. School. Plenty of examples, plenty of role models. Including the goofiest white boy ever and the foxiest girlfriend on the planet."

He realized he'd spent his life trying to understand Billy. But had never really understood himself.

"A part of you always knew that what you were learning was wrong. And you resisted what they taught you. You're stronger than any person I've ever known."

"What they did to me—"

"Other people have been abused. They had problems. *You* have problems. But they don't all grow up to—"

"I know. I know that. Now." He wished he could sit up, wished he could take her in his arms. "I know what's ahead of me. All the pain and the struggling. The survival. But I know something else, too—I made it this far. I got here. Here and now. And I'm still the same person. They made me, but they don't own me. They don't get to decide who or what I am. Only I get to decide that." His voice had risen and cracked. He forced himself to relax.

"Only I get to decide that," he said again, much more quietly.

"Maybe that's the first step," she said.

"Of a million."

"It's not like you're walking it alone, doofus."

He brought her hand to his cheek, reveling in the sensation of her skin on his.

"I want to tell you something," she whispered. "Something difficult. I don't know how it will make you feel."

He didn't know if he was up to anything new, to any additional input. His brain, his heart, and his soul were all topped off. No more room for good or for bad. But he gave a lopsided shrug, telling her it was okay to continue.

"It's about your grandmother."

"I know she's dead. My—Ugly J killed her."

If Connie noted the stutter, she didn't let on. "Yeah. Okay, so you know that. They think it was a potassium overdose."

That would have sent her into hyperkalemic shock. Similar to lethal injection. Depending on when the doctors saw

her, they wouldn't have even realized—she would have pre-
sented like a heart-attack patient. Jazz hoped it had been
painless.

"They tried to save her. They worked really hard. And
they even resuscitated her for a couple of minutes, but she
was too old and too weak."

"I see."

"When she had those few minutes, she said something,
Jazz." Connie's bottom lip trembled. "Do you want to know
what it was?"

Did he? The better question was, *should he?*

"Go ahead."

"She said, 'He's a good boy.' That's all. 'He's a good boy.'"

Jazz expected tears but thought he had no more to give.
And besides, Gramma wasn't lucid on her best day. On her
deathbed? She could have been talking about Jazz, sure. Or
she could have been talking about Billy, Grampa, or the Eas-
ter Bunny.

She could have been talking about Jazz.

He squeezed Connie's hand. "Thanks for telling me."

❦

How long they spent together, he couldn't say. There was no
clock in the room, and no one counted off the seconds.

They compared scars and bandages, prescriptions and
doctor's orders. They talked about how much school they'd
missed and would continue to miss. They laughed at the
absurdity of Howie lusting for Samantha, then laughed

harder at the idea of it actually happening. They avoided talk of the last week, speaking instead of their shared past and the future.

Eventually, it had to end; the door opened, and Connie's father walked in.

"Sweetheart, it's time," he said.

Connie clutched Jazz's hand even harder. "Not yet." She held on, tight and resolute.

"I'm sorry, but now that he's up, I have to speak to my client."

Nodding with sad defeat, Connie leaned in as best she could and kissed him again. "Soon," she whispered.

He wanted to believe her, but as she wheeled out, he couldn't help thinking it was the last time they would ever be together. If the criminal justice system didn't see to that, then her father would.

Mr. Hall gestured to the deputy. "You, too. Attorney-client."

The deputy left. Jazz felt less safe, cuffed to the bed, at Mr. Hall's mercy.

"A little surprised," Jazz said defensively. "I thought for sure G. William would visit before you."

"You're not talking to any cops at all. You're invoking your Fifth Amendment rights. That deputy they've stationed in here? Only here because you proved yourself so dangerous in New York. I fought like hell against that, and the judge says if you say anything to him at all that he's under strict orders to summon a doctor immediately and have you sedated so that you can't incriminate yourself. That's how serious this all is."

Mr. Hall dragged over the chair Howie had used and sat down. "I want you to understand something," he began. "In New York, I agreed to be your lawyer. That means I'm your lawyer forever. Even if you fire me, I still can't act against you. Do you understand?"

Jazz nodded.

"Good. With that in mind, realize that you'll need a criminal attorney at some point. It's been years since my days in the public defender's office, and that was in Georgia, not here or New York. You'll need people who can act on your behalf in those two jurisdictions, and I'm not that guy. We still clear?"

Jazz nodded again.

"I'm part of your team until you don't want me. I know, go figure. I never imagined myself in this position, defending you. But here I am. And right now, Jasper, I'm your best friend."

"No." Jazz shook his head fiercely, no matter how much it hurt. "Howie's my best friend. Always."

"Howie doesn't have a law degree and a daughter saying, 'Daddy, please help him.'" Mr. Hall took out his phone and thumbed through it. "Now, I've spoken to Howie, in my capacity as your attorney, and he tells me that you found some evidence. Something that implicates your parents and others."

The book. Billy's book.

"Yeah."

"Do you know where it is?"

"Yeah, we—"

Hall held up a hand. "Don't tell me. I don't want to know. You broke the law when you dug up your grandfather, and technically I might have to tell the court where the fruit of that crime lies. Just tell me it's safe."

"It is."

"Good." Mr. Hall sighed. "Jasper, you broke a lot of laws. And not for the first time."

Jazz knew it was true. He couldn't even keep track of all the laws he'd broken, but he was sure someone, somewhere had kept a tally. His day in court would be long.

"But," Mr. Hall went on, "I know that a good trial attorney could get a jury to look at what you've done, to look at your past, and probably get you a pretty decent sentence at the end of the day. Plead you down pretty low, even. You might never have to go to court, under those circumstances."

That was about the best Jazz could hope for. The right jury—lots of mothers—would go easy on him. Still, with the sheer volume of charges against him, even "going easy" would add up.

"But with the evidence you've found…If it's as good as Howie says it is, I'm pretty sure we can trade it for getting a slew of charges dropped or pleaded out. Or maybe some sort of probation."

It took Jazz a moment to process what was being said. He wouldn't get off scot-free, but the idea of keeping his freedom under *any* circumstances…That was more than he'd ever dreamed possible.

"Are you serious?" He half expected Mr. Hall to shout *Psych!* and chortle at Jazz's cluelessness.

"New York is a political disaster right now. The evidence in the Hat-Dog case is severely compromised, and the DA wants the book closed on that. For good. They're willing to give you immunity on the crimes you committed up to Oliver Belsamo's death, in exchange for your testimony."

Jazz pondered. That still left everything he'd done *after* Hat plugged Dog in the face. "What about the rest of the stuff I did in New York? Assaulting the cops? Everything else? And I probably broke some federal laws, too, when I fled across state lines." He swallowed. "My parents."

Mr. Hall spoke slowly. "We have testimony that what... happened to your mom was in self-defense. And as for Billy...Well, the knife that caused his wound was wiped clean when the police checked it. No prints. And Billy isn't talking. There's nothing concrete to implicate you, as long as you keep your damn mouth shut."

Billy must have wiped the knife. Protecting his son to the last. It was so magnanimous and so twisted that Jazz couldn't process it.

"You didn't kill anyone," Mr. Hall went on. "I've seen the crime-scene report of what happened in the storage unit, and it bears out your testimony that Duncan Hershey killed Oliver Belsamo and Agent Morales. They have you stone-cold on a whole passel of misdemeanors and things like breaking and entering, assault, but I bet we can get it all knocked down if you trade that evidence Howie's hiding."

"It seems too easy," Jazz said doubtfully.

Mr. Hall leaned back in the chair, arms crossed over his chest. "It isn't easy. It's damn hard and you know it. That's not what's bothering you."

"You don't know what's bothering me."

"I've been around my share of defendants. I know exactly what's bothering you. You feel guilty. Guilty about what you did and guilty about getting away with it."

Jazz looked away.

"Do you think you deserve punishment, Jasper? Is that it?"

Did he? Was that it? He had done wrong. Much of it in the service of doing right, but did that really matter? He clenched his jaw, which tugged at the sutures in his face, spiking him with a moment of pain.

Pain.

Yes, pain meant life. But the symmetric property did not apply: Life did not mean pain.

"All right," he said, turning back to Mr. Hall. "Let's do it."

"I thought you'd see it my way."

"So, that's New York. What about the feds and the stuff I did here in the Nod?"

"In exchange for your testimony against your father and mother, as well as producing information relevant to multiple unsolved serial killer cases, I can get a lot of that pleaded down to lesser charges. You'll probably end up with probation." Mr. Hall paused. "It's going to be the mother of all probations, don't get me wrong."

"So I flip on the Crows, help the cops and the feds solve some old crimes..."

"Roll up some bad guys out there, resolve some lingering crimes committed by your parents..."

"And I get sent to my room without supper."

"Repeatedly."

"That's the same deal Billy made," Jazz said quietly. "He gives up information, he stays off death row. Like father, like son."

"It's not the same thing," Mr. Hall said with a heat that surprised Jazz. "Your father murdered a great many people. And he made a deal not to die. You didn't murder anyone. At worst, you assaulted people. And I'm not saying that's not serious, but every last one of them is fine and will continue to be fine. You stole some things that can be replaced. You'll get serious probation, but you'll walk. Because at the end of the day, the good you've done has outweighed the bad."

"That's not the way the system works."

"Today it is." Mr. Hall actually cracked a smile. "Because you have a really good lawyer."

Jazz drew in a deep breath that tested the work they'd done to stabilize his ribs. "So, I guess this is the part where you tell me that the price of you helping me out is staying away from your daughter."

Mr. Hall stared at Jazz for a protracted moment that would have been unnerving and uncomfortable for anyone not the son of two Crows.

"I'm going to be brutally honest with you, Jasper. I don't know where to go from here. The law stuff is almost simple compared to this. I don't like my daughter with someone like you, someone who seems magnetized to danger. But even before that, yeah, I never liked my daughter with a white kid."

"I know."

Mr. Hall seemed to be struggling, helpless in the claws of something he couldn't explain. "It's visceral. It's not in my brain, Jasper. It's in my gut. It's history and it's still haunting us and I don't like it."

"I can respect that."

"You can't know what it's like. You don't know what it means to be black in this country, so you can never understand."

They said nothing. Words ran through Jazz's head, but they seemed impossible to form, to say. He couldn't arrange them into anything that made sense.

So he just started talking.

"You're right. I don't know what it's like to be black. And I never will. But here's the thing: Everyone's different, right? And sure, there are common experiences, but everyone sees the world at least a *little* bit differently. Everyone filters it their own way. You know *your* black experience, and you know so much more than I'll ever know, but you can't know everyone's experience. Because if you think people are the same, if you think our experiences are interchangeable, well...that's almost thinking like Billy. We are all individuals. People are real. People matter. Each one of us matters, for our differences as much as for our similarities."

Mr. Hall grunted. Jazz wasn't sure if what he'd said made much sense or if it was even relevant, but he felt better for saying it. He couldn't go through life classifying people. For him, at least, that way lay the madness of Billy Dent.

"I've wondered my whole life what it would take," Mr. Hall mused, "what it would take for us as a people, as a society, to become truly equal. To reconcile the sins of the past."

"I don't think you can reconcile the sins of the past."

"Exactly."

Jazz pondered. "Forgive, maybe. Forget, maybe."

When you forget someone, Connie had told him once, *the forgiveness doesn't mean anything anymore.*

"I can't do either of them," Mr. Hall admitted. "But here's one thing I know for certain. For *certain.* I look at you and I look at Connie, and I see how much she cares for you, and now I see how much you care for her. And I think maybe I was looking at it the wrong way. It's not about us as a people. Or as a society. It's about us as individuals. One white boy and one black girl at a time. And maybe someday we—all of us—don't forgive or forget, but maybe we just get a little better, and you folks get a little more tolerant and maybe I get a little less angry, and maybe we all don't think about it as often. Does that make sense?"

"Makes sense to me. Then again, I grew up with two lunatics in the house."

"You grew up fine, Jasper."

Jazz gritted his teeth. He didn't want Mr. Hall to see his tears, but they came, anyway.

Person to person. Just like Bobby Joe Long, letting Lisa McVey go.

One at a time. One person at a time.

Hall politely said nothing about Jazz's tears. He just held out the box of tissues to him.

"You asked before if this was the part where I tell you that you can't see Connie anymore. No, Jasper," he said. "This is the part where I tell you that..." He paused and shook his head. "Where I tell you that I feel so sorry for you. I just feel so damn sorry for you, son."

There was a quality in Mr. Hall's voice that was unfamiliar to Jazz at first. After a moment, he placed it.

It was fatherly.

For the first time in so long, it soothed him, and he felt himself drifting toward gentle sleep.

"You rest now," Mr. Hall said. "Everything is going to be okay. You deserve it. Rest."

CHAPTER 60

Jazz closed his eyes.

Epilogue

Five Years Later

It was an ugly day. It was an ugly room.

Except for the body.

The book made Jazz rich.

A Murder of Crows: My Life Inside the Serial Killer Conspiracy by Jasper Dent (as told to Ricardo Sloan, Jazz's enthusiastic ghostwriter) debuted at number one on the *New York Times* Nonfiction Best Seller list and stayed there for sixteen weeks. It took eight months for the book to drop out of the top five, and another thirty months before it dropped out of the top ten. At random points in time, it would bubble up onto the list again for no particular reason, stay there for a month or so, then drop off. Until the paperback hit, and then the cycle started all over again.

The over-the-top subtitle had been insisted on by the publisher; Jazz hated it.

Jazz didn't let the money change him. Other than renovating Gramma's house in the Nod, he tried to live the life he'd always craved: quiet and simple. He would—on those occasions when the mood struck him and the case seemed particularly intractable—offer his services to the FBI or some local police agency that seemed stymied by a killing. After all, there were still a lot of Crows out there. The deciphering of Billy's "journal" was a difficult affair, involving language experts, cryptographers, handwriting analysts, and—when all else failed—Jazz himself.

The tattoo across his chest—I HUNT KILLERS—still peered out at him every time he looked in a mirror, and sometimes it was still true.

But most of his time was spent overseeing the house renovation and working on his own pet project: a victims' fund for those left behind by Billy Dent and Ugly J. He had to do it in secret. He didn't want people to think he was buying forgiveness or understanding.

Those two things should not be for sale, at any price.

Howie, who had graduated college by now with a degree in business administration, was helping Jazz set up the fund. They spent big chunks of the day together, inevitably dissolving into idiotic juvenile laughter. It was like being kids again.

Except Connie wasn't there.

Connie was in New York, an understudy in a well-received off-Broadway play. She usually got to go onstage a couple of nights a month, and her reviews had been good so far. She and Jazz spoke almost daily. He missed her, yearned for his other half, but he couldn't take her dream from her. Love could burnish dreams but not substitute for them. She came home to the Nod as often as she could. Jazz visited New York rarely. The city held too many memories for both of them, but only Jazz could cause a minor riot by showing his face anywhere in the five boroughs.

Jazz knew that right now they were on separate paths. This was a good thing. She had seen and suffered too much being at his side. Now she was finally ready to be on her own. Those separate paths would meet again, would intertwine.

He could, of course, manipulate her. Control her. Draw on all those old tricks, those old schemes, so easy and readily available, like the house keys that come out of your pocket almost on their own as you approach the door, without conscious thought.

He had the keys to Connie's mind and soul and heart. They jangled in his pocket every time he thought of her. Twisting up her emotions, making her cleave to him and making her think it had all been her own idea...Bringing her home for good, her dreams forsaken...That would be the easiest thing in the world.

But that's what a sociopath would do.

And Jasper Francis Dent was not a sociopath.

Aunt Samantha had vanished. It would not be difficult to find her—innocent people don't know how to hide—but while Jazz yearned for his only family, he could not bring himself to force himself back into her life. If there could be one Dent living beyond the taint of Butcher Billy and the Crow King, then let that be his aunt. She'd grown up with Billy. And as someone who'd done the same, he decided she deserved her privacy and her anonymity.

Most days—unless something absolutely prevented him or he was out of town—Jazz drove out to the Kettle/Herrara Care Institute, roughly a forty-five minute drive from the Nod. It was the best, most expensive long-term care facility in the state, a Gothic castle–looking edifice on a field of rolling hills, cherry trees, and oaks. Jazz paid good money to have his mother housed there, hooked up to the machines that breathed for her, fed her, dripped medicine into her.

Alive, but in what the doctors called a "persistent vegetative state." Lack of oxygen to the brain for a prolonged period of time.

He was such a fixture that Dr. Indari, responsible for his mother's care, joked about getting him an employee badge.

Kettle/Herrara was expensive, but not luxurious. The room in which his mother lay was ugly, the walls painted a sick green, the lighting dim and bland. He stood over his mother, watching her as she slept the sleep of the brain-dead. He knew that there was no activity in that head of hers—if he didn't believe the docs, the EEG by her bedside told the tale—but he liked to think that somewhere deep down, she could hear him. Sense him.

"Hello, Mom," he told her, as he did every time he visited. "It's Jasper."

Dr. Indari said that it was a very human thing to do, talking to someone when you know they can't hear you. If he still had concerns about his own humanity, this would have allayed them.

Beautiful Janice—Ugly J—was beautiful no more. Her skin was dry and sallow, her cheekbones sunken. Machines beeped out her life.

As her only living blood relative, Jazz had medical power of attorney. As Indari reminded him often, he could pull the plug at any time.

A stroke of a pen to sign the orders. That's all it would take to send Ugly J out of this world.

Every day, Jazz came to Kettle/Herrara CI and sat with his mother. Every day, he listened to her machine-assisted breath, watched her chest rise and fall, watched her closed eyelids occasionally flicker and jump from muscle spasms. The order to pull the plug lay on a clipboard by her bed, a pen sitting atop it.

Every day, he came here. Every day, he thought of what she had done.

"I could kill you anytime I want," he whispered in her ear, like a lover.

Every day, he decided: Not today.

Acknowledgments

One more time...

Thanks again to Detective Paul Grudzinski of the NYPD and to Dr. Deborah Mogelof for law enforcement and medical advice, respectively. Where I got it right, it's all them; where I got it wrong, it's all me.

I also want to thank my agent, Kathy Anderson, and everyone at Anderson Literary Management for holding on during this wild ride.

I have more gratitude than you can imagine for everyone at Little, Brown who supported this quite crazy endeavor, especially not knowing where I was headed from the very beginning. My editor, Alvina Ling; her team, Bethany Strout, Nikki Garcia, and Pam Gruber; my production editor, Wendy Dopkin; the Sales, Publicity, Marketing, and Promotions folks (including Victoria Stapleton, Faye Bi, Jenny Choy, and Andrew Smith); the foreign sales team, including Amy Habayeb and Kristin Delaney; the designers and production team, who made these books look as creepy and as powerful as possible; and publisher Megan Tingley. Thank you all so much for your care, your professionalism, your attention to detail, and your faith in me.

Special thanks to Eric Lyga and Morgan Baden for reading the early drafts, and to Libba Bray for "Two Writers, One Bullet."

Last but not least, thanks to *you* for reading this.